Praise for *The Big Seven*

A SCIBA Regional, MIBA, PNBA, and
Heartland Indie List bestseller

Highlighted in *Esquire*'s "Major Crimes: Five
Outstanding Novels About Murder, Treachery,
Calamity, and Revenge"

"Wry, lively and sneakily thoughtful."
— *San Francisco Chronicle*

"The book could easily be read as a mystery and many would enjoy it as such. But the discerning reader will find several layers of enjoyment and intrigue beyond the basic plot . . . It is anything but ordinary . . . Harrison writes simply — he's telling a story as if he were sitting on a porch in a rocking chair. Yet there's a depth of feeling. A quiet passion. Many believe that Jim Harrison is one of our greatest living writers. No argument here." — *New York Journal of Books*

"Jim Harrison delivers another rowdy — and raunchy — mystery . . . A fun read." — *Outside*

"Jim Harrison is one of the unsung heroes of American literature . . . This is a Harrison tale. Whodunit ultimately matters far less than when to fish, what to have for dinner and more important, how to make sense of a life where most all behavior falls so far short of any ideal, including one that echoes from a pulpit . . . Among the most enjoyable parts of the book are the reflections on the craft Harrison has practiced with such mastery across a variety of forms — poetry, novellas, journalism, essays and screenplays — for nearly five decades." — *Oregonian*

"Harrison's new book, *The Big Seven* continues many of his primary concerns as a writer—mortality, masculinity, and the search for a spiritual existence chief among them—following a retired police officer as he assesses himself and his relationship with the seven deadly sins. The ex-cop, Sunderson, is no saint. Nor is Harrison. But they have some great stories to tell."    —*Interview Magazine*

"A storyteller of the first rank. Harrison has created a memorable, quirky character in Sunderson who, despite his faults, is irresistible."    —*St. Louis Post-Dispatch*

"In this shaggy-dog mystery, the 'big seven' deadly sins of the title loom large: especially the ones having to do with food and sex. A carouse with a master."
    —Barnes and Noble Review

"Like the whiskey in the flask he carries, Sunderson may be an acquired taste. But once hooked, it's hard to wriggle free of this mesmerizing angler who trolls the shameful impulses and moral hypocrisies within us and our society."
    —*Jackson Clarion-Ledger*

"When our hero is neck deep in his quest for justice, snooping while also considering the seven deadly sins (hence the title), Harrison proves once again that he is an inimitable, inexhaustible talent."    —*Publishers Weekly*

"Harrison throws real evil into Sunderson's path . . . Harrison sprinkles all that skillfully into the narrative, never deviating from the distinctive, conversational tone he has crafted for his hero . . . Entertaining."    —About.com

"Supported between such highbrow influences as literature, music, and food, and the atavistic tendencies of desire and revenge, Harrison takes his story, as he's done countless times before, along a path punctuated by humor and philosophy . . . In *The Big Seven*, Jim Harrison illustrates yet again, with familiar backdrops, that introspection is successful when coupled with humor and large appetites. Good reading. Rating: 5 out of 5."                —*Petoskey News*

"You can't help but like feckless, unpretentiously intellectual Sunderson, inclined to tie himself in metaphysical knots when not fishing or otherwise engaging with the natural world whose splendors, movingly described, succor him in a way nothing else can."                —*Kirkus Reviews*

"After prolific Jim Harrison mastered other genres, he turned to the mystery . . . Harrison's trenchant, straightforward, nearly comma-less prose mirrors his detective. He's smart and honest, clear in his thoughts and feelings. Harrison lovingly shows us how this 'lucky old fool' of a man tries to navigate the seven deadly sins, death and evil in rural Michigan."                —Shelf Awareness

# The Big
# Seven

## Also by Jim Harrison

# JIM HARRISON

# *The Big Seven*

## A Faux Mystery

**Grove Press**
*New York*

*Published simultaneously in Canada*
*Printed in the United States of America*

ISBN 978-0-8021-2466-1
eISBN 978-0-8021-9212-7

Grove Press
an imprint of Grove Atlantic
154 West 14th Street
New York, NY 10011

Distributed by Publishers Group West

groveatlantic.com

16 17 18 19   10 9 8 7 6 5 4 3 2 1

For Peter Lewis

# Chapter 1

Sunderson must have been about ten and was burning up with fever from strep throat and still had to go to Sunday morning Lutheran service. His mother had her antennae out for malefactors and only Berenice who had broken her leg tobogganing had recently succeeded in avoiding church. It was dreadfully boring and that particular week they had a visiting pastor from Escanaba who was far too loud to allow Sunderson to drift off into a doze. He was thinking of the sausage and pancakes that he would have at home after the service and the likelihood of going ice fishing with Dad in the afternoon. The pastor's resounding basso boomed out the Seven Deadly Sins: Pride, Greed, Envy, Lechery, Gluttony, Anger, and Laziness. On the way home in their old Plymouth with the bumpers and fenders rattling with rust he asked loudly what "lechery" meant and his dad said, "You'll find out when you're fourteen," a typical answer wherein all life was an unearthed hostage to the future. He had a clue because the high school girls referred to the male gym teacher as a "lech" and there must be a connection. When they got home he checked the dictionary and found out that lechery meant unrestrained sexual desire. He couldn't totally leave it alone and at breakfast asked if the sins were deadly how soon would you die? What if you just forgot and committed one, did you deserve to die? The doctor's son had the best bicycle in town and you would die if you wanted it. At his age this was less abstract than sexual desire. When you looked up the teacher's legs under her dress in fourth grade could you drop dead? Could just looking be lechery?

It must have been thirty years before he figured out that it had been the high fever that made the experience so vivid if not lurid. There had been a surreal light cast over the service which made it permanently memorable though also confusing. If Mary Magdalene could be forgiven for being a whore why must others die for visiting her? It was confusing but then he couldn't remember paying any attention to anything a pastor had said before this point. He didn't get to go ice fishing because of the fever but had been forced into church. This was the kind of injustice that weighs heavily on children who collect injustices for later possible use.

Fifty-some years later he was brook trout fishing well up the Driggs River west of Seney when his cell phone made a modest gurgle. He knew from experience he was out of reliable range but saw from the screen it was his beloved Diane, his ex-wife, with whom he was still in contact. She blurted "call now" before the connection died so he quickly got out of the stream and hiked to his car knowing the state

highway a dozen miles south would be his first point of re-
ception. He worried all the way there because Diane rarely
called and only if it was very important.

It was half an hour before he could get through—the
curse of the cell phone was its convenience and frequent
use. The news was bad indeed. Their adopted daughter
Mona had taken off from the University of Michigan in
Ann Arbor with a rock band from LA headed for New York
City. Diane was overwrought and confused and wouldn't
stop talking about the semester being nearly over and Mona
losing credit and all that work. Sunderson said goodbye
and called Mona's roommate Emma, a case where the name
didn't fit the big rough-and-tumble girl from East Detroit.
The news from Emma was grim. The band members were
"lowlife scumbags" but currently *hot*. She offered to go along
if he was going to New York City looking for Mona. His
heart jiggled left and right with a tinge of pain. He loved this
lost girl, his neighbor for most of her life, abandoned by her
parents, then adopted by him and Diane simply because they
all liked each other and thought they might as well become
a family since her own parents were utterly indifferent.

In a little less than twenty-four hours he had hit
LaGuardia then a small hotel with no name on it that Diane
loved on Irving Place a couple of blocks from Gramercy
Park. He restrained himself from asking if the hotel had a bar
because he was crying out of fear for Mona and the bar was
only another inept compulsion of his. In the landing pattern
his seatmate pointed at the gap of the missing towers as if by
knowing he was part of history. A writer-drunk-sportsman
over in Grand Marais in the U.P. believed a giant aviary

should be built in their location in memoriam but the real
estate turned out to be far too valuable whatever that meant.
Memory has no enduring value?

Never having been in New York City Sunderson felt
profoundly out of context, as they say, at the hotel desk
where a fey and elegant young man seemed to wince at his
dowdy and rumpled clothing. "Business or pleasure?" the
young man asked with a smile. "Neither," Sunderson said.
"My daughter has been kidnapped and I'm looking for her."
That put a stop to everything except the figurine of a toy
poodle in a diamond necklace on the desk seemed to yap.

Sunderson's room was named after Edith Wharton
whom he slightly remembered from American literature in
high school. The rooms were expensive by his motel stan-
dards but then Diane had wanted him to be comfortable
and there was an indication of her having spent time in this
room. He was too hungry for his habitual nap which put
him in a small dither. The cab had been trapped at a bridge
and he sat there craving a cigarette. They were stopped so
long he stepped out on the bridge, had a quick puff and got
vertigo from the height. The cab nudged forward a few feet
and he tossed away the barely started cigarette and jumped
back in, feeling foolish when they stayed stationary. With
cigarettes up to eight bucks a pack it was such a waste.

He went down the stairs to the Spanish restaurant next
door called Casa Mono which featured small and medium
plates. He liked whenever possible to order what he had
never eaten with an air of authority. He ordered a bottle of
fine Priorat red wine, some cuttlefish, razor clams, a softshell
crab, a piquillo pepper stuffed with meat and roasted. He

ordered a second bottle of wine, first calling Diane on his cell because he didn't want booze to be obvious in his voice. She told him to check the messages on his cell, which he never did, because Emma had called with the name of the bar on the Lower East Side where the band regularly hung out. Sunderson was so pleased to be eating such delicious food and drinking this superb wine that he had been devouring it. The lunch crowd was thinning and he noted how sallow everyone looked before their summer vacation. Once in his senior year of high school he and a friend had proven their bravery by taking off on a lark and driving the friend's '49 Ford on the long trip down through Wisconsin to Chicago where people also looked sallow. The outside, in his terms, had totally been taken over since then by what he thought of as the inside.

After a two-hour nap he awoke feeling a *crunch* as if none of his body parts knew how to work together. He drank a two-ounce vodka shooter from a tiny bottle in his briefcase kept for such emergencies, a kind of motor oil, as it were. He had three cups of expensive coffee on his post-nap stroll thinking it was cheaper to have a Saturday night drunk in the Upper Peninsula than to try to wake up in New York City. At the third coffee shop he talked to Emma who added another bar as a band hangout, more specifically a favorite of the drummer, who Emma had learned was Mona's post-concert inamorato. This second bar was in the Carlyle hotel where the drummer's mother lived upstairs.

In the third coffee shop the young woman next to Sunderson was a tad homely but friendly. She was working on her laptop and she was kind enough to look up photos of the band, which was called Arugula of all things. She said that they were "scumbags" or so she had heard and that the two bars he had to check out were practically at opposite ends of Manhattan.

The first bar was called Toad in the Hole and Sunderson reflected on entering that it smelled like a very dead toad in a very shallow hole. The bartender's face was gray and flaccid and an immensely muscled man was sitting in the middle of the bar monopolizing the area, so Sunderson took a stool closer to the door, generally a good idea for safety's sake.

"I'll have a double Beam with water on the side. I heard the band Arugula hangs out here?"

"I don't talk to cops," the bartender said, pouring light.

"I retired two years ago. When am I forgiven?"

"You guys are like marines. You never get over it."

"I'm their spokesman. What do you want?" The other patron swiveled toward him on his stool and Sunderson noted that his huge upper body was out of balance with his long, very thin legs.

"You don't look like a spokesman," Sunderson quipped.

"Fuck you kiddo."

"Your drummer left a mess behind in LA. I'm looking into it for a friend."

"Lorin is too careful. He even goes to church." Sunderson had the sudden idea that if he had problems with this guy he'd use a Munising High linebacker trick. You come in low and drive a shoulder into the knees. Bones would crack like timber logs, no question. He doubtless carried a pistol but you can't aim well with broken bones.

"I'm telling you he committed a felony. Your drummer Lorin boffed an underage girl in Westwood." The girl from the coffee shop had mentioned Lorin's taste was an open secret and Sunderson figured he was on safe ground improvising.

"I never heard of the word *boffed*."

"To be more exact he fucked her in the ass in his BMW after choir practice."

"He was avoiding a paternity suit. She probably told him she was nineteen."

"A nice check for the parents or cash and he can avoid a felony charge."

"I'll pass on that news."

"I'd be in a hurry if I were you."

"We leave on a European tour tomorrow."

"Lorin is not going to Europe. We either work this out or he's in jail."

The bartender called the big guy Ben. Ben made a cell call and walked to the door for privacy. The bartender poured Sunderson a freebie glad to be in on a hot secret.

"He doesn't know about any girl, you made that story up," Ben came back.

"He can save that for the judge. Everybody is innocent but I'll take fifty thousand by midnight." Sunderson mentioned his hotel and then walked out and hailed a cab.

He spotted Lorin the minute he entered Bemelmans Bar at the Carlyle. He looked like a young girl about twelve and was close to being a dwarf, maybe about five-foot-six when he got up for the toilet. He was sitting with an older woman who resembled him and was likely his mother. Sunderson abruptly turned his head away because Mona came in through the lobby door. His tummy quivered at the sight of Mona wearing fancy clothes he had never seen before. He of course had to stop this trip to Europe. He took out his pocket notebook and wrote "you'll be arrested at the airport" on a page, gave it to the bartender with twenty bucks, and pointed out the recipients. He quickly walked out through the Madison Avenue entrance thinking his nap hadn't covered the duress of this trip.

Back at the hotel after a slow and expensive cab ride he took off all of his clothes, had a bourbon shooter and a shower, and called Diane. He explained he had seen Mona at the Carlyle and explained what he was doing with the blackmail project which frightened her.

"You always played it legal," she said.

"But I'm not a cop anymore," he replied.

"Why didn't you confront her?"

"Wrong time, wrong place. She has to be alone. She looked in love with the fucking dwarf."

"Then it's hopeless. You remember how much my parents didn't want me with you?"

"I got the feeling she is staying with the mother."

"It's a hotel for very rich people."

"Then security is tight. It will have to be outside."

"What if she goes to Europe tomorrow?"

"I guess I'd have to follow. It would be harder."

On his way back downtown he stopped back at Toad in the Hole on an oblique hunch. Huge Ben wasn't there but the same bartender was. He brought Sunderson a free drink for the hot statutory rape info which he had sold to a gossip columnist. Sunderson tried to ride the newly found goodwill.

"Why Europe?" he asked. "I thought all the money was here."

"Lorin wants to take his new girlfriend to France for a week. He's the boss. He wants a break before they start a ten-week tour. Their tour schedule is on their website."

Up in the room he called the nice girl from the coffee shop. She was surprised to hear from him and said she would fax the schedule to him at the hotel. Within minutes there was a knock on the door. A five-buck tip and he had the schedule which wasn't immediately useful except that they were leaving tomorrow afternoon for a sixty-day stint and the singer had tweeted, whatever that was, about Air France. He felt once again that it was irksome to be computer ignorant. Even Indian grannies in the Upper Peninsula were hot on emailing each other. Looking at the tour dates he wondered what was the human toll to be in Hamburg, Germany, one day and Stockholm the next.

He took a break and walked ten blocks to take in a movie called *Melancholia* and then was pointlessly angry when he disliked it. Planets were bent on colliding and some rich Swedes were having a wedding at a country house. The world would be destroyed so that meant the end of brook trout fishing and Diane. Two unbearable things not to speak of Mona who had fallen for a midget. It was sad to ponder the idea that one had virtually no control over the main feature of one's life. When he was Mona's window-peeking neighbor of course he loved her. How could you not? Bright girl with lovely supple body is friends with and spied upon by retired state police detective during her yoga and other matters. He slowly became her dad and now she had fled the university for Sodom and Gomorrah.

On the way back to the hotel in midevening he stopped at an upscale cocktail lounge and the Big Seven arose again. He wondered what had made him demand the blackmail money and concluded he was jealous of the dwarf. All of the men in the lounge were uniformly beautifully dressed and he felt darkly envious at their clothes, far beyond his budget, and the splendid women the clothes doubtless attracted. He wondered what it felt like to look expensive. He ordered a dry martini and it cost fifteen dollars, a stunning amount.

"Back home this same drink is three bucks."

"Where's that?" the bartender who was also dressed nicely asked.

"Way up in Michigan."

They then launched into a fishing discussion. The bartender was from Maine, also a fine brook trout state or so Sunderson had heard. The bartender, somewhat of a hick, had come to New York City as his own father had done in the fifties but found it was unlikely that he would find his fortune while tending bar. Sunderson felt a bit sad at the whole thing perceiving the boy wasn't "quick" enough to make his "fortune." He should clearly be back in Maine wading a trout stream. Of course that was where Sunderson ached to be himself. He suddenly had what he thought was a bright idea, to wit, pretend to be a detective from LA and try to make an appointment at the Carlyle with the diminutive mother of the dwarf drummer Mona was in love with.

He hurried back to his hotel and made the call. She seemed a great deal shrewder than he expected.

"Is he in trouble?" Any mother's question.

"Possibly. Or slightly. I need to cover some details with you. Anything you say will be confidential and not used in a court of law. We think some bad people might be after him." He was putting up the tease of blackmail and kidnap. "It's important that he not go to Mexico."

"The group is headed for Europe tomorrow," she said.

"Avoid Italy," he huffed.

"I'm not in charge."

"Everyone knows your son is. It would be smart if the trip was delayed for a day."

"That's not up to me, sir. I'm booked tomorrow. I could see you at seven a.m. breakfast in the main dining room."

"Fine by me," Sunderson said reluctantly, having planned a leisurely pub crawl of the neighborhood but now faced being out of his room at dawn. He hung up. Back home in Marquette he had had to forgo public drinking having convinced Diane that he was close to quitting. Now he couldn't gamble on drinking very much if he wanted to wake up in time for the meeting. With age the vaunted inner clock he had always depended on had begun to fail him. Just the other day while camping near the Driggs River he had expected to wake at first light, about 5:30 a.m., but with extra sips of his flask by the campfire his eyes had popped open at a shameful 8:00 a.m., thus missing the best hours for fishing in the early morning. He was despondent all day. What happened to the man who could drink most of the night and fish all of the daylight hours? His capabilities were disappearing. He used to set up camp and rig the fishing gear in less than a half hour. He was not so much despairing about natural aging but missing the pleasures of the old disorderly life. Everyone knows the old saying that pigs love their own shit but Sunderson's problems were a bit more radical. All of his routines tended to be self-destructive except fishing and his thoroughly unchallenging walking. He had often reflected that habits were easy to begin but brutally difficult to deal with. He had wept a number of times in the process of quitting smoking and always started again. After the divorce he discovered he no longer liked it as much as he used to. The final straw had anyway been when you no longer could smoke in your office at the state police post. He would still have a cigarette, but no longer the pack a day he used to. Drinking was more problematical. Without question there were times that he desperately needed a drink though never when fishing for some reason he couldn't parse.

He and Diane managed to adopt Mona together, but he had the gravest doubts that Diane would ever move back in with him. She had inherited a lovely home on the death of her second husband, a local doctor, and their only genuine contact was Mona's well-being. Up until dropping out Mona had been doing very well at the University of Michigan.

Promptly at midnight there was a soft rap at the door. Through the tiny peephole he could see an enormous black man and mumbled, "May I help you?"

"I got your money."

Sunderson opened the door cautiously. The man shoved a cloth bag at him. "Count it."

Sunderson began to shut the door on him.

"I said count it. I can't be accused of skimming."

Sunderson dumped the money on the bed thinking that $50,000 looked very large even in tightly wrapped packets of C-notes. He quickly drank the shooter from the night table, offering the man one.

"I don't drink. It causes problems."

"Certainly does," Sunderson agreed. He flipped through the money carelessly and ballparked about fifty.

"I should squeeze your head and take the money," the man laughed.

"You should have done so ten minutes ago. Right now I got a nine-millimeter Glock aimed at your dick, a friend you don't want to lose." Sunderson's right hand was in a side pocket though in fact his pistol was in his shoulder holster.

"Relax." The man left hastily, slamming the door for emphasis.

The problem, of course, was what he could do with the money. He had seen a dollar store down the street and arrived at the idea of buying a fanny pack and keeping it with him. He slid five of the C-notes in the front pocket in case he wanted to buy something. For a change he wouldn't have to think about whether he could afford it. He impulsively called the girl from the coffee shop who had helped him with her computer.

"Yes."

"Would you like a drink?"

"I'm in bed. I have to get up at five a.m. for work."

"How about dinner next door at six?"

"Fine. I'll stop at the hotel for you."

He ended up buying a *Peanuts* fanny pack. Sunderson thought he might buy some fancy clothes after having the early breakfast with the mother. He poured a big drink in order to go to sleep early and watched the local NYC news which was problematical as he had no frame of reference. He found a sex channel and quickly turned it off for fear it would keep him awake after viewing a line of lovely butts.

He was awake at 5:00 a.m. and toying with the room coffeemaker which was complicated, something Diane always took care of when they traveled. He called his best friend Marion although it was 4:00 a.m. there knowing that Marion, an insomniac, wouldn't mind. Marion's immediate bright idea was to forget the whole thing, bring the money home, and buy a little cabin over west toward Iron Mountain.

"But what about Mona?" he whispered.

"She knows what she's doing. She's way ahead of you. The best you can do is get her to call Diane."

Sunderson slumped at the table thinking that the pile of money had an oddly fresh odor. He had packed it neatly in the fanny pack thinking that in no year of his life had he made this much.

He got the uptown express subway at 14th Street and got off at 86th. He was quite early so he wandered around near the Carlyle hotel. No one was up on the streets except service employees filtering to work. He thought with pleasure of having his own little log cabin near good brook trout fishing. He might even get Diane to visit. There was no window shopping near the hotel of much interest except a bookstore called Books and Company but he wasn't in a mental mood and settled for a splendid butcher shop called Lobel's. He had never seen such an array of expensive prime meat which cruelly reminded him of his lack of breakfast. He pondered eating it raw with salt and pepper. Diane had bought such meat for his stag retirement party of fellow police officers, plus a case of fine French wine. They all agreed it was the best meat they'd ever had but his friends were mystified by the wine knowing it was costly but preferring beer. If only he hadn't made love to one of the hired dancing girls bent over the woodpile out back. The gossip even reached his cranky mother retired down in Arizona. She lived down the street from his eldest sister married to a muttonhead who ran RV parks for the millions of winter visitors.

The main dining room of the Carlyle was glistening and intimidating. In fact he had never felt so intimidated. Everyone looked like a millionaire but that was likely on the low side. He felt grungy and croaked out the mother Felice's name to the waiting headwaiter. He wondered why she lived there rather than in an apartment. She was hiding behind her *New York Times* in the corner and rose to greet him. For an awkward moment she looked familiar.

"Were you ever at Michigan State?"

"I went to Smith but visited State a few times to see my brother who was on the gymnastics team."

"That's where I saw you. I had a girlfriend on the girls' team. You are impossible to forget."

"Thank you if that's a compliment. My brother ended up dying of a drug overdose in LA just like our father. That's why I keep a sharp eye on my son."

"It happened to my brother in Detroit. He was into music. Once they get started it's a runaway train." Nothing made Sunderson angrier than heroin.

"So they say." Her eyes moistened as did his. She nibbled on a large plate of bacon which she pushed toward him. "They have the best bacon in the world here. Bad for you but then I'm a skinny little thing."

"You're awfully attractive," Sunderson interjected. She was light rather than skinny. He would love to squeeze her.

"What's my son done this time that cost fifty thousand dollars?"

He told her. She sighed and rolled her eyes at the ceiling as if the answer were there. "How did you get involved with something in California?"

"My daughter ran away with him after he played a concert in Ann Arbor where she is supposed to be in school."

"Mona is your daughter? She's upstairs."

"I'm pleased to have located her."

"She doesn't want to see you. She wants to lead her own life. She's grateful but needs some breathing room. I almost called the police when you blackmailed me."

"You'd have spent a lot more if the girl testified." For a moment Sunderson almost forgot there was no girl, at least none he had actually talked to.

"Maybe not. Maybe I should let him go to prison."

"Prison would be tough for a cutie like him."

"As tough as it was for the young girl from Santa Monica?" Sunderson had never said anything about Santa Monica. Maybe there really was a girl.

"I suppose so. Unless she was an exception. It mystifies me why girls want to fuck musicians."

"Only God knows," she said as Mona came through the main door and spotted them. She looked shocked but composed herself and came toward them.

"Dad, I wanted to be free for a while. I've never been free."

"I'm asking you to call your mother," Sunderson said.

"She's not my real mother."

"Yes she is. And you know it. Call her. She's heartbroken."

"No, I couldn't bear it."

"Neither can she."

Mona sobbed and fled. Sunderson said goodbye and walked out.

On the subway car home he thought he saw the black man from the night before in the car ahead through the crowd. Was he being tailed? He squeezed his *Peanuts* bag of money and felt for his revolver for security. He could shout if he had to. He stopped at the office on the business card the coffee shop girl had given him and saw on the desk her name, Sonia. Her office was in an elegant brownstone on Washington Square.

"Sonia, nice name," he said.

"I actually loathe it."

They decided to change dinner to an early lunch and then she agreed to a little walk. Outside he saw the black man across the street behind a tree and waved. The chump couldn't actually believe he could tail Sunderson. Sunderson insisted they head to the bar, ignoring the tail. It would be one of the biggest mistakes of his life but he felt he needed what is called "a pick-me-up," a big shot of booze with a beer chaser. He wasn't adjusted to New York City.

"Why do you carry a *Peanuts* bag?" Sonia laughed.

"It's full of all the money I have on earth."

"Put it in a bank you dipshit."

"I don't know how. My wife did the banking."

"I'll help you. You're a strange man indeed." It turned out Sonia was from Michigan too but seemed much more with it than him.

The top-heavy lout was drunk at the bar and wasn't happy to see them. Sunderson guessed he knew about the blackmail. He ordered a Manhattan and quickly called Diane which he had forgotten. He saw Ben leave the bar out of the corner of his eye.

He said he had seen Mona who wanted freedom. Diane said she had also heard from her with the same response. "She's going to Paris with her boyfriend. I guess that's it." He chugged his drink while Sonia sipped a white wine. In his peripheral vision he caught movement in the back hallway of the bar.

The black man charged out of the hall catching Sunderson with a terrible whack in the middle of his spine and another on the shoulders with a ball bat. Sunderson dropped to his knees, breathless, and crumpled, and slid to the floor with his face on the fetid tiles. He glared up to see that Sonia had sunk her teeth into the black man's hand and he was howling. Now blood was spurting upward and he stumbled dropping the ball bat. Sonia was on him like a cat and swinging the bat at his head. He dropped with a resounding crack, saying goodbye to the world with a thunk. Sunderson glanced up and now the bartender came around the corner of the bar with a pistol. Sunderson was lying on his own, his body crippled. He reached out and tripped the bartender with an arm, painfully wrenching his broken shoulder and back. Sonia was on the bartender thumping him with the ball bat and kicking the pistol across the floor. The bartender rolled over fruitlessly trying to protect his face from the bat. He groaned and slipped into unconsciousness.

Sonia knelt beside Sunderson. He sensed he was badly injured and managed to call Diane on his cell. Several people had tried to enter the bar and fled from the carnage. Diane was immediately alert and was reminded of the man they had met at a convention in Chicago who managed a big hospital in New York City. Despite himself Sunderson had liked the guy, a poor kid from Brooklyn who had done well. Diane whistled when she heard his symptoms, saying, "My God, darling." She said someone would come quickly.

Two parodies of New York policemen had arrived and were trying to look bored and efficient. One stooped by the black man.

"This piece of shit is dead. Head injuries."

"This one is still alive. I know him. He's a crook. He's pretty beaten up. He's slipping out of consciousness." He moved over to the prone Sunderson who said, "Sergeant Sunderson, detective, Michigan State Police, Marquette, Michigan."

"You have no jurisdiction in New York City," the cop said.

"I wasn't on a case. I stopped for a drink and was attacked. It was a setup."

The cops sat down at a table with Sonia who slowly and deliberately told them what had happened.

"You'll be charged with murder. It's a formality because it was clearly self-defense. You're lucky not to be dead. I'm not even going to book you right now, but don't leave the area for a while."

Two paramedics rushed in and knelt by Sunderson. They examined him. "Broken back. He'll likely need surgery."

Sonia rode to the hospital with them holding Sunderson's hand. He groaned mightily.

At the hospital they figured it was safe to give him a shot of morphine which was a tremendous relief.

By the time he emerged from surgery the next morning Diane was there. He had always feared hospitals since he was twelve and had broken his pelvis in a tumble down a rocky hillside. The ambulance crew that retrieved him had fallen and he was further injured rolling downhill over the rocks. He had been put in a children's ward next to a badly burned little poor girl, a victim of a house trailer fire. He heard talk that they were going to move her to the hospital in Marquette but then figured it wasn't worth it. When she died the second day he was there and was overwhelmed. She had talked incessantly of her dog and how he needed her. Her face was bandaged but her voice was delightful. Her mother wept by her bedside in an old tattered dress.

When he got out Sunderson would take food to the dog, a burly mutt who slept out in the grass out of loneliness. One day the dog was gone and her mother came explaining that the cops had "put the dog down" for biting the mailman.

It was a cruel lesson for Sunderson. Girl and her dog both dead. He put wildflowers on the grave of the dog in their yard and sat there until twilight when the mother told him to go home, that his mother must be worried. Another day the little girl's father took him to the cemetery so he could put flowers on her grave and then a brisk walk over to the lake to divert him but he couldn't stop weeping. Her father said, "These things happen to people." He never stopped thinking of the little girl's voice or her brave dog.

Both Diane and Sonia tried to calm him when he emerged from surgery in the semidelirium often experienced by alcoholics after anesthesia. He sharply imagined his own funeral attended by none because he had no children, then he imagined the missing children, a daughter plump and homely but lovable with the same name as his older sister Berenice and a son Robert like his brother. Then he was at a river, Robert was way downstream from him, and he called out to warn him of a small waterfall and rapids but his voice was thin and weak. He could never save him, just like his brother. Then he and his friend Marion were fishing in the Arctic. They were in a deep river under the ice threatened by enormous polar bears. They sang "Row, row, row your boat" to the bear who sat down and smiled. The bear nosed a freshly killed seal toward them and they ate some raw which pleased the bear. It was bitterly cold so they cuddled up along the bear's tummy and Marion spread his sleeping bag over them and they were warm from the bear's heat.

# Chapter 2

When he fully awoke to Diane and Sonia sitting beside him he wept a little thinking that they were his wives gradually realizing no such luck. They wiped his tears and spoke to him softly. He was brooding as the surgeon told him that he had both a fractured back and shoulder and convalescence would be lengthy. He was thinking how he'd miss the rest of brook trout season back home all because he had been stupid enough to stop for a drink. What a costly drink! Sonia had a small extra bedroom in her apartment she offered up to save him money but Diane had already secured a professional place. To Sunderson the idea of such rehab was unbearable but she promised to fly him home as soon as possible. Meanwhile under the lid of narcotics his trunk hummed with dullish pain.

His confused mind couldn't quite focus on what had happened to him, especially his shoulder and back. He had always been a strong man and the total immobilization of a back injury seemed inconceivable to him. He remembered a deer hit by a car he saw limping along the road at the fence, one leg swinging free broken in half. It was early December and the deer would never make it through winter. He stopped and put it out of its misery with his service revolver, throwing the carcass in the trunk for the delicious meat. He had taken it to Marion, his friend, to butcher and had given half the meat to him. The incident finished deer hunting for Sunderson. He could not accept a deer's inability to deal with cars. Sunderson thought a world without cars would be lovely. Back to horses seemed like a good idea. He was a hopeless Luddite with Quixote dreams of a world he would never see.

He hated the mental blur of narcotics and took as few as he could get away with but sometimes the acuity of the pain would level him up into a world of pure wrenching agony. His breath would shorten until he was gulping the nasty air of the hospital. This drove Diane crazy though she understood the impulse. She had worked in hospitals nearly all her life and had seen how people craved narcotics to reach a pain-free state just short of death, a fog of unknowing. They would do anything to get more. As a nurse before becoming an administrator she recalled giving a man with a bad kidney stone too much morphine. She couldn't bear his pain that made his body contract and turn rigid. Her sympathy nearly killed him but a doctor friend helped her revive him. Next day the patient told her it was as if his penis were trying to give birth to a cement block.

Diane went home after he moved from the hospital to a rehab unit in the East Twenties. One day after weeks there he told Sonia he loved her which caused a big upset. She broke into tears and said, "You don't love me. Besides, I'm not beautiful." It was true she wasn't particularly attractive but certainly not homely. She was a country girl from out by Elmira where her dad had been an extension agent in land and water conservation for the government. She had been raised on a small farm and despite city life that was her basic orientation. She wouldn't say anything substantial about her work which he respected though once when they were drinking wine it had turned out what she knew about him was substantial. She finally admitted she worked for a government intelligence agency and could say nothing about it, but she knew the street he lived on, his sisters, his divorce. It made him wonder why anyone collected such tidbits.

He disliked the rehab place immensely. It was mostly full of decrepit sick people. He wondered what Diane was paying but she wouldn't talk about it. He would pay her back but he had no idea how. He was shocked when he learned half the rehab sum was being paid by the drummer's mother with whom he had breakfasted. She had told Diane that she felt culpable. He heard the bartender was still in the hospital with several cracked vertebrae in his neck.

Sonia had her grand jury hearing and was exonerated. Sunderson's inability to testify because of his severe injury was a good point in her defense. The charges against him had been dropped.

Nevertheless, Sonia was depressed to have taken a life. Sunderson told her the man would have killed her in a snap for biting his hand. This didn't console her. The idea was causing a death and she could not be dissuaded. She visited him daily at the rehab center, about the only person under fifty seen there. He had been totally dead sexually, he guessed due to the pain. One afternoon he playfully got her to raise her skirt a little to show off her legs, but she wouldn't make love in the rehab center despite the locked door. He was mindful that he couldn't really move anyway with his still painful back. His thoughts for the post-rehab future had been monopolized by fishing but now he had the image of her legs to entertain him.

Sunderson was looking forward to a wonderful break when he learned his friend Marion would be visiting for a few days. Marion explained that Diane had stopped by with a plane ticket and some worrisome words. He had been to New York once but it still stiffened his posture. He was worried about what he called "vertical living." He had Sunderson tell the complete story, and the result was not good for Sunderson. Marion wagged his head in anguish and said, "Your messiness since the divorce is going to kill you. In the old days if you had seen the black guy out the window behind a tree, you would have walked over, shoved a gun in his snout, and asked, 'What the fuck you got in mind?' Now look at you—you're paying with your life. Maybe it had something to do with your drinking?"

Sunderson went to great lengths to defend himself but his voice was weakening. He knew in his heart that he never should have come to New York. The fancy people and fifteen-dollar drinks—everything in this unfamiliar place depressed him and his wariness died rather than became enlivened. The blackmail had seemed smart but look what it got him. He was a dried pea in a huge machine, rattling around at random. Marion continued, saying that Sunderson had never recovered from his divorce and what was the point in pursuing Mona when she plainly wanted to follow her lover? What was the urgency about getting her back into University of Michigan where she obviously didn't want to go? He and Diane were comparatively old and what did they know about the power of younger love? Mona doubtless at present thought she was leading an exciting life compared to being a student as her parents wished for her.

Sunderson continued to listen to Marion with a lump in his throat for an hour. It was dawning on him that it was all brutally true. With his divorce he had lost the edge he had in life. He didn't know where it went, only that it had gone. When Diane had caught a cab for the airport from the rehab center he had wept. It wasn't Diane anymore but someone else in her body, a second mother perhaps, checking on an unruly child. The love was totally gone for her, not for him. He had driven it out of her with his behavior over the years.

Though the rest of Marion's visit was more pleasant, Sunderson was glad when Marion left a few days later because the truth in what he said made Sunderson's whole being ache. Look where his sloppiness had brought him. The evening after his lecture was the first he didn't bribe an attendant to bring him a pint of whiskey. It was very hard to go to sleep without the whiskey and he had tortured dreams of Sonia's bare legs and the visiting pastor braying about the Seven Deadly Sins. In the sixth grade all the boys sat in front and marveled at the teacher's legs carelessly covered by loose skirts. He knew according to the Bible that could kill him and when he awoke before dawn he tried to sort out what he believed in a religious sense. Not certainly that Sonia's bare legs were sinful. Everything was assumptions held over from his youth. He meant to read the New Testament again when he got home to see if he actually believed it.

He and Marion had planned an extensive fishing and camping trip for his recovery. On the fifth week of rehab he was shuffling in the gym. It seemed like a miracle but ultimately all he could feel was disappointment. Diane flew him home in a medical jet. God knows what that cost. A big Finnish girl stayed with him as a full-time attendant to buy groceries, cook, clean, and help him dress in the morning. He had lost all flexibility and despaired of going fishing. The girl walked with him in case he fell. Each day they walked farther. He fell once on a curb but luckily landed on grass. He feared breaking bones again but was okay when he got up with difficulty. The girl screamed when he fell and people came running so it was embarrassing. He knew everybody and explained lamely that he had broken his back in New York. He saw the Finnish girl naked after a shower but was only slightly aroused. As men say it was too much meat on the hoof with an ass an ax-handle wide.

One morning he walked much more vigorously and was encouraged. He spent hours at the dining room table sorting out his fishing equipment with a fishing song in his heart. He needed an extra pain pill for his exertion. He hated the pills—after all, his problems came from mental fuzziness. But he had to decide that he was lucky not to be dead. He was puzzled by how in the sweep of life we end up where we do. Both our good and bad decisions appear to us in peculiar knots that lack the clarity of our original intentions. He had gone to New York to retrieve Mona which now seemed preposterous. Could he walk around the corner without tripping on a toad? He thought humility could be debilitating but now it was apparent that it wasn't. It was wisdom if anything.

Given his condition one day on his walk two months after his return he and Marion reduced their plan for the trip to going to Marion's cabin for a week to do a little fishing and just hang out. It seemed sensible to reduce their ambitions until he was conclusively okay. Marion was much bigger than he so he could carry most of the gear. When Sunderson gathered his gear for the trip he was upset at its shabbiness, another area of his life he had neglected.

Diane stopped by. She heard daily from the Finnish girl who had told her that he was going camping. She disagreed strongly but backed down seeing he was adamant. She had tears of worry in her eyes as he stumbled around. The Finnish girl had reported that every morning he sat in his studio, pulling a book from the shelf so he could watch the neighbor woman doing yoga in her leotard. Diane didn't care. He had been doing this for years. It used to be nude Mona he watched.

"Marion's big and strong. He can carry me himself if I fall," he said.

Suddenly she hugged him and he shivered.

"I still love you," he choked out. Years after the divorce, she was still never out of his thoughts.

"You have to stop and find a life," she said. "You're a mess."

"I know it. Marion gave me a lecture in New York and I could see my downfall clearly. I even quit drinking."

In truth he had been drinking but very little, just to get him over the hump of sleeplessness. He had however bought a fifth of whiskey for the coming trip as he loved to sip whiskey before the fireplace in Marion's cabin. He had mixed feelings about this. Complete sobriety seemed like *nothing*. There were no mood swings either bad or delirious, and his fantasy life had dwindled to nothing. A fantasy life is a big item for a man. When you have nothing and your mind can make love to the most beautiful woman in the world it can be grand. Or catch a big fish, make a bunch of money.

Sunderson had hidden the money from his *Peanuts* bag in different books in his library, making a list of their titles. He was careful as he dreaded losing the list and having to sort through a couple thousand books to get his hard-earned, considering the injury, cash. He very much wanted to buy a small, remote cabin in the wilderness for his coming old age. He had read Thoreau but that wasn't the whole impetus. Besides he wouldn't be within walking distance of town like Thoreau. He wanted to be really *out there* and there were many areas in the Upper Peninsula that qualified. Maybe someone's old deer shack he could fix up? It was the life of the wild that compelled him; a peopleless universe far away would console him from terrifying failures like losing Diane with his hundreds of mistakes. They say you can't die from love but he almost had immediately after the divorce ending up facedown on the floor and then into the hospital with acute alcohol poisoning.

Fishing repaired him somewhat but a peopleless sport is ill suited to a peopled world. Isolated people can become like the babbling prospectors in old Western movies. They come to town and everything is amiss except the taverns. Many of Sunderson's old drinking buddies had died or generally disappeared and he drank mostly at home alone now which compounded his isolation. He couldn't very well split up his life between a five-month fishing season and the rest of life. New York was the exception and he had certainly been dense and unprepared. Marion was right. He should have gone after the guy behind the tree in the park.

Marion came over for the night before their departure and cooked his celebrated Hawaiian pork chops basted with soy, butter, ginger, and garlic. Sunderson thought that his own hastily prepared meals depressed him, another item on a large list of things he had to change. He looked at the ragged and tattered fishing vest he had been wearing since he was a teenager. Why not get a new one? Why be sentimental over an article of clothing? Marion kept his gear neat as a pin. When Sunderson had opened his fly box the other day all of the trout flies were in total disarray. He disgusted himself. Marion told Sunderson that back in his own messy alcoholic days he had left his best fly rod at streamside but when he went back to fetch it he drove over it in the grass, breaking it. He was heartbroken but he couldn't afford an expensive replacement. Sunderson reflected on what made men so messy. It wasn't just drinking but the corrupt spirit behind getting drunk, a general malaise of letting go of good sense and order in life. It was the deadly sin of greed that kept him swallowing. He couldn't blame divorce because it had started way before and was part of the reason behind the divorce. Sunderson decided it was a faulty worldview that he would have to change. How to do so was a daunting challenge. Diane meditated a half hour early every morning before work. She didn't make a big deal about it. She just described it as a half hour of total quiet so she would be ready for the maelstrom of life. Sunderson didn't quite get that part. Life was just life, rolling on in inevitable disorder. Now, however, he was aware that he had to work his way up through the sludge that had accumulated in his life. It seemed compacted in his soul. He wanted the clear cool feeling of a ten-year-old getting up at dawn for a hike around a lake. It was a purity of intent that he wanted rather than sliding from one confused day into another. He found himself envying true believers, those who believed in the Gospels and the Seven Deadly Sins that he found so murky.

He had finished breakfast at 6:00 a.m., cooked himself because the Finnish girl was packing up to go home during his camping trip. Marion wasn't due to pick him up until 8:00 a.m. so he decided to take a little morning walk. He argued with the Finnish girl who thought she should accompany him as per Diane's instructions. He angrily said "no." He wanted to be alone.

# Chapter 3

A block down the street on a fair late summer morning a runner passed him with a nod. It was a lovely girl in shorts, perhaps in her late teens. It was a warm morning and she was in tight shorts with a butt as lovely as Mona's. He cautioned himself against thinking about Mona's body now that he and Diane had adopted her. It had become the ancient taboo of incest which gave him a slight shudder. The running girl in the shorts had given him the first twinge of lust since his back was broken. This both reassured and confused him. What was he going to do with lust, certainly not return to his old girlfriend, his secretary? The thought of her and their absurd couplings repelled him. The fresh-looking girl with the delicious butt suited him though the odds against finding one were preposterous. He tripped on an uneven piece of sidewalk and fell on the lawn in front of Mona's old house. He couldn't seem to get up with his faulty back. A dapper man half dressed for work rushed out of his house, the yoga woman's husband, and helped him to his feet. Sunderson explained his back surgery and they agreed to have a drink as neighbors. His wife came out in a scanty nightie and asked if he was okay. He said "fine" much taken by her body which was much sexier than at the vantage point of the window in her yoga contortions.

He went back in his house thinking of the $v$ shadow in the nightie. He rechecked his gear, had another cup of coffee, and felt lonely for the old days when he drank a lot and didn't think much. Marion finally came, only minutes late but Sunderson was already irritable from his falling. His mood recovered when he spent a few minutes peeking next door and was delighted that the neighbor woman was doing yoga in her nightie which slipped up so that he saw her whole lower half nude. What good luck he thought with a sexual pang in his stomach as if he were ill.

The twenty-mile trip to the cabin brought him back to earth. The last seven miles through the woods they were stuck briefly in a mud hole which was watery from the last winter runoff. They roared out and were delighted to see a fairly big bear near the cabin. Marion knew the bear and speculated that it had gotten much larger from eating all the deer that had died from cold in the hard winter. The bears normally reached their peak weight in late fall before the long winter but this spring they came out of hibernation to a sort of a waiting deep freeze with plenty of deer meat and had fattened up quickly.

They were anxious to get unpacked and start fishing well before the midday sun and heat. They burned a large branch of cedar in the fireplace to sweeten the cabin air, an old Indian tactic.

Sunderson began fishing where a small creek emerged from a swamp about a mile behind the cabin. Marion plunged into the swamp toward a beaver pond, his favorite place. The rough walking gave Sunderson a painful twinge at the site of his surgery so he sat under a tree to rest and took a painkiller. He hated knowing the pills would make him feel drowsy and goofy but the pain was a poor start to fishing. He felt better in half an hour and made his way, now more slowly, toward the creek.

He caught a few small fish then missed a larger one that sensed his presence fleeing upstream. Maybe later when it calmed down, he thought. It didn't take fish that long to calm down and then you had to put the sneak on them.

He became prematurely tired and sat down under another tree for a rest, a fir with piles of soft needles beneath it. He reflected that in literature our lives were rivers which seemed inappropriate to him. Rivers were unstoppable, of great power. We were primarily creeks or rivulets that flowed into rivers. You could hope your life to be a smooth, clear, strong creek. You could make it so with care. Or you could muddy it up with carelessness. Sunderson had to put himself in the latter category but then nothing was stopping a change. He drifted away in fantasies of a clean life and fine behavior. He would find a retirement job of some sort to occupy his time properly. His long career as a state police detective had worn him out. He dreaded the many cases of physical abuse of children and wives. His gorge rose in the woods.

He did not want to change that much. He was comfortable like most of us in his sloppiness except he didn't want to be drunk anymore. He was tired of being drunk in the evening at his kitchen table with tears in his old retired eyes over his lost wife.

Marion showed up very muddy after two hours with a nice creel full of brook trout for dinner. He was proud to have stalked and caught a big one, about two pounds, nearly a trophy for a brook trout, and a few smallish others, enough for lunch. Sunderson was mildly jealous but there was no way his cripple body could reach the beaver pond in the center of the swamp. Sunderson faltered and Marion carried him piggyback. He was always surprised by Marion's massive strength, which Marion explained by describing a long youth spent as a farm laborer often for twenty-five cents an hour. Indian kids were cheap he said because they were so poor. He spent most of what he made on food because his family had so little, his father gone long ago. He told Sunderson now how proud he was to one day have brought home to his mother a big beef roast from the butcher. His brothers and sisters were delighted with everyone sitting in the kitchen watching TV while the roast cooked with a delicious odor. Once for Christmas dinner they had eaten three roast chickens that Marion had bought live from a farmer and killed. He and his mother plucked them outside on a snowy day laughing at the cold.

His little sister Susan had been in prison ten years for shooting a man who had raped her but Marion felt there was a chance of getting her out this year.

They napped after lunch then drove a few miles to a
bigger stream that also had rainbows and brook trout. Sunderson immediately caught a nice brown trout of about two
pounds, less impressive than a brookie but it put him in
a glowing mood with his actual life left well behind. He
slipped the beautiful wildly colored fish back into the current. Brown trout weren't nearly as good to eat as brook
trout. Maybe he could catch him here next year when he
gained a pound. A thought that goes with all released fish.

# Chapter 4

Sunderson was roasting a chicken for lunch six months later in January when he was startled to hear a car. He went to the window then quickly bundled into a coat and went out on the porch. It was Diane and she was crying. She whispered through her tears that she had gotten an email and then a phone call from Mona in Paris. She was sick with hepatitis, the boyfriend had abandoned her in a hotel, and she wanted to come home.

"I'll go get her," he said.

"Are you well enough?" she wondered.

"It doesn't take much to ride on an airplane," he said. In fact his back was aching and he dreaded the idea but Diane was the manager of the hospital, it was a busy time of year, and she couldn't get away. He was counting on an extra pill to take care of the pain. The reservations were for tomorrow morning fairly early and Diane had gotten money

in anticipation. She also got him a reservation for a night in
Mona's hotel before leaving the next day.

Diane drove him to the airport in the morning saying he
smelled like a distillery. He didn't reply but he had had more
than a touch of whiskey the night before. He had been full
of anxiety over going to a foreign country without a word
of their language. He reminded himself that lots of people
do it but that didn't help much.

He flew via Chicago and felt nervous and out of place
in the fancy Air France lounge. In consideration of his bad
back Diane had bought him a business class ticket for the
spacious seats. When he looked closely at the ticket he had
been appalled at the price. In the lounge he limited himself
to a single Bloody Mary in penance for the night before. He
asked the bartender to go a little heavy on the vodka as a
precaution, a steady drinker's trick. It was a dark dull day
and he had hoped for a weather cancellation due to ice or
snow but no such luck.

He had been brooding about the word "hepatitis" in
connection with Mona. The disease was common among
heroin users with dirty needles and he kept thinking of the
death of his beloved brother through heroin in Detroit. His
brooding circled back to Mona's boyfriend because musicians were big users of heroin.

On the plane he was diverted by what he thought was
a pretty good dinner, washed down by several glasses of
wine, and the fact that he was surrounded in his seat by
French people. This was good as he didn't want to talk to
anyone and he also liked the sound of the French language.
He became a child who understood nothing. They drank a

fair amount of wine but less than he did. He had never been successful at sleeping on long flights so he was pleased to cover himself with a blanket, push the seat well back, and sleep until nearly morning when they were only two hours out of de Gaulle.

He was deeply intimidated by customs and showed his badge with his passport but it went smoothly. He caught a cab and had time to dread seeing Mona. Their conversation in New York had been discouraging. She was staying in a pretty little hotel near the Théâtre Odéon on the Left Bank. A desk clerk showed him to a room next to Mona's on the fifth floor. It had a wonderful balcony on which he intended to smoke and drink. He slipped his revolver from his luggage into his shoulder holster. Handguns were strictly forbidden in France but he did not intend to be unprepared as he had been in New York. He felt icy cold when he knocked on Mona's door. He heard a wispy *Qui est là* and correctly answered "Dad, from America" and she opened the door. She looked thin, sallow, slightly fatigued in a dark nightgown. They embraced and collapsed backward on the bed. He held her while she cried and mumbled. Her boyfriend paid for the room for a month but abandoned her. He wanted her to help him seduce the young French girls who followed the band. She did it once but was hurt and disgusted. They separated. She became ill after using drugs. He found her a doctor and that was that. He was having a good time and she became disposable.

Dizzy with jet lag Sunderson fell asleep and when he awoke she had his penis out and was sucking it. He tried to withdraw and she suddenly sat on it. He was trapped he thought. "I want someone to want me not a fucking twelve-year-old," she said, grinding away. He had his hands on her buttocks but his back was too weak to lift her off. Shame nearly overwhelmed him. Finally he came off with a mighty groan but she continued. Afterward they slept for a while then she led him down to Café de Flore for a snack. He admitted to himself that his guilt intensified the pleasure. The ham and salad were delicious. She slowly ate a bowl of onion soup while he had some glasses of Brouilly. She looked better now, more alive. He hastily got up and went to talk to two cops standing out in front. She watched him show his identification and they talked animatedly. One cop wrote in a notepad and they left in a hurry. They agreed not to make love again and he felt the heat and sweat gather in his face. They took a walk in the Luxembourg Gardens. The gravel paths were free of ice and the day was bright. They held hands on a bench near the fountain and she confessed that she felt stupid. She wanted to get well and go back to college. He said that was certainly possible. Sparrows chased each other around the fountain. Sunderson pictured how lively it must be in the summer and wondered why America didn't create such pleasures.

Back in the room they decided it was a "French thing" that would certainly go away back in America. Sunderson was mystified by his painful vigor. He must have been saving up, he thought. He remembered his vow to limit the amount of messiness in his life and worried about the chance of catching hepatitis from her.

At the Charles de Gaulle he was delighted when Mona translated an article from the newspaper about an "American rock star" being caught in a hotel room with two nude twelve-year-olds and an eleven-year-old. He would be able to get bail but would have to surrender his passport. The paper went on to discuss the seriousness of the charges that would merit fifty years in prison. It was now an international charge and if he made it back to the United States he would have to serve the time there. There was currently through the United Nations an effort to fight sexual predators throughout the world including the men who traveled to Southeast Asia to sexually abuse children there. "He's in deep shit," Mona said. "His mother won't be able to get him out of this one with all her money." Sunderson kept thinking that it was the seemingly harmless mother who was responsible for his wretched back. He was however pleased that he had tipped off the French police to Mona's rock drummer. That took care of him for a long time. The little girls had told the police that he had given them heroin which increased the charges.

When they made it back on the long ride to Marquette Mona was put in the hospital immediately with her hepatitis and Sunderson took three days to regather his back strength. He was put in elaborate traction which was terribly uncomfortable but solved his back pain without medication. He was less dopey but still terribly guilty about his sexual behavior. The guilt swirled through his mind and increased when he saw Diane. He and Diane had adopted Mona, so how could he have committed this crime? Marquette brought him back to the unpleasant earth. His guilt was all the more repellent because there was nothing to do about it. There was also the additional niggling foul thought about how wonderful it had been. It occurred to him it was his all-time record for sloppy behavior. What do you do when you wake up and a beautiful woman is blowing you? Run for it? Get out of there! He mourned for the simple time when Mona was only the girl next door he watched through his secret library peek hole. He had always been a bit ashamed of himself about this but not to the point it stopped him even though he had arrested window peepers on occasion.

After he got out of traction he needed several days of hard rest to get his wretched back workable and then he took to the woods like a madman every day from dawn to dark. He was fairly safe from Mona while tramping around but invariably each day several times he'd be stopped in his tracks streamside to mull over his guilt, churning his stomach and dizzying his brain.

One early evening just as he returned and poured a sturdy drink Diane stopped by with a roast beef she had cooked with some potatoes and onions. Sunderson was suddenly tearful and confessed he had made love to Mona in Paris. "That's disgusting. You're quite the father," she said coldly. "She likely seduced you which couldn't be hard. She was angry over losing her lover to kids." She stopped and stared at him in contempt. "You may not have started it," she added, "but you truly are a sucker, letting a sick girl twist you this way and that." She handed him a tissue to wipe his tears then walked out without looking back.

Sunderson felt better as he ate his dinner, the questionable relief of confession. This is not to say that he didn't also feel stupid but there was a sense that he could also breathe freely again. He reminded himself errantly that he intended to read the New Testament again to see if he still believed any of the stuff from his childhood churchgoing. There had been an unpleasant reminder early that morning when he had pulled the book in his library to watch his neighbor's wife doing some yoga in her nightie and got a clear view of her nude butt reared up in posture. He gasped from the strength of his lust. She seemed to look at him and he wondered if she had caught on. He thought of masturbation but look what his peeking had got him.

Almost comically he began with his last bite of dinner to think of spiritual life. He certainly wasn't sure what it was except in a literary sense. It was the one thing Marion wouldn't talk about. He claimed that the spiritual life gained power by being kept secret. Once they were having a roaring political argument while having lunch at Marion's cabin when Marion had suddenly stopped and laughed. He wouldn't continue to Sunderson's disappointment who was enjoying himself. Marion said, "Nothing but child abuse is more disgusting than the U.S. Congress. Just now I remembered I was having a nice lunch in the middle of a galaxy. Each night before bed I step out and look at the stars. It's good for humility. If it's cloudy I have a childish faith that they are still there so it doesn't matter that it's cloudy." That was as close as Marion had ever come to saying something spiritual. That afternoon while hiking Sunderson remembered what Marion had said about being in the middle of a galaxy. He was an earthbound man and if he had any spiritual life it came from close observation of the natural world. The stars were beyond him. Diane had a nice telescope but he almost never looked through it. Once he had looked at the full moon and it frankly scared him. How can this be, he wondered. The mystery in his life came from water. In school they had clumsily just said $H_2O$, but from early on Sunderson had been hypnotized by creeks, rivers, lakes, though it was mostly moving water that mystified him. He was openly frightened by Lake Superior which had killed men in his family who had been commercial fishermen. Even on a placid summer day Lake Superior seemed endlessly ominous. Maybe it was the moving water being frozen that made him so restless over Mona.

# Chapter 5

That spring Sunderson found himself an inexpensive cabin on a small lake two counties to the west in the area that the Great Leader, a cult leader that Sunderson had investigated, had had his headquarters and longhouse. Marion deeply disapproved saying the area had too much bad blood. Two game wardens had been killed there in the past twenty years, there were many marijuana plantations, and there were quarreling families, all marksmen who were given to shooting at each other, not to kill but the bullet landing close enough to be an effective warning. Marion even told him the middle school had had problems with sixth graders carrying pistols. There had been a nonfatal shoot-out in the school yard between children of opposing families. With all of the mass shootings in the news everyone thought the situation was bound to escalate but there wasn't anything obvious to cure the situation. The reason the cabin was so cheap was that the owner from Iron Mountain was eager to get away from the unpleasant surroundings. Sunderson was not dissuaded because he wanted very much to fish the area and the price was right, about thirty thousand, which would leave him some to spare from the blackmail money, plus as a local he had always been able to get along with backcountry people. In all his years with the state police he had always been known as a peacemaker. The significant thing to Sunderson was that the bullets always missed because prison was dreaded, the loss of freedom the most fearsome thing in life.

Sunderson had decided to look for a cabin after a week when he had visited Mona in the hospital twice at her request, before she moved to drug rehab. This was nerve-racking to him but seemed not to bother her at all. She was looking much healthier than in France in her little white hospital nightie. She got out of bed for the toilet and purposely gave him a little flash of her bare ass which made him almost nauseous with desire. Diane remarked at a restaurant dinner that Mona would always use her sex as a weapon. Sunderson choked on his food and Diane laughed bitterly. It was time to get out of town.

So Sunderson bought the cabin and felt strong and independent. On his second day there when it was finally warm enough to go he was cleaning up, taking down some stupid beer company decals and joke posters of immense fish, when he noticed a pickup at the end of his drive and a tall man in his thirties standing beside it. There was a rifle in the back window gun rack, technically illegal in Michigan but not much enforced.

Sunderson walked out to greet the man, who was sullen and withdrawn, finally saying, "Wood, two cords, thirty bucks." Sunderson asked him to unload the pickup near the front door but the man started to pitch the wood right where he was parked. Sunderson said nothing figuring the man might be deaf or retarded. Besides he was getting flabby after his injury and hauling the wood shouldn't hurt his back. On the way back to the house he stopped when he thought he saw movement to the west of the far corner of the property. A hunter's penchant is to look long. A deer or a human? He felt a shiver when he thought of the local tendency to shoot. Had he made another sloppy decision? He dropped the thought when he stared at the beauty of the cabin. He would play his cards close to the chest and mind his own business. He was here to fish and relax.

Inside he called the previous owner for the lowdown. The man was voluble about fishing then cooled down a bit on the problematical neighbors. "I didn't sell because they spooked me. My daughters are living in Montana. My wife wanted to move there to be close to the grandchildren. My great-grandfather built the cabin in the 1890s. Later on members of the Ames family bought several miles of land between the cabin and the village. The family were distant relatives of the Ames who invented and manufactured the shovel in nearly every household. There were many problems including grazing their cows on State Forest land. They split the land into three sections with more than six hundred acres per family. The families never stopped quarreling and their behavior became more cantankerous. There was an early unexplained death, a dog was shot for tailing cows, tearing the tail off. They were all NRA marksmen and took to shooting at each other, not to kill but landing the bullets close, sort of a coup-counting shooting. Got you! Anyway you're better off avoiding them totally, don't even talk to them." Sunderson mentioned the wood. "That's Ike. He's been brain damaged and was shell shocked in the Gulf, his legs severely burned. He's a harmless sneak but he's got good wood." Sunderson agreed, relieved that he had made the call. "The main worry is that the families will get totally out of control. They're near it. Avoid them."

Sunderson was appalled but pleased to have made the call. He intended to also check it out with several policemen he had known in the area years ago. He could check the names with his old secretary in Marquette. Meanwhile he decided to drive into the village for a drink at the tavern he had seen there. In a nod to sobriety he hadn't brought any liquor with him but now he felt his body needed a drink.

The day was too bright and clear for fishing until late in the afternoon. Meanwhile he'd spend his time getting the cabin in shape and heat up the pasty he had bought when leaving Marquette early that morning amid disturbing religious thoughts. Marion had been talking about the evolutionary nature of religion according to a social scientist that such items as the Ten Commandments and Seven Deadly Sins in the Judeo-Christian tradition had evolved to keep the human race in check, to ensure good behavior and prevent self-destruction. The Muslims had proscribed alcohol and pork which historically were a notorious cause of disease in hot climates. Politicians even learned from religions. For instance the Gin Tax in England was necessary because gin was too cheap and people were drinking too much to go to work. Raise the price and people drank less. Adultery is generally destructive in a society so forbid it. Anyone with a dull eye for the financial markets could see the horror of greed. Sunderson in a somewhat Marxian drift took the thinking into the economic arena: people must be good boys and girls for economic balance.

The three Ames places were virtual triplets about a mile from one another: two-story fair-sized farmhouses the color of weathered wood from lack of paint, ramshackle outbuildings and decrepit porches, the edges of the weedy yards covered with rusty farm machinery and autos. Country people keep old cars believing they'll use them for spare parts though in fact that is a remote possibility. On the second of the three farms the main beam of the barn had collapsed sinking the roof. It wouldn't last long. He understood that five brothers inhabited the three houses along with their families. The youngest brother was childless, but the other four had something like nine kids, some of whom had kids of their own.

The village wasn't much: a small grocery that doubled as a post office, a rickety house, a couple of occupied trailers, a small closed elementary school. The tavern was a big well-built cement block building with burned timbers in the vacant lot from which Sunderson deduced that the previous tavern had burned. Such taverns are the social center of small communities with kids playing in the corner and told not to bother anyone, a small pool table, several pinball machines, and a jukebox. There were three pickups parked in front for those who needed a noon beer or two. Sunderson's first irritating thought was he would have to ship food from home. As a detective he had been in dozens of such bars throughout the U.P. The info about the families came from a newspaper article he recalled that talked in terms of Hatfields and McCoys, though in this case it was Ames and Ames and a long history of mayhem over the years.

In the tavern half the stools at the bar were taken. Sunderson sat down nearest the door, a reasonable precaution if the cabin's previous owner wasn't exaggerating. The floor was filthy and there was a heavy fetor of sweat and manure. In short, a farmer bar. A young man a few seats down stared at him. "You buy the Sims place?" The young man turned out to be a girl in Carhartt farm clothing.

Sunderson merely nodded yes not wanting to start a conversation.

"You going to keep it posted?" she persisted.

"Haven't made up my mind. I don't like the signs."

All of the men nodded in agreement. He guessed they were Ameses.

"A lot of deer on your south end," she said.

"I hunt over east near Michagamee," he said, not wanting them to picture him as a competitor.

"You can fish our water if we can hunt your land," she said.

"I'll think that over," Sunderson hastily finished his shot and beer and left with a nod.

When he reached his car he felt he had done okay. Keep noncommittal he reminded himself. He had sensed a general hostility. If he had been in Alabama he would have run for it before getting shot, or so went the superstitions of those in the North about the Deep South. He had often wondered in his detective work if there was a genetic quality in psychopathology. Criminal behavior often ran in families and you came to the conclusion that it must be in the genes. You can't separate nature from nurture but in this family it seemed obviously both. The shallow genetic pool must have worn out and there was a Brownian movement to berserk behavior. His police work had taught him that poverty was always of consequence but less so in areas where everyone seemed poor. In the area of his cabin there was no mining, just poor farmers on bad land and pulp cutters, loggers who cut small inferior trees for the paper mills. This was terribly hard work at poor pay and tended to produce bad tempers. These were strong men and their fights tended to be long and gruesome. Some he had been able to stop only by firing a pistol in the air.

Easter was late this year and he had dinner with Diane and Mona who was home from rehab. Easter had been his favorite holiday as a child. It was without the acquisition and confusion of Christmas in a relatively poor family. Rich kids in his class would get new bicycles or sleds or tobog-gans and he might receive only a pair of bedroom slippers. On Easter they had a big breakfast with caramel rolls his mother made that he loved. They would go to church, fes-tive on Easter, and then have a big ham dinner which he also loved. At church they'd sing, "Christ the Lord Is Risen Today" which he believed. He still believed in the Resurrec-tion but figured that was because he never got around to not believing in it. If there wasn't too much spring snow they'd drive up to the cemetery as they did on Memorial Day. He

would drift by the grave of the little girl from the hospital
then find the graves of his grandpa and grandmother plus
all of the many Sundersons who had died in Lake Superior
in commercial fishing. The young are often ready-made
martyrs. Death is a mystery not yet real and graves are
perhaps temporary traps. It horrified young Sunderson to
learn that the bodies of sailors most often didn't float to the
surface because Lake Superior water was so cold that the
natural gases from decomposition didn't form to cause them
to float. The graves of many drowned commercial fishermen
were in fact empty. They lay on the bottom of the deep lake
forever. At the shipwreck museum near Whitefish Point he
had seen a photo of a cook in the galley of a freighter that
went down in the 1880s. A hundred years later a diver took
the photo and the cook was still perfectly preserved except
that his eyes were missing, likely eaten by minnows. The
sea was cruel indeed.

During Easter dinner he had made the mistake of describing the Ames family to Diane who was horrified and
became worried that Sunderson would get himself shot. He
should have kept his mouth shut rather than giving Diane an
additional worry. Her smile when she greeted him was tight
and she talked to him without her usual warmth. She had
talked to University of Michigan and they were willing to
let Mona back into school for the spring and summer terms.
Mona disliked the idea of missing summer in Marquette
but agreed. Diane offered to fly her up for weekends, an
expensive proposition, which led Sunderson to wonder just
how much money Diane's parents had left her. They had
always kept separate books and his salary had covered their

expenses and what she saved from salary and inheritance was intended for retirement. She had offered to pay for his cabin before she knew about Mona but he had said no. He had never told her about the blackmail cash which would only be another worry. He had never asked how much money she had and she never mentioned it. Inheritance had certainly never existed in his family and when his father died and his mother moved to Arizona even their house was considered fundamentally worthless. His sister Roberta had rented the house to some poor people who never paid the rent but she was too softhearted to evict them because the husband had Parkinson's. Sunderson had been frugal since childhood. Thus his horror that a martini in New York could be up to twenty dollars when the same drink was three dollars or less in the U.P. Local bartenders told him not to order a martini which was more expensive than a double top shelf vodka on the rocks. Why pay an extra buck for the vermouth that they rarely had.

On the way home he drove slowly to study the landscape and three Ames cars passed him at blinding speed, speed being a habit of many backcountry people. He had been thinking of the long ride home from France. Mona was withdrawing from heroin and was intensely restless but luckily he had some strong narcotic pills, oxycodone, left over from his back pain, which calmed her. She slept six hours and then he gave her some more. He knew it wasn't strictly legal but she was in such pain. She still delighted fuzzily in the fact that her ex-boyfriend had been arrested.

When he got back to the cabin he was startled that the roughly dressed girl from the bar was sitting at the kitchen table. She told him her name was Lily and explained she had a key because she had cleaned the cabin for the Sims family twice a week. He thought "why not?" and hired her on the spot since he was a slob. He took her phone number to tell her when he was coming so the cabin would be spick-and-span. She reminded him that cell phones didn't work five miles south. He offered her a ride home but she took off by foot cross-country. He took a nap which was a bit eerie because of new surroundings, waking up unsure of where he was. He suited up for fishing, slowly trying to regain his balance. He tied on a clumsy muddler minnow fly and immediately caught a brown trout of about fourteen inches in a deep pool on the bend of the river. This thrilled him to an ineffable degree and his skin tingled. This was what it was all about, to own your own cabin and catch a nice fish practically in the front yard. He would tell Marion about it because there weren't many brown trout near his cabin and Marion loved the speckled beauty of brown trout. He released the fish and heard Lily who had snuck up behind him say, "I would have eaten it for breakfast." He said, "Be patient," and quickly caught two brook trout of ten inches, fine eating size, went ashore and gave them to Lily to fry. Back in the cabin she looked nice with her coat off in a worn green blouse. Sunderson felt a slight pinch in his groin. He didn't want to but her butt looked nice in Levi's.

He had to go home that afternoon to say goodbye as Diane needed him to drive Mona down to Ann Arbor to college. Sunderson surely did not want to make the long drive himself and was also quite nervous about being alone with Mona for fear of another sexual incident. The simple fact was that he did not trust himself with something as errant as sex. One moment you were a piece of retired dead meat and the next you were a teenage hard-on whose willy-nilly logic made no more sense than the bedlam of the Ameses.

As luck would have it Diane had managed a full day off and would take Mona south the next day herself. This gave him great relief and he had dinner with Marion who shocked him with news he'd heard on the radio that there had been a shoot-out among the Ameses back near the cabin. There were no details available so he called his old office and found out to his dismay that his house girl Lily had been killed in a duel with her cousin Tom who was badly injured with two shots in the thighs. They had stood off at fifty yards with AK-47s, a pernicious weapon, and opened fire. Lily had been shot three times in the stomach area and had died instantly. Both of Tom's thighs had been blown apart and he had nearly bled to death. Sunderson called the number of the dead girl out of curiosity and got her sister Monica who asked if she could have the cleaning job. She wanted to earn money to take the bus out of town and get away from her terrible family. Monica told him she had told police that Tom had been sexually abusing Lily starting at age nine. She'd come crying because he had fucked her in the barn or out in a field. It occurred to Sunderson that Lily had died trying to get even and tears formed thinking of the improbable injustice of life. Monica was only nineteen but was sure she could survive elsewhere.

Sunderson drove to the cabin early one morning but as expected the area was still crawling with cops most of whom he knew from his forty years with the state police.

An actual shoot-out is a rare thing in the Upper Peninsula where most crimes of violence are of an impulsive nature. Many began with someone shooting someone else's dog but often dogs are virtually family members and shooting one violates something deep within people. It was unforgivable and if vengeance was not exacted immediately it tended to smolder for years and would always finally come out. The Sicilians say that revenge is a dish best served cold. Lily must have had years to think about her revenge, but perhaps the pressure point gradually rose and then there was an explosion.

He wasn't at the empty, now spotless cabin for even an hour before Monica, Lily's sister, showed up. He wanted to go fishing but talked to her for a half hour because she was grief-stricken. She was dressed better than her sister had been and was actually quite pretty. She said that if Tom wasn't in the hospital with blasted legs she would shoot him herself, such was her sorrow over her sister's death. They had been close for a lifetime and now she had thought of burning down her family's three houses before she left. Sunderson cautioned her that violence begets violence and that someone has to truncate the cycle, though such a burning might be doing the countryside a favor. She began crying and fell into his arms. He cautioned himself against there being any real affection wanting to avoid another disastrous young woman in his life. In fact he felt his cabin should be kept safe from any sort of sexuality. He did note that she looked thin when she took off her farm coat but in his arms she felt pleasingly fleshed. She was too young, of course, at nineteen.

By the time she left in ten minutes he was erect in his pants and a little disappointed in himself. He wanted to take a nap and then go fishing but a nap was out of the question so he decided to drive to the valley and talk to a cop.

It wasn't hard to find one he knew. They stood in front of the grocery store–post office and talked. "I think we're charging the guy with murder one. The prosecutor said he organized the duel. He'd been fooling with her since she was a kid. The mother's in the nuthouse and the father was in the marines. The whole compound are gun nuts. I'd watch myself around them. They're volatile and have had a lot of assaults. How's the fishing?"

Sunderson said it was fair rather than very good. He didn't want any company other than Marion whom he had called about the brown trout thinking he might be past his distaste for the area. He was thinking again about the possible genetic factor in crime or was it simply learned behavior? He thought of the firm feeling of Monica's butt when he embraced her. There was a modest jolt in his groin that meant he wasn't safe. He went home and fished until dark and then made a clumsy dinner with a bottle of French red Brouilly that Diane favored. The wine saved the breaded pork steak and broccoli from the grimness it deserved. Diane wouldn't drink California wine but preferred simple French vintages she bought at a local store. She wasn't snobbish but confessed to a horrible trip to California in her late teens with a boyfriend. His parents she described as "horrid parvenu." He didn't know what this meant but it must have been pretty bad. They were furious at their son for refusing to go to law school. He was troubled but that was why she liked him. He finally turned out to be gay but they remained friends. He visited Marquette once and Sunderson thought he was wonderful and even told him what bar gays hung out at in Marquette.

Sunderson slept poorly, intermittently waking to think of Lily and become angry, not a good sleep aid. The bottom line was an unjust death. His late afternoon fishing was ruined, haunted by the unremitting vision of Lily sitting at the dining room table. He gave up trying to sleep before dawn, drank a pot of coffee and thought about vengeance, always a dismaying thought because nothing satisfactory could be done. When the outside got barely light he fished poorly for a couple of hours and kept one good-sized brook trout for dinner.

When fully awake he decided on impulse to visit Tom, the murderer, at the hospital in a nearby town. A cop had told him that Tom actually required better medical help but had no insurance. When he reached the hospital he flashed his expired detective ID and got right in. Tom lay in the hospital bed with his thighs in big casts. He was a total whiner complaining that the county wouldn't pay for adequate care over in Marquette. It was as if he had forgotten that he had murdered someone or couldn't care less. He said that Lily's bullets had shattered his thigh bones. Without the correct surgery it was unlikely that he would be able to walk for a long time and then poorly. Sunderson listened with feigned interest resisting an urge to shoot him in the head. He was a strong young man in his early twenties but you could see the strength seeping out of him in the lassitude of the hospital. He further complained that no one in his family had visited him. The cop had said that Lily was liked by everyone and the opinion around town was that it was sad that Tom hadn't been killed.

Before leaving Sunderson falsely assured him that he would see what could be done about his medical care. In fact he didn't give a shit if the man rotted to death with his shot-up legs. On the way home Sunderson was amazed at the dislike he had generated for the man in a short visit.

Back at the cabin he needed a nap to purge him of the hospital visit. Monica was there at the stove saying she was making a little beef stew for his dinner which delighted him. She was in a blouse and short skirt and the rear view at the stove was enticing. He dozed for an hour and woke up with her beside him crying. She talked about Lily mournfully and he embraced her with his hands sliding down to her bare thighs. He quickly removed them and she asked him if he didn't need some "affection." He didn't know what to say but she removed her shirt and his hesitation went out the window to live amongst the clouds. Her body was even younger than Mona's and he was hesitant. Her breasts were small and pink nippled. He didn't last long but they lolled around the bed talking until he was hard again. This time she was very active and he thought she must have a boyfriend who started her early.

She dozed and he lay there feeling mildly ashamed though it was she who had been persistent. Why didn't he just hug her and console her with words? With all the hours he had spent brooding about the subject! The mystery was in the passion that suddenly overcomes one. One moment you feel normal and then it rages within you. You become stupidly breathless and erect. Afterward there's a bit of "what was that all about?" In college he had made love a couple of times to a girl he didn't even like but was sexually attracted to. She was a brash sorority girl, not the kind he was normally drawn to. She walked with a limp and they had nowhere to go so made love in the trees along the Red Cedar River with him on the bottom so she could avoid grass stains. When he saw her at a grocery store later when she was pregnant and married she broke out laughing hysterically near the meat counter. He asked her "what's so funny?" and she only said "us" and walked away.

So what to think of his situation as a divorced retired detective of over sixty-five? No answer was forthcoming and why should he sexually fast when Monica's body was so slender and lively. What about her was the question? Was he doing her any harm? What about her malevolent family? He didn't want to get his ass shot off for sex but he doubted that anyone in her family cared about him except for the NO TRESPASSING signs he intended to take down. He had a sudden insight into the absurdity of sexuality. When you trout fish all day from dawn to dark and forget to bring along your sandwich by evening you are ravenous with hunger. You finally get home and you cram the first thing in the refrigerator into your mouth, even a piece of dry, stale bread. You are quaking and beside yourself with hunger. Sex is like that. The body is suddenly out of control and the brain has fled to parts unknown. You are young and stupid again and the body wants only to mount the woman. You are a mere animal his gonads told him. Sex is the first bite of something good when you are starving.

Monica told him to leave the stew on very low heat and left for home. She kissed him goodbye which he appreciated. He was tired of his mind but it was too bright and shiny for good fishing, so he went on a two-hour walk ripping down NO TRESPASSING signs on the property border. When he was young he hated such signs. A downstater would buy ten, twenty, maybe forty acres of woodlands and post it for no reason. It defied freedom of movement. While he was tearing off signs near the road a pickup stopped with two older Ames men he hadn't met yet. They were pleased he was removing the signs because otherwise the game warden would kick them off the property. They offered him a drink from a flask which he took with pleasure and said they were burying Lily at the cemetery at five o'clock if he wanted to stop by. One man who said he was Lily's father said he would shoot Tom but maybe his bad legs were enough. Sunderson said, "That boy isn't going to be walking."

Back home he was distraught at the idea of Lily in the cold, cold ground and took a restless nap, waking at four and having coffee, a little of the delicious stew. He got to the cemetery early but the funeral home hearse was already there. An old man leaned against the front door and said that he had known Lily through his wife's activities as a 4-H leader. "She was a fine young woman and this is a damned shame. The whole Ames family should be locked up in a madhouse." He huffed and puffed, reddening, sorely vexed. Sunderson noticed the grave had been dug in the sandy earth and the straps to lower the casket lay across it.

Soon enough the three Ames pickups crowded with people showed up. Country people believed in pickups not cars. The Ames men carried the casket across the rumpled ground and on to the straps above the grave. The funeral director said a few words for lack of a preacher. "Our dear friend Lily was taken from us suddenly. May God hold this wonderful girl to his breast and console her for the violent failures of life."

Monica came over and stood beside him holding his hand. She sobbed and he hugged her shoulder. The other children wept while the Ames men were sullen and stony. None of them looked at him though Monica said they were pleased that he took down the posted signs. The south end of his property was a deer route, deer being creatures of habit which sometimes gets them killed. Being creatures of routine also gets other animals in trouble, like us.

On the way home from the funeral his heart sank into his belly. There is a dreadful finality when a casket is lowered ever so slowly. No one can imagine what comes afterward if anything and our sense of injustice gets full play. Why should people who have suffered all of their lives die without justice? The most brutally simple statement in the human race is "it's not fair." He readily recalled the old *Life* magazines his mother had saved and the photos of the Warsaw Ghetto and the prison camps. To the mind of a child the photos were incomprehensible. For untold reasons they are also incomprehensible to adults. Is it us doing such things? But as a student of history he knew you could barely turn a page without coming upon a new horror. A good portion of his impulse in becoming a detective was to lessen horrors. His friend Marion was an expert on the Indian Wars which he had pointed out were massacres rather than wars. The march of conquest across our land had a striking resemblance to Nazi Germany. They aimed their rifles low into tents to make sure they got all of the women and children not just the obvious warriors. The editorialists of the East were behind the notion of "kill them all and let God sort them out." Sunderson found reading in this area unbearable partly because in Munising he grew up with many Indians so the deaths in books had human faces.

# Chapter 6

When he got home he treated himself to a beer, a taste of the stew, and got out a notepad. Mona was a whiz at computers and had done a lot of work for him on the theory and practice of cults. Why not get her to do thorough research on the Ames family background? It was his understanding that they emerged from Boston but in their more recent past it was a remote part of rural New York State and also Frankfort, Kentucky. He sadly wished he could email her but settled for a phone call. He had steadfastly held out against the computer revolution but now thought of it as a stubborn mistake. His former secretary was relatively incompetent but Mona was an ace hacker and could come up easily with arcane information on anyone. He called and she said she was finally feeling well, walking a great deal, and pleased to have an assignment for which she would charge him a minimal amount. College was okay but a trifle boring and she spent much of her free time wandering the splendid library. After he hung up Sunderson worried about heroin. Ann Arbor was close enough to Detroit so it must be readily available.

Within two days he received an ample FedEx with her initial findings on the Ames family, an offshoot of the prosperous group who stayed in the East. It's often forgotten that those who settled the West were doing poorly in the East. The progenitor of the questionable branch of the family was a man named Simon who had murdered a neighboring farmer but the court ruled self-defense. The dead man was popular and Simon was generally despised so he set off on a whim for Frankfort, Kentucky, with his young wife and three children. It amused Sunderson to read about this brute who shared his own much-loathed first name. Frankfort went badly with the only land he could afford being poor indeed. They held out for twenty largely miserable years with the accumulation of six children working at thoroughbred stables around Kentucky. Simon heard that there was cheap good land in Michigan's Upper Peninsula. It was cold up there but he had dreamed of fertile land at a low price. He had an old flat rack truck and built a cover for the back to house the kids. The two eldest stayed in Kentucky which angered him as he was losing free labor for farming. The oldest son to accompany him was his namesake, Simon Jr., who was twenty-one and had started his own family. The youngest was only eight. They headed north on a cold spring day. He bought three sections of cleared land from a lumber company for cheap. The problem was the hundreds and hundreds of stumps left over from the timbering. It took a couple of years to clear them with dynamite and a team of big Belgian mares he also bought from a lumber company that had no more use for them hauling logs. Simon put his family in a worthless abandoned house in town that he still had to pay rent on. He later blew up the owner's car with dynamite and he wasn't caught though everyone seemed to know he had done it. This started the Ames tradition of havoc in a new location. It was easy to figure out who did it with Simon the only one in town who had dynamite. He felt justified because his worthless rental house was unheated. It was a cold spring. April isn't reliable that far north and sometimes brings the last of the year's blizzards, and his family was uncomfortable not getting enough to eat. Simon illegally shot a couple of deer for meat plus one of the recently bought calves died so they ate it. The meat of the sick calf made them ill so they gladly returned to venison. It was soon after World War II and he drove way over to Escanaba and loaded up on war surplus blankets to keep from freezing. None of this really explained his blowing up the landlord's car. It was us against the world in the small community, a tradition of self-righteousness that criminal families share with each other, and they were off to a solid start. The family now living in the houses were all sons and grandchildren of Simon Jr., who by all accounts was even meaner than his father. None of the adults cared for their children. The kids got along fine with playmates and so did the daughters who made themselves useful sewing and cleaning the houses of the town's few prosperous families. The daughters, unlike the sullen and irascible sons, were pleasant and popular.

It occurred to Sunderson while reading that likely the bad Ames blood emerged from this vicious grandfather. Now there wasn't an Ames male that would suffer even a teaspoon of regret if he shot Sunderson. They were a "live free or die" kind of family and the only real horror in their lives was the prospect of jail or prison. The dumbest of Simon Sr.'s sons drove to Iron Mountain, robbed a bank, and was promptly caught, receiving a sentence of fifteen years downstate in Jackson State Prison. He got out during the recession of the 1970s, robbed another bank over in Superior, Wisconsin, got caught, and this time got twenty years. No one ever visited him over which he was quite bitter.

The bank robber made a strong impression on a young nephew, the youngest of Simon Jr.'s five sons. Ten years after the uncle was sentenced, his nephew took to robbing a handful of banks and later bars throughout the U.P. He was quite successful until he was caught in an ambush and wounded a prison guard moonlighting for bank security over in Sault Ste. Marie, which got him twenty years. He was now in his fifties. He had gone away again five years ago for a couple of years for parole violation and had been released only recently. Sunderson determined that he was the smallest of the Ames men. Oddly, by reputation he was thought to be smart because he had done so much reading in prison and was an excellent "jailhouse lawyer" which proved useful to his miscreant family.

Simon did well in the beef grazing business. There was a plenitude of green grass between the stumps and his cattle quickly got fat and sassy. The family did well up through the Korean War when a couple of the sons were arrested for dodging the draft. They avoided prison by joining the navy and had a wicked time in the South Pacific in the months after the war ended.

The beef business was excellent in the postwar years and the family had built the three big houses by the time the sons came home from war. Simon was now old and couldn't keep pace among his sons so the two thousand acres were split in three sections to no one's satisfaction.

The sons fought physically and one shot the other in the leg in a local tavern but got away with it by claiming they were "horsing around" and the pistol misfired. Even the shot man didn't want his brother to go to jail. After old Simon's death in the late sixties the brothers settled down. Other than try to cheat each other on the fenced borders there was peace between them for a while but not their children who had learned violent play from the parents. All three wives left eventually for parts unknown due to wife beating. Somehow the brothers continued to find new women to marry or shack up with. Eventually they all moved away and Simon Jr.'s burgeoning family spread out to occupy all three houses, but the pattern of violence had been established. Young Tom, Simon Jr.'s grandson and the eventual shooter of Lily, was the worst. He abused all of the girls, not just Lily, and thought of himself as king of the hill.

Sunderson rechecked the source of the information, much of it from an odd long confessional and accompanying family tree–style notes in the police file and prison records Mona had hacked of the brother with the curious name Lemuel, Simon's youngest son who had spent so much time in prison reading. Sunderson guessed that the twenty years or so away from the family might have done him some good but he was unsure.

Sunderson, quite fatigued with the Ameses, went fishing for two hours late in the afternoon, confident of his beef stew dinner. By coincidence he ran into a man he learned was Lemuel downstream, expertly casting his fly into a large pool in the bend of the river. They talked for a while. Lemuel turned out to be well spoken, the opposite of what he usually found in ex-cons who are habitually aggrieved, sullen, hurt as if crime had been visited upon their innocence. Lemuel said that he hoped to become a crime novelist as that was his only level of expertise. Sunderson wasn't sure about getting further involved with the Ameses but he figured what harm could a writer do after reading his pathetic family history. Lemuel said what Sunderson had been thinking, that there was "bad blood" in certain families. He owned a small English setter being the only Ames who hunted game birds and everything the dog knew was apparently in its good breeding. It was born with the ability to hunt. He applied this to the criminal impulse and said that Simon had unleashed a criminal family on the earth. The seed was bad. He was heartbroken over Lily who had been his favorite member of the family. They had even spoken about marriage though it would have been illegal as he was her uncle. Once he had saved Lily who was being raped by Tom out in the woods by hitting Tom over the head with a big stick. Tom got up and beat the shit out of him, knocking out several teeth, but Lemuel said it was worth it because Lily was in such pain from Tom's big penis. He and Lily had been close ever since, until her recent death. He hated Tom and hoped to kill him when he got out of the hospital. Sunderson pointed out that if he got caught he'd be spending the rest of his life in prison where there was obviously no fishing. Lemuel thought this over in silence then generally agreed though he thought he should avenge the love of his life. Sunderson joked that he could easily spend a lot of time making Tom miserable, tipping over his wheelchair and that sort of thing, and then his vengeance would be slow and deliberate. Sunderson said he should try to fall in love with the sister Monica and Lemuel interrupted saying that Monica was a young "nympho" fucking everyone in town including relatives. This made Sunderson feel a tad less unique though he didn't really mind. He was curious about the idea that Lemuel would write a crime novel about his family.

When they finished fishing they had a pleasant beer at the cabin and Lemuel recognized the odor of Monica's beef stew saying she was the only Ames who could cook, though one of the young cousins had promise. Everyone wanted to eat Monica's food and the wives were jealous and nasty to her. He had advised Monica to wait another year until she was twenty to run away to Escanaba or Marquette or way over to Sault Ste. Marie. He would personally give her a ride in his old 1947 Dodge.

Lemuel left but to Sunderson's irritation was back in a half hour in his Dodge and presented Sunderson with a dozen pages of his crime novel then left quickly in embarrassment. Sunderson normally had a little nap after dinner especially when he had been fishing but built a small fire in the fireplace because his legs were cold from wading the stream. He admitted his curiosity about the chapter. He was not optimistic about a new, inexplicable fiction writer and the chapter title, "The Deflowering of Lily," was un-promising. *Deflowering* was an antique word and he guessed that Lemuel read some old-fashioned novels in prison, possibly George Eliot whom Sunderson disliked in college and Thomas Hardy whom he loved.

### The Deflowering of Lily

*It was a warmer spring afternoon and there were, I think, seven of us kids out in the edge of the woods playing hide-go-seek. Lily had matured early and at eleven or ten had a fine set of legs in her bright yellow short shorts. I mention this because she asked me to rub mosquito dope on her legs. I did so and it gave me a warm buzz in my tummy that I didn't recognize. Tom was also out in the woods stringing barbed wire between trees to contain the cattle so they wouldn't get lost in the deep woods that went on for miles. When I remember this wretched incident I recall that Tom spent a lot of time staring at Lily in her brief yellow shorts. Tom put down his fencing tools, walked over and grabbed Lily and ripped off her shorts leaving her nude from the waist down. He pushed her down onto a small pile of dogwood and pine branches and she finally started screaming. Before that she was in shock and didn't know what was happening to her. He raised her ankles up to her shoulders and took out his big penis. At first it wouldn't go in her but he kept ramming and it finally did at which she screamed louder. All the kids had come running but they just stood there, the boys were anxious but no one tried to do anything. Finally I picked up a big heavy stick, swung it hitting Tom on the side of the head. He collapsed off of Lily, knocked out cold. He had stared at me as the stick approached his head. The girls helped up the sobbing*

*Lily and they all ran for the house with the boys behind them. I should have run for it too because Tom revived, got up and came at me. I didn't have time for another blow. He grabbed the stick and knocked me down swinging it against my legs. He pounded me in the face with his fists until I had two black eyes and a couple of broken teeth. He finally quit beating me when he hurt his knuckles on my teeth. I walked home slowly with a bloody face and a broken nose which is still crooked.*

*All the three kids told the three sets of parents what happened but there was virtually no reaction. Lily's father Bert was in a stupor but then he was the severest alcoholic in the big family of drunks. They bought vodka in bulk gallons which did not last long. Even the women drank far too much, probably in defense from their husbands. No one took Lily to the doctor even though she bled a lot. The real reason for ignoring Tom's wicked violence is that he was the hardest worker in the families, taking care of the beef business himself except for branding and the October roundup when cattle trucks arrived to take mature cattle to the slaughterhouse. In short, no one wanted to offend Tom.*

*My weak defense of Lily caused a permanent bond between us. She put hot compresses on my wounded face though she could barely walk. After the experience she went without boyfriends in high school. We finally made love in my car the night we graduated from high school, very slow and gently. We didn't do it regularly but at odd times her emotions dictated. This all explains why I have to kill Tom.*

Sunderson noted that Lemuel had written as if he were Lily's age. Was he delusional enough to believe this? The last sentence was more or less a confession of motive. True, it was a work of fiction but the sentence would turn on a reasonably good detective. The chapter had been short but hair-raising, fatiguing Sunderson. The death of Lily now loomed larger in Sunderson's mental collection of injustices. He wouldn't mind killing Tom himself.

There were nine more pages of another chapter but he hadn't the heart to read it now. It was an introduction to Simon, the Ameses, and Simon's tainted progeny. Sunderson was sick of the tainted and looking out at the beautiful landscape it was hard to imagine the violence that had taken place there. Marion had mentioned that the location of many Indian massacres had been quite beautiful and it had been difficult to imagine so many deaths. Sunderson had watched a movie called *Rabbit-Proof Fence* about mixed-blood Aboriginal children taken from their families and put in a wretched school. Three little girls spent six weeks trying to walk home across the desert. They made it but were seized again and sent back to the school. It nauseated Sunderson who was enraged far from the scene in snowy northern Michigan. It was like Mexican migrants dying of thirst trying to reach America while the leaders in Washington drank iced tea and entertained lobbyists to get rich.

He hoped sleep would heal his brain but it didn't last long after he woke the next morning. Lily's death was a canker sore in the brain that needed no probing to reactivate. For once he dreaded seeing Monica, reminding him as she did so strongly of Lily. He resolved not to make love to her anymore. He continued reading Lemuel's description of the Ames brothers.

Bert, the father of Monica and Lily, was the oldest and since his early years a confirmed alcoholic, Lemuel wrote. He was easily the worst of the drinkers in a family of big drinkers. Even one of the women had fallen flat on the floor without her hands out and severely broken her nose and a couple of teeth. Bert was even worse but when he got messy or violent it tended to be directed outward. Monica had told Sunderson that her father had once tried to make love to her but he was so drunk she pushed him out of bed and he was still on the floor in the morning.

Sprague, the second son, was the quietest. He was lazy and seemed genial enough but had the meanest temper of the brothers. To the disgust of his father Simon he had gone to Missoula and gotten a bachelor's degree that he never did anything with except substitute teach on rare occasions. He would sit in his bedroom and brood for days and then emerge from his bedroom acting as if he had been very busy. He had been married briefly but after six months around the Ameses his wife had fled back to Missoula, taken a graduate degree, and was now teaching over in Houghton. Sprague would drive over and visit her which ended badly and he always returned bereft. He clearly hated his father and they had rarely spoken. Sprague had the shortest rap sheet, possibly because he tended to take out his temper on women and children rather than in a fair fight. He had been questioned several times about brandishing his gun in public. Most of the neighbors thought he was the most likely to turn the violence on someone outside the family because he would fly into a rage so easily. Sprague was of limited use on the farm except he liked fencing which no one else did except Tom. Sprague was Tom's father and the mother, whom Sprague had never married, was mean-minded and shrewish as well and Tom was always being beaten as a boy. They had two other children, a son who was turning out as nasty as Tom and a mousy little girl everyone feared for. "The blood was bad as I said," Lemuel concluded.

Levi was taciturn but tough as a scorpion. He was obsessed with science, the only one in the family to have any aptitude except old Simon. They shared a subscription to *Scientific American* and bored the family with their science wrangles. Levi was a bit of a genius on hard sciences and the high school science teacher was bitter that Levi didn't go on to college but Levi was stupidly stubborn, saying that he didn't want to go to college, he just wanted to think about science while doing farm work. If you said hello to Levi you might get a lecture on quarks or neutrons. Wordless Ike was his son. Levi was compassionate about cattle and tried to invent mittens for them for winter. But cattle have thick hooves and don't want mittens. He settled for building them an enormous storm shed to get out of the winter weather. At first they wouldn't go in his shed despite a blizzard so he baited them with hay.

Levi and John both loathed their father who they believed didn't get their mother proper medical care during her stomach cancer when they were quite young. Simon was too cheap and believed she was going to die anyway, not necessarily true as stomach cancer victims have a high survival rate and can live for years with proper care. Levi learned this when he got a little older and challenged his father, but Simon didn't believe it. This added nastiness to those science quarrels. Ever since his mother's death Levi drank more and was prone to getting in fistfights at the tavern. He always won.

John was the biggest of the brothers, quite mouthy and a glutton. Simon called him a genetic outcropping and joked that maybe his wife had "gone to the woodpile" with a passing bozo. No one thought this was funny. From early times John handled the two milk cows and would drink up to a gallon while milking which helped account for his size. The only triumph of his life came at the county fair when he won the dead lift at age eighteen with five hundred pounds, slightly astonishing to beat all the other "biggies" in the county. John's wife was the best of the wives, partly because he was kind and gentle to her. In good weather they would go to the beach for picnics with their two children. Sometimes they would go camping way over to the Porcupine Mountains or the beautiful Keweenaw Peninsula. In other words it was no mystery why John had the only happy marriage among the brothers. John's three sons had grown up to be just as big and had all gotten out of Michigan by joining the military, but one had left two young children behind to be raised with their cousins after his girlfriend died. None of the brothers was able to figure out why but they envied John.

"It all comes down to me," Lemuel continued, "the unsuccessful bank robber but I don't feel like talking about myself this morning. I want to write books about other people. I've forgotten about old Simon, *the keys to the kingdom.* It was an admitted relief to everyone when he finally died."

Old Simon would sit in his easy chair, crippled with arthritis, every morning and give orders to his assembled sons on what work needed to be done. Afterward he'd have a glass of vodka and some aspirin. He could barely walk even with two canes. He cursed nonstop. Levi was the only son with a good idea of Simon's past. You could say that Simon didn't have an ounce of generosity in his system and that included concealing his past. Once during a drunken argument about a piece in *Scientific American* about deep ocean thermal temperatures Simon became rabid at the idea of water recycling at a thousand degrees when he was sure the maximum temperature was 212 degrees. They finally made peace and Simon waxed sentimental which he never did. Levi was amazed to learn that Simon Sr., his grandfather, had done two years at Harvard before getting the boot. This was because Simon's father was remotely tied to the Eastern Ameses who always went to Harvard and had gone there himself. The closest Simon Jr. had gotten to an education after leaving Kentucky was his enthusiastic exploration of alcohol, whores, and blues clubs in downtown Chicago after the harvest. Lemuel wrote about Levi resentfully, and Sunderson wondered if he envied his relationship with Simon.

Sunderson was irritated that all Lemuel said about himself was that he was an "unsuccessful bank robber," a poor choice in a sparsely populated area where everyone tended to recognize everyone. But there is an urge in all of us to have a somewhat secret life, some much more than others.

In his long career as a state police detective Sunderson had heard of a number of crime families dotting the vast wooded expanse of the Upper Peninsula but none so dramatic as the Ameses. He was sure that if you could get any of them to sit for an interview, an unlikely prospect, none of them would admit to accepting a single law. They were their own culture, their own civilization. Other than going to the tavern other people didn't exist in any real sense. Much like grizzly bears trying to imprint the future of their race the Ames men kept an eye out for any pleasant girl reaching the eighth grade. They would occasionally attend the girls' basketball games to keep an eye out for new talent. As one of the few prosperous families in an impoverished area it was easy to attract young girls with a little money. Nothing was too debased for this family. Simple rape was merely a joke on the girl for whom there was no recourse with the few decrepit local law authorities, the sheriff in his seventies who was only concerned about lobbying the county commissioner for an ample retirement plan.

It had occurred to Sunderson that maybe his curiosity about the western branch of the Ames family came from wanting to know how they got that way. He remembered a sociology class he had taken as a sophomore where they had discussed, mostly wrangled about, nature and nurture. Everyone in the class seemed obsessed with blaming their shortcomings on someone else. If you added the idea of trauma to the stew it became richer but messier. Everyone wanted a trauma, real or invented, to explain the inexplicable. A mere parental spanking in the past became being beaten to within an inch of life. Sitting on Grandpa's leg was invariably sexual abuse. One attractive girl tearfully admitted that a stepbrother had begun screwing her at age seven. No one wanted to believe this because it trumped everyone. They questioned her veracity until she was a grim puddle of sobs. The teacher finally made them stop. One young man boldly confessed to screwing his cousin at age seven and she *liked* it. Sunderson with no youthful sexual adventures felt left out. After the knowledge he looked at the girl in class with great sympathy. Once they had coffee together and she told him that she intended to never have a sexual life. She was now nineteen and pretty but it seemed not to matter to her. He took her statement as a warning though they remained warm friends. She ended up marrying a gay friend, a convenience to please both their families who he hoped did not want grandchildren.

Sunderson reflected on the horrors we commit against each other, sometimes just verbal but they can loom large. He recalled an ugly incident with Diane during their marriage. He had a couple of big doubles which he needed at the Ramada Inn bar where they poured large, and at dinner Diane had the blues because a friend at work had died in an automobile wreck out on Highway 28 near Seney, a bad stretch. Sunderson was babbling about his wicked workday wherein he had answered a domestic abuse call from a professor's wife. He got to the trim and tasteful little home near the campus and her face was bloody mush. Diane had asked him to *please* not talk about it but he couldn't seem to stop. He had gone over and arrested the husband with his bruised knuckles right in the classroom. The man's dignity was affronted or so he said. He and his wife had a little "quarrel" at lunch hour. "Yeah, you beat the shit out of her," Sunderson replied putting cuffs on the man to further humiliate him in front of his students. When he had taken her to the ER at the hospital it was determined that she had received two facial fractures, one on each cheekbone. Sunderson had the urge to shove the man out of the speeding squad car but settled for taking him to jail which outraged the snot. Meanwhile Diane had tried to stop him telling her for the last time, left the dinner table in tears, and went upstairs to her small room, her private hangout full of art books which she could look at for days on end when he drove her crazy with his insensitivity.

# Chapter 7

Monica came in with a casserole of ham and scalloped potatoes and put it in the oven for his dinner. She leaned over just so which turned him on so they made hasty love but post-orgasm he became depressed, remembering his vow to leave her alone. Out the window he watched Monica walk back home. He would have driven her but she always refused.

Mona had FedExed a large packet including the lengthy rap sheet for the entire Ames family which she had compiled via her computer, several pages each from police departments in several jurisdictions. Many were Fish and Game violations. One year an undercover agent determined that the Ameses had shot seventeen deer. There was a big fine but no jail time because an otiose judge figured the men were needed on the farm. Many of the deer were shot by Simon out his upstairs window in the remains of the garden. They always planted a couple extra rows of carrots to bait deer who loved them. There was also an apple tree they fed off which the family wanted for cider in the fall.

Sunderson was disgusted with himself. He had bought the cabin for fishing and now suddenly the table was covered with Ames-related papers. His curiosity was intruding on his fishing. He went fishing but quickly stepped in a beaver hole and cold water flooded in over the tops of his waders. He became very cold, got out of the river, slipped out of the waders, and lay in the grass in the warm sunlight. Getting soaked was the nastiest peril of trout fishing. He dozed in the warm grass with pleasure thinking of Monica's pretty fanny which partly redeemed the abysmal family. He wished she was back here for an outdoor tumble in the grass with the bright sun shining on her lovely butt. Sunderson reminded himself he had yet to fish downstream through the Ames property, but then he didn't want to get shot at for a joke.

He concluded that with the Ameses he was dealing as Marion had insisted with a human junk pile. With the possible exception of Monica and the good influence of Lily the young people were surly and foul-mouthed like their parents. If their lawlessness was down to nurture rather than nature, he suspected the complete absence of any religious training or impulse. There was no real explanation for his sick fascination short of observing life on another planet.

He understood that things had further disintegrated when Simon had died at eighty-eight shortly after New Year's this year. On his deathbed he spent his last week yelling out "Why do I have to die?" Without Simon's daily instructions at dawn every morning everything began to slide except Tom looking after the cows, the primary source of income. When it came to splitting up the money everyone, of course, thought Tom was cheating but in fact he was honest to the dime. Tom couldn't help being cruel. It was simply in his blood like a bird dog hunting birds. Despite the pleas of the wives none of the three houses was ever painted and looked worse every spring after another arduous U.P. winter. The wives would occasionally paint an interior room, usually the kitchen where much of the life of the household took place. The pantries were stacked with cartons holding gallons of vodka which was mostly drunk at the kitchen table though each man kept a spare in his bedroom for middle-of-the-night thirst. The one bill Simon had never objected to was the large cost of the vodka supply because he needed several large glasses a day himself. Sunderson had never heard of a family more consumed with overdrinking. Tom, the murderer, was the lightest drinker but he used his light drinking to control the others. Much of this inside information about the workings of the family came from what Lemuel told his jailers. He seemed to feel little loyalty to his brothers and father.

The men were lazier but generally more relaxed after the death of their father. He had a high-pitched cracked voice that kept everyone on edge. He minutely went over the bills the family received and the cost of paint for the kitchen could bring on an outraged tirade so out of proportion that people hid. With Simon you had to believe in the old-fashioned word wicked.

Sunderson fished well for a couple of hours carefully avoiding the beaver pathways that would have got him wet again. He was ironically disturbed because he was thinking too much and trout fishing was supposed to be a total relief from thinking. He was wishing he was still married to Diane and had the pleasant, easygoing life they had carved out for themselves. Without her his life had become abrupt fits and starts. A simple trip to the grocery store could become a nightmare. He tried mightily to avoid the liquor store but often failed.

About halfway through fishing Sunderson wondered what the endgame was to this Ames business. Was he fascinated because their disarray was reflected in his own? With Diane it had been easy to control his behavior because their marriage depended on a certain solid etiquette as do most successful marriages. It was usually not the big things that destroyed marriages but the day-to-day treating each other poorly. He and Diane had mastered civility but finally his job and drinking had wrecked them. He was no fun anymore and didn't read as much as previously and she missed their extended book talks. In the summer they used to camp a lot in lovely places which she thrived on but he became too tired from his job and alcohol, a huge consumer of energy.

Despite the pretty good fishing and pleasant ham and scalloped potatoes Sunderson's evening was full of dark thoughts, premonitions in fact, which he had always disliked as they defied rationality. Life wasn't organized so that the random future could be predicted. All of his life when he had had dark thoughts about the future he had ignored them. Along with the Ames rap sheet with a stupendous seventy-three violations Mona had sent a newspaper editorial that claimed the county would save money and time by

incarcerating the entire family, including the children, two
of whom had tried to set fire to the local school. The alert
local volunteer fire department had minimized the damage but two Ames children were standing there smelling
of gasoline watching the blaze with pleasure. It was hard
for the county to press arson charges against the children
when everyone was frightened of the parents. The Ameses
had a habit of gratuitously beating up anyone who crossed
them, in public and without warning. Few pressed assault
charges for fear of future beatings.

Stormy weather arrived including late spring snow so
Sunderson went home for a few days. He was delighted on
arrival to be invited to dinner with Mona and Diane. As
a putative parent he hadn't acted like one, and he hoped
the invitation meant Diane might be thawing out. Mona
immediately told him she had heard that a French court
had given her rock musician a sentence of seven years. He
appealed but they denied him bail thinking he might escape
to Brazil in a reverse Polanski move.

Diane had made his favorite pot roast, a beef chuck
cooked slowly with potatoes, onions and red wine to which
she had added rutabaga out of habit, a U.P. peasant food
sturdy enough to grow in the wretched climate. Sunderson
would tease her about her lack of peasant roots and she
resented this so in went the rutabaga whenever possible.
In fact, Diane disliked rutabaga but he and Mona loved it.

Marion had said on the phone that Diane seemed to
have a lot of suitors. This was highly irritating to Sunderson who knew it was related to the rumor that Diane had
private money, exciting to any bachelor who wanted to be

supported. At dinner Sunderson told Mona that she could slow down on her Ames research and she repeated an ancient rumor obviously nerve-racking to Sunderson that early on in Kentucky Simon Sr. had fathered a child with his oldest daughter. He was prosecuted for this but the daughter went mad and couldn't testify. Simon celebrated, then a local took a shot at him which winged his shoulder. Simon was all outraged innocence though most people stopped talking to him. He simply could not take his crime seriously though the daughter never recovered.

Sunderson continued to have premonitions through the largely happy dinner. Mona was up from University of Michigan where she was studying art history and musicology. Sunderson stupidly asked her what kind of job that would get her. She pertly replied that she planned on living in France on his retirement money going to museums and classical music concerts. She wanted to hear a famous organ down in Aix-en-Provence. Sunderson felt chastened by her answer. They talked late and when he got back to his house he noted that a raw chicken he had forgotten to put in the freezer was stinking and bluish. He threw it in the backyard hoping a stray dog would eat it. If he had put it in the garbage the whole kitchen would have stunk in the morning. He put an open box of baking soda in the fridge which Diane said consumed odors. The phone rang and he was tempted not to answer it but then it might be Marion. It was Monica who said that Tom had died that morning in the hospital from poisoning. The police said no one had visited him. The authorities refused to announce the murder for a while until the local police could get the state police up to speed. Sunderson remembered that Tom's room was on the ground floor and that next to the large open window there was a blooming lilac bush, always a treat after winter. Anyone could have entered that way. Sunderson was embarrassed that he smiled about the murder but then he had valued Lily highly. He had glanced at Tom's X-rays when he had visited and noted the femurs blasted to shreds by the AK-47 and thought it would be difficult to learn to walk again but now the asshole was dead, and he was sure meek Lemuel wasn't the only person who'd wanted him gone. Any agile person could have crept in concealed by the lilacs and shoved some cyanide in his mouth.

When he drove to the cabin the next afternoon after spending Saturday morning with Marion he took along a cooler of fresh meat for his stay, including a big roasting chicken. He was still pleased that Tom was dead and something, presumably a dog, had run off with the stinking chicken in the backyard, two events of equal value in his mind. Rotten Tom, rotten chicken. His name would be on the register at the hospital and a cop visit was to be expected.

Marion was in fine fettle after fishing with the mosquitoes early in the morning. He cooked half a dozen brook trout for lunch with homemade bread and butter. His wife wouldn't eat brook trout being Apache who he knew didn't eat fish at all, but in their area they weren't in large supply. The Great Lakes tribes were lucky. If deer were scarce you could eat five pounds of fish for dinner.

Marion did not share his curiosity about the Ameses. He said that in his reading every state seemed to have a couple of such families. Marion also explained that he grew up on a reservation full of malcontents so it was a family that behaved well that had his curiosity. Sunderson couldn't argue with this it was so novel. Marion said that such people always seem to end with a virtual explosion and thought Tom's death might be the first of many.

# Chapter 8

The next was Levi. No one thought anything of not seeing Levi because he often spent the whole day drinking in his room or out in the box stall in the barn with Ralph the aging gelding draft horse, an immense but absurdly friendly animal who enjoyed Levi's drunken company. Levi was found on the floor of the box stall by one of Bert's irascible twin sons. Their mother had given up on the hyperactive and uncontrollable twins who often injured themselves. Simon hated medical expenses thinking that everyone should suffer in silence. He claimed to be keeping track of the expenses and the twins would have to pay up when they became adults.

So there Levi was on the box stall floor among the horse turds deader than a doornail, as they say. The county coroner said it was a clear case of poisoning with traces of cyanide in the half gallon of vodka which he had barely started before the poison took effect. Monica looked down at him without pity thinking that the horse was the only one who liked Levi. His wife certainly didn't.

Naturally with three down recently paranoia arose in the family at large. Two dead had dug quite a hole in the daily familiarity and no one had taken over all the work Tom had done with the cattle. This was a danger to the general livelihood. No one was totally above suspicion except each to themselves. The idea of a second family murder got the state police interested without results. Some in the family suspected that one of the wives was guilty and they were treated even worse than usual. There was something feminine about poisoning compared to a club or gun.

Sunderson spent a long time thinking about the crime and came up with John for no solid reason other than he was the most decent of the males, a sort of reverse logic wherein the most unlikely seems most likely. Others thought of Levi's widow Sara who seemed to hate everything and everybody to do with the Ames family. Having been deprived of sexuality by her drunken husband she had an open affair with Tom when he was still in his teens. Levi never noticed. Tom screwed Sara and moved on to raping Lily, but the rape alone was worth his eventual execution not to speak of Lily's murder. Sad that someone can't be executed twice.

He fished farther downstream than ever before, well into the Ames property. Their water wasn't as fine as his own, being too straight and monochromatic to be good trout habitat, though he caught a couple of good browns in deep pools. The ancient ancestor of the owner he'd bought from had picked the best water but then he was first by five decades. Sunderson was just getting out of the water to walk back home when something unbelievable caught his eye. Lodged in a small jam faceup was the body of one of Bert's twins, a big vigorous boy in his teens, so freshly drowned that he looked like he could be alive. Sunderson did a quick furtive examination rolling the boy over because his eyes were open. As a longtime detective Sunderson knew it was his responsibility to report the death but he wasn't up to it. Suddenly he was cold and walked the two miles home shivering ignoring a playful rifle shot that hit near his feet. When he got home Monica was there with a batch of good chili. He was paying extra for meals but loved the lack of bother. When tired from fishing you didn't want to spend an hour at the stove. He didn't want to but told Monica about the body of her younger brother. She winced but didn't seem to care. "Half brother. He was a horrible person. Dad made him that way," she said, "and that crazy woman he took up with after Mom. I'll tell the others." Sunderson gave her exact directions and let her use his phone. He was relieved to have it in another's hands but nonetheless feeling a little shabby as an ex–police officer. He hadn't seen any marks on the body but if it was poison again there wouldn't be external marks. He jumped the gun on dinner and had a small bowl of chili, then made love to Monica who was already on the bed. It seemed as ordinary as going to the grocery store though she held him more strongly than usual. The question was how do you make love to a girl after you announce you have found her dead brother in the river? But after she slipped off her jeans and sweater would it have been more hurtful to refuse? He walked a couple of miles with her on the way home. A rifle bullet hit a tree they passed. She said,

"That's Teddy. He doesn't understand his brother is dead. They were nearly inseparable."

In the twilight Sunderson saw in the distance a cop car driving across the field followed by the coroner's car. Not a good job on a summer evening. There would have to be two cops to haul the body up the riverbank as the coroner would have a struggle just to lift his fat off a sofa. Monica called at midnight with the news that a dead coyote had been found nearby with the remains of the boy's lunch, a clue that it was poison again. Sunderson immediately thought it was sad that a coyote had to die in this creepshow. He couldn't recall having exchanged a word with the boy but had noted that he was tremendously surly like the rest of the Ames males. He also evidently started drinking vodka as a child under his father's care.

Sunderson woke abruptly before dawn thinking about writers. He had learned to read at age four. His curiosity was about the adult world not children's stories. Luckily when he was in sixth grade a school friend would steal his older brother's *Playboy* and *Esquire* both of which transfixed him. During his long marriage to Diane he had been to dozens of arts and letters events at the local college, Northern Michigan University. They were always early in the evening and it was a struggle to keep awake after a long day of work but Diane loved these visits from novelists and poets so Sunderson pretended to, too. When he learned the full résumés of the visitors he thought it odd that they had full tenured positions at universities on the basis of a slender book of poems or a critically admired first novel. The poets read in strangely affected voices poems about their largely bourgeois daily lives. The novelists were worse, if anything. They would read a chapter from an upcoming work, never about crime or anything interesting, often about a boy who was too sensitive for words always with parents who misunderstood him. It was a little like having your mom read to you as a child. The peculiar thing about visiting novelists was their absolute self-obsession. There was one world and it was limited to their curious point of view. It was a real yawner and Sunderson wondered why they hadn't spent more of their lives out in the world doing something interesting like running guns to Mexico or Mali. There was frequently a small party afterward to which he and Diane were always invited, and the novelists always flirted with her thinking there was a possible score and always looked hangdog when they left. The best he could say about the novelists was that they were better company than he expected, professionally curious about everything.

Lemuel was another matter. Was he doing the killing to add verve to his crime novel about the family? It was certainly logical if a little far-fetched. Sunderson searched his mind for any hidden clues. Monica had told him that Lemuel had had an affair, discreet, with her mother Silvia. The wife of a severe alcoholic is evidently fair game and when Silvia was attentive to herself she was quite attractive.

At first light Sunderson went out to pee in the yard but it was chilly, not quite forty, so there was no hurry to fish. He spent a half hour making himself a pan of fried potatoes. His eye caught movement far out in the pasture which told him that Lemuel was headed his way. He had been thinking that as a boy the nude photos in *Playboy* had been quite a shock. They were too monstrous to be desirable. The huge breasts troubled him reminding him of his mother and sister Berenice through whom he learned to dislike huge breasts. He liked Monica's modest breasts which were nearly identical to Diane's. He was reminded again of the Seven Deadly Sins. And when he saw a woman's hairy pubic patch in those same magazines he got quite a jolt. He was slowly developing his own pubic hair but it hadn't occurred to him that women would have it. It seemed vulgar.

His mind was muddy that morning and irked at Lemuel for dropping in. He could always clarify it by an hour of fishing but he had long since abandoned fishing when it was 40 degrees or under. His brain mud which started in a fit of insomnia the night before was comprised of the idea of taking Monica to Marquette to get her away from her awful life but what would it look like with him living with a nineteen-year-old girl. It wasn't illegal and she was unlikely to walk around saying, "Yes, he's fucking me." But what would Diane think? Though they were no longer married, and perhaps it wasn't her business except in his mind. The second intrusive thought that stopped him from falling back into the sweet sleep that is the last hour of every morning was about the Seven Deadly Sins. He wished he had ten bucks for every time they arose in his mind and then he could buy a new car. After that youthful exposure they could be labeled *post-traumatic stress disorder* for all of the mental damage they had done. He had only gotten back to sleep by planning to write them down and see how he fared in an honest assessment, and was awoken again with thoughts of

writers and Lemuel. Now as Lemuel approached the back
door he strewed some papers on the table to make it look
like he was busy.

He poured Lemuel a cup of coffee and he glanced at
the table.

"Am I interrupting something?"

"I was doing my monthly books." This was an outright
lie as Sunderson never did books. Diane had kept track of
his finances except for his checkbook which was always
such a mess she didn't want to touch it. For some reason
a check stub was beyond his filling out. The bank always
called when he was overdrawn. Diane pointed out that his
yearly overdraft penalties were enormous. That didn't help.
He hated to be in a grocery line when someone ahead of
him was laboriously filling out a check stub at the counter.

"This is a chapter on Bert I thought might interest
you." He handed Sunderson a sheaf held together by a big
paper clip.

*Before his long decline after Vietnam Bert was a key
worker. We were very friendly when young, hanging out together fishing and hunting. He told me when he got home
he had killed some wrong people by mistake. That's why he
couldn't hunt anymore. He couldn't even eat venison because
it reminded him of dead bodies. Bert started each day with a
big glass of vodka before breakfast.*

Lemuel got up hastily to leave glancing again at Sunderson's strewn papers.

"I've always hated paperwork," he said.

"Me too." Sunderson in fact had very little of it since retirement and generally ignored it.

With Lemuel gone Sunderson pushed the Bert material aside for the time being. With minimal exposure he disliked the man intensely. He had heard that once on a hot day Bert had tethered his daffy wife to a post in the yard and left her there until a kid came along and cut her loose with a jack-knife. He had chased the kid down and beat him. Meanwhile Lily had driven her mother to the ER with heatstroke.

He carefully made out a list of the Seven Deadly Sins on a long, yellow legal tablet: Pride, Greed, Envy, Lechery, Gluttony, Anger, Laziness. He resolved to be honest and as brief as possible in his self-evaluation.

*Pride.* Most men are prideful for no particular reason. They carry themselves as if they were directing the United Nations when they are real estate agents or bookkeepers. Real estate developers are particularly prideful as if they were the economic key. Early on when I was the only ace detective in the U.P. I would put on a clean shirt and beam in the mirror. The thought of it now embarrasses me. By and large I flunk on pride. No matter how bad my behavior I am still full of pride even after my wretched but justified divorce.

*Greed.* I can give myself a fairly high mark on this one having been raised the way I was. My father made enough for the basic support of the family, no extras, and that was that. I made my own small amounts of

money by mowing lawns, washing cars, shoveling walks
in winter. My father made me continue shoveling the
walk for an old lady who would only give me a dime. She
couldn't do her own, he pointed out. I never washed a
car as an adult because I did too many for a quarter as a
kid and it generally took two hours which meant about
twelve cents per hour of work. The only exception was
a real estate developer who would give me a buck to
do his Buick, the cost of a car wash over in Marquette
in those days. The developer was from downstate and
I figured that was what they paid down there. Such
youthful labor teaches economic realities, but I was
simply never oriented to money. We lived fine on my
detective salary and Diane saved her hospital paycheck
for travel and our retirement which as it turns out will
not be together. She has mentioned the unfairness of
this and told me to tell her if I need money. I nearly
asked her for a Toyota 4Runner, Sport model, which
would be fine for the rough country I encounter fishing
and hunting but stopped short. She would go to France
and Italy every couple of years usually with a friend. I
didn't go except once because I doubted an airplane's
ability to fly across the ocean and I'd rather go fishing.
It will cost me money to move Monica to Marquette
but I don't care. Call it compassion.

*Envy.* I don't get this one very clearly. I mean I am
unsure what it covers. Envy for Diane's husband,
maybe—which means I envy a dead man. I once read
an article about American women traveling solo to

Europe to get fucked by French and Italian men who
I envied. I brought it up with Diane once when I was
drinking. She laughed very hard and said, "Why would
I do that when all I would have to do is go to downtown
Marquette in the evening? They must be desperate.
You already do it more than I like which I tolerate
because I love you."

Writing this down had upset Sunderson so he decided
to take a break and read a little of "Bert." The upshot was
that well into his teens Bert was a fair-haired boy. He was
a fine high school athlete and would neither drink nor
smoke. He did one year at the state college in Bozeman,
Montana, didn't like it, got drunk and joined the marines
with no idea of the horror he was entering. He spent the
last two years of Vietnam, the waning years of the war, as
an NCO in the north. "When I picked him up in Marquette
from his flight home we had to stop at several bars. He
said, 'Lem, none of it was worth it. None of the war was
worth a single American life. Our country betrayed us.'"
The girl Bert had married before he shipped out promptly
called an end to it.

Lemuel then went on for several pages on Vietnam
with nothing new or original. As a lifelong student of history
and noncombatant Sunderson had read too much of wars
starting with Alexander the Great and even the Indian Wars
which disgusted him. The only ones who came out good were
Red Cloud, Crazy Horse, and Chief Joseph. Nothing was
so contemptible in American history as our fatal pursuit of
Joseph and his people, except possibly Vietnam.

Anyway what recovery Bert made was down at the tavern, according to Lemuel. "He married the lovely Silvia before he totally maimed himself. It was ugly to watch a good-looking young man become a bloated monster. His wife was a profound Catholic and would not leave him with the children he totally neglected. Bert's case was the clearest I've ever seen of alcoholism as a disease though other family members are close. In sheer quantity it was dumbfounding, never less than a quart a day unless he had flu and was vomiting. It was a shock to me that his lovely wife, of whom I was overfond, took his daily abuse."

This was not new to Sunderson. He had handled dozens and dozens of spousal abuse cases, and it seemed similar to people who adapt to living with chronic pain. Unless the woman had a considerable network of close friends helping her, the trap continued indefinitely, especially for Catholic women to whom divorce is such a taboo. For women the law could not protect, their suffering became like an act of God. After being tied up in the yard, however, Silvia cracked and finally got away from Bert.

Sunderson was tempted to put the "Bert" chapter off to the side, there being nothing unexpected, including a thirty-day jail term for severely beating three young men at the tavern who were persistently harassing him. One was the mayor's son, the mayor of fifty people, if that, known for a wool pinstripe suit left over from the fifties he loved to wear on special occasions of which there were next to none. This man's loutish son and two other boys were taunting Bert on the subject of Vietnam over which he had no sense of humor.

Bert was everything to excess including alcohol. I know that many days he must have come close to consuming a half gallon but then he was the largest of the brothers. Twice I recall he totally collapsed and had to be hospitalized for alcohol poisoning. He dried out during his 30 day jail term but actually camped next to the tavern when he got out of jail. He was always bedding tavern tarts. Locally it was a homely selection but I guessed there was some sort of camaraderie in the woebegone.

I speak with mildly improper authority on alcohol. There's so much of it to observe in my family at large. I've only been truly drunk twice in my life and it was long ago when I was a freshman at University of Montana in Missoula. At the onset of the school year I sat around with my new roommates for hours drinking beer. In the morning I vomited for an hour and warned myself not to drink again it was so unpleasant. About a month later I became the lover of a young woman from Kalispell. I had no experience to speak of and her sexual ardor scared me. Her father had sent her off to school in a new Ford convertible, an unsuitable car for Montana except for a few summer months. She was extremely proud of her car which all the students looked at with envy. One evening we were parked on a country road with a six-pack. It was so cold outside but the car heater was on high. She was humping me face forward with the ceiling light on, a lurid sight. Suddenly I felt ill, pushed her aside, and vomited on the dashboard. That essentially ended the relationship. It was unthinkable that anyone would puke in her new car. As penance I never drank another beer in my life. A few years later when she would talk to me again she said it was awful that year in winter because every time she turned on the radio the dashboard would heat

*up and the car would stink. I sympathized but there was no*
*way she would make love again.*

Monica brought in a pot of ham hocks and baked beans
for dinner which didn't smell as good as possible given Sunderson's reading. They talked a bit about her planned escape to Marquette. She now wanted to leave as soon as
possible. That morning one of the wives had slapped her
hard when she set out breakfast. The wives had long abdi-
cated any cooking responsibilities, shoving it off on Monica.
They had so many chickens and eggs she would scramble
a couple dozen every morning which the men would eat
with Tabasco. She used plenty of butter and cream trying
to kill them with cholesterol. They all loved her chicken and
biscuits which she hated making because she would have
to kill and pluck five chickens. She liked the chickens and
it was hard to cut off their heads.

Monica said that they would have to use stealth to escape
to Marquette because everyone would try to stop her. She
said that twilight would be best because by then usually
everyone would be too drunk to act. He agreed. They made
love hastily with Monica bent over the table, her favorite
way to avoid undressing and dressing.

It was too cool and windy to fish well and coinciden-
tally, when Monica left, he discovered he had aborted his
Seven Deadly Sins project with *lechery*, perhaps a subcon-
scious act, wanting to avoid an item over which he felt guilt.

*Lechery.* Perhaps one of my downfalls and I don't know
why. Most men, I think, talk more about sex than they

actually feel. I never talk about sex except in humor-
ous terms with Marion. On our honeymoon I made
love to Diane ten times one day and she talked as if
something was wrong with me. Maybe. My prostate
acted up so when fishing I had to keep a hold on a
tree to pee. Admittedly I did a very wrong thing with
Mona in Paris. And should Monica seem in question
at age nineteen? I told her there was no obligation and
she said, "I thought we were lovers, like in books I've
read." What do you say to that? Still it nags at me. Her
butt is beautiful but is that an excuse? I should look
for a girl at least in her twenties or thirties of course. I
consider Mona a sexual disease that started years ago
with my peeking out the window at her next door doing
nude yoga before school. I was so vigilant in my lust
checking the window nearly around the clock by pulling a book from the bookcase that covered the window.
After a while I knew that she knew I was looking, and
sometimes I mistakenly left a back light on but that
seemed to encourage her. I think of the sexual urge
deeply coded within us, ingrained, and predisposed
to make us fools. I think Mona was curious, charmed
by my stupidity, pleased with her power over an older
man. Obviously the world has to be populated thus
nature has given us these barely controllable impulses
that begin early and continue into advanced age. This
is copping a plea a bit. But then I can't very well withdraw my offer to help Monica just to avoid making
love to her. Perhaps I'm not being entirely honest. My
generosity to myself knows no bounds! The very idea

of sex on occasion fills me with unrest and torpor as if I want it to end.

*Gluttony.* I am absolved of this sin though when I finally get something good I'll eat it to near exhaustion. I am a poor cook. Good ones like Diane and Marion always have a mixture of patience and imagination. Even when I do something as ordinary as chopping garlic I could be droning the "Song of the Volga Boatmen." In a dozen tries I've never made a chicken pot pie where the crust didn't collapse into the stew. Actual tears fell. Trying to bone a lamb shoulder also brought tears. I did research and drew the bone structure on a piece of paper with no luck. What I am insinuating is that poor cooks are poor eaters. One night during deer season I missed a decent dinner while drinking and talking about the hunt with other nitwits. I ate a big pile of bar food, pickled turkey gizzards and a wretched frozen pizza which was asking for trouble. Shortly before noon on the next day's hunt I was eating my favorite baked bean and onion sandwich and the diarrhea struck with breathless intensity in the middle of a blizzard. I crawled into a small pine plantation swearing off pickled turkey gizzards. Luckily every hunter carries toilet paper, a great invention if ever there was one.

The other day Marion made me a venison carbonade, a Belgian dish that seemed the best single thing I'd ever eaten, a stew made with lots of onions, garlic, and dark beer. I have had a fantasy of simply going to France (without Mona) and Italy for a couple of months and eating well. Diane thinks this is a great idea and even did some restaurant research for me and sent me a little book, *The Best Bistros of Paris*. She said I was temperamentally ill suited for starred restaurants or what she calls *haute cuisine*. They would "put me off," she said. My mother was an ordinary to poor cook so I didn't develop sophisticated tastes like many do. She regularly made pot roasts but not good ones like Diane. My mother would put the pot in the oven and cook the hell out of it so the meat was dry and tough and the onions and potatoes denatured. The only thing that survived with taste was the rutabaga of which she used a great deal because my father loved it. So do I. Naturally she didn't use the essential cup of red wine. I don't recall ever seeing wine in the house. We were poor and doomed in a culinary sense. Even the Thanksgiving turkey or any roast chicken was dry and tough. She was killing everything twice. Now I imagine that there was an American Housewives School of Dry Cooking to which she adhered. Quite naturally my own tendency is to never cook things long enough. I've had altogether too many pink-jointed roast chickens, too many underdone pot roasts wherein the secret seems to be long low heat. In any event I'm innocent of the sin of gluttony.

*Anger.* I'm up in the air about the sin of anger. I've always believed in "righteous anger" but I'm in doubt about what direction it's in. Obviously when I was still working I would get very angry at wife and child beaters but this can rapidly descend in other areas. The expression "I blew my top" is quite lame or "I was real pissed off." Maybe rage at inanimate objects is excusable — fury over the flat tire, a furnace that quits on a cold night, a car that won't start, the meat that you burned — but I find so much of this questionable. Anger gobbles up so much of the energy that could have been used correcting the situation. I except wife beating or child abuse. I'd answer a call and the wife was a mess with the shit beat out of her face, the husband sitting at the kitchen table crying into his hands. Why is he crying? He did it. Sometimes the husband would still be angry as if your answering the call was the cause of everything. Sometimes they had to be restrained. The same with the beating of children. The man would cry as if he were to be pitied.

More than anything as a detective I learned that human behavior was an endless puzzle, especially bad behavior. Good behavior is obvious. It also saves oceans of time. You always feel the fool when you're mad at your car. I rarely ever got angry with Diane except occasionally when she would adopt her father's right-wing opinions. "The poor don't work hard enough." I've never known anyone as desperate for work as the poor. Welfare Diane was mixed about. Apparently there is welfare fraud but not nearly as much as many people think. I saw a few cases of it but the majority of welfare recipients were hopeless people who simply couldn't take care of themselves, often for reasons of low intelligence or mental illness. I think that often a stupid man would marry a stupid woman and breed a family that would never be able to take care of itself. Food stamps are wonderful because we can't let them starve. So I would get mad at her limited views.

*Laziness.* Is up and down. Too often in a bad situation I just sit there instead of getting out of it. My father wouldn't just mow the lawn he would attack it with our old-fashioned mower. When I grew older I was expected to do the same but didn't have his strength, partly because some of the lawn was uphill. But he said he went to work at manual labor at age twelve so was very strong right into old age which he refused to recognize.

Monica called saying she had to get out of there ASAP because Sprague had punched her hard in the face that morning when his eggs were cold. Bert threw him against the wall but then Sprague, a champion fistfighter, punched Bert several times until Bert got him in a choke hold on the floor. Bert had to be restrained because it looked like Sprague was being strangled to death. A family breakfast, Sunderson thought. They agreed to meet at 8:30 p.m. in the twilight this close to the solstice at the foot of the road. Monica thought she could get away after serving dinner because this was the time of day the men were the drunkest. It was agreed though Sunderson was upset. These warm, muggy days were supposed to be the best for trout fishing and he had ruined his vacation by getting involved. He fished the rest of the day through dinner hour, Spanish rice Monica delivered that he never liked due to its heavy presence on the school's hot lunch program. Monica's, however, was good with lots of chicken thighs in it not the chintzy school variety, and lots of garlic which he loved. He dozed, woke up and made coffee, then fished for a while.

It was time to fetch Monica. As a precaution he wore his pistol and shoulder holster under a light sport coat. He was bathed in the mist of having caught his largest brown trout, probably four pounds, and had been so transfixed remembering the beauty of its coloring that he burned his lips on the coffee and dropped the cup, jumping back to avoid splattering. He wasn't angry, he just felt inept. He cautiously poured another cup and thought about what he hoped to do. He thought of buying her a hotel room at the Landmark Inn, the best hotel in town, then thought it would be more awkward than staying at his house which had the advantage of being more private. He imagined someone trying to stop him getting Monica out of there and made himself pointlessly angry.

There she was in a skirt and blouse and a small cheap suitcase at the end of the driveway. She had tears in her eyes but still managed a smile. They were barely through the village when he saw in the rearview mirror Sprague's muddy white pickup truck giving chase. About a mile out of town he pulled up beside them and Monica screamed, "Don't stop!" Sprague bumped their left front fender fairly hard and Sunderson nearly lost control. He drew his pistol and blew out Sprague's windshield lowering his tolerance for cool evening wind. Sprague slowed down to get behind them then accelerated up on the inside with a shotgun out the driver's window. Sunderson yelled "duck" to Monica and quickly shot Sprague, it looked like in the shoulder, and the shotgun dropped to the road. Sprague's pickup swerved off the bumpy shoulder and into the thicket of young maples where it stopped. Sunderson slowed to a stop, got out, and approached Sprague's vehicle slowly in case he had another gun. He was sitting in the front seat holding the bloody shoulder with his other hand.

"Where you taking her, fucker?" he muttered in pain.

"I'm sending her to my sister in Tucson tomorrow morning." Sunderson was pleased with the lie.

"Who is going to cook for us?" Sprague whined.

Sunderson was stunned. Was this all about food?

"You'll have to take cooking lessons," Sunderson said lamely. "Meanwhile you want a ride to the hospital?"

"I doubt that it's that bad. Give me a ride home."

"Not a chance. You can hoof it." Sunderson imagined that anything near an Ames house could bring fire from a .30-06 rifle.

"You're a dead man," Sprague bellowed.

"I'll take that chance." Sunderson shoved his pistol in Sprague's mouth and cocked it. Sprague's eyes were wild with fear. Sunderson walked back to his car and consoled the sobbing Monica.

"You should have killed him," she said.

"It would have been too much of a mess afterward," he said. "Filling out papers. That sort of thing. Death is very bureaucratic."

She slumped in the seat and tried to calm down and doze. Her skirt was well up her thighs which didn't help his

driving. He leaned far forward for a craven look upward.
God never made better thighs. Or butt. What a lucky old
fool I am, he thought.

They reached Marquette before 10:00 p.m. and the
kitchen at the bar at the Landmark Inn was still serving
food. He talked to the chef extolling Monica's abilities and
he went back to the office and got a blank job application
which Monica held as if precious. Sunderson had his favorite
fried whitefish tail sandwich and a beer.

At home he put Monica in Diane's lovely private upstairs room. He had moved a single bed in there and the
toilet and shower were next door. She wanted a shower so he
went downstairs and poured a modest drink. At first he felt
nervous putting her in Diane's precious room but then she
had abandoned it when she left him. She came downstairs
in one of Diane's huge expensive towels. They had a quick
one on the sofa and the immediacy of sexual desire surprised
him. A moron friend sophomore year in high school used to
say, "If we didn't fuck the world would get empty." Everyone doubted that the boy had done the deed but it turned
out his neighbor, a great big senior girl, was screwing him
often for her own purposes. When she got pregnant she
was too embarrassed to admit he was the father but he told
everyone who would listen. He was proud. Sunderson was
amused remembering this. There is someone for everyone.

It was pointless to get too analytical about sex, and no
one had done so satisfactorily that he knew of. They liked
to say "it's in the brain" but where else would it be, down
the street? He was ill equipped in the sciences anyway. He
was just curious at the electric effect Monica had on him not

to speak of Diane in the past. The very thought of Diane filled him with unrest and even the next day he wandered around the yard to check on this and that on his list of tasks to be done. He always disliked yard work having done it so cheaply as a youth. His neighbor was hanging up clothes in a sexy robe. There it was again! They chatted a moment. She was wondering where he spent so much time and he told her about the fishing cabin. She hoped that sometime she could go along. They were from Ohio and quite unused to the natural beauty that she was seeing in the Upper Peninsula. Her name was Delphine, a name he'd never heard before. He couldn't imagine her husband letting her go off to his cabin while he worked but perhaps they were a "modern couple." He had heard of such things but not locally. Besides his plate was full with Monica.

Marion stopped by and had a cup of coffee. He seemed delighted to meet Monica who was getting ready to go off and look for work. Marion was going to help Sunderson look for a used compact to buy for her. Sunderson was too impulsive and dumb about cars and needed help. She left, borrowing Sunderson's car after the two men gave her tips and directions to likely restaurants where she might find work. She was worried that people might know about her background but they thought this unlikely. When she left Sunderson told Marion about the Sprague story. He was not amused and wondered if the Ameses might invade Marquette to get their cook back by kidnap. Sunderson said that Lemuel had promised to call and tip him off if he saw any movements in this direction. Marion was still full of doubt. Nothing was beyond these people in his opinion.

Marion suggested he keep himself well armed and Sunderson agreed.

Monica stopped back briefly with groceries so he could have lunch. She hastily made him a bowl of pasta with lots of garlic at his request. He meant to do some minimal work in the yard since she was using his car and he couldn't drive around aimlessly which he liked doing. He weeded and trimmed Diane's herb patch and perennial beds. His neighbor stopped over and gave him advice. When she stooped he saw up her legs clearly and blushed. He reminded himself again, "Stay away from this one." He also said to himself, "Act your age," but this was quickly followed by the question *why?* Everyone says it and surely there were some absurd older men. He had once arrested one in Escanaba for consorting with a fifteen-year-old poor girl. The man refused to admit to doing anything wrong. He was sixty-eight and said that in the "old days" he would never have been arrested. Sunderson merely said that these were no longer the old days. He had always thought this would never be in his character. What had he become? His neighbor however must be in her early forties, the prime of life.

He went inside for a rest after his dizzying work on his knees. Lemuel called to say there had been some talk led by Sprague about recapturing Monica and getting good food again. Bert, her father, was the only one who agreed. The others maintained that kidnap was too serious a charge to play with. Sunderson was painfully aware that at nineteen she was just barely an adult and they could accuse him of kidnap instead, but he couldn't imagine the Ameses going to the police.

He was in an agitated state despite knowing Bert couldn't simply grab Monica if it involved what police call "a breach of the peace" which it certainly would. The times Bert had tried to fuck Monica when he was drunk would look bad in court.

Monica came back at about 5:00 p.m. and began preparing dinner, a meat loaf and baked potato. She was jubilant having got two jobs for a total of sixty-five hours a week. "What about me?" thought Sunderson though he acted pleased for her. The one in the kitchen at the hotel bar was as sous-chef six nights a week from five to eleven. The other was at a diner Sunderson considered worthless. He spent the evening arguing that the hotel would be enough and was a classy place good on a résumé. The diner would only be slinging workingman's hash and do nothing for her. She wanted to save money to move to New York City and work in a famous restaurant and leave her family far behind. This utterly appalled Sunderson. He claimed that he had lived there though it had been mostly in a hospital and rehab clinic. He had forgotten that he had told her exhaustively about his experiences and she said that his life in New York was scarcely typical. He quickly offered her a hundred bucks a week to cook for him and take care of his house. That would take care of turning down the diner job. She said she would sleep on it. She didn't think he could afford it but he told her otherwise. He couldn't bear the idea of her being gone sixty-five hours a week plus commuting time but what was he really offering except money.

Monica had spoken of suicide several times which frightened him. It was the old saw that if they talk about it they might do it. Sunderson had known three suicides in his life with one being flatly justified, a schoolteacher with the always fatal Lou Gehrig's disease. The first one had been in high school, a girl he liked a great deal. She was kind to everyone expect herself. She seemed very intelligent but lonely with her only good friend moving downstate and her own parents going through a nasty divorce. She had hung herself, a violent and too often unsuccessful form of suicide he had learned. It was in the tenth grade when all girls are too sensitive. The whole class was saddened and perplexed except two boys who joked about it and whom Sunderson had beat up during noon hour. Later he realized that the suicide had embarrassed them into humor. He apologized but it was not accepted. The third suicide was a successful local businessman. It seemed incomprehensible though later he heard that the man had gay tendencies he didn't want to surface and also his wife was having an affair plus he wasn't nearly as successful as he appeared to be and the walls were closing in. Many were upset because the man was such a pleasant person. Sunderson wondered about how rarely we truly know each other but then perhaps it's right that we remain essential mysteries to one another.

# Chapter 9

The next morning reading over his Seven Deadly Sins material he found that he had been less than completely honest. Why lie to yourself? Why fool God if there is such a creature? His father used to be quite irate with the Catholics who he believed were trying to monopolize Christianity historically. His own Christianity seemed nominal but despite his education being limited to high school he was very well read and a Library Friend with Marquette's splendid Peter White Public Library being a wonderful resource. On winter weekends Sunderson's father would drive them over to Marquette and go to the library, the origin of Sunderson's own love of books. Diane was amused because as an adult Sunderson's book buying often exceeded the cost of their mortgage. After the library they would stop at a bar and have large delicious hamburgers which never tasted that good again in his life. His dad would have a couple of beers and on the way home they would stop in front of St. Michael's, the huge Catholic church, a monument that Sunderson found very impressive though he had no idea what went on inside. Parked in front his father would rant about Catholicism, especially what he saw as the malformation of the New Testament in Lyon in the eighth century when some apocryphal gospels were left out. In his mind the appearance of Luther should have destroyed the Church. He had a love of the scholarly gossip about the sexual promiscuity of some early popes. Sunderson was taught to think of them as the biggest businessmen in the world. His father believed that all churches should pay property taxes excluding the Lutherans. Sunderson made no effort to try to understand the parameters of his father's beliefs. His ranting had a definite entertainment value. His own father, Sunderson's grandfather, had been a schoolteacher against whom he rebelled by refusing to go to college. It was a regret and made him strongly urge Sunderson to go to Michigan State. He had heard that the University of Michigan was full of snooty rich people and as a populist and left-winger that wouldn't do for his son. His own life had been somewhat blighted, he thought, by an early family and hard labor.

He was in a funk thinking of rewriting his Seven Deadly Sins when Lemuel called warning that they were leaving late that afternoon to retrieve Monica. Fine, Sunderson thought, she would be at work at the Landmark Inn. He called the detective who had replaced him, Smolens, and described the situation. Smolens knew about the Ames family and whistled. He said that he would be there by four with two patrolmen and wait it out. Sunderson got out his pistol in case they arrived early. He started rewriting his lechery portion because that was the most interesting.

> *Lechery*. In my work we kept lists of people for when we would tell sexual malefactors that they needed "professional help," ministers and psychologists and one psychiatrist and suchlike. I rarely could imagine them going but would tell them the judge would go more lightly if they were seeking help.
>
> At one point, early in our marriage, Diane had suggested that I was a sexual obsessive and should definitely see a psychiatrist. I wanted to screw her butt which she wouldn't allow saying it was perverted. I was hurt and tried to show her literature that said it was a fairly common practice. This meant nothing to Diane who was adamant. I did not show her a rather racy piece in a men's magazine saying that the practice was popular with Brazilian girls who wished to save their virginity for marriage. This boggled. I was in my randy thirties at the time. What was stopping me from going to Brazil except I was married with a job? I thought of trying it when she was sexually carried away but didn't dare.

He was unable to concentrate on the Seven Deadly Sins given the mortal threat he was under. Smolens and the two officers arrived promptly at four. He made a pot of coffee for them thinking that a drink would be more appropriate. While fussing over the coffee he took a gulp from one of his many hidden pints in the kitchen. The men selected their hiding places, Smolens in the entry cloakroom, one officer in Sunderson's study around the corner, one in a dining room closet. Smolens told him to offer the Ameses a drink or a cup of coffee. He also told Sunderson to put away the pistol he had left out on the dining room table but Sunderson forgot to do so what with feeling the deep warmth of his gulp of whiskey. He was also amused that this whole thing was basically about food. They had lost their only good cook and couldn't get by. The wives had lost interest in it after a lifetime of being brutalized. If your husband ties you up in the hot sun you're unlikely to make him a nice dinner. If your husband is drunk why slave at the stove. Steady Monica had just kept on cooking because she loved it despite Sprague punching her because his eggs were chilly when he was late for breakfast. John was the earliest and sometimes ate all the sausage before the others arrived. No niceties were observed. Simon had complained about the grocery bills but she bought the best sausage that he loved. John was the biggest and strongest of the brothers in physical terms but slow moving and often tired when he worked which wasn't much. His essential good humor could turn radically sullen in a second. Sunderson was sitting at the table feeling a fast and irregular heartbeat and staring at the pistol when there was a knock at the door. He opened it and Sprague barged in shoving him out of the way. He was followed by John and Bert who acted less aggressive.

"Where's Monica?" Sprague shouted.

"She's at work," Sunderson said quietly.

Sprague looked as though this wasn't part of his plan which was *Get Monica and take her home.* He looked at Sunderson's revolver on the table and pulled his own.

"You promised no guns," John said.

Sprague was swaggering around the table. "Where is she working?"

"I'm not at liberty to say. A long ways, actually." Anything to discourage them though you could walk there in five minutes.

Sprague was obviously enraged. He pointed his gun from a close distance at Sunderson's head. "You'll tell me right now or you'll be dead. You guys go outside and turn the car around for a quick escape."

"Don't do it," John begged.

Sprague looked at him with scorn. "I said get out. I don't want you to witness this."

Sprague's left arm was in a sling from where he had been shot. He came close again pointing the pistol at Sunderson's head. "I'm counting to five. At five it's goodbye to you unless you tell me where Monica is." He got to four and then Smolens shouted, "Drop your weapon!" causing Sprague to turn the gun toward him and cock it. A hail of bullets from the three policemen twisted him this way and that. He screeched out and dropped his revolver which Sunderson grabbed. The three men came out of their hiding places and looked down at the riddled body.

"I didn't want to do it. But this nutcase had it coming. Get the other guys."

Sunderson nodded in agreement as the two policemen rushed to the door with their guns still drawn. Sunderson followed with his revolver. John was sitting peaceably in Diane's porch swing. "Sounds like my brother is dead," he said, holding out his hands to be cuffed. Bert was leaning against the muddy pickup smoking a cigarette and drinking from a flask. They approached him cautiously but he took a last gulp and held out his hands.

The ambulance and coroner came fairly quickly. Sunderson poured himself an ample drink and stared at the blood on the floor. The coroner stayed by the body and said, "You can't weep over an Ames." They loaded up the body so they could do an autopsy and left after Smolens gave them a brief statement promising to write it up immediately. A newspaperman arrived and Sunderson turned him away saying, "Please get the fuck out of here. Police business."

# Chapter 10

Hours later when everyone was gone, with Bert and John in the back of the squad car and Sunderson's home declared no longer a crime scene, Smolens had a big drink saying his workday was over though he would go home and write up a report. Sunderson reminded Smolens in John's defense that John had said to Sprague he had promised no guns. Smolens helped him clear up the copious blood with an entire roll of Brawny paper towels that had an absurd picture of a "rough and ready" guy on the package as if to communicate their purpose. Sunderson took the blood-soaked towels out to his burn barrel (illegal because of clean air rules) but they wouldn't burn properly until he added some kerosene from the garage, kept there for a camp stove. His neighbor Delphine waved and headed his way. Smolens was just heading out the door and her flimsy outfit caught his attention. It was a warmish late afternoon and Sunderson thought it was sad he wasn't fishing instead of burning bloody paper towels. But he always believed he should be fishing when something unpleasant was at hand. It was a bit boring. Her light robe parted revealing a glance of her pubis. Sunderson thought wisely that her neighborly outfits had to be worn to attract his attention. In the old days it would have been called a "prick tease" outfit. He introduced Delphine and Smolens.

"Did I hear firecrackers?" she asked innocently.

"No, we were shooting a bad guy who was going to shoot your neighbor."

"Oh my God!" she shrieked covering her face with her hands, parting her robe up to her belly button.

He didn't know about Smolens but to Sunderson this combination of sex, bloody towels, and death was uncomfortable. The burning towels smelled odd and he thought of cremations on the riverbank in India.

"Right next door someone was killed!" she gasped.

There was a fine light line of hair going from her belly button to her pubis. These accidental flashes were far more attractive than strip clubs. Smolens turned away briefly then looked back.

When everyone was gone and the bloody paper burned Sunderson went back inside and poured another hefty drink and put a tuna fish casserole from the refrigerator to the oven. Monica had made it that morning putting in double the ordinary amount of tuna fish like she did at home. Men often feel cheated by this dish but Sunderson loved it, which reminded him of the sin of gluttony. He would eat an extraordinary amount of this dish. It was up there with spaghetti

and meatballs for turning him into a hog. His father had
the patience to grill chickens all brown and beautiful which
thrilled the family on summer Sundays. When Sunderson
served chicken pink in the joints once too often Diane had
quoted St. Augustine, saying, "The reward of patience is
patience." He was unsure of this then the meaning dawned
on him. It was true and helped him cook chicken properly.

He sat at the table staring down at the floor where
Sprague died with what he estimated as nine holes in him.
His eyes had flickered and flickered and then stopped flickering. The image was interrupted by Delphine's open robe.
He had never seen a man die close up with gunshot wounds.
He had been with his father when he died from his heart but
that wasn't noisy. All of that gunfire in a closed house was
deafening but what was Sprague seeing when he died? It
was hard to imagine him shooting up to heaven. What hap-
pens when you die anyway? This called for another drink.
He used to hope when he was young that he'd shoot through
the galaxies. Recently his religious thoughts had only been
the ordinary Seven Deadly Sins which were not encouraging. The afterlife seemed up for grabs and life herself an
improbable puzzle. Of late he had pondered the invention
of trees, a magnificent idea. Humans also were an invention that took millions of years to perfect and then it wasn't
perfect. Here he was an older man drinking whiskey and
thinking about religion while the tuna casserole cooked.

Are we worthy of an afterlife? So many that fate has
made to suffer through this life are more worthy. A doctor
friend showed him a photo of black children's bodies piled
like Tinkertoys outside an African clinic. Or the Syrian

children's bodies he had seen on TV. It was all unbearable. Who could shoot a child or starve one? The world was full of things he couldn't deal with even by fishing. He had thought of going to Africa and helping out but what could he do? Arrest people? Meanwhile back at home children were always in jeopardy, every cop's least favorite call. Time for another drink. As a child he had been confused by angels and when he asked his father he had said, "That's a Catholic thing." His confusion increased until late in his teens when while sitting in the woods staring at a river in the spring two migrating warblers had landed on him. At that point he decided that birds had to be angels and felt blessed. He had sat still in the woods many times since during the migration period but it hadn't happened again. Even the lowly crows and ravens were holy to him.

He dozed for a while at the table and got his casserole out a half hour late but it wasn't burned. The edges were crunchy which he liked. He ate an unholy amount with a jar of hot pepper dills that Marion had given him. He fell asleep on the sofa until Monica came home from work. She raised her skirt above the sofa. What beauty.

"I need some affection. I worked hard. It went well."

"That's good," Sunderson said, thinking that it was a wonderful way to wake up. They had some rather hasty affection.

"My God you ate a lot of tuna casserole. Are you okay? You ate pounds of it!" She examined the remains on the table. "You hardly have any leftovers."

"I'm a little drowsy. My body is struggling to handle it. It's hard making love on a full stomach at age sixty-six."

"You should have said no."

"I couldn't. The view was beautiful." Despite all, he found that this evening he was a little worried about the relationship of ninety billion galaxies and religion. Was there a connection? The cosmos was too much for an ordinary man to handle. He got a clear case of vertigo when he had seen the first multicolored photos from the Hubble telescope. Right now they went out in the warm evening to see the burgeoning stars. Marquette didn't have enough ambient light to totally ruin it though if you really wanted to see the Milky Way it was best to be camped way out in the backcountry where there was none. The same was true of the northern lights if you wanted to see them in their full glory. He didn't want to but he had to tell her about the shooting of her uncle Sprague and the incarceration of Bert and John.

Sunderson told her the full story of the shooting and midway she grabbed his hand and held it. He left out the number of times Sprague was shot thinking it too brutal to repeat. And the flickering eyes stopped flickering.

Mona stopped by while he was still talking. She sat down next to Monica. What a pair.

"I saw on the Internet that there was a shooting."

"It was my uncle Sprague. He's dead. When I was young he was the only one who would take me sledding. We'd drive a couple miles to a good hill on a country side road. He was like a kid. He loved to sled."

"I'm sorry," Mona said.

"Don't be. He was going to shoot my old lover here," Monica continued.

Sunderson felt smugly serene being described as her "old lover." He certainly wasn't a young lover and needed to be something definite.

Next morning a judge released Bert and John. They were told they would be jailed again if they came close to Sunderson's house. A week later the body still wasn't claimed so was buried locally. The autopsy revealed that Sprague indeed had nine bullet holes, six potentially fatal. Sunderson thought it a grim way for a life to end but what can you do? He was confident that Sprague would have shot him for not revealing Monica's location. You can't lose a good cook.

# Chapter 11

Early next morning Sunderson packed for the cabin. Now that it was safe, Monica would stay behind to work. To his delight she had stayed up late to put a pork shoulder on slow heat that he could warm up for his dinner. She had rubbed it with garlic and ground chiles. He loved this cheapest cut of pork because it was one of the few things his mother cooked well. She had also packed a box of groceries with explicit instructions for cooking. He packed his revolver in a shoulder holster unsure of his welcome in the neighborhood. He knew the trip was a bit foolhardy but craved to go fishing. Since the shooting, when he dozed he'd wake up quivery to the sound of gunshots. He wondered how his underused brain could imitate the sound so convincingly.

Astonishingly enough Monica had said that she was occasionally homesick. When questioned she said she missed her room with its double locks and all her books about

Mexico. It was her dream to visit someday. It was the first time she had mentioned Mexico to him. A couple of books had come from Lemuel who had gone to Mexico trying to recover from prison in Jackson where he was denied enough sunlight. Sunderson vowed to take Monica there someday.

When he got to the cabin it felt empty without Monica and he had an attack of melancholy. He felt doomed that it was either one female or another that dominated his interest. On the way he had stopped to fish two likely looking creeks and caught half a dozen brook trout for lunch. He let the largest go because it was too beautiful to eat. It was deeply colored from living in dark water in the swamp. Fish were the one thing Sunderson could cook with total competency. There was a fine line between cooking it too much and too little but he was very familiar with this fine line even when roasting large lake trout or whitefish. He was eating the last of several brook trout with bread and butter when he noticed out the window Lemuel headed his way across the pasture with a sheaf of paper. It irritated him to be interrupted while eating but he judged he would finish before Lemuel reached the cabin. He was a dawdling walker and a birder so often slowed to lift his battered binoculars to his eyes. He thought unpleasantly that when he told Monica that he would take her to Mexico she had burst into tears. It reminded him of the meager lives most people lived while others could vacation in Mexico on a week's salary. There was the errant thought that maybe Lemuel was killing members of this family to have something to write about. On the way into town he had stopped for gasoline and heard one of the wives had died, John's wife, when he had been away in

Marquette, but she wasn't tested for poison because she had midstage ovarian cancer. This sloppy police work irritated Sunderson. Of course, given the family context, she should have been tested.

Sunderson had judged correctly. Lemuel hit the cabin's doorstep just as he finished his last bite. He again strewed some papers on the table so he would look busy and yelled "come in" to Lemuel's knock.

Lemuel was distracted and out of sorts.

"Are you busy?"

"Not terribly. No more than usual. I think I've been sort of busy since birth." What a lie I just told, thought Sunderson. The piece of manuscript was called "Thoughts of a Writer" and Sunderson inwardly groaned.

"I always wondered what Raymond Chandler actually thought," said Lemuel naively.

"What he thinks is the whole of the novel," Sunderson said with ire. "A novel is a different form of thinking."

"Well, read it or don't. It's idiosyncratic and I think you might find some parts interesting."

Sunderson walked Lemuel back across half the pasture with two stops for birds, a shrike and a kestrel. Lemuel agreed that John's wife should have been tested though he said she was on her way anyway. He also said that there aren't any survivors to ovarian cancer. As he walked back to the cabin, Sunderson reminded himself to check this with Diane. He often zoned out on cancer talk because he hated the use of military metaphors ("I'm battling cancer" or "I fought cancer to a draw") but also because Diane's hospital stories gave him chills. One day you're okay and the next you're dying.

Sunderson felt like an oaf for becoming so fond of Monica and missing her so much at the cabin. He wondered if his compassionate desire to "get this girl off the farm to where she belongs" was in fact social engineering of the kind he had always dreaded, sort of "let's get the poorest into high-rises. Life on the ground floor is dangerous and dirty." Sunderson was singularly ignorant in all aspects of love. Monica certainly didn't raise the all-encompassing feelings he had had for Diane but here he was at the cabin with the sharp pang of missing her. Something had changed when he moved her to Marquette. It embarrassed him when she treated him as if he were her savior. When he protested she would simply say, "How else was I going to get away? I couldn't do it all by myself." She had only been to Marquette once on a school trip as a senior. Now she bounced along as if it was a natural stepping-stone to New York. Once in bed she had said at some point she would like to have a baby. His whole body shivered with dread and he asked, "What about New York? How are you going to take a baby to New York?" She was charmingly naive. One evening she had asked him to describe the Empire State Building in his own words. In truth he hadn't noticed it. "It's a huge ass building. If it fell over it would destroy the city," he had said. She was thrilled. The Empire State Building had figured large in her imagination as a child. Once in the car she had sung "Give My Regards to Broadway," which she had learned early in school without any idea what Broadway was.

Did he love Monica? The whole culture claimed to be in love with someone or something, maybe a football or baseball team, a girl, a woman, a man. It seemed a form of hysteria. Maybe with Monica he was absorbed in that slip-stream. It was not what he intended but what did that matter? Or maybe these peculiar niggling feelings we generate toward one another are called love. They enter our minds willy-nilly like bees around a sweet pop can. He had once been bit in the mouth by a yellow jacket that was hanging around the perforation in his beer can—was there a lesson here?

Sunderson sat at the table glancing with dread at Lemuel's manuscript, "Thoughts of a Writer." He was sick to death of the whole Ames clan. Why couldn't they behave? Lemuel had told Sunderson he was confident that Sprague had killed a game warden who had been found dead by a hunter way back three miles into the woods. The game warden had been shot once in the back of the head with a pistol. The authorities had questioned whether someone had snuck up on him or had walked around behind him when he was examining a license. It occurred to Sunderson to call the station to recommend Smolens compare the ballistics of the game warden's death to the few shots Sprague managed to get off in his house before he was blown away into eternity. He could dig out bullets with his jackknife but it was best to leave it to the forensics guy in the department. A ballistics match wouldn't surprise him one bit. Knowing that delay was impossible he called Detective Smolens immediately. Smolens thanked him profusely and promised a call back on his suspicions.

The day was bright and sunny, bad for fishing unless he used weighted streamers but he preferred the grace of dry flies floating down from the sky to be sipped or gulped by a rising fish. It was a matter of aesthetics. He was abruptly nauseated with the Ameses when he reread the first paragraph of Lemuel's manuscript wherein he described his childhood and how his friends in school were never allowed to come to his place. People in town heard all too much gunfire coming from the three Ames places. Even the men who visited the saloon like birds to a feeder kept a safe distance from the Ameses. The question, Sunderson thought, was why the dad never learned to behave.

Sunderson decided he himself had behaved rather well though he wasn't setting the bar very high and it was obvious that the seeds of his destruction were in alcohol and lechery. Diane, of course, had perfect behavior and so did Marion though his was learned after early alcoholism and fistfighting. Right now he was at a conference of middle school principals at Michigan State in East Lansing. That made Sunderson want to pull up stakes and fish out of Marion's peaceful cabin rather than endure the implicit threat of the Ameses which was in the air everywhere like mosquitoes. So the urge to cut and run was actually there but so was the uncontrollable ego that resisted it.

Anyone sensible would take the next plane to Chicago and simply walk around and eat in restaurants or to Montana and fish around Bozeman near rich stockbrokers. He imagined the three Ames homes suppurating with mayhem and possibly planning his own murder. If he went to Marion's cabin Monica could go out with him in the day and it was close enough to Marquette, thirty miles, that he could still get her to work on time. But letting fear drive him away from his beloved cabin seemed worse than the threat of nuclear attack. Ego again, or one of the Big Seven, pride. He reminded himself that the cabin had been free, bought with highly illegal blackmail money from New York City. He was ever so slightly ashamed of the blackmail matter after a lifetime of legal purity, his first time on "the wrong side of the law," but he was glad again that Mona's misbegotten rock 'n' roll boyfriend was doing ten years in a French prison for fooling with girls in their early teens and preteens. He had no idea about French prisons but hoped they were nasty.

He still had some blackmail money left for his French-Italian eating trip or taking Monica to Mexico, maybe both. He had once dreamed of something truly adventuresome like going into the jungle and capturing an enormous reticulated python or anaconda by himself, but these were the fantasies of childhood and had nothing to do with a retired careworn cop. Why would he want to catch a huge snake? He had seen photos of these monsters and there was the question of why God made them. A question not to be answered in a lifetime, similar to why did God make Hitler.

Some things in creation were altogether too messy, including the cosmos. What on a side street in Marquette was he to do with ninety billion galaxies when he couldn't comprehend nearby Lake Superior? Diane had explained to him all about the melting glaciers. It was appropriate that humans felt insignificant contemplating the cosmos when our own historical record was so appalling. You needed only to read about the inception of World War I to feel navy blue shame for humankind. The thought of millions upon millions of the dead would send one running to the woods to stare at a simple creek. Dead Sprague on his floor was just one. Meanwhile what were all of us minuscule orphans supposed to do on earth after we endured the so-called miracle of birth? He had read an endless amount of history, his den was full of it, simply to see what had happened. He had heard that hundreds of historians had committed suicide. Our universities should be charnel houses.

Little items like literature suffocated in the sweep of history. He did recall that the summer after graduating from college before he joined the state police he had read Shakespeare. It was the pure language that stupefied him. He would be in a diner reading *A Midsummer Night's Dream* and his acquaintances were confident he was studying for some test. The test turned out to be the nature of his mind. Shakespeare seemed even truer than history. Literature was against the abyss while history wallowed in it. Now, forty years later, he remembered the pleasure of going fishing while thinking of *Hamlet*. The mental music while fishing was always the cello. It still was.

He had to come up for air. Despair over the Ameses was driving him crazy and he had to put an end to it. Diane could always decompress him but she was off on her own and he preferred not to think of what she was doing. Did curiosity about the Ameses drive him? Or was it the fundamental question of evil on earth? Who in this wretched world had any answers to anything? He had never seen or heard of a family that lived in such disarray, legal or otherwise, the grotesque way they treated each other and their wives. He was thinking of paying them a neighborly visit which he had never done.

He was diverted by a line in Lemuel's manuscript on the table: "My father used to beat all of us with a simple willow stick for misbehavior, real and imagined but he stopped beating me when he discovered I was learning about science and could talk about it with him. He never paid attention to anything else I had to say. The grade school science teacher, Mrs. Sedgwick, taught us slowly, carefully and gently. That way it stuck and aroused our curiosity, for some of us permanently. I was never smart about science like Levi but where it came to life for me was birding. Simon and I would take short walks to teach him bird watching. He knew physics well but knew he was weak in the natural sciences, so it made him irritable but was something we could talk about. He believed in Darwin but questioned why evolution had created so many different species of birds which was messy indeed. The habit helped his old age because after the obligatory and somewhat cruel early morning meetings with his sons he would be off in decent weather to the pastures and woods to see birds. This seemed contradictory to his essential mean mindedness but he never spoke of it except to me."

Lemuel seemed the very definition of an unlived life. What would it be like to spend your twenties in prison? He continued, "I missed my talks with Simon when I was in prison for my bank robberies. Simon would write me short notes about any new birds he saw, the only mail I got in prison. I wrote letters to an imaginary girlfriend. The only sex in my life at the time was with one of Bert's girlfriends who took my virginity after I got out of the bathtub with a hard-on. This did not urge me toward other women because I could only think of one at once."

# Chapter 12

The bleakness of Lemuel's manuscript had given Sunderson the urge to see how he lived at present. Before he could change his mind he put on a coat, his pistol in his shoulder holster, and headed off to the houses he had seen only from the road and never visited. They looked absurdly large and spread out from the road but maybe they wanted to keep distant from each other after a lifetime of fistfighting. He walked fairly fast downriver at the beginning but then his legs seemed to weaken with his courage and he slowed down. The first house seemed to be moving toward him in the manner of a ghost. It was a huge box on prairieland. It hadn't been painted since it had been built and on the south side where the weather was the weakest you could still see a little raw lumber out of the sun. A little boy about ten popped out from behind a bush holding a real life pistol.

"You're trespassing," he shrieked.

"I'm looking for Lemuel," Sunderson said holding up his hand in peace.

"You're not from the government?" the boy said, calming down.

"No, I'm your neighbor from upriver." Sunderson pointed.

"You're the sonofabitch that stole our cousin Monica. Now we only have shit to eat. I ought to shoot you." He was genuinely irritated.

"Why shoot me and spend your life in prison, far from this beautiful place?"

The boy looked crestfallen and turned away.

If anything the second house was junkier than the first. It was a mile down the trail as each house sat on a section of land more than six hundred acres. The screen on the back porch was torn in several places and the porch itself tilted severely to the south. A log pole was holding it up none too well. A little girl who couldn't be more than seven came around the corner of a shed aiming a big .44 pistol at him. It was so heavy she had to hold it with both hands.

"You're trespassing," she said in a wee voice. "Uncle Lemuel is writing today. Don't disturb him unless you have to."

It occurred to Sunderson that if she fired the pistol the recoil would knock her down. She pointed the pistol at the third house in the distance. "He lives there," she said with a sudden smile which startled him. The smile made him forget the trashy background and the gun. Two big coon hounds were investigating tipped-over plastic garbage barrels. A pit bull was snarling at the end of a long chain tether but couldn't reach him which was lucky as he didn't want to shoot it. It was preposterously muscular.

Lemuel's house looked very trim compared to the others with a recent coat of gray paint and a nice back porch, screened to get away from the mosquitoes. Lemuel was watering ornamental bushes with a hose which he dropped in shock after noticing Sunderson.

"What a surprise," he said.

"At least you don't have a pistol on me like the other places."

"The kids are trained as guards because if they shoot someone they're too young to go to prison."

"That's convenient," Sunderson said.

They went inside and had coffee in a big spotless kitchen.

"This was Simon Jr.'s house. He bought part of the land when Big Simon bought the rest. Monica did her cooking here. I received the house in his will that I forged. The other two houses are pigstys."

They toured the house including an ample library with a bed. "I like to sleep with my books. The only adult I let into the house is Levi's wife. We still make love but never more than once a week." Upstairs there were four bedrooms, one with a huge rococo bed. "This was Big Simon's bed. He brought it up from Kentucky, doubtless stolen."

Sunderson was amazed at the house. So clean and rather feminine.

"Simon was ill a long time so I finished him off with a tincture I devised."

He said this with the airiness of someone announcing good weather. Sunderson wasn't surprised. In this family

killing your father didn't seem terribly serious. Back down
in the library Lemuel pulled out a volume on violence in
America. Sunderson told him he already had the book. Perhaps after spending most of a lifetime as a detective it wasn't
strange he was obsessed with violence and a family that had
spent so much time beating the shit out of each other and
others. Bert had done a year's time for beating up an IRS
man who had shown up on the steps. Sprague had shot out
the tires of the census taker's car. Political canvassers before
elections were simply thrown off the porch.

"Violence is a rich tradition in America," Lemuel said.
"History books in schools don't teach us about the thousands
of lynchings or this tradition of shooting low into teepees
to kill Indian women and children while they slept. Many
newspapers argued that all Indians should be exterminated
like the Nazi press in the 1930s with the Jews."

Lemuel had hit on some of the history that most disturbed Sunderson. He could think of nothing to say except
that the tradition of gunfights made police work difficult.
And mass shootings were a mentality his mind had never
grasped and nothing he'd read offered a firm clue either.
Hate was as common as fingernails among the human race,
and though Lemuel seemed civilized his brothers were far
from it. He felt very tired thinking about it and how weak
the law was as a consideration. He didn't want to walk home
thinking about it and accepted an offer of a ride from Lemuel.

On the way home they detoured to the tavern to get
a drink. John and Bert were sitting in the corner drinking
the unvarying vodka. John came slowly over with no signal
in his face of what he had on his mind. He suddenly kicked

their Formica and metal table over splaying out their shots and beer. He aimed another kick at Sunderson's chest but Sunderson had the wit to catch his foot and lift it high. John went over backward with his head hitting the floor with a resounding crack. He was still. Now Bert rushed over but Lemuel stood and met him with an astounding array of punches. Bert shuffled away, his face bloody and shamefaced that the smallest brother had kicked the shit out of him.

"My black cellmate in prison taught me how to box," Lemuel said.

On the way out Sunderson remembered he needed to replace the pint he had exhausted at home. First things first.

"No fighting in here," the bartender said as they left. "You Ameses never learned how to behave."

"Very sorry," Lemuel said. "We were under attack."

After the liquor store Sunderson couldn't talk. He took a swig of his pint. He was thinking that violence should be the eighth deadly sin, and then unpleasantly it occurred to him that he was almost fifty years older than Monica. If they did have a baby he would be eighty when it graduated from high school. Not good, he thought. This was all a mortal blow about which he had to do something.

He packed up and left the cabin that afternoon after having a cup of coffee and another drink with Lemuel who startled him by showing no aftereffects of the violence except some bloody knuckles. Maybe that was partly it. Sunderson was shaken and had the urge to flee, but these Ameses simply didn't react to the evil of violence or any other kind of evil. It was mysterious. They were born and lived that way from the start.

# Chapter 13

On the long drive home he impulsively called Diane on the phone. He lamely wanted some advice on Monica.

"Of course it's absurd but it's not the dumbest thing you've ever done. Maybe it's okay in South America and you should move there," she laughed. Her voice sounded relaxed talking to him for the first time in a long time.

"You know I hate that word *absurd*," he said.

"What else is it? Forty-five or fifty years' age difference is absurd. Even the French say that seventeen years is the max. My husband was ten years older than me and that was quite a gap."

"You mean sex?" he asked.

"I'm not answering that, you old fool."

Now they had truly irritated each other. She never called him a fool unless she was pissed off. And she knew he had long hated her use of the word *absurd*. This had begun

decades before when he had gone ice fishing with friends on
a terribly cold January day. They had a few whiskeys and
fished after dark. That evening at home at bedtime Diane
discovered that his entire body was cold and said, "What
an absurd sport. Your body is still freezing cold. This must
be bad for your health." He took umbrage. Ice fishing was
a way of life. At bars in early winter before the ice was safe
men were anxious to get out on the "big ice." Out near the
oar dock and power plant men would fish off the edge of ice
in the open water. Sunderson pretended otherwise but he
had never felt comfortable doing this. When a friend insisted
he said he didn't feel well. The few times he had done it he
was semiparalyzed with fright.

The wrangle with Diane had spread far and wide.
"Why not just buy fish and avoid suffering from the cold?"
she said. He could not convincingly explain the pleasure of
the sport to her, the beauty of frozen lakes, or the endless
vista of frozen Lake Superior. You spudded a hole with effort
and dropped down your bait and would occasionally catch
a nice lake trout or whitefish. They were delicious drawn
from extremely cold waters. She had segued to his health and
nagged him insufferably about his physical condition saying
that he was an early heart attack "waiting to happen." Well,
it hadn't happened though he was a little worried when an
orgasm with Monica over the table made him so dizzy he
fell down. He had better settle for the bed, he thought after
crashing to the floor.

The evening brought a call from Lemuel saying that
big John had died from a heart attack that may have been
precipitated, according to the doctor, by the concussion from

falling backward in the tavern that afternoon. Sunderson felt as if he had killed someone but what was he to do about the kick that might have reached his face? Still he was nudged by guilt. It was the eighth deadly sin of violence, impossible to avoid when you're attacked. He mentioned all of this to Lemuel.

"No, it was the sausage," Lemuel said. "That sucker ate at least a pound for breakfast every day with a half dozen scrambled eggs. Sometimes he repeated it for lunch. Sometimes I'd cook for him because he simply couldn't. He wanted short ribs and would eat all the fat first. I called the resident doctor who I play chess with to get his cholesterol checked for the sake of curiosity."

Sunderson felt foolish coming home for no reason other than that the tavern incident the day before had been so unpleasant. He could have been killed by a kick in the face. Instead the other guy died forever. Violence was wretched indeed. He reflected that he had no theological authority to add it as the eighth deadly sin. Who did? Not even the pope.

He called Monica at work thinking probably she wouldn't know her uncle had died but Lemuel had already called her. Sunderson had an extra drink feeling a little morose. He went out in the backyard to try and shake his cast of thought and there was Delphine on her knees in a flower bed, her ass in blue shorts bobbing in the air like a house cat's. He guessed her to be in her early forties, more his proper age range. He sat in the lawn chair to watch her. Monica had told him that there was a small chicken pot pie in the freezer he should put on thaw cycle then bake for half an hour at 350 degrees. He loved chicken pot pies as much as women in blue shorts. Marion came quietly up behind him and startled him.

"Haven't seen you in quite a while. I stopped at the hotel for a fish sandwich and Monica said you came home."

Sunderson gave him a litany of poor fishing, violence, and death.

"You better get out of there before you get your ass handed to you on a plate," Marion said, following the line of his vision to the gardener. "Pretty good porn movie. Did you know you're fifty years older than Monica?"

"I've been thinking of that as we speak. Something has to be done."

"Get her a nice room or small apartment. Stop fucking her. Wean her from your company. Tell her to find a boyfriend not on the lip of an old folks' home."

"What if I'm in love with her?" This sorrow was quite sudden. Sunderson felt woebegone.

"You were also in love with your current stepdaughter. You keep on like this and you'll end up in jail or on one of those registries. Pick on someone your own size." Marion pointed at the neighbor wagging her tail.

"Monica takes care of me. I can't quite do the job." Now Sunderson was a little plaintive. He had never told Marion about his time with Mona in Paris.

"You're being a fucking brat. If it was someone you knew with such a girl you'd be horrified."

This was definitely true, even if it wasn't technically illegal. Many rural girls got married by sixteen or earlier, but to people their own age. He admitted to himself that any other retired man living with a nineteen-year-old would have horrified him. What's love got to do with it? In terms of the shadier side of life Monica had seen it all. Once more love in America disgusted him. What could it possibly mean? Monica playfully nude on her hands and knees was irresistible. But so was peeking at Mona through the window nudely doing her yoga. Look where that got him. Diane had been a paradise of guiltless affection. The best that marriage offers. Until it ended, a personal Nagasaki for him.

He and Marion went in the house when the neighbor finished her gardening. The movie over, Marion talked about the burdensomeness of sexual attraction. He was faithful to his wife because the alternative made him feel weary. There was a third grade teacher at his school who had attracted his full attention. She wasn't any great beauty but was quietly attractive and supple. Sunderson hadn't thought of it before but to Marion the sky to eroticism was intelligence. That was true of Diane, he thought, but didn't figure in his lust for Monica who was smart enough but was basically unlearned except for her rich knowledge about Mexico. She had been grumpy lately because the head chef at work kept hitting on her. Sunderson wondered if she wasn't telling him because she actually was interested, and said, "Don't let me stop you." It might have been an errant moment but he meant it. It would be good if she got out and around. At her current rate she said she would have saved enough by fall to move to New York City. She had read enough to know she would have to settle for a simple room. An apartment might be forever beyond her reach, especially in Manhattan. Sonia's apartment sitting there on Washington Square would make her envious, but it would make nearly anyone envious. Sunderson had guessed the property was owned by the FBI in its impulse to "gather facts" about each and all, including Marilyn Monroe and Martin Luther King. Reading a book about either the CIA or FBI was disturbing.

Sunderson had the breath knocked out of him when he stepped into Diane's old room, now Monica's, and saw a pamphlet sticking out of her suitcase. With his obsessive curiosity about the printed word he had to check it out. It was called *A Handbook of Poisons*. He reassured himself that she was just reading up on the subject, though his detective's mind protested weakly. Lemuel's name was on the cover as if it belonged to him. Was it a conspiracy? He knew her incapable of it.

He slipped the pamphlet back in her luggage and grabbed an art book that Diane had temporarily left behind, one of hundreds in fact, which he loved to flip through. Art was a mystery to him. He knew very little about it. He particularly liked Caravaggio, Goya, and Gauguin. He had never thought about why until now. Maybe Caravaggio for the primacy of colors, Goya for the width and depth of his work, and Gauguin partly for the romantic idea that he ran away to the South Seas. Diane had gone to Chicago for a big Gauguin show but he was too embarrassed to accompany her. Why all that money when he had a book of Gauguin on his lap? In short he was a stupid prick. There was also the slight fear of being overcome since sometimes when he gazed at the Gauguin book a long time in the evening he would get a lump in his throat as if he couldn't quite handle the work. It was too powerful. He got the same lump for difficult reasons looking at Goya's *Horrors of War* and its eighth sin of violence but then the pope had killed a boatload of Jews by not interceding so they could land in Italy. Gauguin was a great puzzle, beauty that produced a kind of terror. He threatened my life, Sunderson thought.

His thoughts were disturbed by two calls in rapid succession. Lemuel reported that John's cholesterol was in the four hundreds, the highest the doctor had ever seen, doubtless due to a lifetime of excessive sausage. And then Smolens called to say the bullet in the game warden's head had come from Sprague's pistol. Murder solved. There was however an additional nonfatal .32 in the game warden's back, perhaps a coup de grâce when he was prone. Who did Sprague usually hunt with? Sunderson knew the answer. It was always Bert. Together they were widely known as the champion violators — Mona's long rap sheet was covered with their names. They would drive the swamp toward each other and Monica said that one day they shot six deer. But Sunderson had a dilemma: how to test Bert's .32 for the ballistics to the other bullet? Sunderson could readily imagine Bert shooting the game warden on the ground. He knew that Bert carried the pistol to the tavern and said so to Smolens. He had seen a sag in the coat and one day got a glimpse of the grip. He suggested that Smolens have two of his biggest, strongest cops stop Bert's pickup when he left the tavern and do a body check, confiscating the pistol as Bert certainly wouldn't have a rare permit to carry. Smolens thanked him.

He went back to gazing at the Gauguin book while heating his chicken pot pie. The South Seas women and girls were slightly chunky for his taste but he couldn't deny their allure. Maybe he should go there? He had thought frequently of buying a set of paints but was too timid. It was presumptuous. He had seen the wretched products of Sunday painters in Munising and Marquette. Like writing you have to give your life to it or stay away. He had told Lemuel that his chapter "Thoughts of a Writer" lacked any elements of a story, therefore must be left out of the crime novel. Everything must contribute to the story. "Read Elmore Leonard. He's the best right now," Sunderson advised. He felt dishonest suggesting Leonard to Lemuel as he could scarcely aspire to him. Perhaps Lemuel would realize this on his own, although he had told Sunderson he'd read "hundreds" of crime novels so the possibility was remote.

In his mind Sunderson could still hear John's head cracking against the cement floor, in itself sounding fatal. But there were hours between that and the evening's heart attack. He hadn't been able to read crime novels when he was a practicing detective, but on retirement he looked into Diane's strongest recommendations. First in line was Raymond Chandler who knocked him out of his chair. He also enjoyed Elmore Leonard and John D. MacDonald who were writers of a different sort, albeit wonderful. Chandler could make you want to take a shower and go see *The Sound of Music*. He was so foreboding at times that you sharply drew in your breath. Leonard in Detroit, MacDonald in Florida, and Chandler in California all made him wish he had been a detective in a more interesting place than Marquette. There wasn't a single unsolved murder during his career. And now the Ames family arose after his retirement.

# Chapter 14

After an awful, restless sleep caused, he felt, by too little whiskey he and Monica made vigorous love in midmorning. They dozed on the bed afterward and he awoke looking at her uncovered back. Her skin was a lovely light olive and her strong back tapered nicely to her butt which was utterly appealing. Not too big, not too small, but just right and smooth. Men will follow good fannies everywhere, even to the ends of earth. He had followed one woman through many aisles of the supermarket with an empty cart until she caught on and suddenly turned her cart and came right at him. He was paralyzed and lamely picked a can of butter beans off the shelf that he didn't want. She passed closely without comment and he caught her lilac scent. He passed the checkout counter when she was leaving and she gave him a deep smile. When he got home at midday he heated up the butter beans which were fine with lots of Tabasco.

His groin lurched as he ate. Clark Gable would have known how to make contact. "Let's go someplace so I can look at your butt" wouldn't do.

While looking at Monica's butt his thoughts turned naturally to the Seven Deadly Sins. He had no sexuality left and was in a clinical state of mind. He knew he should feel guilt but rarely did. He had largely lost his capacity for sexual fantasy but Monica represented actuality. He had read that some famous theologian had had an affair. So did Einstein. Could he do less? But you can't have an affair unless you are married and he had lost a wondrous woman. The divorce still made his heart ache and occasionally brought tears to his eyes. She had been utterly burnt out on his drinking and usual cop depressions. He had steadfastly refused to go to the counseling she had insisted on. The last straw had been when cleaning his den she had come upon a big cache of shooters, about fifty of those small bottles airlines use. This upset her a great deal. Their marriage had been open and when he had wanted a drink he poured it in the kitchen. This secret supply profoundly upset her. Enough was enough and she filed. She had left his cache out in the open so he would know she had discovered his secret. They never mentioned it. The language was clear.

His mind slid from Diane back to theology. When a battle was lost during the Crusades the sultan didn't have the enemy all killed, he just told them to go home and not come back. But when the crusaders were victorious the streets of Jerusalem ran red with blood. The Christians were cleaning up home plate. Sunderson had read that currently there was an old desert chieftain still deeply upset by the Crusades.

Why not? It was the beginning of our relationship with the Middle East. It occurred to Sunderson that he still believed in the Resurrection because no one had ever taught him how not to. It was a childhood holdover, still in the air around Easter. "Up from the grave he arose; with a mighty triumph o'er his foes" the hymn went. The world and religion were huge and he had no authority to disbelieve anything.

Smolens called. He was easy to talk to and apparently not jealous of his territory. Mona had been called as a computer whiz and found out that Bert had been close friends with a medic in Vietnam. That was a tie-in, however slight, to poison. Could he imagine Bert killing his brothers, if not his father? Easily.

Smolens also said that the .32 pistol they confiscated with difficulty from Bert outside the tavern was ballistically not the right pistol. Sunderson told him that Monica had said that Bert had a whole big drawer of pistols in his room. Smolens sighed. "How do we get at them?" he asked. Sunderson had no immediate idea. A .32 man was a .32 man and Bert likely had many. He had won many NRA shooting contests, Mona had learned from her latest searches. Sunderson wanted to say "shoot him and get the pistols." Monica could get at them but why endanger her for a dead murder case? "I suppose you'll have to keep arresting him and confiscating his current .32. I doubt he has any permits at all." Smolens agreed that would be the only option. Sunderson called Lemuel to see if he had any ideas. Lemuel said that years ago Bert had given him a .32 because Lemuel as a felon couldn't buy one. Bingo, thought Sunderson, unload your vulnerable .32 on your brother.

He called Smolens with this new development then
drove out to the cabin after calling Monica and saying he
wouldn't be home for dinner. He took the leftover chicken
pot pie with him as a precaution against hunger. He had
tasted every kind of canned and frozen food imaginable
with no luck except Stouffer's mac and cheese but doubted
its health value, to the extent he thought about his health.
Right now he was thinking about fishing and how easy it
was to get too busy. He resolved to go fishing the minute he
pocketed the pistol but the moment he reached the cabin it
started raining fairly hard. Lemuel was already there standing on the porch and he felt obligated to make a pot of coffee. Along with the gun Lemuel handed him another sheaf
of manuscript which he dreaded. This chapter was called
"The Afterlife." Glancing at page 1 as he drank coffee he
didn't need he spotted the dreaded word *karma*. He hadn't
heard that word in use since way back in college, certainly
not in Munising except perhaps by tourists he didn't know.
Doubtless some of the college people in Marquette used
*karma* but he knew very few of them. He wasn't at all enthused about Lemuel's notions of the afterlife. He had told
him to stick to the crime story. If you shot someone or were
shot yourself there was the vision of someone shooting up to
heaven, presumably in a distant galaxy like a NASA rocket.
The idea that some unearthly creature was keeping track of
your bad habits and these bad habits would revisit you to
your detriment in a future life seemed specious. For billions
of people the scorecard would be immense. A beatnik girl,
this was pre-hippie, in college had told him in a coffee shop
where he was eating a hamburger and she a bowl of rice that

he had bad karma and must stop eating meat immediately. She was rather attractive and he had had hopes to see her bare naked but the prospects looked dim. He had heard she didn't shave her armpits or legs and her long hair looked a bit unwashed. He tried to make the deal that he would quit eating meat if she would come back to his room with him but she insisted that he "purge" himself for a month first on a vegetarian diet including lots of boiled almonds. They parted ways without compromise. He never got close as a hamburger eater.

The rain had stopped. Sunderson began putting on his fishing gear and that got rid of Lemuel who left with the interesting point that all the criminals in prison assumed they were going to heaven, even murderers of children. He beat God to the starting gate on self-forgiveness, Sunderson thought. He hadn't waded twenty feet when he stumbled and heard a voice. It was Bert up the bank on solid ground. He grabbed some dogwood branches to steady himself.

"If you start drowning I'm not saving you," Bert said.

"I wouldn't imagine you would," Sunderson replied.

"You got to stop bird-dogging me."

"Don't know what you mean."

"The cops outside the bar that took my .32. I was kicking the shit out of one but the other drew a pistol."

"Yes, I heard you got an assaulting an officer charge. That should get you sixty days."

"Tell it to someone who gives a shit. It means no booze, drugs, and cigarettes. Maybe Monica would come over and give me a blow job through the bars. I'm sure she will. She has before. What a total slut."

Sunderson was enraged and couldn't resist the nee-
dling. He drew his pistol from his shoulder holster, cocked
it, and aimed it at Bert's midriff. "You're her father. Say
Monica's name again I'll blow your guts out your ass." He
lowered the barrel a bit and shot at the ground between
Bert's feet. Bert yelled and jumped which was hard to do
and Sunderson was amused at how often ex-marines stood
with their feet widely apart as if prepared for imminent war.

"I missed," Sunderson said.

"You asshole," Bert yelled. "I saw you lower the barrel." He seemed as much amused as enraged. "You should
get your fat ass a half mile downstream. There are a couple
of big holes for brown trout. Use that big fly called a muddler minnow."

"Watch your mouth but thanks for the tip. I'm just
learning the local fishing."

Bert walked away but just before he entered the woods
he peppered the water around Sunderson with .32 bullets
to get even.

So much for fishing, thought Sunderson, his heart beating wildly in his chest. He crawled out of the river but then
on a hopeless angler's impulse trundled downstream. It was
a warmish day and in his uncomfortable waders he could
feel sweat trickling down his legs. A fine time to think about
death, he thought. He was wheezing with effort to get to the
new fishing holes Bert had mentioned. And there they were
where the river entered the woods, big river holes looking
like brown trout habitat. He sat down in hopes of catching
his breath, feeling greasy with sweat and hard breathing. He
thought about heart attacks. It was altogether natural for a

retired man of sixty-six to think about death, the impending doom that had come to many of his friends. Clyde, an ice fishing friend, had died of a heart attack spudding an ice hole on the bay in front of his house. Clyde always ate a whole package of raw hot dogs when they fished which couldn't have been good for him. Also at breakfast before they fished Clyde would have a double order of sausage, three eggs, and biscuits with extra sausage gravy. His intelligent friends thought Clyde was a walking time bomb and it had proved to be true. The relentless northern march of biscuits and gravy, Sunderson thought, another vengeance for the Civil War. At the funeral Clyde's wife who was morbidly obese wept profusely and told Sunderson that now that her husband died they were going to miss their planned trip to Hawaii. Sunderson told her she could go alone and she was outraged saying that Hawaii was a place for "romance" and it would be meaningless without Clyde.

Death was in his thoughts as he rested up. He would settle for a quick trip through the galaxies as a substitute for heaven which sounded boring. Ever since the Hubble photos were published in all of their splendor he wanted to see the galaxies closer. The other day in the *Detroit Free Press* it said that black holes rotated at a speed of seven thousand five hundred miles per hour which would give the spirit a real quick trip. He had frequently worried about whether he would see Diane in the afterlife. Of course he wanted to but perhaps death made us not care about our worldly life. Would there be trout in heaven and birds? How could these wonders be left out? He had read that in the Middle Ages hell was thought to be a place without birds. And didn't the

Mormons believe that you remain married to your wife in heaven? He'd have to check this out. In their newspaper, the *Heavenly Gazette*, it is announced that a couple have been married for five thousand years, that sort of thing, and there's of course no divorce in heaven. He couldn't come to the conclusion that he had any talent for theology.

Maybe he should write an essay on violence as the eighth deadly sin. Maybe he could become a late-blooming minister? His long experience as a detective had given him plenty to say about violence. Why do some men want to box women who can't box back? He had seen some real bloodbaths. He had hated taking statements in hospitals. You couldn't smoke in the hospital though he had run into a hall toilet for a quick puff. Nothing made you want a cigarette or a drink like talking to a purple-faced woman missing some teeth and with an arm in a cast. If they asked he always recommended divorce. If he beats you once he'll beat you twice. There were an amazing number of repeat offenders. They had only a few cases of professorial wife beating, one an English professor who had severely flogged his wife for having an affair with a graduate student. Sunderson had gotten the idea that if the wife had had an affair with another professor it wouldn't have been so bad but dipping low into the ranks of graduate students was contemptible indeed.

Sunderson had stayed professional except once he tripped a handcuffed man walking off a porch who had beaten his ten-year-old son just short of death. The man hit the cement face-first. Sunderson remembered with pleasure the man flying through the air for a belly landing. In jail the man had sworn vengeance and Sunderson said, "Good, then we can lock you up forever." Immediately afterward he looked nearly as bad as his kid. He had seen the man several times since this incident but the man had just looked away.

As Sunderson got up and began fishing he laughed at himself for the minister idea but still thought of going to Michigan State or University of Michigan for a course in introductory theology. Why not, since he was so interested? He had an immediate fantasy, the first in months, about a little apartment full of college girls which seemed to disqualify him from Christianity. He clearly remembered a course in European history during the Renaissance. The professor was young and cynical and liked to talk about the criminal Borgias, especially Pope Alexander VI who was suspected of many crimes including adultery, simony, theft, rape, bribery, incest, and murder using arsenic poisoning. The young Catholics in the class were embarrassed into complete silence. The Borgias were enemies of the Medici family, an impressive enemy.

Sunderson saw a big brown trout feeding close to a log and despaired of making an accurate cast. He tried half a dozen times without spooking the fish thinking that Pope Alexander had had a good time. To be sure he was evil and a pope shouldn't be evil any more than a minister should screw his parishioners. But that was making it all American-style low rent. Diane had a book that followed the art collecting and patronage of both the Borgia and Medici families. When in doubt build another palace to house your art. The Borgias had enough money and power to get away with evil, a little like New York bankers and brokers in the recent nauseating recession. It was obvious that they didn't care about the millions of families they destroyed. Sunderson felt it was obvious that they should set up a guillotine down on the Battery and execute these bankers and brokers, grind up their bodies and make them into elite sausage.

While wading upstream for a better angle on the brown trout near the log he had to compare the Borgias and the Ameses up the road. The money and power of the Borgias gave them considerable versatility in their evil. The Ameses were born and bred and reminded him of William Carlos Williams saying *the pure products of America go crazy.* By any standard the Ameses were certifiably nuts, a severe genetic mishap. County government isn't prepared to deal with such concentrated chaos. It was without purpose, haphazard. They were what they were. Even the total aggregate of six children under age ten showed signs of disaster except for one, a bright young girl. Lemuel was teaching her math early plus botany and bird watching. A good parent can easily make up for a mediocre school. Lemuel had a good library which meant everything. Sunderson remembered speaking to a class of ninth graders on a career day. Only a few showed signs of leading a life not monopolized by video games and television. Of course he didn't even know what a video game was except that Marion's nephews played them and he found the sound abominable. It was a magnification and concentration of the hospital sounds in New York, hundreds of gizmos beeping their mechanical anguish.

On his seventh cast Sunderson hooked the brown trout, the largest of his life, and thought he was eating his heart. It swirled several times then dove deep in the hole where it bulldogged. His line was too light for him to be insistent so he simply let the fish exhaust itself in the deep while keeping a light tension. He finally beached the fish on a sandbar with trembling hands figuring it was at least five pounds. Twice the size of any brown trout he ever caught. He reached in his vest for a little camera Diane had bought him but found its batteries were typically dead. He stared at the fish to memorize it, then slipped it gently back in the water. It resumed its vigor and shot off for the deep hole. He was drenched with sweat and his flesh tingled in this holy moment in a long angling life. He lay back on the bank and was surprised to doze for a few minutes. He got up covered with mosquitoes and walked slowly the long way home.

At the cabin he poured a big drink and called Marion to tell him about the fish. To his disappointment he couldn't reach him. Monica called to ask if it was okay if she went to a staff party tomorrow night, the day he was coming home. He said of course, reflecting she would enjoy people her own age for company. He was still tingling from his big catch and the drink when a disturbing memory troubled him. When he had been home he had walked downtown thinking he might enjoy his old favorite bar. Monica, of course, had his car to commute to work at the hotel bar and restaurant. He was sure he had seen Lemuel's car leaving the hotel parking lot but Lemuel never said anything about visiting Marquette and when Monica got home she didn't mention it. He had repeatedly forced this from his mind until his will kept it out but this all put the ice of a conspiracy theory in his gut. A defense lawyer would say that there were hundreds of old Subarus around like the one Lemuel drove because they were good in snowy conditions, and Sunderson fully trusted Monica to tell him anything of importance, but the ounce of dread it caused persisted anyway. His detective's mind wouldn't let go of the fact that there had been no deaths without both of them being at large.

Until today. He had gone fishing again in the late afternoon and when he got home Lemuel was there to say that Paul had died, also apparently of poison. Paul was Sprague's son and an incorrigible and destructive young man in his early teens. Everyone out of necessity had to keep an eye on him and he was the only one forbidden to carry a gun. When the truant officer had visited Paul had shot out the tires of his car which caused no end of problems. When Paul was in juvenile court Sprague had raised such a fuss, tipping over the table, the judge had sentenced him to a week in jail. Bert had driven him because Sprague's driver's license had been revoked and the cops were watching him. Anyway Bert was so angry over Sprague's arrest he had rammed a police car parked in front of the courthouse with his own car. This cost him four thousand dollars and thirty days in jail. The sheriff hated to have any of the Ameses in jail saying that they promoted misbehavior among the other prisoners. He was happy when Sprague had died because Sprague had said he was going to "shoot the sheriff" because he liked the song, and the sheriff knew Sprague was perfectly capable of it. Under no condition would he visit the Ames property but always delegated the job to deputies. Paul looked to be following in his father's footsteps and was cruel to the younger children, especially when he drank.

Sunderson reminded himself that an implicit favorit-
ism was often a stumbling block in the solving of a crime.
The simple fact was that he liked both Lemuel and Monica
very much which made him less likely to suspect them of
anything. He was also aware that certain women could be
guilty of the eighth deadly sin with a specific aplomb while
men tended to make a two-fisted bloody mess. There did
seem to be a corner of his dear Monica's mind that was cool
as a cucumber. She had actually asked him if she might find
a man to support her which had disturbed him. He told her
that she was better off with a job than trading her pussy for
a living. Of course there were lots of women, and men for
that matter, willing to loll around being supported. In college
a popular guy borrowed money from everyone and it took
a year for everyone to realize that they would get nothing
back. Most people stopped giving him anything except a few
rich kids who didn't care. Sunderson who had been burned
for twenty bucks, a lot for him at the time, asked why he did
it. The reasoning was straightforward and simplistic: he
didn't want an onerous part-time job like everyone else. The
idea of being kept seemed an atypical question for Monica
who liked to work hard but then, he thought, look at her
background. One evening she had admitted that Bert had
raped her repeatedly when she was twelve, beginning with
her twelfth birthday as if it were a magic number. She tried
to say it casually but Sunderson was enraged. He should
have shot him. Part of him wondered if Monica was trying
to find a better father figure with him.

Marion showed up the next day to fish for brown trout
which he couldn't resist in a new Toyota 4Runner Sport

model, a vehicle Sunderson had always wanted, built as it was on a truck chassis with a powerful V-8 engine, perfect for the rough rides out of doors that he favored. Marion handed him the keys.

"This is a present from Diane. She's calling it a loan so you don't have to pay gift tax."

Sunderson felt a little dizzy as he had just been thinking about the inequity of the marriage. Marion had brought food which was good as he was down to roots and stems which is what dopers used to call shortages. They fished for a couple of hours well downstream driving the new car through the pasture, hitting a mud hole on purpose just to put it in 4WD and get out. Marion caught three nice browns though none as large as Sunderson's. On the way home they stopped at the tavern so that Sunderson could refresh his pint. Marion wanted to go in saying that you could judge a town by the character of its tavern. Sunderson didn't say anything because the place was utterly dismal. On the way into the bar Bert was sitting near the door and sucker punched Sunderson knocking him to the floor. Sunderson looked up to see Marion hit Bert with a right cross that sent him spinning and reeling into the corner table that no one ever sat at.

Bert yelled in a slurred voice, "I told you to stop bird-dogging me!" He drew his .32 from a vest pocket and pointed it at Marion. The bartender leaned over the bar and knocked the pistol out of his hand. Sunderson pocketed it just in case it was the right one ballistically.

"No shooting in here. This is a family place," the bartender yelled. "Bert, you're cut off for drawing a weapon. Get out." Bert staggered around as if looking for his pistol then seemed to forget what he was doing and left. He had plenty. Sunderson looked at the pistol on his lap and was hopeful because it was an older model, which Smolens thought the right gun would be. They looked out the window to make sure Bert was gone but it wasn't over yet. On the way home down the long driveway they took a bullet in the backseat. Sunderson swerved and turned to see an oak tree about three hundred feet up and stepped on the gas with Marion yelling "no." He had seen movement and it was the only cover available. On the way they took two more bullets in the front, probably in the radiator. He drew his pistol from his vest and on the way past the oak shot Bert in the hip. He was aiming at his gut but a jounce in the car saved his life. He dropped as if poleaxed. Sunderson was furious that there were bullet holes in his new car. At the cabin he called the county police and poured a drink. The police didn't want to come if it was an Ames but Sunderson said to bring an ambulance, the man was flat out on the ground. He called Smolens on his cell and luckily he wasn't that far away in Escanaba. He'd come up to pick up the pistol and help on the Bert affair. Sunderson wanted to call the Toyota dealer to pick up his wounded car but then realized it was evidence and it would have to wait. Suddenly Sunderson was trembling wildly and Marion had him stretch out in the back.

"Nice location you got here," Marion laughed.

"Sure is for brown trout. We'll be fishing in the morning. I got rid of the worst one left."

Smolens and the slow-moving cops arrived at about the same time. Marion pointed out the tree and knowing local history the ambulance driver wouldn't move without a cop with him. He gave Bert's .32 to Smolens who was also pleased it was an older model. Smolens counted four bullet holes in the new car.

"Your radiator is fucked," he said.

"Can I get it fixed or is it evidence?"

"No, I've seen it and we would have the mechanic's testimony. I'm going for attempted murder. Put this sucker away for a while."

"Good," Sunderson said. "I really don't want to see him again."

"What's the deal with these Ameses? They're nothing but trouble."

"I'm not sure. I heard the mother was good but she died early. The father raised them after that, and he was a mean-minded nutcase."

Smolens sighed deeply and looked at the sky as if there might be an answer there for the human horror to which he had been overexposed. He had recently got a week off because he had arrested a man for car theft and his wife had attacked with her long nails, digging his face into a bloody mess. He had needed stitches for a flap of flesh she had torn on his cheekbone. He still looked bad but dismissed Sunderson's concern. "It comes with the job," he said. "Did you hit her?" Sunderson asked, thinking the claw marks looked terrible. "A right cross," Smolens admitted, the same punch used by Marion to demolish Bert. Unlike Smolens, Marion was immensely strong from his youth working on farms near the reservation where he grew up. He was barrel-chested with very large arms.

Marion was making a Szechuan stir fry when Sunderson got quite a shock on the phone. It was his beloved Mona who told Sunderson she had been looking into Simon Ames, Sr.'s court activity in the later thirties, early forties. The Ameses by nature were always in court. The bombshell was that Ames wasn't their real name. It was Arnett. Simon had adopted the name Ames as part of a scam in Frankfort, Kentucky. He was a putative Harvard man and would say, "My family made the shovel that built America." Everyone had an Ames shovel so he won a great deal of credibility. He was busy selling large tracts of land he didn't own on the path of progress near major cities. He was an expert at fabricating land deeds and would tell investors they'd end up living in splendor on Chicago's Gold Coast. This especially enthused wives who were bored with Frankfort, Kentucky, and dreamed of being rich in the big city. He got away with it for two years but of course it caught up with him. A reporter who followed the case referred to him as "dapper" and "likable." The judge was left wing and announced early that Simon was the sole support of a wife and three sons under eighteen. The judge in general also disliked the investors who had fought against his appointment. Simon got only a couple of years plus returning as much money as possible. Simon managed to squirrel away a quarter of it in a crooked bank over in Cincinnati and it was with this money that they moved north the next year. Mona had unearthed a few other scams in the names of both Arnett and Ames but Simon was gone with his family and they involved dirty politics that no one wanted unearthed.

When Lemuel dropped by after dinner with yet another chapter Marion was fishing and Sunderson was dozing before fishing. Lemuel said Bert's left hip bone had been shattered by the shot behind the oak tree. Sunderson was pleased and as a joke called Lemuel "Arnett." Lemuel paled saying that the family was still being sought under that name by the estate of one of the investors. They could lose everything.

"What did the investor lose?" Sunderson asked.

"A lot," Lemuel said. "Simon was good at it. But it would be a shame to lose the farm to rich people."

"You couldn't save your house?"

"Possibly. It's in my name while the others can be traced back to Big Simon. They would go for that first."

"Everyone would want to move into yours."

"Not a chance. They're out of luck. I've got no more sympathy except for two of the wives. I'd help get them settled, maybe in Escanaba. They'd be overjoyed to get out of this place." Despite this, Lemuel departed with a worried look.

Smolens called saying, "Bingo, that's the pistol. The charges are increasing. He'll be locked up forever."

"As it should be," Sunderson said. "That is what we're here for."

Marion was fishing and Sunderson still felt tired so he hastily read a chapter of Lemuel's book in which an eleven-year-old girl, presumably Monica, was sleeping with her narrator uncle. She already loved to cook. Sunderson was shocked. It was a novel, supposedly, but Lemuel didn't seem very imaginative and none of his manuscripts had seemed fictional so far. He recalled finding a shred of paper on the floor of Monica's room that said, "Love, Lem," nothing conclusive and likely the end of a friendly note. It had occurred

to him that Monica and Lemuel were the only two competent
beings in the entire Ames clan. Was it deranged to think
that he might be a patsy, or the odd man out in a three-
way love hoax? Monica was too young for him, but not of
course as young as with Lemuel if fiction was actually fact.
Nevertheless it made him uneasy with himself. Why would
anyone but a deviant make love to an eleven-year-old even
if she was extraordinarily precocious? There was a huge
taboo written all over it. He had seen a wonderful movie
about a girl who had been abused and then became a famous
bandit leader throughout the countryside in vengeance. The
old idea of two wrongs don't make a right seemed wrong in
this case. The theory is that the vengeance of the state slows
crime. This was likely true for most but not the Ames-Arnetts.
Bert didn't know about the state. He knew cows and vodka.
Sunderson had heard that the judge looked forward to
the case, having wanted to nail him with something major
for years. Sunderson would have to testify and it would be
hard to keep a straight face when the sentence was meted
out. He was betting on the range of twenty years. At his
own age he would be unlikely to see Bert again. It occurred
to him that there were never enough good women around
to keep them away from the kids. Maybe it was that basic.

Sunderson's mind drifted back to Monica and Lemuel
and the ancient expression *played for a sucker*. He had been
a sucker a number of times in his long career as a public
servant, even reprimanded by his chief for being too "easy."
Since he himself had always been averse to lying he could be
quite gullible with others. A bad kid could whine about not
wanting a record and Sunderson would occasionally let him

go though the kid didn't have the foggiest idea what a record meant to his future. Would Monica cheat on him? Perhaps on the right occasion whatever that might be. Thinking it over they had never "plighted any troth," as they used to say. Would he, in fact, screw Delphine his next door neighbor if the occasion arose? Of course. Everything seems to be a sliding scale. He, however, couldn't imagine a woman sleeping with a man who started her at eleven. Shouldn't there be some resentment? The world of sexuality was mysterious indeed. The *Detroit Free Press* reported that the age of sexual awakening was getting lower year after year. Who knew? Who was being honest about such matters? Kinsey was long dead and Sunderson struggled to tie his shoes and had lost the grandest wife imaginable on the grounds that enough was enough. The fact that he couldn't imagine Monica and Lemuel having an affair was no reflection on the possible truth. He felt disgusted with himself for being jealous. He resolved not to follow in her father and uncle's footsteps anymore and to find someone a more appropriate age.

# Chapter 15

Marion left the next morning so Sunderson went home too, mainly to get his car fixed by the original dealer. The towing charge to Marquette was five hundred dollars, so he got a local kid with a tow bar to do it for two hundred. If he wrecked the car sullied by bullets so be it. He called Diane on the way home to ask why she'd bought it for him, but after he mentioned the bullet holes she was too distracted to answer. It seemed she thought she owed him and somehow it would wipe the slate clean on their marriage.

He had assured Marion that if he ever came back he was unlikely to see Bert again. Marion said that he had run into a number of bad people in his life and Bert was way up there. Sprague was worse thought Sunderson. But then Bert would be charged for contributing to the murder of the game warden and also attempted murder for shooting at Sunderson. It would add up to at least twenty-five years down in Jackson prison.

Sunderson was upset lately the way his fantasy life had tended to dissipate. It likely was his age, he thought. Everything is going away as many older men had noticed, and it was impossible to believe that everything was within reach. The grocery store, where he always saw beautiful housewives, rarely brought on any craving. The snack shop for university kids down the street was mostly empty during the summer but he enjoyed it when the girls were in their late spring athletic wear. They certainly never noticed him which allowed him to stare at them with freedom.

Late last summer he had sat on a bench outside the snack shop on a hot afternoon and watched eight scantily clad cheerleaders going through their routines. He should have been embarrassed but he wasn't. It was too extreme to walk away. For a while Janis Joplin had been his favorite singer and he thought of her song "Get It While You Can." When they left one of them waved goodbye to him and it was difficult to ascribe meaning to the gesture. Maybe it meant nothing. Maybe she was knowing age-old lust but that was doubtful. Maybe she was just a Friendly American. In high school of the four cheerleaders two were marvelous sluts bent on early marriage and two were prim as saints, also bent on early marriage. When he had seen them in later years they all looked like they had had too many pancakes after church, a tradition not to be broken. None of the husbands were successful but they all stayed married and had lots of kids.

Of course he knew that the aging process was bound to kick in with full force but there should be a way to hold it off for a while. The only reliable trigger of lust in the past few months was when Monica came home from work and took a shower, wrapping herself in one of Diane's big expensive towels. Monica was beautiful, not in Diane's classic way but in a sort of American manner like a Big Ten cheerleader. He felt too lazy to cook and hadn't told Monica when he was coming or she would have had something ready. He went for his old standby, possibly the sin of gluttony, and picked up half a dozen pasties, meat pies that he had been fond of since childhood, a local tradition among miners who would reheat them on their shovels for lunch. Diane used to drive him mad with desire but then he was in love with her, and probably still was. What he had with Monica was a lesser form of love.

When he got home in the late afternoon he went to the backyard and sure enough there was his lovely neighbor crawling around in her flower bed. He went over to say hello and look at her at close range. She was wearing blue shorts again, and a halter top that barely controlled her breasts. She mentioned that her husband was in Lansing and she had to cook herself something. He said he had just bought six pasties if she would like to come over for a drink and pasties. "I love pasties," she almost yelled so loud it startled him. "When?" "Now," he said with a slight tremor in his voice.

He poured her a whiskey in the kitchen but she wanted wine so he drank two whiskeys which he needed. She said she would run home to clean up since she was still in her garden clothes so he sped to the peek hole in his study and lo and behold he saw the entire person naked which churned his guts more than Monica.

Here was an adult woman, now in green shorts and a different halter. At dinner the conversation was utterly strange to Sunderson. Delphine and her husband Fred were involved in "sexual freedom" to try to keep their marriage alive. As a teacher Fred's opportunities were endless while she had to deal with a meager supply. Fred had to be careful as people no longer turned a blind eye as they had in the past, even if no one complained. They would visit their house late in the evening in secret and Delphine was expected to stay in her room so as not to upset the little dears. Throughout this monologue Sunderson sensed he was expected to stay silent and not utter any of the wretched witticisms that the situation called out for. They had tried everything to keep their marriage sexually perky: nude dancing, porn films which Freddy liked but she didn't. "I'm not visual," she said. They had gone to "swap parties" but generally didn't like the people. Freddy, as a graduate of both Yale and Oxford, found them unbelievably vulgar. Sunderson had reflected on the idea that academic people found regular people disappointing.

Delphine pulled her chair down the table next to him and flipped one of her breasts out of the halter and into his mouth. He nearly choked what with a mouthful of meat pie. By a miracle he managed to swallow the chunk of pasty, take a quick drink of whiskey, and suckle at her ample breast. Isn't life wonderful, he thought stupidly. She felt his penis under the table which was responding properly to the on-slaught. She had been occasionally discouraged by dicks that stayed soft under the most outrageous stimulation. There was a bit of gristle to her nipples which he found intriguing. She stood up and pulled her green shorts down to her knees. He dove on her as if she were the most fascinating coral reef in the Keys. She leaned far over the table and he went down on her from behind. "Fuck me," she said. Simple enough he thought. Unfortunately she twisted her butt wildly. This caused him to come off rather quickly. "There's plenty more where that came from," she laughed. After finishing dinner and an hour's doze he managed one more and then he was tired, sleeping until Monica came home from work. He woke up barely enough to see her pull up her green shorts. He was feeling pretty lucky in his semi-sleep trance when she said goodbye and left by the back door. He was amazed by how sexy he found Delphine and the idea of a younger woman seemed a thing of the past.

He felt like a true adult and obedient to the law which wasn't technically accurate. He remembered the startled talk in saloons when Jerry Lee Lewis married his thirteen-year-old cousin. Was this where Lemuel was headed? Of course in the north there was a free-floating contempt for anything southern that could only be understood by a new academic term, *geopiety*. There were cities in Italy a mere thirty miles from each other that regarded the food and people of the neighboring city with contempt.

He didn't so much like the idea but his state police boss and a favorite professor in criminology had insisted that he was a fine detective because he could think like a criminal—he was totally opportunistic and understood the preferences of the local element. Any criminal with ill-gotten gains wanted to spend some money. It was burning up his pants pockets and the choices were limited for free spending. Several times he had found them broke and sober in Sault Ste. Marie. The local criminal element had thought that blacks might murder them in Detroit which was anyway a full day's drive. Chicago was also too far. Milwaukee was an occasional choice for those stupid enough to think they were safe in another state. Minneapolis was unknowable and huge and thought to be boring by the criminal population though it would have been smarter to go where they could get lost.

When he was growing up Marquette people thought the strip clubs of Escanaba a hotbed of evil which made Sunderson desperately want to go to them. He announced to his parents that he and his friends were going fishing and camping, but they headed straight for Escanaba to see mysteries revealed. Later in life after a Tigers ball game he had gone to one in Detroit that was far better and more stimulating than anything the Great North offered. There were actually beautiful strippers in Detroit, not tired hags that looked as if they were going to drop dead from drugs and fatigue. The best ever, though, was an amateur night with a good prize in Escanaba where at his very feet a pretty girl had struggled and writhed to get out of her tight jeans. She was a bit classy which increased the lust. He was happy when she won the fifty-dollar prize and tried to imagine her in his sleeping bag beside the Ford River.

Sault Ste. Marie had the advantage of being close, an attractive town with some cheap flophouses and motels. You need only drive across the river to be in the Canadian

Soo which featured an absolutely major league strip club
where you could exhaust your wallet. There were many
girls of startling beauty, nearly all French-Canadian from
Montreal. Sunderson had been thrilled the first time he
went there when he heard them speaking French together
as if he was in a foreign country. Which he supposed he
was. He bought a lap dance with money earned at a buck
an hour. He was only eighteen at the time. The girl was the
best-looking and couldn't have been more than eighteen
herself. She got on his chair nude, straddling his legs on
the chair with her back to him. She bent way over placing
her entire article on his nose. He was thrilled nearly to the
point of fainting. In general he disliked strip clubs but this
was an exception. The girls were fresh and in fine shape.
Unfortunately one of his friends lipped off to the bouncer,
a huge Native American, or in Canada they are called First
Citizens, and got thrown about thirty yards into the parking lot where he was knocked out colliding with a pickup.
The story naturally got inflated to a fistfight but the friend
never would go to the strip club again. He admitted calling
the bouncer "Tonto" and Sunderson quipped, "Must be he
didn't like the name" to everyone's laughter.

# Chapter 16

Monica came home and threw herself on him in the bed. He carefully explained he wasn't feeling well because he had eaten three pasties very fast. She was disappointed especially when she noticed that two people had had dinner and he admitted to Delphine's company.

"That big slut is after you," Monica shrieked.

"Monica, take that back. She's a married woman." He wasn't ready to level with her.

"Everyone in town but you knows that she would fuck a rock pile if there was a snake in it," she said, a witticism from the north.

To calm things down they took a long stroll down to a beach on Lake Superior. It was a warmish evening and the lake was placid as it rarely is. The last time he had been there, there were still frozen mounds of snow on the shoulder and huge mounds of plowed snow piled up in beach parking lots. Sunderson recalled as a child digging in a sand dune near Grand Marais and coming upon a huge trove of snow and ice in July. Sunderson loved the little harbor village of Grand Marais where sometimes they had enough money to rent a cabin for a week or two when he was a kid. It was crowded and he always slept on the floor in his sleeping bag. They swam and fished for a weekend with him helping out his brother who was missing a leg.

Monica sat down on a bench and whispered, "I have to tell you something. I think I'm pregnant," and Sunderson thought he would vomit. She said she thought she had gotten pregnant before she moved to Marquette with him, probably with Lemuel. Her ready admission startled him. Lemuel knew and had offered to take care of her in his big home. It would be pleasant as long as she could avoid everyone else. She felt stupid and careless for getting pregnant with her uncle of all people and wished it had been Sunderson. He couldn't say how happy and relieved he felt that it wasn't, which would have been a disaster at his age. He had to assume that she was being honest about the matter. Lemuel had told him that the buyers' estate had called in the sheriff's office when Bert wouldn't surrender the land. They were on the way and would seize the other two houses but not his.

Sunderson reflected that the rest of this family bumbled and mumbled their way through life while Lemuel pinned it down. It was amazing how many men were slovenly fuck-ups. Diane had always taken care of all details in regard to insurance, taxes, etc., for him and he was sure Lemuel was good at these, too, while the rest of the family was out to lunch. He himself had needed Marion's advice with some of his own paperwork. The world, of course, was full of needless details. When a questionnaire asks for your mother-in-law's maiden name you should look for the dynamite.

His thoughts were confused about Monica's pregnancy. Losing her made him forget his vow, but when he made love to her now he was soft and gentle. In the moment before she dropped the Lemuel bomb he had readily assumed he was the father. It didn't seem all that bad but then he had never fathered a child much to the disgust of his mother who thought all marriages should be breeding factories. Now there was a certain melancholy in the fact that he probably wasn't the father doomed to a hundred years of child support. He could see himself holding the baby and giving a bottle as he had seen men do at the grocery store. There would be a newspaper headline reading "Older Father Completes Spawning Run." What was the source of the melancholy? He reminded himself again not to want things except fishing and maybe his neighbor's gorgeous ass. He could imagine that after a lifelong affair how Lemuel's years in prison hurt Monica, sitting around reading about Mexico and cooking for mongrels, waiting for him to come home.

He received a call from Smolens who sounded delighted that Bert had just received sentences totaling thirty years. Wow. He thought of a childhood song, "If I had the wings of an angel, over these prison walls I would fly." When Bert got out he would be over ninety, too old to shoot. He felt as happy as he had about Mona's drummer being locked up in France. He called Lemuel to suggest that he take Monica to Mexico on a honeymoon of sorts. Lemuel reminded him that he was the sort of convicted felon that didn't have a passport. Could Sunderson do it? With the baby coming it might be Monica's last chance. Lemuel also said he'd be glad to finance the trip but he'd rather they go to Toronto and see museums. Sunderson felt a little deflated after having his bright idea rejected out of necessity.

A few days later Mexico was resolved. Berenice called to say that their mother had had a severe stroke and was in Tucson Heart Hospital and wanted to see him. He doubted the latter not having got along well with her since he was a teen and especially since the little incident with the dancing girl at his retirement party, but he considered that visiting her would put him practically in Mexico anyway.

Late at night a few days later Sunderson was awoken by useless and absurd memories of the past, such as his puzzlement at seven or eight years old over the song "I'd Like to Get You on a Slow Boat to China." While they were fooling around who was going to run the boat? Were they just turning around and coming back? You couldn't fish on these big boats. It was too far to the water. What would they eat? Did songwriters know what confusion they caused among children? His whole class would sing "The Spanish Cavalier" and nobody had any idea what a cavalier was. How many of these kids would ever leave the country? In high school civics they spent an entire month on the United Nations, a real snoozer. The teacher had seen the actual United Nations in New York but couldn't manage to get any of his excitement across. He loved to say "Dag Hammarskjöld" in a heavy Scandinavian accent. He must have sensed the utter futility of what he was doing.

Drifting back and forth in the incoherence of his mind
he had the alarming realization that Lemuel had mentioned
to him in passing that he had had his tubes tied, a vasectomy,
to avoid paternity suits. Sunderson had thought it para-
noid at the time, but now it struck him, how could he have
made Monica pregnant? Had he had the medical procedure
reversed or had he only wanted to raise a child? He had
also mentioned that any child of his would be a good bird-
watcher by age five. Suddenly Sunderson was wide awake
in the middle of the night and felt the need for a whiskey
and a Motrin, a magic combination for sleep. His thought,
of course, was that maybe it was his child but they wanted
it. Maybe that was okay because how was he going to raise
a baby at his age? Lemuel was at least ten years younger. He
imagined his nights broken by a crying baby. Time to heat
the bottle. This was a matter he wouldn't look into very far.
If he really cared he could always have a DNA done from
baby spit or something.

He was pleased by how quickly the trip had come together. Monica was excited, and her boss at the hotel restaurant was agreeable as there were few tourists in spring
when you can get a surprise blizzard. Diane thought it was
wonderful that he truly got out of town. He went to a travel
agent to book tickets for Tucson for him and Monica to
see his mother in Green Valley that wasn't green, a stay at
the Arizona Inn in Tucson for the nights, and going on to
Mérida in the Yucatán via Veracruz so Monica could see
the water. He got checks for a thousand dollars apiece from
both Lemuel and Diane which was kind of them and not

needed because his simple life had not managed to use his retirement checks. He had one more go-round with Delphine in the garage where he kept a cot for the odd very hot night because the garage was under an enormous maple. The mating was fast and uncomfortable as the cot was small and neither of them was an elf. He feared the cot might break and even though it didn't afterward he continued to worry, worrying being habitual behavior.

Lemuel's apparent lack of jealousy was curious. After watching countless nature videos it was easy to see that most of the conflict between animals came from sex. He was particularly horrified by a fight between two bull giraffes over a female. He had never realized that giraffes fought with their heads, swinging them hard on their long whipping necks, knocking each other down with stomach blows. Throughout most of the programs there was the wonderful calming voice of David Attenborough. In "Birds of the Gods" which was filmed in hospitable New Guinea, birds of paradise danced with a beauty that would make anyone in Detroit or Harlem jealous. Why not go to some of these places now that he was retired? At least he was headed for Mexico tomorrow with a stop to see Mother in Tucson. Finally Sunderson slept.

# Chapter 17

Monica naturally was in a dither having dreamed of Mexico so long and spent a restless evening packing and repacking. He had told her that experienced travelers travel light, besides he didn't want to haul multiple bags around in the sure to be hot weather, or so Mona advised him after laughing that he hadn't even checked the Internet for Mexican weather. He had booked the long way around so that after visiting his mother they would fly to Veracruz only because he had always liked the name and had read that Veracruz was the place where cattle were first unloaded in North America, an act of enormous consequences for the future. Sunderson was also enough of a romantic to appreciate that it was on the water.

Lemuel called very late to say that Bert's house had burned to the ground. It was the house closest to Sunderson's cabin. The bank authorities had been there all day to take possession of the house. Lemuel was sure that the burning was on Bert's instructions, and he had doubtless moved his gunnysack of pistols and other arms including the illegal fully automatic M15 with a banana clip. Someone had left strategic pans of gasoline in each room and the big boxy wooden house burned into an inferno. Lemuel had read Bert's mail for him before he was incarcerated and pointed out that an estate intended to repossess their property as assets that had been lost in Simon's swindle. "If I can't have it, burn it," was Bert's attitude. Lemuel had said that all of the land was also being seized except the plot his own house sat on. "That land is mine," Bert said. "Not according to the judgment," Lemuel responded.

In the morning Lemuel called again while Sunderson and Monica were having breakfast before the airport. He said the second house burned in the night from obvious arson. The estate was now furious as they had an investor on the string who wanted to form a trout fishing club using one of the houses as a lodge. This prospect frightened Sunderson for a moment as he had been around rich fishermen from the city several times. They tended to be piggish about what they thought were "their" stretches of river and also absurdly overequipped somewhat like golfers who bought the most expensive clubs thinking they were guaranteed success. Selfishly Sunderson was a little bit grateful to Bert.

When they boarded the plane Monica seemed frightened and he found out she had never flown on a jet before. Sunderson soothed her by assuring her that no one wanted to live more than the pilots which made them quite careful.

She slept against his shoulder all the way to Chicago and then most of the way between Chicago and Tucson. When she finally awoke about a half hour from landing she said, "Jesus Christ, we're up too high and we're starting to fall." "We're getting ready to land," he said.

When the cab took them to the Arizona Inn she was shy and remote but became wildly enthused about the green grass and profusion of flower beds. Sunderson was diverted when checking in by the idea that evil people don't seem to mind doing evil to themselves. It must be a matter of pure anger, he thought, and damn the consequences. Bert must have known he'd get in serious trouble by standing behind the oak and firing away at Sunderson's car. Still, he did it. Sunderson's insurance wouldn't pay for bullet holes which had set Sunderson back more than a thousand dollars so he had a small hopeless lien on Bert for the money. But Bert would be going directly to prison from the hospital where doctors were trying to mend his shattered hip from Sunderson's passing pistol shot. Lucky he hadn't missed or Bert would have had a shot at the vulnerable back window. Monica knew about the first house going up in flames but he hadn't told her about the second. Spite figured large in all of it. Also a big shot detective in Detroit had once told him, "We catch most criminals because they're stupid." He reflected again about children growing up and the old cognitive problem. A lot of people don't get it because they never learned better. Like his neighbors. He imagined growing up in that rabbit warren of fear and horror. "Your mom is tied to a stake out by the doghouse." What did that do to the mind of a child?

He followed the bellhop out into the big flowered yard and didn't see Monica at first, but there she was in the distance stooped by a large flower bed. When he reached her she practically began to babble saying she had tried to grow flowers "back home" but the dogs or the other kids destroyed the beds. In their room which she thought was "fancy" he called room service and they split a club sandwich with a Coca-Cola for her and red wine for him. He regretted telling Berenice that they would come straight from the airport just to get her off the phone when he wanted a snooze and to see Monica nude on the fancy sheets. He read the map while Monica drove them to the Tucson Heart Hospital. She stayed in the waiting room downstairs reading magazines while he went up to the room. Mother was on oxygen and had IV tubes coming out of her arm. Berenice said she couldn't talk but could write notes on a tablet. Berenice looked old and gray and tired and for the first time it occurred to Sunderson that she was closer to seventy than sixty.

   The first question after he kissed his mother's forehead was that he had been seen at the Marquette airport by a friend of hers with a girl. Who was she? He reflected that this was the phone tom-tom again. He decided to blow the situation sky high and said that the girl was his pregnant girlfriend. It certainly worked. They were utterly dumbfounded. His mother quickly wrote a note, "I hope to live to see my first grandchild!" and Berenice kept shrieking, "You're too old!" This dither lasted his entire visit with his mother outraged when she realized that Sunderson hadn't married her yet. Still she was very happy because her most

long-standing complaint was that she had no grandchildren
and all her friends had many. Berenice had never told her
that her husband was sterile because Mother would have
said "Get rid of him." "Who is going to carry on the Sunderson name?" she would ask, as if a Sunderson were like a
Rockefeller or a Kennedy. His mother had looked into the
genealogy of both sides of the family but quit when all she
could find was "trash and scoundrels." One grandfather was
even half Indian which she rejected because she didn't want
to be part Indian like a great share of the people in the Upper
Peninsula. Genealogy seemed to be popular among people
making the largely vain effort to find someone noteworthy
or noble in their pasts. Sunderson never cared. What was
wrong, he had asked his mother, with loggers and commercial fishermen? Even if they ended up in prison for a fatal
fight they were hardworking people. Sunderson had been
addicted to history long enough to like being a peasant. All of
the problems on earth were caused by men who wore suits.

Out in the car in a predictable cold sweat he didn't
remember ever so desperately needing a drink. His younger
sister Roberta was coming into town in an hour or so but
she was always soothing and had been so since childhood.
Unlike Mother and Berenice she had a soft voice and when
he had his first hangovers in high school she pretended to be
a nurse and would bring him aspirin or Alka-Seltzer which
she preferred as it was more dramatic. Meanwhile work had
never presented any difficulties that could compete with his
mother and drawing a pistol never equaled the anxiety she
could cause. Anyway, his mother demanded to meet "the
pregnant girl" in the morning. He said it would have to be

early as they were flying to Mexico in the early afternoon
on a kind of honeymoon. His mother took umbrage at that
saying, "Honeymoons are for married people." And then,
"Can't you do anything normal?" She had liked Diane a
great deal despite her childless condition but had thought
that Diane was too refined for her son whom she ultimately
thought to be a lout.

As he drove to the hotel his mind drifted off to long ago
when an old-time Detroit homicide detective addressed a
room full of state police recruits of which he was a member.
The geezer was impressive and slangy saying that the only
safe place for any of them was a casket and that a bullet
felt like a bad bee sting but you had to immediately check
how much you were bleeding. It sounded grim and fearful
and he was glad that he seemed destined for the Upper
Peninsula or so he had been promised where he would
carry his fishing equipment in his squad car. Of course
at the cabin his immediate neighbors now competed with
Detroit for horrors. Once he had read in the *Free Press* how
police had raided a drug apartment and found eight heads
and no bodies. It would have been easier to stomach the
other way around.

There didn't seem to be a firm theological basis for adding violence to the list of Seven Deadly Sins. All religions
at times seem to officially revel in violence and the Middle
East appears never to have recovered from the Crusades.
The Borgia pope, Alexander VI, hadn't evidently minded
assassinating enemies. Al-Qaeda used belief to oil the skids
of murder. A talented historian could total up comparative
body counts for Muslims and Christians. You wondered

how Muhammad and Jesus thought about the conflagration that was history. Certainly the Gospels didn't defend violence and the pope himself had always been there to excuse Catholic behavior. The only resource one had was private beliefs that weren't worth bringing up in public but how much does silence count for? He meant this coming winter to survey theological opinion on violence. It was so easy to become overwhelmingly discouraged when thinking about religion. When reading Elaine Pagels he had decided he would have been better off living in the time of the Apocryphal Gospels before the hammer of the Church came down.

He was a full hour into a delicious snooze when Roberta called from the desk. The afternoon heat had broken. Monica quickly covered her delightful nakedness and they had a drink with Bertie, as the family called her, on the patio attached to the room. Sunderson became instantly encouraged about life when he saw two quail and a little rabbit. If they could persist in the middle of Tucson life would go on, for a while at least.

A friend had told Bertie about a Spanish restaurant and they had a fine time, Sunderson drinking a gallon of fine Spanish wine. There was an extraordinary young guitarist that the owner had sent to their table and the Spanish music gave Sunderson shivers and Monica tears. Bertie said the music from Spain was called *flamenco* which Sunderson remembered slightly from college. He felt he should take some money left over from the blackmail and cabin and get himself to Spain before he dropped dead. He mentioned this to Bertie who suggested a week in Paris and another week or so in Seville and Barcelona. He was naturally worried about the expense but Bertie said both cities were less expensive than New York and Chicago.

He was at least momentarily enthused. The music had changed and the dance floor at the restaurant was crowded with people doing the samba, a difficult dance. A young man asked her to dance and Monica did very well. When she sat down again she said that she and Lily had spent thousands of hours back home in the evening practicing dance steps after which they would read good books until midnight. It was important to keep your life structured and active or the hellhole they lived in would drive you batty.

The wine woke Sunderson in the middle of the night. Despite being a retired man he had pretty much given up thinking about death. Death hadn't seemed too bad when his father died in the hospital of heart failure and he had been there holding his hand, but when Sunderson had said, "He's dead," Berenice and his mother sitting there ruined it by starting up wailing. Death exhausts the options for an old fool, he thought. He had noticed the gradual thinning out around town and when he asked after someone he would get "Didn't you know he died?" He never did because he avoided reading the obits in the Marquette paper. What he couldn't bear was the bright smiling faces of people Monica's age and younger who had died in traffic accidents. It was simply unacceptable. He often carried a speed gun in his car before he made detective and once on the Seney Stretch, a straight portion of road where people tended to speed dangerously, a car full of young people passed his anonymous sedan doing a flat hundred miles per hour. Rather than chase them he stopped next to their car at the Seney Bar and nailed them. The three young men were smart-asses and the three girls were drunk and began crying. The ticket cost them over three hundred bucks because he had added reckless driving. He couldn't test them for alcohol because he didn't carry a Breathalyzer, but he showed them photos of a 100 mph accident over near Iron Mountain including one of the four young people who died with a head torn off. One of the drunk young girls puked in her lap. Sunderson with his broad experience on drunk driving reflected that it was hard enough driving 50 mph while drunk and at 100 mph the margin of error didn't exist. Suddenly you were airborne, then dead. He had checked their IDs and they were all below drinking age. He let them off with a warning and drove them all home, and then drove up to Grand Marais and took a walk on the beach to soothe his nerves and bought a big lake trout to fillet for dinner. When in doubt fry some fish, one of the few things his mother could cook well. Their freezer was always crammed with fish and venison both of which the family liked.

He remembered having dinner with Diane before her husband died, at a restaurant well out of town toward Munising so they wouldn't have to meet and greet people. The table had a splendid view of Lake Superior on a blustery day, the waves huge and roiling, the kind of day his commercial fishing relatives used to die on. He sat there thinking what a relief it must have been to make it to the harbor on such a day, the relief of getting behind the long lee of Grand Island if the wind was westerly. He still had a secret dread of the lake deep in his system.

At dinner Diane was perky from a recent "lovely" trip to New York City while Sunderson tried to hide his perpetual

melancholy about their divorce. He'd heard the doctor she
was married to had been born rich. They lived in a beautiful
home on the high hill overlooking the harbor. The father
and ancestors had been in the timber business which Sunderson felt was the equivalent of being in the slave trade
in the eighteenth or nineteenth centuries. All timber had
been razed to the ground for money except for a few piti-
fully small patches. Occasionally but rarely while fishing
Sunderson would see an out of reach virgin white pine in a
river gorge and the tree was breathtaking. And sometimes
he would see a great log half buried in the sand where the
water lacked enough volume to float it downstream to the
mill. They were returning in size but then he had seen in
old lumberjack photos puny men next to gloriously immense
trees. It seemed to him that these immense trees were like the
buffalo we wiped out in our western movement when we had
killed some seventy million buffalo, many shot from passing
trains for fun with the meat never collected. Sunderson had
cooked buffalo tongue, a favored part, mail ordered from
the O'Brien herd in South Dakota. It was utterly delicious,
much better than the fatty beef tongue offered by supermar-
kets. He often reflected that people whether individually or
in groups think they are smarter than they are. Why would
a country decimate its best forests and kill all the buffalo?
Because they are collectively dumb bastards, he thought.
And so am I, he added.

He had missed some of what Diane had said about an
"amusing" play about five lesbians trying to live in peace in
a tiny apartment. Sunderson wanted to ask if that left an
odd girl out of the night games but he feared being vulgar in

front of Diane. She had never had any of the rough humor of the north and it couldn't be learned, not that she wanted to. He had found out in their courtship that they often didn't think the same things were funny. She had a complete intolerance for anything she considered "off color" unless it was French or seemed to be French. French-Canadian, the roots of many locals, didn't seem to count though they had virtually founded the U.P. When he had dropped Diane off at her house on the hill he felt he couldn't imagine how much money she and her husband spent on trips to New York City and Chicago. In the latter they always stayed, Mona had told him, in the same suite at the Drake the husband's parents had stayed in, some more profit from devouring the forests. And they had built the so-called beautiful bank back in the 1920s, so ready to skin people during the Great Depression. While waiting for her to finish getting ready for the restaurant he had noticed first-class ticket stubs on the desk. Why sit with the working class? Whoever they were these days, though the paper said they were all going broke and having houses foreclosed. None of this thinking made him less stupid. How had he lost this lovely woman? A bad couple of years of stopping for drinks with cronies and coworkers and not keeping his mouth shut, mentioning a wife beating where the woman's face had looked like a squashed plum and Diane would say, "Please, not at dinner." Or talking about the little boy who had both his arms broken by his father for not cleaning his room. The mother called in the complaint and got slugged in the face for her "betrayal." The father was a well-known problem so Sunderson took Eddy, a huge Finnish patrolman, along. Eddy had accidentally kicked the guy in the nuts real hard when he resisted arrest. The mother rushed off to the hospital with the kid and he and Eddy sat on the steps drinking a nasty orange pop while the father was puking on the lawn from the kick. "We also have to nail him for resisting arrest. How can I understand anyone who breaks their kid's arms? I'd like to hang him, no shit." Sunderson could see the level of Eddy's anger. Cruelty to children is difficult to take. A couple of weeks later he saw the kid at a playground in his bulky arm casts. He felt tears of rage welling in his throat.

About an hour after dropping off Diane from dinner she had called and thanked him saying he had looked good and must be drinking less. This wasn't true but he said it was. Then Diane said, "Maybe we should have tried harder." In that last fateful year she had tried to get him to join AA but he wouldn't do it, unable to imagine no drinks after work. He tried to backtrack when she dropped the divorce bomb but by then she was simply sick and tired of him. Marion had once done an experiment with third graders. He had passed out 3x5 cards to the class and asked them seriously to write down what they were most frightened of. He had expected bears, monsters, and dinosaurs but was very surprised when the majority wrote that they were most frightened of their parents when they were drinking. Sunderson was ashamed to think that might be what Diane felt about him. He began to hate those well-oiled sensations, but when she left it had been far too easy to succumb, ending with Marion finding him passed out on the cold floor — for some reason he had drunkenly turned the thermostat way down. He had to be taken to the hospital to be detoxed. He was deeply ashamed of the whole incident and after that bought his booze in pints rather than fifths in order to stop himself short of disaster. After all those years alcohol was still a bit of a mystery. With their limited income his father had only one drink a week and that on Saturday afternoon. Maybe then he subconsciously resolved that when he grew up he'd have as much as he wanted not understanding that in drinking more is less. Teens in his high school, the males that is, drank as much as they could get their hands on. Alcohol was the culture of glory, happiness, nonsense.

# Chapter 18

After a rough night, in the morning he took Monica to the hospital to meet his mother. Not having had a functional mother herself, now in a state mental hospital, she was very nervous, and Sunderson was dreading it himself. Sunderson had hated it when Diane would say that he had "unresolved issues" and insist on "professional help." People from his class never spent a hundred dollars an hour to talk to a shrink. Among his acquaintances it was thought to be a scam. Only lawyers got that much.

His mother was calm and delightful to Monica and so was Berenice to his relief. No one brought up the pregnancy. When they left the hospital in the late morning he didn't even need a drink. He should have stayed with his mother longer but he craved to get out of the hospital which he viewed as the place of death.

After the visit they took a plane via Houston to Veracruz where they rented a car and took off for a drive. They
stopped in a village where they saw activity in a stadium.
Rather than a corny ball game they watched a marvelous
dance contest for an hour or so. Sunderson had a couple of
cold beers in the hot sun and was mystified by the grace of
the dancers. They couldn't all be professionals, just local people dancing with the crowd cheering the favorites. Monica
was totally swept away and stood at the sidelines keeping
time with the music. When they left she was gibbering with
the excitement of Mexico. Some of the lovely women caught
Sunderson off guard. He had noted that his waning sexual
fantasy life seemed to have died nearly for good ever since
his severe stoning the year before by young people defend-
ing the Great Leader's compound where they lived. Maybe
there was a medical reason centered in the idea that the
mind is much less playful after a severe trauma like the one
that kept him in the Nogales hospital for a week. He had
been a mass of purple swollen bruises from this custom still
in use in the Middle East. He only saw the kids in passing
searching for more rocks to throw. He had passed through
a small canyon, perfect for ambush. Toward the end when
he was prone he saw a close-up of their feet throwing bigger rocks from close range perhaps trying to kill him. Much
later on when he had visited the cult he recognized a pair of
red tennis shoes being worn by a pretty young girl who had
murder in mind. With a cult anything is possible. The only
good that came out of it was the surprisingly good food at the
hospital, plus the view out the window and his crazy nurse.

Their lovely old hotel fronted the water in Veracruz. He took an old man's short snooze and then sat on the balcony having a big glass of very old tequila. He had forgotten in his reading that Veracruz was Mexico's leading seaport and he enjoyed watching the big freighters docked to the north. Evidently there was a big plate in the hold that rotated on an axis so that the trucks offloading cargo need not turn around within the ship. He had thought of the water as romantic but as he watched he felt like a big kid. The location of the first cattle shipped to America, Veracruz also saw the creation of cowboys, many of whom in their wild stage worked their way north to what was now the southwest United States, which was the birth of the American West. The cattle were unloaded in a lagoon just north of town and he meant to drive up there and think it over in a historical sense. He had also noticed a large aquarium near the hotel which excited him. He was clearly undertraveled and overopinionated, or so he thought.

They were hungry and ate early. He had an excellent roasted fish called snook in English and *róbalo* in Spanish. The skin was brown and crisp with lemon and garlic and the inside soft and white. It was an important game fish in Florida and when he asked where it was caught the waiter pointed south and said, "Fifty miles." This gave Sunderson an itch to fish so far from home.

An immaculate Mexican gentleman in an elegant suit sitting at the next table said they must drive over the mountains on a back road to Xalapa, the capital of Veracruz state, where they had, he said proudly, a medical school and also a big Edward Durell Stone anthropology museum in the public park. Sunderson readily agreed to go. They talked until twilight, maybe an hour or so until Sunderson heard music in the distance. The man said it was Tuesday night and they played music so the "old people" could dance. Monica was itching to go.

On a short walk to the *zócalo* downtown Sunderson stuffed the map the man had made in his pocket. Sunderson saw some attractive *putas* near the doorway of a café where they stopped for coffee plus a flan for Monica. He was amused at the critical way they stared at the nonpro Monica. He was also amused that his retirement and his trip to Mexico were further making him forget his profession when he might very well be strolling toward the *zócalo* in Veracruz with a murderer. He had done a lot of thinking about Monica and her long-term lover Lemuel. Was her attachment to him to throw him off the scent? Maybe. No one in the three homesteads except Monica and Lemuel seemed smart or stable enough to pull off the crime wave, starting with her nursing of the fatally ill Simon who might have been hurried to the great beyond. But the main *person of interest* had to be Lemuel as he couldn't imagine her being the origin of the plot. You had to follow your suspicions even if you liked the people involved. He had shared very little with Detective Smolens even back when it began to jell. He could see it all coming but wanted to keep control of the situation. He also didn't want Monica to have her baby in prison.

Could Lemuel, in fact, have organized this whole thing for his mystery novel? It was certainly possible from what he had learned about writers. One professor used to like to quote Faulkner as saying "Keats's 'Ode on a Grecian Urn' is worth any number of broken-hearted old ladies." Hemingway was ruthless with his children but would head to bed with a case of sniffles. Sunderson always thought Hemingway wrote very well but if you peeked under the covers you saw one of the worst pricks in the history of literature. Faulkner stayed home and drank and wasn't into serial marriages. To Sunderson's limited knowledge Hemingway's personal downfall came from wanting very much to be a big shot all of the time. Back to Lemuel who was by far the brightest of the Ameses and whom Sunderson liked very much. There was the ethical question of whether he felt compelled to blow the whistle on Lemuel and Monica. Probably not. He was retired. If Smolens figured it out which was unlikely he could do as he wished. Currently his attitude toward all the murders was *good riddance to bad rubbish.*

They wandered around town until they found the *zócalo.* There was a bandstand set up which they approached from the backside. A rather ratty-looking American next to them said that it was called *El Danzón* and every Tuesday evening the city as a public service set up an orchestra so that the older people could dance old-style. Sunderson and Monica watched amazed at the elegant dancers, and shuffled a bit to the music on the sidelines. Some of the women were using antique fans against their faces to brush away the heat of the evening. One of the passing older women smiled at him and he felt a small jolt at her handsomeness.

He had made two mistakes during the layover at the Houston Airport neither of which he shared with Monica. He had called Lemuel with his cell and found out that after the second fire a crippled child, Levi's son, had been found suffocated on the second floor. The mother had been having a couple of habitual morning drinks on the porch and her first thought was of saving herself. The fire was instantaneous and spread quickly due to the planted pans of gasoline. Once out the mother remembered her child and ran back inside in her robe. The stairwell was blazing and her robe caught fire. She ran back out and was helped to roll in the dirt but was severely burned. Lemuel had heard the casual comment that the child would have had an unhappy life as a cripple. Lemuel had once pushed the little boy along the edge of the woods in a wheelbarrow to see birds. He had taught him bird watching which had delighted him. Sunderson had an instant lump in his throat. He wanted to murder the arsonist with a blow torch.

His second mistake was to errantly read the second item in the Houston newspaper. A fourteen-year-old boy in a Houston suburb had shot a seven-year-old neighbor girl five times in the stomach with a pistol for borrowing his bicycle without permission. She died in the ambulance. He felt his soul wither with the little news item which was actually vast when truly penetrated with the mind. His thoughts drifted back to theology that had nothing to say on the matter. Lemuel had been with the little Ames boy when he saw his first oriole and had told Sunderson he began hooting like an uninvented animal. What about the eighth deadly sin? It should have occurred to someone long ago. He had never believed in capital punishment because too many mistakes were regularly made in conviction but what could you do about a fourteen-year-old

boy who would commit cold-blooded murder? The paper
failed to mention whether he was a Boy Scout or a junior
member of the NRA. There were no clues other than the
implicit one that he was a member of a culture dying of
dry rot. Who was the father of the boy that gave him ready
access to a pistol? Sunderson knew he could drive himself
senseless pondering cause and effect in such a case. The
girl dead with five bullets in the gut and he had the likely
vain hope that the crippled Ames boy would be quickly
reincarnated as an oriole. Back in the fifth grade each student had received a packet of Audubon cards resembling
baseball cards but with photos of birds rather than play-
ers, and they were let out into the woods to match them to
what they saw. An oriole was a prize sighting. Some boys
cheated and sat around in the woods smoking cigarettes.
He told his dad about this and his dad had said, "Once a
cheat, always a cheat." He had pondered what this meant
and came up with not much because he had noticed that
cheaters seemed to do well at everything and being one
might well prepare you for a career in business.

On the way back from the *Danzón* at the *zócalo* Monica
was crying softly and he thought she was happy.

"I love Mexico. It's the opposite of how I grew up where
no one ever danced."

This embarrassed him because Diane had to force him
to let her teach him to dance. Now he liked the illusion that
he was moving well to the music.

Back in the hotel room they made love briefly. He was
suffering from an emotional overload and began to lose interest partway through. Afterward he went out to the balcony

and sat with a very old bottle of Herradura, a treat he bought himself for being a nifty fellow. It was delicious. Far out at sea at the entry to the wide harbor there was an enormous freighter headed for port. It looked like a small, well-lit city in the dark, somewhat melancholy as if it were laden with sadness in shipping containers from China. Despite resisting, his thoughts returned to the crippled boy and the girl with bullets in her stomach. It seemed horrible to die in an ambulance. Was it your soul wailing or the ambulance? He chided himself for not having started his essay. This tiny self-criticism propelled him into taking a large gulp of tequila. Maybe he hadn't read enough about violence but had certainly lived it. He had read a brief smattering of Paul Tillich and Reinhold Niebuhr at the public library in preparation but they made him want to go to the bar. It seemed he had read nothing appropriate to the job. Elmore Leonard couldn't help and he had read nothing else of note of late. One evening Diane had been reading Nabokov's very complicated *Ada* and when he asked her she as a practical joke told him that he'd love it. To her surprise he did like it saying the book reminded him of a beautiful and senseless dream. At the time he had been particularly bored with academic prose, the 1, 2, 3 aspect of historical studies — "Therefore Europe fell with a resounding splat that quivered the civilized world like currant jelly," and so on — whereas Nabokov was splendidly whimsical.

　　He couldn't remember much of *Ada* now except Lucette's wool bathing suit. From what he could figure there was a lot of well-veiled sex in it but not the kind that gave the reader a boner or had a woman panting. Nothing was as simple and appetizing as spaghetti and meatballs, one of his favorite dishes.

Anyway, he couldn't have spent more than a half hour in the library looking at Tillich and Niebuhr but unlike the Michigan State library in college there weren't any hordes of lovely women hanging out. He had checked out the Tillich to please the woman at the desk who was like a car salesman making a sale. Who would read theology (except him) if it was as dry as cremains?

What did you know after you had read that there were eight hundred thousand casualties at Verdun? His relentless reading of history proved disappointing in retrospect, perhaps why he wanted to write about violence as a sin. Eight hundred thousand was just a number in the most fatality-racked battle in human history. He used to idly wonder if a single transvestite had been involved, a young woman who desperately wanted to be a man at war.

In college he had become absurdly fascinated in a class with a girl who seemed to be the most depressed person he had ever met. They had a couple of perfunctory dates going to foreign films at the State Theatre, Bergman films, which seemed to push her deeper into her slump. She didn't drink because it made her depressed so they had coffee at Kewpee's, wretched coffee but a pleasant place after watching *The Virgin Spring* which broke a little ice within her. He tried without success to penetrate her mind but she would only say that "there's nothing in my life worth talking about." He had drawn a blank but a few days later on a fine spring day they had taken a long walk on the Red Cedar River and she became voluble. Her parents had died in an auto

accident when she was twelve. The three kids were farmed
out to aunts and uncles. Her uncle had raped her "a lot."
She told a teacher and he was prosecuted which made her
whole larger family angry with her rather than at the uncle.
This was mystifying to a young girl. After that she lived
with the teacher, an older woman, and she studied hard and
won a scholarship to Michigan State. That evening they ate
a Chinese dinner and she loaned him several of her favorite books: Dostoyevsky's *Notes from the Underground*, Emily
Brontë's *Wuthering Heights*, and Djuna Barnes's *Nightwood*.
As a junior detective he quickly read all three looking for a
clue to depression other than death and rape. He admired
the books but they certainly put him in a slump. How could
anyone imagine the minds of any of them? Heathcliff for
instance, or "I am a sick man, I am a spiteful man," or Barnes
spinning her tale of darkness. Of the three Barnes was the
best stylistically for him to imitate in writing about his eighth
deadly sin.

His attention waned on the balcony because the approaching ship for the time being was more interesting than
literature. He assumed that ships found their way in the
dark the same way planes did. He hadn't a clue about the
nature of radar, imagining that the ship might speed up
and collide with the shore with a tremendous crash. He
didn't want anyone to get hurt, but a part of him thought it
might be exciting. He had a brief fantasy of running down
the shorefront and saving victims. The whole fantasy matter became abruptly clearer. It occurred to him that sexual
fantasies waned to the point of disappearance because age
in itself is a diminishment of possibility. We come to a point

that anything much beyond eating breakfast and going to the toilet is unlikely. The thrill of fishing was that given a modicum of skill you could still catch big fish as you grew older but the fantasy of catching a pretty girl in your sixties was patently absurd. When you were nineteen and your mind was agog with life's possibilities even a resplendent Hollywood actress wasn't out of the question. When Deborah Kerr was bound to the stake in her diaphanous robe in *Quo Vadis* he wasn't thinking of religious matters but of cutting her loose and taking her camping. Monica, of course, was a fantasy come true. Perhaps it was all about the unlived life. It occurred to Sunderson that while he was working mowing lawns and digging post holes his friends were all free to chase girls.

Reality strikes its mortal blows against us all. Once he rushed over to the hospital where Diane worked to get her to sign something urgent. She was in a room talking to the parents of a prone patient, a beautiful girl who was hopelessly paralyzed from a car accident. It made you hate cars and his throat squeezed shut. Diane led him into the hall where he wept. Diane embraced him, signed the paper, and he rushed out, half blinded by his tears so that he had trouble with the doors. Once outside he could see down a long street to Lake Superior which helped a little. Seeing the girl he had only heard about seemed unfathomably unfair. When he said so to Diane she said, "We know from our jobs that life is unfair." That was that, however true. Diane suggested that he stop by and talk to the girl. She enjoyed listening to people. She could talk haltingly and her reading machine hadn't arrived yet, a breath-controlled gizmo that would hold a book and turn the pages. Sunderson said, "I couldn't do that." And Diane had said, "Darling, it's your sensitivities that are paralyzed not hers." He never did go and still regretted it. Before she died a few months later from pneumonia she had said in her last hour, "I think that it's wonderful that I'm going to die." The priest that was there said he nearly fainted. Sunderson was awed by her fearlessness. She had told Diane that she couldn't imagine a life without making love to her boyfriend.

The freighter neared the dock and Sunderson had a last gulp of tequila. He hoped not to topple off the balcony into the black water below. He toasted a goodbye to fantasies for the last time or so he hoped. What did they fulfill? He thought, though, that reality could be unimaginative except in the good old days when he was peeking through the window at Mona. Delphine wasn't in the same league crawling in her flower bed in shorts. And through the window her yoga lacked Mona's grace. It wasn't youth it was just pure grace. Monica when nude was frequently enlivening but less so than a grand fantasy. He was curious at what age his attraction to the female would disappear. It had to happen. He had not rehearsed the inevitable event but hadn't the actor Anthony Quinn fathered a child in his eighties? He wasn't sure. Diane had told him that Mona now had a steady boyfriend down at University of Michigan, a cello player. Sunderson thought this was fine because the cello was his favorite instrument, which he often thought of while trout fishing. He could almost hear it in the river. The sound of cellos and the sound of rivers went well together. So if Mona was with someone better a cellist than a boxer or rock musician. He still hoped her rock drummer was in prison forever.

He had no real idea about the French penal system except when young he had read a book about Devil's Island, a tropical island off South America where the French often sent prisoners. The heat and insects were terrible and it was infested with vipers. Way back then he had sworn that if he had ever got to France he wouldn't commit a crime because of his fear of Devil's Island but then he supposed he had with Mona. That night he had never even thought of Devil's Island, a thoughtlessness he recognized as typical of criminals, including the neighbors of his cabin. He knew that he was missing some good fishing, also he had dreamed of the ghost of the crippled boy floating up and down the river, moving freely at last. Very little had been done medically to improve the boy's life. You couldn't very well cut into the big vodka budget on which the family collectively thrived.

# Chapter 19

Early the next morning he breakfasted solo on a piece of fish and *huevos rancheros*. He went back to bed for another hour until he heard Monica come out of the shower. He feigned sleep and watched her towel off and dress through squinting eyes. It was always a pleasure to watch unobserved. Once early in his career his chief had him follow a suspected bank robber from Detroit around for a week. He deeply enjoyed the job which started early morning in the parking lot of the Ramada Inn, upscale for a criminal where the disguise is often poverty stricken. Five days later he followed the goof into a bar taking the chance that he might get "made" because he wanted a drink badly, a Friday late afternoon feeling. The man had left his car running, possibly to save a low battery, but then he had a shot and a beer and left, walking across the street and into a bank. Sunderson finished his drink hastily and moved to the window of the front door.

The man came running out of the bank with a canvas bag of money. Sunderson moved outside and yelled "halt" and then the man reached in his pocket and pulled out a pistol. Sunderson ducked behind the running car and shot out a back tire. The man's single shot had broken out the big front window of the bar behind him. He peeked over the fender of the car and the man was still coming waving his pistol in the air. Sunderson fired four rounds peppering the cement around the man's feet. He threw the money bag high in the air and went flat on the cement, raising his hands and dropping the pistol. Sunderson heard another shot and turned to see that the bartender was firing out the broken window. The robber was hit in the thigh by one of his shots. It was all a big event locally where no one remembered anyone ever firing a gun in a robbery. Sunderson won an award for bravery and jokingly passed it on to the bartender. Why not? He didn't want an award. He wanted not to get shot and to have a drink in peace.

He and Monica visited the magnificent aquarium for a couple of hours in the morning. The fish all swam counterclockwise that day in an enormous pool encircling the building. Most of the species were unrecognizable to him though he decided that one day he must fish tarpon. The tarpon swimming in the aquarium were wonderful and thuggish, looking impossible to catch. He had seen a movie made by some hippie types in Key West and the fishing looked thrilling. They weren't the kind of people you saw fishing up north but who cared? It was the fish that counted.

The interior of the aquarium was faux-natural and there was a movement next to his head that startled him.

Some nearby children laughed when he jumped and yelped. It was a live toucan with a huge beak, a beak that could crush a Brazil nut. Kids grew up calling these nuts *nigger toes* up north when he was a boy, where there are still next to no blacks except on the university sports teams in Marquette.

When they got in the rental car for the drive up and over the mountains of Xalapa, Monica said Mona had forwarded him an email from Detective Smolens. "Be careful, you are traveling with a felon as is her boyfriend Lemuel. Call me." He thought that Mona had been probably amused to send it, particularly ironic since it went to Monica's iPhone. Monica stiffened when she read it and tears rose in her eyes. He decided to say nothing and had no intention of calling Smolens while he was on vacation. They were diverted by the spectacular drive up to Xalapa, the best of his life, with epiphytic orchids hanging from the phone and electrical lines living on the rich air. He also saw two of the huge monkey-eating eagles he recognized from Diane's book of exotic raptors.

Despite being nearly blinded by beauty he couldn't help but wonder how Smolens reached his conclusions. Did he threaten to revoke Lemuel's parole? That would be a chickenshit move if you were trying to nail someone with a crime, especially a serial murderer. Diane had said she had seen Smolens several times in the Marquette hospital visiting Levi's pretty young wife Sara, the mother of the dead crippled child. Her burns were being slowly treated and Sunderson assumed that she might be charged with fatal neglect but wasn't sure. Sunderson was startled when he first spoke to her and she actually sounded elegant and

intelligent. What was she doing here? It turned out to be
the briefest college romance. His first wife long gone, Levi
had gone back to try college after Ike went to war. He'd
eventually quit school and gone home, then went back and
collected her, convincing her she would love being a farm
wife on a big acreage. She was beaten regularly, or so said
Lemuel with whom she had a brief affair loaning her enough
money to run away to Escanaba. Levi found her and brought
her home bound and gagged. They had a little girl who died
of leukemia, and then the son who was born crippled. The
die was cast with Sara's life taken over with his care. The
story was so grim he could scarcely bear thinking about it
but he supposed that Smolens had got her talking about
her suspicions in the hospital. He wouldn't be surprised
having noted in his career that patients are often talkative
out of boredom.

They didn't reach Xalapa until midafternoon because
they kept stopping so Monica could get photos of the splendid hanging orchids. Though quite tired they went straight
to the Museo de Antropología de Xalapa, which swept him
away. There were huge Toltec statues of stone somewhat
resembling Buddhas though far less serene and reassur-
ing. Sunderson thought they must have been sculpted to
engender fear. An assistant said that they had been found
and transported up from a swamp fifty miles to the south.
There were literally hundreds of small works of the faces of
women morphing into jaguars. Did they know something
about women we refuse to admit he wondered? It all upset
Monica who hurried outside. He soon joined her after asking
the woman at the desk for a hotel close by. He didn't feel

up to driving all the way back to Veracruz on the coastal highway. She made the call for him and gave him directions in English. He was grateful as his Spanish was nil. He went outside where Monica was sitting on the spacious lawn leaning against a tree.

"Does it upset you traveling with a felon?" she asked.

"Not at all. I don't believe it." He sprawled on the grass.

"It must be Sara talking to Smolens."

"Why do you say that?"

"She was guilty because I was always entertaining her poor son. Pulling him around in his red wagon, singing to him which he loved."

"Is that all?"

Now Monica was embarrassed confessing something he already knew. "Once she caught me and Lemuel in bed and she was jealous. This was early on. Maybe I was thirteen. A day later we went for a walk and she said to me that I was lucky to have a lover because a woman has sexual needs and her husband hadn't made love to her in years. He was always drunk which gave him what she called a *limp dick*. Is this true?"

"Likely. If you have a few drinks you're fine. If you have too many your article isn't in working order."

"Well, she was happy when he was murdered. He would beat her at the drop of a hat."

"Did Lemuel kill Levi?" Sunderson could barely get this question out.

"I doubt it. Lemuel's the only nice man in the whole family. When he does have a drink he sits there smiling. He never shouts or hits a woman."

"How about you. Did you kill him?"

"I wouldn't know how."

"What about that pamphlet on poisons I saw in your suitcase?" Sunderson was practically choking interrogating someone he loved.

She laughed and then said, "That was stuff I found on the Internet then sent away for it to help Lemuel on his novel. He asked me to help him do research."

Sunderson wanted to accept her explanation, but he still couldn't dismiss the ice in his heart. He let it go but something didn't add up.

They walked up the hill to the hotel crossing a bridge over a deep gully. Far below women were washing clothes in a narrow river. Sunderson couldn't quite believe his eyes but was charmed. He had the traveler's temporary displacement when "Where am I?" became "Who am I?" They reached the hotel after a strenuous walk up the hill at which point lovely Monica remembered that they had left the rental car at the museum. He slapped his own forehead like the classic dummy. She took the keys and trotted off reminding him of the vast difference of their ages. Was he a fool? Yes, of course. The entire lobby was decorated tastefully in Mexican antiques and there was a burbling fountain in the middle. He asked the desk clerk for a drink and the man said that they didn't serve liquor. Sunderson put an American five-dollar bill on the desk and the man quickly poured him a nice glass of Hornitos tequila from a bottle in the desk. Sunderson sat down in a chair near the fountain with a groan of fatigue. He sipped the much needed tequila and dozed. The desk clerk came over and refilled the glass with a smile.

He felt curiously displaced again. It seemed that nothing in his life turned out as expected. He had certainly planned on being married to Diane forever, however long that was. Her absence was similar mentally to a missing limb, waking each day and not hearing her below in the kitchen making her pot of tea. The dread of absence rose in him again. How can you fill your life without murdering your spirit? He had planned a long slow retirement of fishing and contemplating nature then ran into a buzz saw next door to his cabin. He meant to act out of ordinary compassion for Monica and now she was pregnant and with him in Veracruz, Mexico. Maybe the trip was also an act of compassion, outside of his planning as was the coming baby. It seemed irrelevant whether the baby was his or Lemuel's. He would be sad to lose her, but it had to be taken care of. He couldn't be a father now, no matter how nice it seemed. How could he stay remote from his good emotions? People do. He certainly was good at enacting his bad sexual emotions.

His overwhelming motive in life was to write out the eighth deadly sin. But who was he but an ex-gumshoe from a poor family in Munising, Michigan? His hubris frightened him as it got him into many messes in the first place. The sin of pride obviously. The question was how could he write the essay? He might start with the biblical quote "Cain rose up and slew Abel." The Bible was full of sheer gore and certainly his job had given him a great deal of experience in the color of blood. Blood was the lubricant of history. Early on he couldn't read about the American Civil War unless it was in the mannerly prose of Shelby Foote. The carnage was unendurable and even entered his dream life. Wars were like that to the innocents back home if a little imagination were applied. He knew his essay on the eighth sin of violence would be up close and personal because he didn't have the writing skills to exceed that. Sometimes you couldn't study history without first amputating your imagination. He had been still in high school when he read about the Siege of Leningrad. He recalled trying to fish when his mind was drowning in the idea that the world was a madhouse and had always been one.

This introduction to consciousness was unwelcome. Living in a remote part of the country the newspapers tended to ignore the bad news but in college he could walk into the smoke shop in East Lansing and buy the *New York Times*, read it with coffee, and his mind would immediately begin to whirl. And when the blood began to drench your own locale you became fearful. Must I shoot my way out of here? If Lemuel were indeed guilty maybe he hoped to gain peace and quiet by murdering the rest of his family. Progress had been made. It was clear indeed that he didn't think his family was worthy of life. And what about Monica, beaten and raped since childhood? The most elementary forms of vengeance came to mind. Any dog remembers who beat it, all of its life it remembers. On the dog's deathbed this person would draw a growl. He wasn't thinking justifiable homicide but the mere reality of Monica's life was undeniable. He had never been offended to the point of real vengeance but our minds readily imagine it in the manner that cats treat imaginary threats. They are always ready unlike us who are compelled to brood through our lives.

# Chapter 20

Mérida was wonderful. He was pleased to learn that when he was a young man Fidel Castro had stayed in the little room next door to their spacious corner room. Down the street there was a beautiful cathedral that made him appreciate the Catholics more. Each morning they heard a dulcet marimba beautifully played by an old man who towed it with his bicycle every morning to a little flowery park in front of the hotel. Sunderson couldn't recall ever hearing a marimba in real life but it certainly was a pleasant way to begin the day. He ordered coffee from room service and they brought a pot on a tray with a small container of yogurt and some fruit he didn't recognize but which was delicious. He sat on the balcony listening to the marimba thinking how crummy records were compared to someone actually playing the music. The man was very old and Sunderson speculated that he may have been playing back when Castro lived next door well before the blood began to flow in Cuba. Batista was such a swine that for a change he could overlook the blood and the fact that revolutions tend to increase the power of the state.

The desk clerk told them there were eight musical events in Mérida that Saturday and made a list with his recommendations and they were off. On the way Sunderson saw a huge roast of pork spinning on an upright BBQ through a bar window and he had to stop. The man behind the counter carved him a goodly pork sandwich he ate with a beer, choking a bit when he used too much habañero salsa. Still he loved it. Monica didn't eat because they had had shrimp and also a wild turkey sandwich at the market in the morning. Sunderson, however, delighted in this foreign food and saw no reason to be controlled by a waning appetite. He could cut back when he was home if he cared to.

The desk clerk had been on the money. Their first event was on the far side of the *zócalo*. It was a dance club of local young people, mostly in their teens, doing a history of Mexican dance accompanied by an orchestra under the shady colonnade. Monica and Sunderson were somewhat stunned by the skill of the dancers. Sunderson couldn't stop staring at the whirling of the most beautiful girl. She had crooked teeth that she tried unsuccessfully to cover with her lips which set off her beauty. This seemed against logic but was true. Meanwhile he was amazed at her skill and remembered he must go to Seville in Spain to see the Gypsy dancing. Americans, he thought, seem to think it a virtue to spend their lives in one place. Many of his friends were like that. "I'm here. It's good enough for me." If they were doing well they dreaded their wives wanting to go to Hawaii. It was either Vegas to see the shows or to Hawaii to take in the sun. "To sit there and bake," one friend said, "because my wife wanted to come home brown and showing signs of Hawaii." He reflected he had barely thought of home since arriving in Veracruz. And why should he?

The problem of Monica and Lemuel was clearly preposterous but he had decided to try to distract himself from it. They were, in his mind, good people, and he was retired. Did he have to pursue people he liked? He knew that he was ordinary indeed but maybe if he traveled more perhaps he could become less ordinary if that were a worthy pursuit. Everyone wanted to be above average whatever that meant. He readily admitted that going fishing was his primary impulse. What was more peaceful than standing in a river up to your hips in your waders? What was more holy than a river though man had butchered them everywhere with dams and sewage, including the worst kind, chemical sewage? To Sunderson it was worse than shitting on the altar of a church.

They saw a splendid event where a large group of girls did a reenactment of the history of Mexico in dance, and it seemed like someone was playing classical guitar on every corner. After the last event they had a pork sandwich at the same bar. Monica wanted something simple after an elaborate Lebanese dinner the night before. She hadn't his tolerance for overeating but then few people did. He had noted that the back half of the bar was an Internet café full of youngish Mexicans working on computers. Monica was curious why they didn't work at home and he explained that the average wage was less than three bucks a day and they couldn't afford to own a computer and also support themselves. She was embarrassed at her own insensitivity.

Once again he was choking over his sandwich having added too much habañero sauce. Over the noise of the bar he was sure he had heard a Charles Mingus number, of all things. The street was now crowded and he stepped outside and saw the Mingus music came from the cathedral steps where to his wonder there was a brass quintet and a drummer, all old ladies in their seventies. From a passing vendor he bought their CD, the first of his life, for five bucks. He went back into the bar to pay his absurdly cheap bill, less than the CD, and fetch Monica. They went out on the street with her carrying her leftover half-sandwich. She broke into tears when she saw the old ladies. The bartender had told him they had been playing together nearly fifty years and had known each other since they were school friends. One had been a waitress in a lounge in LA and learned the music, then came home and taught her friends. A skinny stray dog jumped up and snagged the rest of Monica's sandwich. She laughed very hard and said, "He needs it more than I do." He pointed out that the mutt was a female. She looked at them apologetically as she chewed. He went quickly back into the bar and bought the dog another sandwich. This time she seemed to mull over her good luck then wolfed the sandwich down. Naturally Sunderson identified with stray dogs.

He huffed and puffed his way up the hill to the hotel while Monica trotted along without drawing a deep breath. He felt slightly reassured when he felt the pint of tequila he

had bought in his jacket pocket. His mind was in a whirl and
he was bone tired from their music day. When they reached
the hotel after listening to the fountain burble he was thirsty.
The desk clerk poured him a liberal tequila which gave him
the tinge of a thrill. Just when a man needed it most, or so he
thought. The elevator was on the blink so he had to stumble
up four flights of stairs. He was gasping but once again
Monica wasn't even breathing deeply any more than she did
on the steep hill in front of the hotel back in Marquette. He
secretly hoped that she didn't need lovemaking. A gentleman
doesn't say "no." He noticed again that the door was hand
carved which he had only vaguely observed when they had
checked in. It was admirable work. When they got in the
room he noticed for the first time that protuberant female
buttocks were carved in the headboard with a calla lily on
each side. The buttocks gave him a tingle in the balls and
he revised his feeling about making love.

     He checked his luggage for a last-minute book Diane
had given him for the trip, *The Poems of Jesus Christ*, the
words of Christ retranslated and arranged as poetry by
Willis Barnstone. Not very diverting for travel like say an
Elmore Leonard but he appreciated Diane's good intentions.
She had been surprised by his recent theological bent. He
had quipped when they had dinner out that everyone thinks
of themselves as Christian but then everyone also slips. Halfway through their marriage she had wanted him to take a job
teaching history but he couldn't stand the idea that would
be half his pay. Then she would say, "I have money," and
he would say, "That's not the same thing." And it wasn't for
the old-fashioned way he was bred. A man makes enough

money to support his family. Of course this was largely no longer true in America. It was the sin of pride that blinded him. Despite his expertise in the area he could barely ever apply the knowledge to himself. Pride is hard to notice. It's in our bones and can't easily be shaken out.

He pulled up a chair in front of the open window at the back of the room. He took a deep swig of his tequila pint because he feared he was having a fit of sorts. He thought it might be his fatigue but when he closed his eyes he was hearing all the music of the day at once in his head. When he was listening to music he always saw flashing multicolored lights. He had once asked a doctor friend about this phenomenon and the doctor said not to worry and that many people would be envious. The doctor had an old name for it that Sunderson couldn't remember. You could drown it out with alcohol but he hadn't the heart to endure a hangover with a long drive coming up the next day when they would pass through the fishing village of Alvarado. So he sat there enduring his light show with many sips of tequila.

He must have dozed a little because he heard a rustle and then turned to see Monica nude on her tummy on the bed. Should he do his duty, obviously called for? He felt semiparalyzed in the chair thinking of an article he had read in the *New York Times* about the danger of death in early retirement, mostly caused by idleness and the body delaminating. He was sixty-six and felt that on any given day he could die in a split second. His friend Marion got up early before work, had coffee, then walked a fast couple of miles before breakfast every single day. Marion had also subdued his passion, shared by Sunderson, for a massive patty of pork sausage for breakfast. Sunderson hadn't been able to do so. When he was married and had tried to substitute Diane's wretched granola there were a few tears of denial in his eyes. He had lost twenty pounds on the Atkins diet but his cardiologist had warned that there were long-range health consequences to eating that much meat and recommended the Mediterranean diet which was fine but a little light for his taste. At least Marquette had fresh fish from Lake Superior. Nonetheless, he felt a bit "fruity" on the diet as if one morning he might wake and start flying. The day the cardiologist pronounced him in excellent condition he went out and bought the first fresh pack of cigarettes in a month, a pint of whiskey to hide in the car, and two take-out pasties he ate in the car while watching a lake freighter unload out by the power plant. His decline was ominous and fast. Diane noticed it and said, "You worked so hard. Why are you in a hurry to put the weight back on?" He wasn't, he thought, but he wanted freedom not self-punishment.

Pasties, meat pies, were a golden dream, the one dish where his father stepped in and helped his mother. As a boy he had helped cook in a lumber camp and rolled out the lard dough with a false sense of expertise and chopped up the difficult rutabaga, also potatoes for the filling, fairly good beef, and some tasty kidney fat to drizzle in the tiny holes at the top of the dough. They were the best pasties he was ever to have and had frequently thought of making them but Diane as a downstater didn't care for them. Now with her gone he had no reason not to. The dish was meant to fuel hard work not the sedentary retired detective. Still, when trout fishing he would pack one or two along, and a small pan, and heat them up over a fire, then doze for a while. There was nothing as good as waking to the sound of a river nearby. He was teased by everyone over his dozing but the answer was easy: at any given time half the world was wisely asleep. Any more wakefulness would cause fatal mischief. The best thing he could do for the world, therefore, was nap. Few gave him credibility but what the fuck did he care? Store-bought pasties were but a dim reminder of homemade but much better than nothing.

He sat there blearily at the window finishing the pint of tequila he had meant to save. His mind had become less frantic and he was luckily hearing simple guitar music from a nearby house. He proudly identified the composition as from the Spanish composer de Falla. He had heard it on Marquette NPR which Diane always had on when he would just as soon have been listening to the Ishpeming country music station which charmed him with its white trash blues. He didn't know what to make of certain maudlin aspects or what if anything they had to do with him but he loved the mournful cry of George Jones in "He Stopped Loving Her Today." It turned out he only stopped loving her because he died. How was that different from the story of him and Diane? Love was preposterously corny. This was a simple fact. People had bleeding hearts to the ignorance of the universe. God couldn't possibly keep up with the prayers muttered in despair. He finally went to bed when the de Falla turned to rock 'n' roll. He never really comprehended rock except the Grateful Dead's "Weather Report Suite" which Diane had given him to liberalize his taste.

When Sunderson came to bed Monica was wide awake and talked at him evidently in a confession of murder. "I helped him, I helped Lemuel, and now everyone's dead," she wept. However, he was too bleary to really listen. He finally said, "I don't really care who killed those assholes, but think about what you're saying. Do you want to have your baby in prison?" He was thinking that right and wrong and ethics get so murky out in real life compared to the ironclad principles of criminology and state police ethics. Besides, he knew that Lemuel was behind the whole thing with his wretched novel idea. If your brothers get in your way, kill them. That put him in mind of his own intent to write the eighth deadly sin. He wasn't a writer and he knew there couldn't be anything harder than writing well. People spend their whole lives on it and fail. They used to say write about what you know, which meant he should write *A History of Naps* or *All About Rain*. He was a virtual technician of naps, preferring the wholehearted nap suggested by Henry Miller with all the clothes off and under the sheets. Don't hold back! And for God's sake don't try to sleep with your socks on. His father's Sunday midafternoon nap required him pulling off his socks. Live and learn. Only think about sex vaguely or you'll agitate yourself. Thinking about nature and fishing or birds works very well. Above all don't count sheep unless you know them personally. He recalled bottle feeding one of his grandpa's infant lambs that had been ignored by the mother who had borne triplets. He was startled by how fast the little creature could down a bottle. It began to follow him around whenever possible. It was a girl and he named it Julia.

Why had Monica chosen this odd moment to confess what he already knew in his heart? He got in bed and still heard the lovely de Falla in his head now that there was silence out the window. It was one of those rare times that travel achieved the magic it is reputed to own. Why should he stop? He still had some of the blackmail money left plus his ample retirement. Next stop Paris and Seville. He would take along his unread *Poems of Jesus Christ* and maybe one skin magazine to remind him of earth though in recent years they did nothing to arouse him. In the dim light he could see Monica's eyes glistening with tears. He said jokingly, "Good night, cyanide." She stiffened so he embraced her long and hard. He was now sure Lemuel had approved of her going off to Marquette to try to divert him from the truth. He would call Smolens from an airport on the way home to avoid ruining their vacation any more than it already was. He would say he had grilled Monica exhaustively and try to pin all the blame on Lemuel who could write his novel in a lifetime of prison. His possible first child wouldn't be born in a hospital ward in a prison.

The fishing village of Alvarado he would always think of as his escape hatch on earth. It was on the mouth of a huge estuary and there were many colorful houses, docks for the fishermen, and relatively small fishing boats. They caught a number of fish and shrimp but they were basically after *róbalo* (snook) which was a favored fish for restaurants. Sunderson ate it roasted for lunch with some wild shrimp which were wonderfully better than any cultivated variety. From his vantage point at lunch he could see across the estuary to the great swamp where an archaeologist had discovered the Olmec heads. He was troubled when reading about the matter that it took many months of brutal peasant labor to dig out the big stone heads and transport them to solid land, then ship them north to the museum in Xalapa. He tried to imagine the laborious process but fell short. Was it worth it? Probably. It reminded him of the forgotten men who had built the pyramids, and the peasants who built the vast cathedrals of Europe or the Borgia palaces for that matter. He had worked as a laborer in the summer in Munising and recalled what it was like to be utterly fatigued and drenched with sweat ten hours a day. His mother would pack him three two-sliced sandwiches for his lunch and that barely covered it. He was a shovel man for a construction company, digging forms, well pits, mixing cement. He made a good wage and gave his parents twenty bucks a week for his keep which only seemed fair. Even early on he lacked a trace of venality.

He found out that Alvarado was named after one of Cortés's men. He tried to imagine Mexico without the invasion of Cortés but couldn't do it. He sat there on a bench on the dock dreamily while Monica strolled around town. He thought over and over "I have found my favorite place." They went back to Veracruz late in the afternoon. He had talked to a real estate agent about a cottage for sale for three thousand dollars. He took his card thinking it was certainly not beyond the realm of possibility. A winter fishing place, he thought, where you didn't have to pretend you liked ice fishing and freezing your ass. Sunderson ignored the real estate agent who said the cottage might be too small for an American. Sunderson thought it was just right though the

bathroom could use a little work, easy enough to arrange if
you paid a fair wage.

Back in Veracruz he drank a little much on the balcony
watching freighters. He and Monica ate a last roasted fish.
He speculated he could cook a Lake Superior whitefish
the same way. Start very hot rubbed with olive oil then
turn down when it begins to brown. Butter would brown
better. He would experiment, maybe cook it for Diane. He
caught himself doubting that she would come over to his
old house, so junky compared to her present one. He had
been more than a bit irascible questioning Monica in the
car as if he were a detective at work. "I need to know with
absolute accuracy what you did to help Lemuel." He felt
sure Lemuel was the mastermind and intended to separate
her activity from his. He could see it wouldn't be easy as her
story emerged. She had plainly enough served the victims
cyanide-laced food, but she seemed unaware what it would
do to them. Sara in the burn unit was a big problem. He
would visit her. Likely Smolens had said he would prosecute
her for child endangerment unless she told everything she
had noticed. Sunderson would visit and snoop around in a
friendly manner. Right now he had no idea what Smolens
really knew. Monica kept saying, "I should have known,"
but insisting she didn't, and he couldn't get any sense out
of her after that.

Sunderson fell asleep a tad drunk on the balcony and
Monica helped him to bed at 2:00 a.m. They had a ghastly
flight day ahead. Veracruz, Cancún, Houston, Chicago,
Marquette by midnight. Trying to fall asleep he was haunted
by the worst mental image stored in his head, his brother

Bobby's leg in the dirt near the railroad track at the paper mill where it had been cut off nearly fifty years before. What could be worse for a young person short of getting your head cut off? It was tragic but not surprising he had problems with heroin later on. When Bobby died he had been doing well as a soundman. Sunderson drove to Detroit to claim his body and his friends told him that Bobby had been drinking a great deal to avoid heroin. So drinking has some use, he thought, even if it was ultimately unsuccessful.

On the way home he called Smolens from both Houston and Chicago later in the evening after Smolens had visited Sara in the burn unit at the hospital again where she seemed to be failing. She had told Smolens that Lemuel had said he hated his family and that none of them deserved to live except a few of the female children. The boys also deserved to die. Smolens had talked to the prosecutor who refused to start work on what he called hearsay evidence using the famous Shakespeare quote he always trotted out to make himself feel important: "You have but a woman's reason. You think it so because you think it so."

Smolens added that there was no one left who could have done it except Lemuel and Monica.

Sunderson said in reply, "You should make that just Lemuel. I questioned Monica exhaustively under the most relaxed circumstances on our vacation. I had found a pamphlet on poisons in her room at my house."

"You should have told me, for God's sake," Smolens nearly shouted.

"She had a perfect explanation. She's been doing Internet research for Lemuel for his detective novel."

"Anyone can get cyanide in a day," Smolens said. "It must be hard to think about your girlfriend in prison for life."

"Don't talk like that! I may be retired but I'm a cop at heart," Sunderson said sternly, though if he was honest he was less so than before.

"Sorry. Anyway, the prosecutor won't move until we get some hard evidence. He's ambitious politically and has no reason to move on something everyone thinks is obvious. And all the locals in the county feel that we're well rid of the murder victims. Myself I can't bear the idea that anyone should get away with serial murder. Another problem is that Lemuel has retained this hot defense lawyer from Lansing. I wonder where he got the money."

"He likely embezzled it from his father. He kept the books and there's no other source. I know he had a trust officer, Bissell in Escanaba. I'd guess he has a pile and he's sitting pretty with the only house left. The rest of the family is camped at that trashy old house in town where they started. Lemuel won't let any of them in his place. They're living on welfare. And Lemuel told me he bought the seized land back cheap at an auction in Chicago."

Smolens whistled saying, "A smart cookie."

"Dumb financial people. Burn sites aren't popular with big city buyers. They should have had the land auction in Escanaba. It's a moneymaker, especially if you put cattle on it."

"Cattle aren't fast enough for people making money. Most people can't think of future burgers. My cousin is in the business in Indiana. Prices are up."

"Yes, wheat is easier and more profitable. Or so I read," Sunderson said, bored with the conversation.

"Sara said Levi was sure Lemuel would try to kill him. He was real scared for a drunk. Forensic evidence said that there was cyanide in the sausage patties John and Paul ate. That points to Monica."

"Anyone could poke a hole in a sausage patty and put a pinch of cyanide while she was serving someone else. The kitchen is largely invisible to the dining room where they ate but a swinging door is all that separates them." Sunderson felt a little sweaty.

"Are you fighting for your girlfriend?" Smolens was in a huff.

"Cut the shit. You remember all of those death row prisoners in Illinois who shouldn't have been there? That's a rush to judgment."

"That's not fair. I admit we need hard evidence. I'm just speculating, so stop changing the subject. Sara saw Monica drop a vial of white powder in the kitchen."

"Probably cocaine," Sunderson said knowing it was unlikely that Monica had ever been close to the stuff. "We have to look for hard evidence. I'll call from Chicago."

"Okay, but you better play it straight with me. Call my cell. We're going out for a picnic on a sailboat. It's a hot one here."

Sunderson brooded from Houston to Chicago. The flight was two hours late and they missed the Marquette connection. They rebooked on a morning flight and he thought of a downtown hotel but was too tired. The desk agent made him a reservation at the airport Hilton across the courtyard.

Monica was absurdly impressed by the Hilton. He had a whiskey from the room bar and a short nap. She stretched out checking all the TV stations with the sound off. On waking he recalled that his friend Marion had told him from his travels with his busy wife that there was a first-class steak house in the Hilton with the unlikely name the Gaslight Club where the waitresses wear garters. Sunderson thought that might attract horny travelers though the average man might never have seen a garter except at a wedding. He called for a reservation. They were booked except for early. Sunderson accepted a 6:00 p.m. reservation. It was nearly 5:00 o'clock now and he was already famished. He regretted the first-class ticket because the plane lunch was a chicken pastrami sandwich. He took umbrage knowing from his trip to New York City that true pastrami is not made from chicken. He was, after all, a veteran of the famous Katz's Deli. He was still in a minor snit about this food setback. It was therefore quite a solace to have a big, fatty rib eye steak and a bottle of old Barolo, a wine he remembered from his ill-fated retirement party. He certainly had never ordered a sixty-dollar wine before in his life but then the dinner was the swan song of their vacation and Monica loved it, studying the label as a mystery. Back in the room they made love briefly. Monica teased that the scantily clad waitress had inspired him which, of course, was true. He finished half a pint of tequila while staring out at the night.

Morning came abruptly early. Monica had luckily pre-ordered breakfast at 6:30 a.m. from room service. Who wants to look presentable at dawn? Women learn that early. At the gate there were a lot of people he recognized bound for Marquette. Many seemed to be staring at him and Monica. He introduced her as a niece to a sort of friend art dealer who had a twinkle in his eye. Sunderson slept all the way to Marquette. What put him to sleep was overhearing two people talk about the big Russian plane that had landed at the Marquette airport, a former SAC base, at the end of the Cold War. About half a dozen passengers and crew ran for the woods, which were vast. It was obviously a well-planned migration. He had been sent to look for them with the rest of the police but all of them had gotten lost without compasses and the local search and rescue squad had to be sent out to find them. None of the Russians was ever found and their plane is still at the airport, the Russian government not wanting to admit that such a thing was possible.

# Chapter 21

He slept on their arrival until late afternoon when Diane called. She wanted to hear about the vacation about which she was jealous. They had never traveled anywhere until their forty-year marriage was nearly over. He was too busy, as they say. He read history books, watched sports on TV, and drank too much. Now he had the itch. They arranged to have a light supper at the Landmark Inn where Monica worked. Diane wanted to meet her.

He only had one drink before he left thinking Diane's alcohol antennae would be sharp as usual but when they met she untypically ordered a martini and he said, "Make that two." Perhaps she was loosening up her rules after her husband's death. She finally got the husband she wanted and he disappeared within a year after they were married.

Sunderson had met the man several times, a retired surgeon. His ex-wife couldn't bear Marquette winters and had moved back to New York City, where she was from in the first place, with their daughter. Sunderson admired the man but he couldn't help the absurd fantasy that now that he was gone maybe he and Diane could travel someplace, Paris and Barcelona, separate rooms of course. If you push a fantasy too hard it will self-destruct of its own weight.

She was pleased to hear about Mérida as she had always wanted to go there and it was high on the list of destinations she kept and checked off, a list that began in her girlhood so that when her parents took her to New York City for her twelfth birthday it had enormous meaning. The jump from Ludington, Michigan, to New York City is immeasurable to a girl, or boy, of twelve. You are finally out in the world after the semi-suffocation of home. When she finally walked into the Metropolitan Museum she broke into tears. She wanted to stay so long she wore out her father who walked back to their hotel, the Carlyle, for a nap. Her mother absorbed her daughter's enthusiasm and hung in there. One of Diane's few regrets was that after five years of trying she had no talent as a painter, a dream that trip to New York had inspired. Her friend had the talent but didn't particularly care about art. It seemed so unjust because it was. All Diane could do was stare at art books with love and envy. The envy part embarrassed her but she had no power over it. Eventually she learned to find pleasure in it.

Monica came out and sat with them during her break. Sunderson could tell immediately that they liked each other. You either like someone or you don't. At first Diane acted a little motherly knowing that Monica was pregnant. She and Sunderson had tried unsuccessfully to have a child, then she chose a career over adoption. In any event she would love a child in the family or whatever it was, somehow still a family. Monica was voluble about Mexico and talked as if she were the first person ever to go there. She told the funny story of Sunderson using their pocket Spanish dictionary to try to get another pillow over the phone at the hotel. A room service waiter had brought an omelet and a glass of wine which were good. He showed the waiter the pillow from the bed and the waiter brought five of them, all blue and green.

When Monica went back to work Sunderson confessed to Diane his secret project, writing about violence as the eighth deadly sin. His problem was getting started. She approved and told him he must buy a journal and write anything about the matter that came into his head. It would take shape later. "In short, writing causes writing. Thinking causes more thinking and is not necessarily helpful. Just write an hour or so each day."

They ended the evening on a woozy note having added a bottle of wine to their martinis. It was almost romantic with glances that said "we blew it." When they got in their separate cars tears of frustration formed in his eyes. Life was so unforgivable. She recalled that in his last days her husband could only eat soup, peas, beans, or barley. Otherwise he couldn't keep down his myriad of pills. He was miserable and considered euthanasia at one point. She ate sparingly herself but loved to cook. Even when she and Sunderson were still married she was always looking for an occasion to cook a French or Italian meal. She never watched television unless a chef was on. She loved a big round red-haired guy from New York. She had all his books. Sunderson never read the recipes but liked looking at the food photos. His favorite was called *osso bucco*. After the divorce he quickly lost thirty pounds. He struggled to cook well and nothing was as tasty as when Diane would cook.

Early the next morning he heard steps on the front porch. When he got up he found a red leather-bound journal made in Italy inscribed to him with "Good luck. Love, Diane. Bought this in Perugia." He ate a light breakfast knowing that too much food steals brain power. He washed the jam off his fingers and took the journal and a cup of coffee to his study. He couldn't resist watching Delphine doing her nude morning yoga. Her bare ass seemed to be aimed at him. He had a hard-on which is not a good way to start a writing day. He opened his journal and wrote.

> *Cain rose up and slew Abel. The first human brothers. Not a good start for the human race. It was over jealousy, Cain's anger that Abel's gift was more acceptable to God than his was. So he killed him. Daughters would have been easier than these two guys. Is violence basically a "dick thing" as girls say these days?*

Looking these words over cast Sunderson into despair. He had wanted something elegant on the order of the Sir Thomas Browne he had read in college. What to do? Keep writing, Diane would advise, but then what had she written? He had never looked at the journal she kept in a desk drawer in her room. The act could be too craven like any marital snooping. A friend thought his wife might be cheating so he followed her one day. She stopped at the apartment of a

bookstore clerk for an hour, he told Sunderson. For lunch?
He doubted it, more likely for what is called a *nooner*. However, the friend couldn't confront her as within his own ethic
he shouldn't have been following her. "If she's cheating on
me I finally don't want to know it," he concluded.

> *Cain rose up and slew Abel. From time immemorial men*
> *have murdered each other, in this case over jealousy. Abel's gift*
> *was more pleasing to God which angered Cain. These were*
> *purportedly the first human brothers, born of Adam and Eve.*
> *Centuries later the streets of Jerusalem ran red with blood*
> *after the Crusades started. Evidently some Arabs were still*
> *vexed by the Crusades despite their having taken place over a*
> *thousand years ago but then there is no statute of limitations*
> *for murder. Just lately we expected the Indians to celebrate*
> *the anniversary of Lewis and Clark despite it spelling their*
> *doom. The whites are a confused race indeed. It has been to our*
> *collective advantage that scarcely any of us knows our own his-*
> *tory. The cheers of Fourth of July could be dammed otherwise.*

Sunderson was confused because he had dreamt about
Kate, a spindly girl of twelve years with big ears who was
Sprague's daughter. Perhaps he ignored her out of guilt
because her father died in his home. Kate was quiet and
pleasant, helped Monica in the kitchen, and Lemuel had
taught her bird watching. Sunderson idly wondered if Lemuel had made love to her. Lemuel had a taste for *young stuff,* as
they say. Another idea arose. Could Kate despite her youth
be a coconspirator? She kept herself as remote as possible
from everyone else. She was especially welcome at Lemuel's

house. She and Lemuel would pack a lunch and walk far back in the forest to a small lake where there was a family of loons which thrilled them with their querulous cries.

His own mind was a bit twisted on the subject. Monica was only nineteen but seemed a woman in every respect. Every female is different but there must be laws, he thought, to protect them from predatory males of which there were many. Meanwhile Kate ignored everyone and everyone ignored her. At least Lemuel didn't beat her into a prune. Sunderson had heard that once Sprague beat her severely for pouring a bottle of his vodka out on the ground. To her vodka was the obvious curse of the family. Oddly, he thought, Lemuel never mentioned her. Monica said that Kate was helpful and had alphabetized the spice rack. Sunderson wondered if it was still intact. Maybe he should take a look?

He was suddenly bored with his cop mind when he should be pondering the eighth deadly sin. The Old Testament was full of horrors he remembered from when he read it in high school, skipping through the nonsense of Deuteronomy and Habakkuk. It was during a religious phase when he was trying to help his brother Bobby through a profound depression. The coach was angry at him because Sunderson had quit the squad when he was their roughest tackler at middle linebacker. At the time Sunderson was very strong and known for being able to push a powerless lawn mower up the steep hills of Munising and for shoveling snowy driveways faster than anyone else. Every time there was a snowstorm there were many calls for his services. But he had quit the football team because after school in the fall

Bobby liked to ride on the lumber barge over to Grand Island. Bobby would stumble along the beach on his artificial
leg and they would look for rare agates among the rocks,
put them in a pail, and Bobby would sell them to tourists
in the summer for good money. One day they missed the
barge's return to the mainland and Dad had to come over
and pick them up. Berenice was on the beach yelling at them,
as always. Sunderson was having a difficult time. He had
lost his popularity when he quit the team. Everyone was
mad at him, including teachers. He had fallen in love with
a transfer student from Flint who came north so her mother
could take care of her infirm grandmother on a small farm
on the way to Trout Lake. Both Marilyn and Sunderson
were juniors. She was sexually experienced and he wasn't.
She let him see her nude on a warm early October day out
in the woods. He had to lean against a tree to avoid fainting. It was a much rawer experience than he had expected
in his relentless fantasies. She was a precocious city girl
and had stolen some condoms from an ex-boyfriend. She
put Sunderson through his clumsy paces. He still felt it
might have been the best sex of his life. One day Marilyn's
mother went shopping in Marquette and the grandmother
died when Sunderson and Marilyn were supposed to be
looking after her and not fucking on the living room sofa.
Out of guilt Marilyn no longer wanted to see Sunderson
despite his relentless efforts. Soon after her mother sold
the farm and had an auction for the belongings. She and
Marilyn drove back to Flint in her newish blue Buick she
had bought at a discount while working at the Buick plant.
Once on a hot July day he and Marilyn had made love in

the sweltering backseat of the car and he still had memories of the odor of her sweat and the new car smell.

Next morning bright and early he shopped for groceries in Escanaba and drove to the cabin to hopefully fish which he did immediately on his arrival. He caught a few small rainbows and one good brown on a caddis fly. When he returned to the cabin he was irked by Lemuel and Kate showing up wearing their bird-watching binoculars, but he gave them coffee and didn't act cross. They were headed upstream for the afternoon and Sunderson realized that gave him free time for snooping. Kate offered to make spaghetti for dinner seeing that he had bought some Italian sausage. He gracefully accepted and waited until they disappeared out of sight upriver before driving over to the second burned house. No one was around and he entered the burned-out kitchen. Luckily the fire truck was parked on the back drive and the pantry was scorched but pretty much intact. He put on rubber gloves to avoid marring any prints or leaving any of his own. He was very gentle when he discovered that the small amount of alum didn't smell like alum, used for making pickles crisp. He knew what it smelled like because as a child his mother would dab on alum when he had a canker sore. The only other light-colored spices were dried mustard which was definitely dried mustard and a tiny amount of garlic powder that was transparently not garlic powder. He put all three in his coat pocket and left pronto fearing to get caught. He drove up to a hill where he could get cell service to call Smolens who was thrilled with the story and the work. It wouldn't be admissible unless they could sneak it back into the kitchen, but maybe it would help get a confession. He said he never thought of Kate when he did prints of anyone working in the kitchen because she was too young. He added that he still hoped to find the prints of Monica and Lemuel on the bottles. Sunderson let it pass knowing how hard it is to change your mind when you think you have solid suspicions. He'd send someone out immediately for a pickup.

Sunderson was irritated with himself over the Kate situation. In his very necessary mental rehearsals of the crime scene he had foolishly bypassed her, maybe because of her age as Smolens said. Irrelevant, dammit. Lemuel could very well have engineered the poisonings through her despite the idea that Monica was more obvious.

The deputy reached the cabin in the record time of a couple of hours just as Lemuel and Kate returned from bird watching. Kate saw Sunderson hand the deputy a small paper bag.

"What's this all about?" she asked, naturally curious.

"Just some evidence from your house." Sunderson stopped himself from telling her they were dusting for prints. She looked startled.

Kate whipped up a fine pasta sauce working at a speed incomprehensible to Sunderson. He kept a close eye on her while she was cooking to make sure everything came from his kitchen. She was masterful at chopping garlic which made her attractive to him since he was a clod at garlic and onions. She was however slight indeed and if Lemuel was making love to her there was something clinical going on. Lemuel was a little *off* and had probably overheard their interchange about evidence. Sunderson was having a bountiful glass of whiskey while Lemuel had a little wine. Kate refused a beer saying sharply that she intended to never drink a drop in her life.

"Look what it did to my family," she fairly hissed. "My father would be alive now if he wasn't a mean drunk who had to be shot."

"I'm so sorry. It couldn't be helped." Sunderson had a lump in his throat despite the fact that Sprague had had it coming. Him or me was the conclusion. Monica had since told him that Kate's mother was terrible calling her U.D. for Ugly Duckling while her father had frequently taken her fishing and hunting. She was very good at finding the grouse and woodcock he shot in heavy cover. She would also pluck the birds and get them table ready. In Sprague's mind she was a third son and a fine substitute now that Tom and Paul were gone.

Sunderson allayed his melancholy by drinking faster. Lemuel's spirits picked up talking about birds. They had seen two local rarities, a lazuli bunting and a black-headed grosbeak. Then he talked about getting out of prison that first time after doing seventeen years. He had been crazed for nature after being penned up that long and had bought a used Subaru and drove to a great birding region near the Mexico-Arizona border in late March and had added one hundred and nineteen species of birds to his life list in two weeks. He said this with such an air of triumph that Sunderson was almost moved and thought too bad you'll likely finish your life back in prison. Sunderson was ultimately without sympathy. You can't just go around killing people no matter how bad they are, but as a claustrophobe Sunderson

dreaded the very idea of a prison cell. Death would be better, or so he thought for the time being. As a retiree he was
surprised how little he thought about death, the end of the
story. That wasn't a flip idea but a truth favored by Native
Americans. Your story had a beginning, middle, and end
like all stories. He liked the epitaph that the anthropologist
Loren Eiseley had written for himself, "We loved the earth
but could not stay." What could be more beautifully concise?
Maybe he'd have it engraved on his headstone. He must
instruct Diane. Who else could he ask?

They had finished a fine dinner when Smolens called to
say that all of the prints were Kate's and complimented him
on his good work. Kate and Lemuel looked at Sunderson
quizzically when he hung up the phone, thinking to himself
that they were perfectly capable of killing him if they thought
it was to their advantage.

It was early on the warmest morning of the year when
Lemuel dropped Kate off for fishing continuing on to Escanaba to see his broker or so he said driving off. Kate
evidently didn't have waders and had on short shorts and
hip boots. There was a five-inch gap of bare thigh between
the tops of her boots and shorts and there was a bit of the
electric in her rounded butt in her short shorts.

They fished for about two hours before he had to climb
the bank and cool off under a maple tree. He was sweat-
ing hard under his waders so he took them and his pants
off and sprawled under the tree in his boxer shorts. Kate
joined him sitting against the tree in front of his face with
her legs cocked up, her dainty crotch aimed at his nose. He
felt his cock rising underneath him, Old Mister Fool. He

reminded himself that to fool with her could be actionable
and was forced to acknowledge that Lemuel was brilliant
in his conning. He knew that Monica liked him a great deal
but he also knew that to a specific degree even she was a
setup. Lemuel was an obvious pimp with these girls and
Kate could be held against him as leverage if he was stupid
enough to touch her.

"It must be in the eighties. I'm going to take a dip."

She stood and quickly shed her clothes, having an awkward time with the tight hip boots. She trotted to the river,
screeched at the cold water and paddled out to a sand bar
where she stood shivering and flailing her arms for warmth.
She came back and sat nude against the tree on her T-shirt.

"Did I give you a hard-on?" she asked lightly. "Let me
see it." He could tell she was putting on bravado but there
was a quaver in her voice.

He said no. It was the first piece of ass he'd ever refused,
young or old. These oversexed Ames girls were making his
stomach churn. Kate should be worried about school and
when she'd develop, not being used as her uncle's honey trap.

They fished for another hour in the hottest part of the
afternoon, then walked back to his car in the shade of the
woods across the river. He carried her shorts, T-shirt, and
hip boots across the river in his waders and she swam.

When they got back, Lemuel offered him a vodka and
orange juice which he drank thirstily, having surreptitiously
watched to be sure it came out of a sealed bottle.

"I found four cases of half gallons in the root cellar,
more than enough for my lifetime. You take this one." He
pushed the half gallon of vodka toward Sunderson who said

thank you. He never drank vodka which was just tasteless alcohol and only valuable in a pinch. He preferred the flavor of Canadian blended whiskey like VO.

He took a three-hour nap, very long for him, and toward the end he was only half asleep and thought about the Seven Deadly Sins and also *The Poems of Jesus Christ*, the book Diane had given him. This was all in comic contrast to his day so far. There was a knock on the door and Kate entered carrying a casserole dish.

"I was making a *choucroute garnie* for Lemuel and made some extra for you. It's just sauerkraut, sausages, onions, potatoes and one pig hock in the bottom. I didn't have any dried mustard to make you hot mustard."

Sunderson reflected that the dried mustard could have killed him. Her brash pronunciation of *choucroute garnie* was sweet, just like Diane's when she made the dish which he loved. There were enough Germans in the Marquette area that good sausages were readily available though Diane had said that the dish had crept north and east from Wisconsin.

They were sitting at the table with her dishing up the meal when she said, "I think Sara did it. Levi let all the men beat her, even the male children. No one could have endured what she did and forgive it. She was stuck-up about her nice hands and was always wearing rubber gloves to protect them. Maybe she didn't want to leave fingerprints? She was always trying to help Monica or me with the cooking but she was totally lame at it except for washing dishes."

Sunderson stopped in mid-bite wishing he had hot mustard for the sausages but quite startled at the idea of Sara. He hadn't thought of her because Monica had never told him she helped in the kitchen, and she was always lethargic, drunk, or both.

"Lemuel admitted to me that after prison he had had a long affair with Sara," Kate continued. "She was depressed when he threw her over for Monica, all the more reason, I mean her anger, to try to frame Lemuel and Monica."

Sunderson was thinking that it would be easy to open a spice bottle without leaving a print. Naturally Kate's prints were on the bottle because she was doing the cooking. How easy it was to kill one another! And without the vulgarity of guns. Even the popes used poison. He called Smolens with the new possible developments being careful because he knew Smolens had been having marital problems and had a definite soft spot for Sara. Would it never end? Probably not. Sunderson disliked this sort of irony except in himself. You could get a crush on a burned woman and visit her every day in the guise of police work.

He stared at Kate and thought that she and Monica and Sara all reminded him of the hundreds of statues in the Xalapa museum whose faces were turning into those of the dread jaguars. He also thought that despite his retirement here he was in the middle of a murderous spree.

# Chapter 22

The next morning there was a relentless cold rain. He heard it in the predawn sleepless hours. He went out with his coffee, standing under the eaves and seeing the rain was going to sock in for the day. He packed up and started to drive home, calling Diane halfway there in case she could have dinner. She was bereft and missing her husband. Sunderson actually felt morose for her. Her new marriage had gone so well for a year. They had a glorious trip to Italy, Spain, and France. They even went to China for God's sake, a trip well beyond Sunderson's interest. Her obsession with art could carry her anyplace.

The day Diane's husband died Mona had called about 10:00 p.m. to tell him. He had the Miami–San Antonio NBA game on and was exhausted watching them run up and down the court. Mona told him not to bother but he drove over to the hospital. The night was black and cloudy but still a glint of light to the west. There was a little rain as he walked from the parking lot to the hospital and he was able to press down his unruly hair having forgotten to brush it. He was wearing old clothes and a shirt with food stains on it.

There were several of Diane's friends in the waiting room with her. When he walked in she hugged him very hard and sobbed. They all drove over to Diane's house and Mona opened a couple of bottles of Richebourg which was so delicious he thought it nearly made you forget the occasion. Mona also put a gentle Mendelssohn CD on. Three of the women who sat on the sofa were also widows. He sat there stiffly thinking about their husbands, hard-charging men who overate and all died at his age in their early sixties. Probably none had avoided the fat on their pig hocks.

The women all talked softly and Sunderson followed Diane into the kitchen where she and Mona made up a cheese platter. Sunderson shyly offered her a platonic camping trip wherever she liked. She shook her head and said maybe someday, smiling sadly.

Now Sunderson reminded Diane of their conversation and she admitted that she would like to see his cabin. It gave him hope. He sometimes thought perhaps he was a widower himself with the actual spouse alive seven blocks away. Human loneliness is a huge item and Monica couldn't begin to compensate for his love for Diane. A hopeless love at that.

He thought of the number of times he had been rained out when fishing. When he was a junior in high school he had sat in a cheapish pup tent two full days in the rain until he and all his bedding were soaked. He persisted, catching trout for his family's dinner. When wet you can only get a little wetter. Now he reflected that the odor of sex was as powerful as that of a butcher shop. At the cabin it was cut only by the blossoming of a chokecherry outside the window, an odor he had always loved. In the spring he liked to travel to an area to fish where there were hundreds of acres of blooming chokecherries and be overwhelmed by them.

Now, suddenly, in his car approaching Marquette he thought of copying passages from *Nightwood* and *Ada* under the idea he would thusly learn to write. Why not? He had the paper and pens. What was stopping him? He doubted this was a surefire answer but was worth trying. He didn't think it constituted cheating. He certainly needed not to die before he wrote about the eighth deadly sin. For a very big change he felt necessary to the world. He knew if he could get it right the essay would change everything.

Back in college there was a year after the rage of existentialism that it was commonly held we are all guilty of everything. Sunderson, however, was drawn in very little on this one for common pragmatic reasons. He tended to see the entirety of the United States as an Indian graveyard but could not see how any of it was his own fault. Maybe his ancestors were at fault and he didn't have any descendants.

He nearly ran a stop sign when he had the absurd idea that perhaps Sara, Monica, and Kate were all guilty. Lemuel was a junior Svengali. Sunderson couldn't admit Monica might have known what she was doing and stopped at the IGA, buying a very large package of pig hocks. Back in the parking lot he called Diane's cell phone to see how to cook them. He was disappointed to find out that the pig hocks took three hours at a slow simmer. Maybe he should nuke them first. "Absolutely not," she said. Naturally he wanted more immediate results. He walked across the street and stocked up at the liquor store seeing a beautiful girl ride past with the seat of the bicycle stuck in her butt, or so it seemed. Boys used to tell girls they wanted to be their first bicycle seat and he wondered if they still did. What was there about a shapely fanny? The taste must be deeply embedded in the brain.

He put the pig hocks on the stove in the big Le Creuset, had a drink, got on the sofa for a snooze. He intended to spend the evening copying parts of Barnes and Nabokov. He awoke in three hours to smell pork fat. He leaped up and saw the water had boiled away and his beloved hocks were frying in their copious fat. He refilled the pot with water deciding that the hocks weren't fatally injured. He got out his books by Barnes and Nabokov with the religious sense that he was in touch with greatness. Mona walked in without knocking because she saw him in the kitchen. She asked after the "dreadful" smell and he said, "Fucked-up pig hocks that I'm restoring." He averted his eyes because she looked particularly lovely. Her boyfriend the cellist had parents with a house in Naples and they had gone there on August break. Mona's long bare legs were tan as were her arms and face.

"Did you sunbathe nude?" he teased.

"Of course not." She turned then raised her skirt and pulled down her panties revealing a lovely pale butt. She pranced around wagging it.

"Don't do that," he said. "It reminds me of our unforgivable sin in Paris."

"Oh bullshit! You'll live." She flopped down on the sofa with her skirt on her chest. He bolted out the back door. After five minutes she came out with a beer and sat beside him. "I'm sorry I'm wicked. My current boyfriend can't make love unless he's wearing his bedroom slippers. I suddenly wanted to do something old-fashioned nasty."

"I'm in a murder mess in my retirement. I can't afford mentally to fuck up now."

"Diane told me you were thinking of going to Spain. You should go tomorrow."

"I'm sure it takes a lot of planning," he said lamely.

"Don't be silly. I'll go in and call the travel agent."

He followed her inside as she booked him to Paris for five days then Seville. If he didn't like Seville he could take a train or plane to Barcelona, and his flight home was from there. She also booked him the same hotel near the Odéon he had stayed in when he came to retrieve her. May as well give him some memories. To irritate him she got him the most expensive hotel in Seville. She helped him pack and reminded him to pick up cash and the tickets in the morning. He kissed her goodbye and gave himself the treat of letting his hand brush across her tight ass. She had always amazed him with the immediacy with which she lived. Compared to her he existed totally on a diet of reverie and fishing. He was also proud of actually running out when she tempted him though there remained a nugget of regret. When she left she said that she wished she was going with him and his mind constructed an absurd headline, "Man Fucks Stepdaughter Across Europe."

Monica stopped by to take a shower before work. She had been sailing on the bay with friends from the hotel. She was running late but he nagged her into some quick sex. Mona had built up a head of steam within him. After she went to work he had another drink and hastily made some hot mustard out of the dried. He sat down and ate with the prompt conclusion that they weren't as tender as Diane's but much better than no pig hocks.

Of course he was brooding about his possible trip. He could see that he was damned if he did—could he get the considerable sum back for the tickets?—but even more so damned if he didn't. He couldn't come up with a single other reason not to go. The TV had said that a week of coolish weather was due which meant there wouldn't be bug hatches for fly fishing. Other than fishing and his little adventure tracking the Great Leader, his life in retirement had been quite aimless except, of course, for taking Monica to Mexico. Right now he wished he were in Veracruz or Mérida, then he wouldn't have to fly to Paris, where the ghost of Mona waited. His last trip had been frantic on the way with worry about Mona's musician and on the way back there was the regret and immense guilt. What they had done was clearly a strident violation of one of the Seven Deadly Sins. Mona made his mouth dry and his heart pound.

He had waited until Monica came home late to tell her about his trip. He gratuitously lied to her, saying an old friend from college was getting married and asked him to stand

up for him. The friend was paying for the ticket. He began
to believe the lie himself. He was already irritated because
Smolens had called earlier to say that the prosecutor was still
unwilling to proceed despite the new evidence. His point was
obvious: Kate was in the kitchen all the time so of course her
prints would be on the spice bottles and even more damning
was that the two bottles that supposedly held poison contained
small amounts of comparatively harmless cocaine, one cut
with the popular Italian baby laxative Manitol, the other with
a teaspoon of ordinary talc. The prosecutor was pleased with
the coke and wanted to pin it on someone because it was the
drug that put him on the warpath and strong action against
it was popular with voters who were ignorant that the real
threat was speed. Sunderson had always been amazed how
drug dealers as businessmen cheated their customers and
still stayed in business. A recent big bust in Detroit flopped
because the three kilos of cocaine that had been seized had
been devoid of any actual cocaine.

Meanwhile he tried to console Smolens who was heart-
sick and threatened to quit the case. "No one gives a shit
about these people," he said. Sunderson replied, "You can't
let a murderer go free," and Smolens said, "Yes I can, just
watch." When Sunderson said "a murderer" the image of
Lemuel flashed in his mind. There could be no other en-
gineer of the whole matter. In the mail Lemuel had sent
him another chapter, called "Doom," of his wretched crime
novel. Maybe he should actually be reading it for clues but
the punishment was truly bad prose. Lemuel's prose was
absolutely devoid of any charm, one of the main reasons
you read. If he found a clue would he recognize it while

half asleep and bored? Lemuel would never be a good crime writer. He wanted to inform the world not describe it.

In the morning he cleared his credit cards in preparation for the trip. He stopped at the bar across the street from the travel agent. Suddenly worry hit like a sledgehammer. What if Diane wanted to go camping while he was wandering aimlessly in Paris, Seville, or Barcelona? What a disaster. He'd wait a day and call her tomorrow.

At the travel agent's he delayed his trip for two weeks, not easy as it was a busy season and planes and hotels were getting booked. He was forced to book business-class tickets to Paris for a fortune but then he viewed the remaining blackmail cash as "funny money" like winning big at a poker game. The prospect of taking Diane camping was emotionally too large to miss. He had waited over sixty years to go so a couple more weeks wouldn't hurt him.

Smolens stopped by for a chat and a drink. He was frazzled and generally bereft.

"What do you generally think happened not considering our lack of evidence?" Smolens grimaced with the size of the drink he had poured for himself.

"Well, it's pointless to speculate but I see Lemuel spearheading the whole thing possibly using all three of the women not incidentally because he was a lover of all three. Lemuel was on the offense of course and besides he's likely smarter than us. With the right preparation a perfect murder is easy and Lemuel possibly did a lot of research. He's not going to break and I don't see any of the women breaking. Too much is at stake. And I don't see anyone suffering from conscience. The victims were too ghastly as humans."

"I can't believe that a hayseed outsmarted us college guys who wear guns." Smolens smirked.

"Well, he's very well self-educated. Don't forget that he had fifteen years of reading time in prison. They have a pretty good library."

"I simply don't understand the power he had over the women. He's an ugly little twerp." Smolens was in a state of umbrage.

"He was the only one in the compound who listened to them. He's not even having the two burned-out hulks of the houses removed. He told me he likes to look at them. The remnants of the family are living on the east side of Escanaba on welfare though I know he helps them out. He's sort of rich."

"I wish I was," Smolens said begrudgingly. "I'd buy a small farm and dawdle on it. I'd quit this shit job like you did but I'm five years from possible retirement. My wife wants to live in Hawaii. I don't."

"Why Hawaii?" Sunderson was curious.

"A childhood dream, I think. She always wanted to grow coconuts near the ocean." Smolens was obviously in despair.

"How do you grow coconuts?"

"I have no idea. I think you have to grow a tree first. It might take a hundred years. Luckily that leaves me out of the marketing."

"Maybe we could look into Lemuel's taxes."

"Very hard to do. Even for a Mafia don or a political candidate."

Their lack of ideas evaporated their withered spirits. They poured another drink and went out in the backyard and watched Delphine next door weeding a flower bed wearing knee pads. Smolens stared with curiosity. "On a certain level women can be quite basic. Of course so can we. Like lonely stray dogs who are still horny."

That did it for Sunderson. He choked on his drink and had to spit up a precious mouthful.

When Smolens left Sunderson had a headache and poured yet another drink. He remembered a professor saying in a criminology course that some crimes are meant never to be solved. He thought, it's always darkest before it gets even darker.

Monica had left him a small T-bone bought with her own money as he had forgotten to set out the grocery money. He errantly cooked it too long while fiddling with the TV to get the Bulls-Heat game. He was irked with himself and also the world. Only a fool didn't know how to cook a steak. He had lectured junior officers countless times about their level of attention. The steak was pretty good anyway. He drank too much whiskey and after the ball game which LeBron won in the last minutes he treated himself to a quick peek at his neighbor's evening yoga. From here, her ass looked a bit large but smooth and in good shape.

He almost overslept the next morning but was luckily awakened by an early call from Smolens who had had a bright idea that woke him in the middle of the night. He had had breakfast at the diner and run into the prosecutor who ate oatmeal and raisins, a repulsive combination. He took

the opportunity to broach his idea to the prosecutor: offer
Sara, who was refusing to testify, immunity from a prison
sentence if she turned state's evidence against the others.
The prosecutor agreed. Smolens admitted to Sunderson that
he had told Sara he would divorce his wife and marry her.

"That won't get you a promotion after a criminal case
with her," Sunderson pointed out and Smolens said he didn't
give a shit. If he went up any further he'd have to transfer to
Lansing which he wouldn't do at gunpoint. Smolens said he
had been to the hospital early to broach the idea with Sara
who so far was noncommittal. She had said, "But Lemuel
was the only one who was nice to me." And Smolens had
answered, "Well right now he's fucking your kid niece Kate."
Sara didn't know this and got quite angry. She was Kate's
godmother and had dressed her for school.

Sunderson's head was light and hungover but the news
was good though how could he separate the pregnant Monica from this? When the evidence was in he was sure Kate
and Lemuel would be revealed as the main malefactors.

Sunderson had always thought it was a good idea that
justice moved slowly as the potential for mistakes was in-
finite. He himself had engineered the withdrawal of a case
against a young man who had been charged for underage
drinking with the naked daughter of an important family
along with three other naked boys at the gravel pit swimming
hole at night. They all ganged up on the poor boy saying he
had supplied the beer and whiskey. However Sunderson had
noted that the beer was an expensive import, not the kind
kids buy, and the whiskey was a scotch, Haig & Haig Pinch
with the wire around it, not available locally. He interviewed

the girl in a car after school to avoid bringing her to the station and ruining her life. She was terribly attractive, wild
and destined to get wilder. She wore a short dress and put
her stocking feet up on the dashboard so that her legs, her
trump suit, might get him confused. Sunderson was already
in the middle of a patented lecture on poor kids but they
were parked near the Coast Guard station and he was really
watching the sunlight glitter off the big waves. He explained
that though the poor kid was very bright he would likely lose
his chance for a college scholarship. She broke and started
crying in sympathy. She said, "Mike brought the beer and
I filched the whiskey from Dad's liquor cabinet." The case
was dropped now that it had become complicated with rich
kids' lawyers. Later he heard that the poor kid had gotten
her pregnant and her mother had taken her off to Chicago
for a medical procedure. Unfortunately she had wanted to
keep the baby and after this she got wackier and wackier
and didn't want to come home for several years. He had
lately seen her coming out of a lowlife bar looking like a
very premature hag. Could she drink the baby back alive?
Not likely. Her parents had died and left her a good deal of
money all of which she spent in Chicago. Sunderson tried
not to care but the arrest and then the abortion had marked
her life terribly.

Lemuel called to say he understood that he was to be
prosecuted with Sara's testimony.

"Why would you think that?" Sunderson was concerned about the leak.

"An old girlfriend of mine works in the prosecutor's
office. Always be nice to ex-girlfriends. They know a lot

about you. Anyway you should leave the girls alone. I don't give a shit about myself."

"No one will believe you did it all by yourself."

"I basically did. I admit we had a little club called the Murder Club. I put it together for my novel. If a woman loves you she'll do anything for you."

"You're proof of that," Sunderson quipped. He thought Lemuel was full of captious shit.

When Sunderson hung up with Lemuel he found himself amazed at how calm Lemuel sounded except when he said, "I'm not going back to prison. There aren't any birds there." Was he talking about suicide?

Sunderson was irritated that this had intruded on the day of the solstice which was as close as he got to a religious occasion. He was usually camping and fishing on that day. He was awake and staring at the eastern sky for the first glimmer of light which this far north was shortly before 4:00 a.m. And in the evening he'd find a good place, usually the bank of a river or a comfortable stump, and sit there for an hour for the last of the light to leave the western sky about 11:00 p.m. It made for a nineteen-hour day. When they were quite young his little brother Bobby was obsessed with the idea that everyone got murdered or died in the dark. Obviously this made the summer solstice the best day of the year, the day you were least likely to die.

One year when he was camped he had the spectacular combination of a full moon, huge pale green northern lights, and a big thunderstorm coming from the west. Did this mean he was going to die? He sat on a log actually trembling until the storm hit and he was immediately drenched. He toweled off in the tent and dozed for the mere five hours of the storm with his Glock pistol ready in case this was a sign for any prospective murderers. For years afterward he was prone to think of this as the most sacred night of his life apart from his wedding night with Diane, if only he had had the knowledge to take advantage of it. He dropped that line of thought because what was there to take advantage of, the full moon, the northern lights, and a thunderstorm. It was the sheer luck of being in the right place at the right time. He couldn't remember the name of the philosopher who said, "The miracle is that the world exists." You had to be in the right mood to believe this but it happened not so infrequently.

He remembered another night of camping when a half mile across a clearing he had seen a lightning bolt hit a tree. He was over there at first light to look at the still smoldering tree that had been vertically split in half. Marion told him how lucky he was to see such a thing as his people revered a tree that had been split by the gods. Sunderson had revisited the now dead tree a number of times and always felt a little eerie.

# Chapter 23

The shock of the day was when Monica came home late from work and said she had seen Lemuel who had asked her to marry him. In short she was asking Sunderson for permission.

"Why are you asking me?" he stuttered.

"Because you've been taking care of me."

"You can't marry him, he's your uncle."

"I'm thinking it over. I don't want my child to be a bastard and you're not going to marry me."

"Why do you say that? It's possible."

"Because I can tell you only want to be married to your ex-wife."

No matter how true that put Sunderson in a hole from which he couldn't emerge despite struggling to do so. The rest of his life would be cursed by this missing woman, however long that was. Monica was only saying she couldn't step in between. Lemuel probably thought that he would do better with the judge in his upcoming prosecution if he was married to a pregnant girl, but how could he think the marriage would be legitimate? Sunderson was abruptly sorry that Sara had agreed to testify as his life would have been better with Monica's future settled. There was an ounce of forgiveness in his heart when he thought of Sara's only remaining child dying in a house fire probably set with Lemuel's knowledge, another motive. The boy was too crippled to run for it. He had crawled to his open door but the stairwell was ablaze. He doubtless heard the screams of his mother as she got burned.

Monica sat across the table with tears in her eyes. "Life is so hard," she said. He asked her to pour him a drink. She looked beautiful. It would be hard to lose her. Their life together had been comfortable but so what? Even now he smelled the beef stew that she had put on to slow cook while he was with Smolens.

"I think you should go with him. He told me he has good savings. Maybe he'll take you to New York so you can be a real chef. Anyway, he'll take care of you well. You have my blessing." Sunderson nearly choked on the word *blessing* and poured himself a big drink. She'd be confronted with reality soon enough but maybe if he didn't go to jail they could move to New York and have a decent life away from anyone who knew they were related.

"Thank you so much." She went to the phone and called Lemuel and merely said "yes" before hanging up with "I can't talk now." Then she went upstairs to get ready to go back to work.

"Why go to work?" he called out.

"They need me," she called back.

He sat there in a fresh kind of doldrum. He recalled that after his father had first met Diane and they had gone brook trout fishing his father had said, "Isn't she a little classy for you? You're just a poor boy who went to college." His father was always frank and he thought about this for a long time. What did *classy* mean after all? He decided that his father's generation after the Great Depression and all of that was much more conscious of social inequities. His father's main hero had always been Walter Reuther, the labor leader, and Sunderson shared the admiration, but this was a period when business types referred to labor as "communistic."

When he first went to Diane's parents' lovely home on Lake Michigan near Ludington not a thing seemed out of place. Her father had gone to Dartmouth and her mother to Vassar. What he noticed most was that they never used slang when they talked. He always felt like a bit of an oaf in their company. Once when he ate lunch there he found out that they had no catsup in their home. This amazed him but thereafter he thought of his passion for catsup as lower class.

He sat there for a full hour after Monica left for work. He was thinking about the consequences of her decision. It came down to sex and food, both of which he would miss. He couldn't make a good beef stew at gunpoint, he thought, smelling the delicious air. There was a knock on the door and through the oval glass he could see it was Diane of all people.

"I was feeling tingles as I walked over. I should have called."

"No you shouldn't have. Who is more welcome than you?"

"Maybe a dozen bathing beauties," she laughed.

She asked him if they could take a long walk. She needed to talk to someone other than her women friends to whom having money and no husband was a perfect world. "Everyone seems so unhappy and I want to be an exception," she said.

He suggested that they should drive to his cabin which she wanted to see for a "platonic" night. He admitted there was only one big bed and she said she would bring her tent and a chicken cacciatore which he loved.

He was giddy by the time he picked her up at noon the next day. Naturally he hadn't slept well with his mind a whirl of unlikely possibilities. She was sitting on her front steps with her gear piled beside her finishing a call on her cell.

"My friend is scandalized that I'm going off overnight with my ex-husband. I teased her and said that if you want good sex you head for a man in his sixties. And then I hung up." She thought this was very funny while he felt mildly ridiculed.

They talked softly about nothing in particular for many miles. He felt it was important not to act what some called "needy." She said it might do him good if Monica left him. In her mind he needed a more intellectual woman, someone who could divert him from himself and give him new ideas to ponder. She used to think it was odd to be married to an intellectual detective, one who was always thinking of the exception rather than any rule. They stopped by a creek to eat ham and Swiss sandwiches. He saw a fair-sized rainbow trout near a boulder and would have fished for it had he been alone. Now it didn't seem important whereas the woman next to him in the front seat seemed critical to his future in a way that he couldn't bear to think of. Often he regretted having to retire. What in God's name did people do with all of their free time? Now that he had endless free time to fish he wasn't doing as much of it as he planned. He thought he should try some new rivers farther west. Even buy that new edition of Sibley's bird book. He was currently very sloppy, actually incompetent, at bird identification. When fishing he'd remember where he saw the bird last rather than its name. He wondered oddly what birds called themselves then dismissed the question as silly though interesting. He had long been fascinated with the big northern ravens and their obvious intelligence. They were thought to roost on the outstretched arms of Odin in Scandinavian mythology which he preferred to Greek as it was more his own and less remote. Of course there were creatures in the deep forest no one ever saw. You sensed them.

Diane had always been a hard news junkie. He had read up on Syria in case she brought up the subject. He was mostly interested in weather forecasts which was typical for someone from the U.P. The subjects of the news never seemed to touch the U.P. while the generally horrid weather was with them every day. So when he saw Diane he would freshen up on health care or Afghanistan. Afghanistan particularly enraged him. He would think, why don't we help Mexico rather than waste our money way over there?

It was a very warm day and Diane's skirt was over her knees which naturally gave him an itch. The weather said a colder front was coming through this evening. Maybe it would force her out of her tent and into the cabin he thought hopefully. She could have the bed and he would sleep on the floor in front of the little fireplace. He had quite a pile of dry hardwood—beech, maple, oak—to burn. Rather than nervous he was giddy. This was the woman of his life and he had blown their relationship to hell. She began talking about Mona, not a totally safe subject for him, but at the moment the sins of the past did not seem to burden her. For once he knew he had done a terrible thing.

Mona had sent her two papers for which she had received perfect scores. One dealt with molecular biology which Diane couldn't really read but the other came from her course on astronomy. The professor had written on the top of the paper, "You write beautifully." It was about the future of black holes, a subject of which Sunderson was unsure. This reminded him that he had packed along his copies of *Nightwood* and *Ada* in case Diane went to bed early.

Diane was delighted with the beauty of the area around the cabin except for the burned-out phantoms of the two houses. Lemuel had gotten in a landscaper from Escanaba and now his house was surrounded by many lovely flower beds and some transplanted bushes. Sunderson morbidly thought that when Lemuel went to the big house for life without parole Monica would have to take care of the place assuming she wasn't in prison herself.

The cacciatore was wonderful as expected and afterward they took the remains of their wine out front and sat near Diane's assembled tent. He told her that she could have his bed and he'd sleep in the tent but she said she

wanted to. Early in their marriage they had done a great
deal of camping and should never have stopped. She hadn't
camped as a child and loved it as an adult. He tended to
focus on her discomfort although when he camped alone
or with friends discomfort was just part of the experience,
the tormenting mosquitoes, the can of beans they used to
carry to heat beside the fire, the sardines for breakfast.
He always worried so much about her smallest complaints
that he began to hate camping. Actually Diane had always
made it quite pleasant and if it was too warm she would
pack along sheets and a blanket, sleeping bags like steam
heat being tolerable only if it was cold. And with Diane
the food was always masterful.

They had eaten late so that after staring for an hour
into a small campfire he had built the stars slowly began to
emerge. Diane could identify all of the constellations, another thing about which he was totally unsure. In the detective business he had had to be accurate and hard on details
but that didn't apply to the rest of his life except fishing
where he could identify dozens of streamside insects, then
pick out from the fly boxes the closest imitation to what the
fish were feeding on that day. Trout could be improbably
choosy in what they ate so you needed to find as precise a
match as possible. Sometimes the flies you tied on were so
tiny that you could barely see them other than infinitesimal
humps or dots on the current. The trout had no trouble
seeing them because it was lunch or dinner, pure survival.

"We should have bought a little cabin early in our marriage. You were always uncomfortable camping," she said
softly.

"You're right. If we had we might still be married." He immediately regretted saying this. His plan had been to stay away from hot topics.

"That's possible. Nobody understands their marriage until it's too late to save it."

"I remember when we were thinking about trying to buy that cabin on a river near Grand Marais. It was too expensive."

"That was my fault. I could have gotten the money from my dad overnight. But you wouldn't take money from him because of pride."

"So we lost the cabin and lost the marriage." Sunderson was pissed to have it on his lap. "Of all the Seven Deadly Sins pride is the hardest to figure out."

"That's partly because you're afflicted with it and can't see the details. It must have come with your job. At all times you needed to be brave but also safe."

"Of course," he spit out, irked at the obvious.

"People who think about safety all of the time get buried to the point of suffocation in their egos. The world exists only in terms of their safety. I have a friend who I really can't see anymore because she is so obsessed she might get breast cancer that it's become the sole subject of her life. No one will give her a mammogram anymore she's had so many. In short, she's a nutcase."

Sunderson laughed. "I hope I was never that bad. I suppose that pride is directly tied to narcissism."

"I'm sure it is. It's one of the Seven Deadly Sins for its disastrous consequences. All of the cheating husbands I've met have been full of pride for no apparent reason."

They were startled when Lemuel walked into the fire-light. He sensed it was awkward and left quickly after Sunderson introduced him to Diane.

"What a lovely damsel you are," Lemuel said.

"Why, thank you. I've never been called a damsel."

Lemuel handed Sunderson a fresh chapter of his book and then walked back into the dark along the river.

"Is the novel any good?" Diane asked.

"I've only read a little of it."

"You might check it out. Beginning writers invariably write about themselves. You might get a clue."

Sunderson shined his penlight on the sheaf and groaned when he saw the chapter was called "The Murder Club."

"You read slow and I read fast. I'd be glad to read the manuscript for you," she persisted.

"Okay. Okay. But he can't be dumb enough to write about murdering people."

"It's not dumb. It's self-infatuation. We're back to pride again. Prideful people tend to think that everyone in the world is dumb except themselves. I've seen men at the grocery store picking up a loaf of bread who can't do so without saying to themselves, 'I'm picking up a loaf of bread.' You see them overdressed in line for the movies. When I was growing up our neighbors had peacocks. These men remind me of male peacocks who never stop saying 'I am a male peacock.' They might as well add, 'I have a huge splendid ass.'"

Her words gave Sunderson a murky feeling knowing how often on certain days he could manage no esteem for anyone but possibly himself. He naturally didn't admit it.

"One of my biggest problems at the hospital is the number of smug and prideful doctors. You could suspect they were born that way if it weren't possible. I actually think it's in the training. If you can make your way through med school you feel generally superior. That's why they are so miserable at their own investments. They think their superiority in the medical field also applies to finance. You would be appalled at the childishness of the complaints I get. I don't argue, I just listen until they wear out which is usually pretty fast. I say, I'll think it over, which is hard to argue with."

"I was thinking that they make so much money they should be pretty happy."

"You know that's not true, darling. The only rich doctor I know who is happy is also an amateur naturalist. He spends every available moment in the woods, swamps, beaches, hills with his guidebooks. He built a tiny cabin, also near Grand Marais, about fifteen by twenty feet. I've seen it. No power or anything. He never takes his cell phone. He got lost last year and found himself thirty miles from his cabin down near Newberry. He basically walked around the clock including the night of the full moon. Now he never misses his moon walking. He's made friends with an old female bear who often walks with him. If he stops for a rest she stops and snoozes too. Anyway he is the happiest doctor I know. His wife and children are flagrant spenders but he seems not to care. He took them to an expensive resort in Costa Rica, dropped them off at the resort hotel, and then wandered the countryside. He got bitten in the left foot by a fer-de-lance and knew he had to cut his toes off to avoid death. He did so and now he walks with a limp but it doesn't slow him down much. He is the total opposite of prideful because he's obsessed with the natural world outside himself. You were always obsessed with the natural world, but you could never stop trying to make it safe and comfortable for me."

This all made Sunderson feel tawdry and lazy. He used to take very long aimless walks and realized that afterward he often forgot to have a drink. Marion teased him about this. Marion knew a Zuni poet who had walked all the way from southern Arizona up to Pine Ridge in South Dakota. Sunderson had pondered heroic walks of this sort but then forced himself to admit he wasn't a hero. He mostly imagined sore and blistered feet. Every boy fantasized about being picked up by a girl in a hot red convertible and so forth. This likely never happened on earth. The truth was that everything you do is what you do. No plus or minus. It was a college coffeehouse argument taking place in your own head.

The talk meandered into his essay adding violence to the Seven Deadly Sins. Violence made glandular lust look pathetic.

"How far along are you?" she asked.

"Just a few pages of notes," he admitted.

"That's not writing. Every morning when you get up don't do anything except drink a cup of coffee until you've written a page. I used to use this tactic on term papers I didn't want to write. Just do it and I'll help you edit it."

"I'll try." Now he had a down-to-earth motive if writing the damn thing gave him more time with Diane.

"Don't say *I'll try*. That's too weak. Just say, *I'll do it*. Start tomorrow morning. We're in no hurry to get back early."

"Okay. You may remind me."

"Oh bullshit. You're thinking about it all the time instead of just doing it. You're paralyzing yourself with interior jabber."

He had rarely heard her say *bullshit*. Maybe a couple of times in a forty-year marriage.

"I can't seem to express what I intend in my mind," he said petulantly.

"Of course you can't. It takes a lifetime of work to write well and even that's not enough. There are hundreds of thousands of writers in the world and only a few can write well."

"Then what am I doing? I quit."

"You can't quit when you haven't even started."

"A man who beats his wife is slapping God in the face."

"That's pretty good if you believe it."

"I do. I have a secret religion."

"You've managed to keep it totally a secret. You could be a spy," she laughed.

He brooded for moments that it seemed ridiculous to her that he had a secret religion. He recalled that in an undergraduate philosophy course at Michigan State, the sage Santayana was said to have claimed that we all had secret religions to accompany our ordinary one. It made sense to him as he had often felt the implicit secrecy of life, especially since he had lost Diane and now a truly intimate conversation was impossible. Now there was a lump in his throat and his heart was beating too fast while sitting next to her before the fire.

"I'm sure you have secrets too. Why make fun of my secret religion?"

"I'm just an ordinary Presbyterian, not a very imaginative group. I can't even imagine going to church. Of course I had secrets. Every girl does. When I was thirteen my cousin Tom showed me his erect penis. He was angry when I wouldn't touch it. I thought, why would anyone want to have anything to do with something like that."

"You finally did touch one."

"It took some getting used to," she said and laughed.

"That's not much of a secret."

"Tom was a peacock. He still is. He was married three times and blew through his inheritance. Now he deals in scrap metal."

"Tell me a secret that will make my heart beat fast."

"Well, when we got divorced I still loved you but I couldn't bear the idea of living with you anymore. I was sick to death of you. I wanted to live in a nice little house down by the water all alone. So I did."

This wasn't the kind of secret Sunderson had had in mind. "Then you married a rich guy," he interrupted.

"I guess it may have looked like that to others. He was the biggest catch in town before he got sick. A very nice rich man with a beautiful house."

"I've deduced that you could afford a beautiful house on your own."

"Too much of a bother. Who needs it? His only daughter is coming next week. We're going to list it and split the take. She's worthless and lives in Aspen. You could call her a *playgirl*."

"I still think of you too much. I haven't found anyone to love."

"What about you and Monica?"

"She's barely more than a kid. I like her but she's going back to Lemuel. A home for the kid. That kind of thing."

"I had fantasies about you but you're too much of a kid for an affair."

"I truly resent that." He felt his body swell in anger.

"I mean an affair calls for grace and secrecy not emotional explosions."

"I won't drink a single drop."

"That's charming. You must like me more than I thought."

"You're the biggest, darkest failure in my life."

"Let me think about it until you get back from Europe. Maybe we could give it a trial run. We could start in that motel on the hill in Grand Marais."

"What about the motel down by the car? I'm up for anything. I'll even drive to Detroit."

"Have you forgotten you're going to Europe next week?"

"Not really, but right now with you here I can't think about Europe."

"Well, you need to open the window and let some oxygen into your life. Lately you've been acting like a classic depressive. You wanted early retirement and now you seem not to know what to do with yourself. I was thinking that if you went to Barcelona first while l have my ex-husband's daughter I could meet you the following week in Paris. Remember, I was always trying to get us to Paris together?"

"I don't know why not. I just hope I won't die in Barcelona and miss you in Paris," he laughed.

"That's not funny. You simply have to get out of the U.P., darling," she said softly.

That brought him to a stop. It had been years since she had called him *darling* as if she meant it. He felt a tremor he controlled with effort.

"I'll fix it at the travel agent tomorrow."

"We'll leave after you write a full page."

"Fine by me." His voice was drowned by a crash of thunder. They looked up to see that the lower third of the stars had been abolished by the coming storm. The big moon was behind them casting an eerie light on the forest to the west. The storm looked like a big line squall, a real bruiser. "I'll sleep in your sleeping bag on the rug. You can have the bed."

"I want to hear the rain on the tent first."

"Suit yourself. I'll bring in more wood."

Then a very large gust of wind ripped out her tent stakes and blew the tent against the cabin door and Diane gave in. He was quick to drag the tent in and toss her sleeping bag onto the bed. Wind was driving some smoke down the chimney so he took a poker and parted the logs so that they would burn less intensely and the smoke cleared. Now it began to rain hard and hail at the same time and the lights went out. He was prepared and lit three large candles from the closet so that Diane could read the Lemuel chapter. The hail rattled noisily against the tin roof of the cabin. He was pretending to write about violence in his notebook but the

candlelight flickering against Diane's face was diverting.
He copied what he had written before to appear busy.

> *Cain rose up and slew Abel, an astounding way for God to*
> *begin human history, perhaps showing that He's not in full*
> *control and doesn't want to be. It's up to us. The first two broth-*
> *ers on earth and one killed the other. God knows why or maybe*
> *not. Mental freedom is mostly invigorating but sometimes not.*
> *There were no girls to chase in the Garden of Eden, often a*
> *diversion from violence. The Old Testament, mock history,*
> *is indeed a murderous book. The Greek Senate prevented an*
> *intended war by proclaiming that each senator had to commit*
> *a family member to the battle. That stopped the war. As an*
> *aside it is interesting to note that young men from Ivy League*
> *schools hardly ever died in Vietnam. Violence is apparently part*
> *of what used to be called the* class struggle. *The lower the*
> *class the more likely you are to suffer from violence.*

"I love this storm," Diane said. "I'm overprotected in
my big house. I'm going to try to buy my little one back
where I could hear the rain and wind and snow."

"You can hear snow?"

"Of course. Meanwhile you have to read this chapter.
He confesses everything."

"I doubt that you could introduce fiction into a court
of law."

"Maybe not but it tells you how he did it. He evidently
convinced the women that he was only trying to make the
victims sick, so they would become nicer, more pleasant
creatures."

"I'm tired." Sunderson nestled into her sleeping bag on the braided rug. The bag had the odor of lilac, his favorite scent.

"I assumed you might want to fool around," Diane said. "Fool around" was her euphemism for making love.

Sunderson got out of the bag and onto the bed feeling quite strange as if his skin were pricking and his heart beating fast. They embraced and he felt nothing from this act long sought, only despair. In fact, he couldn't move.

"Is something wrong?" she asked.

"I feel paralyzed. Too much anticipation."

"Maybe you should have a little drink, relax."

"I think I will." He got up and poured a stiff one. Just imagine her suggesting he have a drink.

He drank quickly and got back in bed but the drink did no good. They were in an embrace but his body was dead. He imagined that he was a cold pork shoulder in the butcher's case. Soon enough he heard her slight, vague snores, somehow charming, but he wasn't aware of sleeping himself except briefly at dawn when he smelled cooking sausage.

Diane woke him. He grabbed her but once again felt a sexless paralysis overwhelm him. She finished cooking breakfast while he pretended, at her insistence, to write about the deadly sin of violence. He was cheating again and asked silently, "Why am I a cheat?" He found himself writing willy-nilly about a terrible accident he'd witnessed as a child. Mack was a friend of his brother Bobby, a daredevil. He was small for his age and had run at a very slow moving freight train to pull one of his favorite tricks which was to run at the space between the moving railroad cars, jump up on the coupling and jump down on the other side. He had done this a dozen times including once for cops in chase who had to wait for the passing train at which time Mack was home in the basement in his old hideout, the root cellar. This time he stumbled on the coupling which was rain wet and fell on the tracks, scrambling out of the way of the vastly heavy wheels except for his right arm which was severed. Sunderson could still hear in bad moments the crunch sound. Jake, a friend whom they called "Boy Scout," made a tourniquet out of his T-shirt, pulled off Mack's shirt, and shook out the arm with a quizzical look. Jake applied the tourniquet and ran over to the train station for help. Mack was pale white and Sunderson had watched as Bobby knelt beside his friend and looked over at the severed arm which seemed very isolated in the ragweed. And that was the end of Mack's normal life. Sunderson had thought, the fastest boy in the Munising school system became the slowest.

Sunderson wondered idly how many lives had been taken by trains and then he switched to cars and traffic for which he had attended a series of lectures in preparation for police work. Car accident calls were the only thing that competed with wife beating in terms of the loathsome. Helping paramedics get the wounded bodies out of a wrecked car could spoil lunch to say the least. Hard to wash the blood from your hands and impossible on the clothes. He always packed a pair of bib overalls. The deaths of young people in particular squeezed his heart. Once he was giving a young girl mouth-to-mouth resuscitation. It looked bad because the back of her head was soft from fractures. She coughed up blood, filling his mouth, and then she died. On the way home he bought a pint of whiskey and drove into the country and drank the whole thing. Diane chided him for being semidrunk but forgave him when he told her the story, including the fact that the girl's blood had a copper taste.

Now Diane was making sandwiches for the trip home. She looked nice at the kitchen counter in a pale green summer skirt. He was pleased she had brought along ham and cheese because he usually stuffed himself at a pasty place and felt ill the rest of the day. He said he was done and she wanted to see what he had written. He said no as it needed some work and largely didn't exist. He was transfixed by his dead pecker and the amount of mechanical violence in the world. He had left out Dresden, Hiroshima, and Nagasaki in his thinking in favor of the symbol of Cain and Abel. The Germans mechanized violence at Buchenwald and the sheer horror made one forget the Warsaw Ghetto. We liked planes because we could kill at a safe distance and now we don't even need to be in the drone. This was the worst part of being history adept, knowing the history of violence which was the history of man.

When they left the cabin they saw Lemuel back at the edge of the woods with his binoculars. Lemuel called out, "Three orioles!"

They waved and Sunderson pondered.

"He watches birds every morning."

"How nice."

"For a murderer?"

"Birds are more likable than people," she said.

"Remember when you were trying to plant peas and blackbirds were in the row behind you eating the seeds? You were so pissed."

"Let me repeat, you have to read Lemuel's chapter. The whole technique of embedding poison in a sausage patty is there. The women believed he was just trying to make the victims sick because such a small amount is needed. Toward the end with victims dying he did it all himself."

"Hard to believe the women were that gullible."

"Oh bullshit. You like the idea they were suckers." Diane was coming down hard on him lately.

"Maybe so," he laughed. The fact of the matter was that it takes such a small amount of cyanide to kill someone it would be easy to believe it wasn't a serious threat.

On the way home he made modest detours to show her some favorite fishing places. She pretended to be interested but how could she be as a nonfishing person? Like Lemuel her neck was always craned for birds. In late May the great arboreal canopy of the U.P. is flooded with warblers and these tiny, unique creatures had always fascinated her.

He was still distraught over his sexual paralysis but it was as dumb as regretting your suicide. What's over is over. Sunderson mentioned that Smolens had told him Kate was fourteen and not twelve—she'd been a sickly child and remained skinny so no one figured it out.

"He's still her uncle, and she's still a child. Lemuel should go to prison for sleeping with her."

They had reached their lunch place, a lovely park rest stop near the bridge that crossed the middle branch of the Ontonagon River. Before eating their sandwiches he led her

on a longish, steep path down to a fine stretch of the river.
He stumbled twice but managed to stay afoot. Diane was
surefooted. On summer vacations with her parents they
always visited vacationing relatives in Jackson Hole, Wyo-
ming, and Diane had learned rock climbing early. Diane
was thrilled seeing a heron across the river. Everything was
fine until they turned around and Sunderson had difficulty,
slipping on the steep path. She did what she could to help
his huffing and puffing and efforts to get a solid foothold.
She was ahead of him pulling on his left arm and at one
point he stumbled and fell grabbing her bare calf. A bright
light went off in his head and he was suddenly aroused.
The calf had been so palpable. Near the top there was a
small tussock of soft grass and he dragged her down. She
couldn't stop laughing hard but he quickly made love to her
and she responded energetically. His heart actually soared
rather than fluttering. At lunch never had a ham and cheese
sandwich tasted so good. She acted natural as if nothing had
happened though she kissed him.

When they got home in two hours they made love long
and languorously in their old marriage bed. Afterward she
had tears in her eyes. "We really screwed up, didn't we?"
she said. Now he teared up as well and muttered, "Yes."

"I could never get married again."

"Why?" he asked with an ache behind his voice.

"I noticed as I get older it's hard enough to take care
of myself let alone adding a man. When I was nursing Bill
I was exhausted all the time though it wasn't much work.
We couldn't find another nurse he could abide. He said
the problem was that when you're dying you can't stand

banality. So when a nurse would say her dishwasher broke or she thought her grandson was smoking dope it would drive him batty. In those last weeks he kept talking about his glorious dream life in which he could see death creeping up on him while he was whirling free through the universe which he loved. He told me how he was able to visit many of the ninety billion galaxies out there. He would say, 'If this is death it's not bad.' That aspect was quite encouraging. I mean he had always been a doctor, a scientist of the body, and quite the cynic about anything religious. Now he was talking about visiting galaxies and hearing the voice of God in the explosion of a black hole that had the power of five million suns."

Sunderson's curiosity but not his comprehension was piqued by any information about black holes. He had read about the one with the power of five million suns but what could he make of it? Was this where God lived? There was also a constellation surrounded by five million stars. How did they count them? It had to be an estimate, he thought pathetically. He had read a couple of books by the astronomy writer Timothy Ferris that left him chewing the air as if it were food. The man had once appeared at the local university to give a lecture. That helped to humanize it a bit though all the details were still beyond him. In childhood Sunderson and his friends had the usual dream of inventing a time machine. If he had one he would mainly use it to revisit his best days of fishing. So many years later after the divorce he kept wanting to go back to certain times with Diane like one night camped on a deserted beach miles east of Grand Marais when the northern lights were so spectacular that for the first time he had felt at one with the universe. Usually it was at two, three, five, ad infinitum. In truth, like most men he lived his life in pieces and remembered only fragments.

They stopped at the travel agent in Marquette to synchronize her trip to Paris with his own. He didn't mind heading to Seville first, then Barcelona and on to Paris when she arrived. She told him she'd picked out a relatively inexpensive hotel with a room overlooking a garden that she and her husband had loved because she could watch birds and there was little street noise. When he looked he realized she'd chosen the hotel where he stayed with Mona. It was now easy to admit that it was the worst thing he'd ever done in his life.

Sunderson dropped her off at her grand home that she was eager to leave. She kissed him on the lips, an instant thrill.

"See, we don't need to get married. We can have a nice affair until we die."

# Chapter 24

At home Sunderson was pleased Diane had given him the Le Creuset of leftover cacciatore. He saw Monica's bags packed near the door and no longer regretted that she was moving away to be with Lemuel. There was a phone message from Berenice in Green Valley that said his mother was dying again but there was no point in his coming out. The doctor thought she would die soon from her stroke and pneumonia. He was relieved that she didn't seem to be in pain, though he could not imagine his mother absent from earth.

There was also an angry call from Kate who was furious that Lemuel was kicking her out in favor of Monica. Kate was now willing to tell him anything he wanted to know about the "murderers" as she called them.

He hurriedly called Smolens who was overjoyed with the news. He would send a car early and take Kate's statement at headquarters as the location would encourage her to say everything. Smolens said that they would be able to hold Lemuel indefinitely on sex abuse charges. Could Sunderson bring her in, since she seemed to trust him? Sunderson wanted to say no but couldn't very well do so since he had broken the case. Smolens admitted he just didn't get Lemuel's motive. Sunderson told Smolens about Lemuel's overwhelming hatred and shame, how he wrote of endless abuse from other members of the family, describing himself as runt of the litter.

There was a note from Monica. "Lemuel is picking me up late this evening. I left a rib steak in the fridge for your dinner. Love, Monica." Sunderson liked the idea of living alone again. If it wasn't Diane it was settling for less. He was nervous indeed about her idea of a lifelong affair but then suddenly he perceived she did not want to be tied down like a housewife, a position that had never appealed to her. He remembered again his mother's struggles to think of something for dinner that everyone would eat. Bobby was the most difficult. He only wanted a piece of fried meat with Worcestershire sauce and cottage cheese. Mother had a partial deliverance when she met their neighbor Mrs. Amarone, who taught her about Italian cooking. She realized that lots of garlic and basil, thyme, and oregano turned the corner for her. For several months the family wouldn't tolerate anything not Italian. She made massive pizzas in the oven though Berenice and Roberta wouldn't accept the anchovies that males loved so she had to mark the sections of pizza that were anchovy free. Roberta claimed her boyfriend nearly "puked" when kissing her with anchovy breath. No wonder Diane didn't want that job.

Sunderson couldn't imagine life without his mother. Berenice said that they would cremate her rather than go to the pointless expense of shipping her whole body back to Munising. Berenice had always counted her pennies and worked at a soda fountain after school. She also sewed drapes for people. Sometimes when Dad was particularly broke she would loan him money from her savings. But in this case her penny-pinching made Sunderson feel maudlin.

After Monica got home from her last shift, they were chaste from eleven until midnight when Lemuel showed up. Sunderson helped him take the bags out to the car, a new blue Yukon, perfect for the snow. They sat at the dining room table with Sunderson having a drink. He offered one to Lemuel who refused it. He was careful about drinking because of his rotten family.

"So this is where Sprague died? What a gift," Lemuel said, "to humankind."

Sunderson pointed to the spot on the dining room floor where Sprague had fallen in an actual hail of gunfire.

They talked peaceably until the subject of Kate came up and then Lemuel grew angry. She in revenge had torn up his favorite book, a big folio of Audubon reproductions.

When they left there were tears in Monica's eyes. After all it was Sunderson who liberated her from her awful family. Lemuel was a bit embarrassed but possessive of Monica now that she was pregnant. Sunderson sat there a long while steadily drinking and pondering the vagaries of life. His family was without descendants to the disgust of his mother but he thought this was meaningless. At least he would never have to tell his mother that Monica's baby would not be her

grandchild. Roberta at one point had adopted an unruly
Pawnee boy but he had run away and hadn't been found for
years until she located him back on his reservation where
he wanted to stay. Now she was putting him through the
University of Washington in Seattle. It occurred to him that
if Diane was going to regularly visit the house he should do
some cleaning, sanding, painting or, better yet, hire it done
with blackmail money. It was all insignificant to Diane who
had had money since she was born and never felt the pinch
of normal people.

He was up bright and early to be fully conscious while
helping Smolens with Kate. He had stayed up late reading
Lemuel's murder chapter at Diane's insistence. There it was
clear as a bell with all of the cracks of doubt filled in. The
whole crime was concocted early and well thought out—it
gave him new respect for Lemuel's intelligence. He was
the movie director of the crime organizing the dosages for
the girls to pass out, deftly stuffing them in food. A pinch
of cyanide could sink the ship. He would pass the chapter
on to Smolens and the prosecutor. They would be slow to
read it because it was fiction, but he knew Kate could cor-
roborate the details.

He felt melancholy entering the police station for the
first time in so long. Smolens had his old office but now it
was spick-and-span. He had good take-out coffee on a tray,
a relief to Sunderson as Kate had insisted he be there which
suited Smolens too. Interrogations often made him doze.
The problem was that both sides lied as much as possible.
You were trying to build a case for yourself and so was the
putative criminal.

Kate turned out to be much more intelligent, well spoken, and acerbic than they expected.

"When did Lemuel first make love to you?"

"What does that have to do with the murders?" She practically spit this out.

"We have to start at the beginning." Smolens was undeterred. "We have to establish that Lemuel was thinking of these murders for years. He needed coconspirators so he would start affairs to get them."

"Lemuel was kind and no one else was. I think I was twelve and the two of us were off mushrooming and bird watching. None of the other men paid any attention to me except to force me to blow them. Anyway we two were way off in the woods and he bent me over a stump and pulled down his jeans. It hurt a bit. He was the only person who was ever nice to me!"

"Did you know it was wrong?" Smolens persisted.

"What's right or wrong? Everyone in my family is drunk all the time, and all of us girls knew sex would come up sooner or later. No one ever told us it was wrong and no one cared whether we liked it. It was like eating to them, whereas with Lemuel he actually cared. I read in the newspapers about a man going to jail for making love to his sixteen-year-old daughter and that was the first time I knew anyone thought it was strange."

"Did you at any time refuse to help Lemuel?"

"He didn't force me, if I didn't feel like it. But he told us we were doing ourselves a favor by making them real sick, so they'd be civilized and peaceful rather than drunk and violent."

"Didn't you ever feel that he was actually raping you? That's what it is at your age."

"No, though I gradually realized that our compound was another country."

"What about school?"

"School is nothing out there. I was self-educated better than my teachers. For teachers our school is the end of the line. A clique of loutish boys run the school. Disgusting young men, all of them athletes. I keep my head low."

"When the first couple died what happened to the prolonged illness plan?"

"Lemuel can talk brilliantly about science and medicine for days. And he was the only one I could turn to out there. My parents were puking drunks, and Lemuel was kind and gentle. He said we made a mistake in the dosages."

"Still, they continued to die."

"Look, if you're in prison and only one person is kind to you they're all you have and you have to believe in them."

And so on. Sunderson had nothing to contribute. Of all the dozens of interrogations he had taken part in she was the hardest case, absolutely unapologetic for what she'd done and that she was blowing the whistle on Lemuel because he had chosen Monica over her.

Kate seemed to be comfortable talking without him now so he excused himself and went out the front door for some fresh air. Standing there on the steps smoking his first cigarette of the day he remembered reading Freud's *Civilization and Its Discontents* at the insistence of a girlfriend, a very bright sorority girl. He had gone to a Greek dance with her after which slick young men and girls greeted him in the halls. The book hadn't given him much that was new. He had long since come to believe that the world was fucked and always had been. He imagined himself one of the several thousand Polish cavalrymen who charged German tanks on their horses and were wiped out. Or that other one on the Crimean War, the Tennyson poem, "Into the valley of death rode the six hundred." He was tempted to simply move out to his cabin to live except for the affair with Diane. His mind was such an unresolved mishmash of historical texts that he swore he would read only fiction and poetry in the future. Keats for instance.

It was raining lightly and he was transfixed by the sound of cars on the wet streets. It was certainly time to go to Seville and Barcelona. He hurried across the street and had a quick double whiskey then returned to the station. Things were winding down with Kate giving full assurance that she would be "happy" to testify against Lemuel in court. Smolens was very happy himself. He actually glowed. The police were putting Kate up at the Ramada Inn at the top of the hill. Sunderson offered to give her a ride up there. She needed something to read so they stopped at Snowbound Books on the way. He bought her a couple of Loren Eiseley books that he revered. While she further browsed he went out and bought a pint of whiskey. She made him want a drink, or so he thought.

He drove to her motel and stupidly went to her room to pour himself a decent drink. She went to the bathroom and took a hasty shower saying that she felt dirty after talking to the police. He sat by the window with his drink looking out at the banality of rooftops. He felt amiss because he

hadn't done the daily page promised Diane. He had meant
to get up early but hadn't. He would go home now and get
his work done. Kate came out of the bathroom carelessly
wrapped in a towel. She dropped the towel and lay on the
bed completely nude on her stomach.

"I have to go," he stuttered and fled.

He was barely home with his papers out on the desk
when Diane called.

"How did it go?"

"Very well. I don't see how the prosecutor can resist
Kate's testimony. I'm bothered by the idea that Lemuel has a
spy in the prosecutor's office. That means Lemuel will know
everything Kate said. I hope she's not in danger."

"I got a note from him in the mail saying he was pleased
to have met me and to come out and see his osprey which
are nesting on a phone pole behind his house. He also said
that you were the most wonderful man he had ever met."

"You should take the recommendation of a multiple
murderer," he said, concerned that Lemuel had found her.

"Oh, I do, darling. I'm sure honest men also commit
murder."

They agreed to meet the next day for dinner. He continued to worry about Kate and the idea that Lemuel might
take vengeance for being ratted on. Maybe he could drive
out and try to talk sensibly to him. Monica seemed safe as
he had chosen her as a bride.

With a leaden heart Sunderson sat at his desk to write
his daily page, perceiving the irony of trying to write about
violence when the last few months with the Ameses had

dragged him into so much. Diane had put stars near the last few paragraphs of Lemuel's chapter where he'd written well describing the osprey nest near his house up on the cross arms of a phone pole. It was a slow process getting the mother and chicks to accept him by trapping and taking up the pole a pocketful of mice which they loved to eat and a dead garter snake they ripped into pieces. After a while they apparently recognized him and were pleased he was bringing lunch. Sunderson could imagine Lemuel dangling up there with his first love, birds. In another chapter Lemuel had claimed that two of his brothers cornholed him and once he had to go to the doctor for rectal repairs. Shocking to Sunderson John had been there and not saved him. He had had trouble believing this at the time but as he learned more about the family it seemed possible or even probable. The accrued insults that led Lemuel to murder.

Smolens called and interrupted his writing, actually his cheating, as he was copying passages from *Nightwood* and *Ada* that should help him write well. Smolens was joyous because the prosecutor had agreed to proceed with the prosecution of Lemuel after reading Kate's statement. He also knew that Monica and Lemuel had gone to the courthouse yesterday afternoon to try to get a marriage license. They were turned down, but Monica still wanted to spend her life with Lemuel and was refusing to testify. Sunderson said that they should have enough evidence with Sara and Kate testifying. Smolens was pleased that for the time being the prosecutor wouldn't come down on the women. Smolens was still carrying a torch for Sara.

Sunderson told Smolens that Lemuel had an ex-girlfriend in the prosecutor's office and therefore would be aware of their strategy. Smolens was appalled but said he thought he knew which woman was the spy and it couldn't have done any real damage.

Sunderson was chewing his fingernails which he hadn't done since grade school. He couldn't stop worrying about Kate. At least Sara was safe in the hospital. He removed a book and took a peek at his neighbor at her afternoon yoga. It wasn't all that stimulating but then no woman could compare to Diane. He didn't particularly want to drive all the way to the cabin but his mind was full of frightful intuitions and he'd feel better knowing where Lemuel was and that Monica was all right.

Berenice called the next morning to say that the doctors didn't think Mother would last another night. She was just a few days from her eighty-seventh birthday, although when you're on your deathbed what do birthdays matter. With typical efficiency Berenice had already contacted the funeral home in Munising to request next Tuesday. This seemed ghoulish to Sunderson but Berenice said that Mother had requested her ashes be dumped in Lake Superior and agreed with Berenice about cremation and saving the money it would have cost to ship her whole body back to Munising. Berenice said that pneumonia is thought to be an old person's friend as the death is comparatively easy. Sunderson noted that Tuesday was the day before he was to leave for Seville and Barcelona thence to Paris to meet Diane. He lacked enthusiasm for this trip and worried that the bars of Spain would be difficult, typical of an American drinker worried about his future drinking.

He bit the bullet and called Diane about the necessity of his speeding to the cabin. She agreed. On the way out of town he picked up a couple of pints of whiskey and some cans of stew he didn't actually like, then as an afterthought bought a pasty for dinner. He would sorely miss Monica's cooking.

On the way out of town he got grim news from Smolens. Lemuel tried to poison Sara the night before but luckily because she was already in the hospital they were able to save her. Smolens had asked that Lemuel not be allowed to see her but the hospital didn't heed it. He hadn't even been called immediately because he wasn't a direct relative. He was furious. Even worse a poor family was walking the ditch out near Champion that morning picking up bottles redeemable for a dime apiece and came upon a large garbage bag of the type used on construction sites. They were going to use the bag to haul bottles but there was a body in it, nude Kate with a bullet through her temple. Smolens had just heard this and sent a squad car out to pick up Lemuel. Sunderson said he was on his way at top speed. What if Monica was next? He had stupidly forgotten his pistol. Smolens told him to wait for the cop but he had no intention of waiting for anything.

Sunderson made it to the cabin in record time. He hurriedly swerved onto the two track that led along the river through the pasture toward Lemuel's. He noted that it was too windy for good fishing — the wind blew the insects off the water the trout fed on. The two burn sites had also been cleaned up.

He saw the horror from a fair distance. Lemuel was hanging by a rope around his neck from the crossbar of the phone pole, next to the osprey nest in fact. Sunderson wondered irrelevantly if he had fed the birds one last time. Probably. He rushed in the house and found Monica loosely tied up in the library amid the torn-up pages of Lemuel's big book of Audubon reproductions. Monica had nearly got herself loose and was crying.

"He told me what he was going to do. He tied me up so I wouldn't try to stop him. He said that he killed Sara and Kate last night because they ruined his *life's plan*."

"Sara didn't die. They revived her. A good thing it was ricin and not cyanide."

Sunderson read Lemuel's note left on the desk. "I bequeath my home and money to my wife Monica. Now she can afford to go to New York City and learn how to become a great chef after she has the baby."

They went outside just as the deputy from town roared up. He mentioned unnecessarily that Lemuel's face was purple then used a ladder to reach the hand grips and made his way up to the crossbar where the mother osprey pretended she was going to attack him but didn't. Lemuel hit the ground with a horrible crunch that Sunderson would always remember. Monica fainted and they helped her inside to a sofa and a glass of cold water. The deputy called an ambulance and Sunderson used the house phone to call Smolens.

"Shit," Smolens said. "We were going to win this one."

When Monica could speak again she asked if she was going to prison and Sunderson said that he doubted it, as the prosecutor already thought there was not enough evidence she was what he called a coconspirator. A jury with women would never convict anyway and the county couldn't afford a fishing expedition just to convict an unwitting accomplice. Sara was still in a coma and Monica couldn't be forced to testify against herself. The case was toast as they say in the trade.

# Chapter 25

Sunderson drank whiskey for several days. Monica cooked small meals because the weather had become hot. They slept together without touching except for a hug or two. He asked what she would do about the baby and she admitted she was never pregnant, that it was only to make Lemuel choose her. Now that her predatory father and uncles were removed home didn't seem so bad. Sunderson was a bit shocked but relieved he didn't have to worry if the child was really his.

On the third day they picked up Lemuel's ashes down in Escanaba and that evening they strewed the ashes in his favorite bird-watching areas. Lemuel had said concluding his suicide note, "It looks like I will go to prison forever. There are no birds there. I can't live without my birds every morning." Sunderson's stomach with this note plummeted. Lemuel's dependence on birds made no sense until it occurred to Sunderson that Lemuel was the much-abused runt of the litter and birds were likely his only true companions as a child. Curiously Lemuel was a murderer who meant well. It was sad that he couldn't simply have a nice life but then like so many he allowed the idea of vengeance to overwhelm it.

Sunderson recognized that he was in very bad shape when Lemuel's purple face immediately entered his dream life. Diane perceived how bad it was from his phone calls and drove out to the cabin, where he'd stayed after scattering the ashes. When she arrived he was weeping and couldn't stop. Earlier he had tripped into a deep hole in the river with strong current and nearly drowned. He crawled along the bottom getting handholds on the rock with his breath nearly gone. His dying breath was water until he reached the riverbank and puked up a gallon of it. The bank was steep clay and he barely made it to the top flushing a family of Canada geese. He watched the little ones run away shielded by their mother. He realized his mind hadn't cared if he died. Everything had been his body's innate struggle for survival. The steep clay bank might as well have been Everest. He gouged handfuls of dirt on the way to the sought-after top. He told all of this to Diane who listened with a worried frown. They were sitting outside looking at the river, he with a drink and a box of Kleenex to subdue his weeping. She told him over and over that he was taking too much blame. He had the idea that if he had minded his own business and kept remote from the Ameses everyone would still be alive.

"But Lemuel was already writing his book with that ghastly last chapter," she insisted.

He was buried in it: stealing Monica and then Sprague was shot. His cop's mind couldn't let anything go. You had to drive deeper and deeper into the wilderness until the road simply ended. You passed the corpses virtually without notice. Kate told everything and ended up with a bullet in her head. Perhaps Monica would be okay in the long run.

Over dinner Diane reminded him that his mother's funeral was the next morning in Munising. In his state he'd forgotten. Monica said if he wanted to drive with Diane she could drive Sunderson's car and drop it off at Diane's house. She had an old boyfriend from her job who would drive her back home and to the Jeep she had inherited from Lemuel. Sunderson was amused that Monica had managed to have a boyfriend behind his back. The sheer guts and ingenuity of women amazed him.

"You said you didn't care if you died in the river. Did you forget our lifelong affair and trip to Paris?"

"Only momentarily. You are keeping me alive."

"Don't say that."

He tried to explain to her that in the months since he had the idea of writing about violence he had been wallowing in violent death. He had to wonder if his own snooping had urged Lemuel on in his dark project. He had been an interloper.

# Chapter 26

At his mother's funeral they sat in the family pew except for Berenice who chose to sit alone in the front row. Diane and Roberta held hands which he found charming. He hadn't been in the church since his father's funeral a decade ago when they all held hands and comforted Roberta who was particularly fragile. His skin prickled because he was in the exact place that he had heard his death sentence over fifty years before in the Seven Deadly Sins sermon. Luckily Diane was with him. She protected him from the fear that had constricted his heart way back then. He remembered dropping his pencil, a Dixon Ticonderoga no. 3, to look under the table for the telltale dark shadow at the top of his teacher's thighs. Most often she somehow caught on and quickly crossed her legs and gave him a stony look. She knew her boys. And then he was left with a glance of thigh, not his visual ambition. There was a rather homely girl who would go out in the woodlot behind the school and raise her skirt. The price was a dime apiece for each of the boys who chose to join the expedition. If you didn't have a dime you could hide behind a big fir tree and try to catch a glimpse. When he accidentally saw his sisters naked upstairs he felt nothing but this big-thighed girl in the woodlot set his stomach buzzing. In college in a philosophy class he thought about the mystery of sex way too much but then it wasn't on the academic agenda. It was certainly more interesting than Immanuel Kant's *Critique of Pure Reason*. But here he was with his ass on a pew brooding about that fatal sermon over fifty years later. He remembered his mother's sternness with him when he first discovered sex, and again after his retirement party. Sin obviously had great energy and it was a surprise that it hadn't killed him. It was all the trauma of fear he supposed. Maybe by trying to write about the eighth deadly sin he was trying to compensate for his failure at all the others. They, the preachers, talked about people going to hell for eternity but he wondered how hell can hurt if you don't have a body?

He squeezed Diane's free hand and she squeezed back which immediately changed the nature of his mind. Why the hell was he going to Spain tomorrow without her? But she had a houseguest, her stepdaughter from Aspen who smoked dope constantly in the backyard rose garden. Diane had used the term "exhausted" to describe her. When they were introduced the Aspenite stared at him with no effort to conceal her boredom over his existence. Diane had said that she hung out with movie stars but then Sunderson rarely went to a movie. He watched a few on television but the commercials derailed his interest. His favorite he had gone to once with Diane had been an actor named Nicholson in *One Flew Over the Cuckoo's Nest*. He loved the main character and had felt better for days afterward. The idea was that you could find personal freedom even when confined. Diane disagreed saying that he had missed the point that the ax always falls on free men. This distressed him so he stuck to his own interpretation. He would have voted for McMurphy for president, anything to escape the ghastly boredom and habitual lying of politicians. Any ex-cop could tell when he watched them on television that it was all lies. They all had an ex-con's self-assurance.

He was all packed at home in a single modest suitcase with wheels. In truth it contained everything he owned that was wearable in public. He also had some emergency one hundred dollar bills and a couple of credit cards in a fat wallet zippered in his pocket to stop the many pickpockets he was sure littered the streets of Europe. As a matter of fact he was never approached on the street because he looked much rougher than he was. His head and shoulders were overlarge and his legs a little short. It was the build of a tugboat.

Sitting in the pew listening to the preacher spew inanities about his dead mother being "in a better place" his mind segued to the great mystery in his life, moving water. Lakes were okay but nothing compared to creeks and rivers. As a child he would drive his father quite batty asking him where the water came from when he was looking up a creek or the Laughing Whitefish River. Even now he never understood Faulkner's line "A drowned man's shadow was watching for him in the water all the time." He liked reading Faulkner though he frequently hadn't understood him. But what was the point, he thought, in reading Hemingway's "Big Two-Hearted River" when he had fished that river himself dozens of times? He was overfamiliar with the material. He assented to the fact that the river must have been a thrill after having a hard time in World War I.

His thoughts were severely interrupted when the preacher said that his mother was kind or kindly, he wasn't listening closely. This wasn't really true. Especially after his father died who was the only one capable of moderating her behavior. They had always been Democrats but since she moved to Arizona she blamed everything on Mexicans. Up north she was sometimes the same toward American Indians. Mexicans frightened her like they did many older white people. Anyway, she decidedly wasn't a nice person. She was a cranky old lady who went out of her way to be difficult. He himself hoped not to become crankier than he already was. He remembered his mother cooking the endless Italian meals with lots of garlic that delighted him even though she didn't really care for it. Maybe this was love too.

In view of his early departure he had a light goodbye supper with Diane at the hotel café. He doubted that he would have another fried whitefish sandwich until he got home. He told Diane that he would pick her up at de Gaulle when she arrived. She told him not to be stupid, that Paris morning traffic was horrendous. She would take a cab. Meanwhile their supper was uninspired, and he regretted not getting his favorite. He had found the funeral emotionally exhausting. After the service there had been the usual slovenly potluck lunch in the church basement. He hated these as a child because he wasn't allowed near the dessert table until he'd eaten some of the casseroles, for instance, hamburger and noodles bound together by various canned soups. Afterward they waited for Berenice to finish talking to old friends then drove down to the dock for Grand Island and dumped Mother's ashes in the water. It had been her decision because so many of her relatives who had been commercial fishermen had drowned in this water. She normally spoke of these men with contempt because they hadn't saved their money and gone to college. Of course she hadn't done either of those things either. She hadn't been capable along with his father of coming to his graduation at Michigan State because the speaker was Richard Nixon. His father when he could find listeners loved to fulminate against Nixon who he thought was a crook. It was a big day for him when Nixon had to resign. He bought a whole case of cheap beer.

Diane and Sunderson went out to Presque Isle in Marquette Park and walked a couple of hours, an old habit for when they were having a marital argument. It always worked for lowering the cabin pressure as it were. It was such a lovely place with deep woods and stormy cliffs and quite full of bird life. He once dozed off out there and woke up with a deer staring into his face from a few feet away attracted by the sonority of his snores.

As they walked and chatted it occurred to him that she increased his love of life while he had decreased hers. Did he have no natural talent for marriage? Marriage required the etiquette of an hour-by-hour getting along, something that dawned on him too late. In short, real work. He dropped back to tie his shoe and watched how gracefully she walked. He wondered again why stumbling and grabbing her calf while struggling up the hill near the Ontonagon had caused instant sexual arousal.

He had to sit down on a park bench. His stomach churned and he felt a bit faint. It was a delayed reaction to the church and the memory of the nausea of fear after the Seven Deadly Sins sermon that was virtually shouted at him. For weeks he had expected to die at any moment for his sins. He didn't of course, but the damage was done and he never again was able to think of Christianity as a peaceful religion, and he always felt like someone was watching him even though it's ridiculous to think that God cares about our genitals. He thought God was probably habituated to saying "no thank you" to the millions of requests he gets every single day. Sunderson could imagine the prayers blubbering skyward, so few of them worthy. His biggest ally on earth, his father, had told him to take the sermon with a grain of salt, but it had already marked him. He could tell that his father disapproved of his choice of a career but never said so. His father was a redoubtable leftist and stood strongly against authority. He had been beaten by the police during a demonstration in Chicago in his youth. The much later misbehavior of the Chicago police during the Democratic convention was thoroughly foreseeable, according to his father.

Right now, there on their pleasant hike around Presque Isle, Sunderson was convinced that the early curiosity about evil that eventually led him to become a detective likely began with that execrable Seven Deadly Sins sermon. It depressed him that he could be so predictable. It had been a great mistake not to become a high school teacher as Diane had wanted. She was sure that his problems with alcohol began and ended with the relentless daily unpleasantness of his job. As usual she was right though she seemed not to comprehend the drop in income going from detective to neophyte teacher. She was simply trying to save their life together. But still, here they were on a nature walk together, even after the ineradicable mistake that had chopped their marriage in half.

He had simply been raised in a culture of hard drinking. As if he didn't know, his sociology professor at Michigan State had given him a monograph on the Upper Peninsula being a hard-drinking place ever since it was populated mostly by miners and loggers. Sunderson's father had been a light drinker simply because the family budget couldn't handle it. For a brief period his father had been a local school board member, the only proletarian on the board, he claimed. At Christmastime a bus company had distributed gift baskets to board members that included several bottles of expensive whiskey. His father invited over several poor friends, retired injured railroaders and miners. The group of them sat at the kitchen table until they had drunk everything and were exhausted and drunk with that much alcohol. There were also fancy cheese and crackers in the basket but no one in the family liked them compared to the ordinary sharp cheddar made ninety miles southwest in Rapid City. In the following days his dad would say that he was glad they got rid of the liquor. Sunderson had never had his father's ability to deny himself. Maybe he was a glutton after all.

Diane and Sunderson sat at the last bench on the point of the island staring out at the immensity of Lake Superior, the largest body of fresh water in the world. Michigan residents were sure that other states wanted to steal the water of the Great Lakes and were combatively protective.

Diane spoke briefly of Lemuel's suicide and admitted that one day he had stopped by for a chat, something Sunderson didn't know. It made him retrospectively angry. She said she hadn't expected a serial murderer to be so charming. She thought that it was only fair that Lemuel commit suicide after he had shot Kate. Sunderson didn't know what to say. What is fair in double deaths? But he knew what she meant. Lovely little Kate's death needed to be answered and the answer in the cosmos is always no.

He held Diane's hand. Hers was dry while his was sweaty. She seemed on the verge of saying something that could upset him.

"Marriage was lovely compared to the glories of courtship," she sighed. "But remember that fine week after we bought the house?"

She was referring to the second year of their marriage when they moved out of a depressing apartment near downtown and into his present house which had been owned by an old alcoholic couple. Diane had researched them to satisfy her own curiosity. She couldn't believe a drunk couple could live well into their seventies. Her parents had been steadfast members of AA. By her teens she often thought that their only accomplishment in life was to quit drinking. Her parents had visited the house when Sunderson and Diane were scrubbing, mopping, sanding, and painting.

Sunderson came off his high horse and allowed them to pay for a new kitchen for the young couple. The kitchen had been so embedded with filth as to be hopeless anyway. The previous owners had taught literature at the university then retired and moved to Arizona. The rehabilitation had taken his entire vacation and Sunderson sorely missed his trout fishing. For a change he was truly his father's son and often worked a dozen hours a day on the house. They were young enough to still make love a couple of times a day, once on the floor where they had rolled into still wet varnish. When they finished they camped the entirety of each weekend near a river so he could recapture some of his lost fishing. She spent her time applying insect repellent to her body, feeding their campfire and reading. They took at least two long walks every day which rejuvenated them. With these long days he slept harder than ever in his life. It didn't matter if it rained because Diane had bought them a first-rate, expensive tent, the first in Sunderson's life that didn't leak. With his modest youthful savings he was always buying war surplus crap, thinking if it was good enough for soldiers it was good enough for him. He thought of them in far off New Guinea encamped in this very equipment or in France breaking off the necks of bottles so they could drink the wine they found in bombarded French basements. Despite these romantic dreams everything he bought either leaked or malfunctioned and the store wouldn't take anything back. This was what Diane called a false economy. A canteen smelled like a skunk had pissed in it though years later he realized a soldier had put tequila in the canteen. So if it rained they were quite happy in their big waterproof tent. He brought in wood and stored it inside the front of the tent so they would have dry firewood after the rain stopped.

They chatted for a long time out on the bench at the tip of Presque Isle. She urged him to continue his nonexistent writing in Europe. She wanted to see what he had done but he said it would intimidate him and temporarily ruin his productivity. She backed away and he felt a strong shame over his fibbing. They walked back to his house which was closer because she had said she could use some sex, a bold statement for her. They made love on the sofa. He went down on her because she used to love it. Her butt moved to the rhythm of his tongue. She made modest screeching noises with her eyes wide open as if she could see straight through the back of the sofa. When they were done she sat up and her face tightened.

"I hate this fucking house." She had never used the F word to his knowledge. "Remember how we loved it when we spent three weeks fixing it up? It was downhill after that. I never told you the previous owners died in an auto accident in Arizona. They were drunk of course. Maybe their ghosts came back here. You would come home from work after a few drinks somewhere. You would wolf down your dinner, then flop on the sofa and, more horribly, I would take a walk to get away from you. You always treated alcohol as if it were your life's performance-enhancing drug. I'd go on long walks in spring and summer way down to near the campus and watch the college boys practicing soccer. I had a crush on one and he finally figured it out. He came over to the sidelines to say hello and said that we ought to visit each other. I agreed that it would be nice but I told him I was a married woman with children and if any of them found out my life would be ruined. He smiled, gave me a hug and a kiss which impossibly turned me on. He went back to the game and I immediately started regretting it. I used to imagine I had children all the time. When Mona came along I was so happy. I'll never really forgive you for what you did, but I had to try to forget it because I loved Mona and you, and you less so perhaps."

# Chapter 27

He was off to Seville and Barcelona via Paris early in the morning. His mind was chilled a little by fear and his extraordinary independence which was rare in his life. He thought that once you got on a plane you abandoned your usual support system. These odd feelings persisted through a lengthy wait in Chicago and a very long night on the plane to de Gaulle and stayed with him in the transit lounge at de Gaulle. This was a little bit, he was sure, of what it feels like to be an orphan which in a way he was, having lost his parents and wife. A big old boy on the loose in very thin air. He ended up loving the wide comfortable seats in business class and decided to upgrade on the way home. What was he saving for? Not Lent. He was generous in his contributions to the poor and the unemployed and to the Humane Society in honor of his little dog Walter who died so long ago.

He had always loved dogs, but after Walter he didn't get another because the chief had ruled that state police couldn't have their dogs riding with them while on duty. The world is plagued with chickenshit rules. He first greeted the dogs in any home he visited and on walks he said hello to any dog loose on the street or behind fences in yards. Dogs liked it and on future walks they ran out to the fences to greet him. The dogs of the guard dog ilk took longer to warm up but finally managed to wag their tails and smile broadly as dogs do. Marion had an old Lab that never stopped smiling who would sleep on the bank when Marion fished.

It consoled him in the de Gaulle transit lounge waiting a couple of hours for a plane to Seville that he had packed along *Nightwood* and *Ada*, those marvelous books that were intended to help him write marvelously. Thus far it hadn't worked but he still had a smidgen of faith. Diane had also given him two small volumes of poetry written by Lorca and Machado. Sunderson wasn't much given to reading poetry, if at all, but Diane had assured him that these two poets would give him the spirit of Spain. He very much wished she was with him rather than entertaining that dipshit Aspenite. He was worried that forty years of writing police reports had permanently corrupted his chance of writing well. Police reports were gibberish shorthand like emails. "Just the facts, ma'am," as Joe Friday used to say. From reading so much history he knew that the facts alone didn't do the job.

He went into a cafeteria and had what he thought was the best salad of his life. It looked ordinary with very good greens but the chef had dribbled small roasted pork bits called *lardons* all over it, and a poached egg in the middle, and a wonderful tart vinaigrette for a dressing. What a tonic after the awful plane food, doubtless made in a dark basement in Chicago.

He had a large glass of so-so red wine and reread a letter he had received a few days before leaving. It was from a rich couple he barely knew who lived well on their inheritance from their old timber families that once controlled the Huron Mountains. They had a son as well as twin daughters at the University of Michigan. Both of the girls had joined a strange Buddhist cult and dropped out of the university, any parent's nightmare. They were hoping since he was now retired he could look into it quietly. Sunderson called Mona to check it out rather than drive all the way to Ann Arbor himself. She would be less noticeable while he might be looked at as a spy. The master of the quasi-Zen group had achieved perfect satori at the Detroit Zoo while listening to a large cage of howler monkeys. Naturally he was inspired and gathered a group of mostly students and those drawn to any religious exercise. Mona called him an asshole on the phone for having her go through an hour of group howling which was an amount of howling from which she would never recover.

The group howled six days a week and spent one whole day in total silence. Sunderson had no interest in these batshit ninnies beyond the ample reward the parents offered to get their twins back actively into their university studies. In fact the reward offered was equal to his cabin price and would fully restore his blackmail fund. He thought perhaps he could become a world traveler but then the time spent in the transit lounge wasn't all that pleasant. Mona had teased that he could become a crime novelist and write as his maiden flight "The Case of the Howling Buddhas" and she would help. He allowed himself a gentle fantasy of becoming a famed and wealthy crime writer only he would begin with one called "The Family Down the Road" about the past year of his life. The fantasy descended into shambles when he remembered that despite weeks of effort he hadn't been able to write a simple essay on violence as a deadly sin. He couldn't imagine anything harder to do than fail to write. It was exhausting and thus far *Nightwood* and *Ada* hadn't helped one little bit. He had read once that John D. MacDonald wrote several books a year when he was starting out which was beyond Sunderson's comprehension. Sunderson wondered if because of his career he was overfamiliar with crime and found it boring. It was not so for evil, as he had found with the Ameses, the kind of evil which educated people seemed never to have their noses rubbed in. He had barely recovered from it. Maybe the secret to writing would be to get down all the stories Diane had hated hearing, to make some sense of them.

Finally he boarded the Seville flight which not surprisingly was full of Spaniards. Across the aisle were two dowdy American schoolteachers chirruping about how expensive Paris was. Sunderson felt confident with the thatch of C-notes in his wallet. He had cashed in five for euros at the Chicago airport but doubted it would last long.

The red wine put him to sleep and he didn't wake up until the plane landed in Seville. A cab took him to his hotel, Alfonso XIII, which Diane's guidebook reminded him was the most expensive in the city. He was comforted to see a large bar in the corner of the lobby. It was past drink time back home. He was embarrassed by the well-dressed men in the lobby who could even button their suits across their tummies which he definitely would never do again. He was embarrassed again in his big room which was elegant beyond anything he had known, and it was two doors down from a suite reserved for the king of Spain when he was in Seville. If he ran across him, Sunderson thought, what would he say? "Hello, King"? He hastily changed his sweaty shirt, washed his face, and went down to the bar. He had one Canadian whiskey which was expensive because of import taxes. He backed away to wine which he found he liked because of the gentleness of its effect compared to whiskey. The bartender spoke perfect English and they talked about politics in the empty bar. The bartender said that his father was a journalist and had been imprisoned by Franco for most of the bartender's childhood. Sunderson had been eyeing a big ham on the shelf next to the liquor bottles, and the bartender took a big knife and sliced him a number of paper-thin slices, giving him the provenance of the ham. It had the best flavor of any ham Sunderson had ever had. It was made from black pigs that ate mostly acorns in the forest. The olives were also unbelievably pungent.

Rather than take an intended walk after the drinks he went up to his room for a nap and to wait for the day to cool off. He woke in two hours and failed to recognize where he was. When it dawned on him his brain felt a couple of degrees cooler than usual when he looked out the window. He was in Seville not Marquette. His usual support system had disappeared and good riddance he thought. He was

empty at last. What was a support system but an overfamil-
iarity with one's life that was ultimately suffocating? Once
when Diane was particularly angry with him for drinking
too much she gave him an essay on alcoholics written by
a famed therapist in Los Angeles. He threw it toward the
open side window of his study but missed which made him
want a drink. Failure again, this time in throwing. He left
it on the floor for weeks to make sure she saw it there, then
one evening when she warmed his heart with a rabbit cac-
catiore he finally read it. It was a rare honest evening. The
writer said that the true emotionally crippling factor in the
alcoholic was the complete dominance of the self-referential.
The drinker was the intense center of his own universe, his
perceptions rather lamely going outward but colored utterly
by the false core.

  Good enough, thought Sunderson, wandering slowly
toward the Guadalquivir River that ran through the center
of the city. He hadn't imagined that his sensibilities were
that truncated by a few drinks, then admitted there had been
more than a few drinks. It seemed he had to have them. Of
course that's what the article Diane had given him was saying. Nothing is allowed to stand between the drinker and
"a few drinks." After he had arrived he had that expensive
whiskey and two glasses of wine. One would have been
plenty.

  He arrived at the walkway along the river and saw a
lovely girl in a green skirt but she was walking too fast for
him to keep up. Her legs were brown and when she sat on
the bench for a few minutes her skirt flashed up a bit in the
breeze off the river and his heart felt a pang at the bareness

of her legs. How hopeless. When does it stop? The Guadalquivir at this point was broad and placid. It occurred to
him it was hard to think about yourself while staring at a
river. In fact you couldn't do it. A river overwhelmed the
senses, at least they always had with him since childhood.

He had only once forgotten to respect a river. When
they were kids his dad had taken him and Bobby to his own
favorite camping spot on the Escanaba River where it was
very broad and fast. He and Bobby were told to fish from
the bank and Dad went off downstream. Sunderson tried to
wade anyway and quickly was swept away in the strong current. Bobby stood screaming and his dad waded out farther
and intercepted his struggling body, dragging him to shore
and booting him in the ass. After that throughout his trout
fishing life he had been a cautious wader. This was close
after the dreaded sermon and he naturally thought while
tumbling through the water that he was being executed for
breaking one of the Seven Deadly Sins. This increased his
fright because you could plummet straight to the bottom
of the river. Much later in life when Diane wanted him to
seek professional help he tried to imagine telling a shrink
that the biggest trauma of his life along with seeing Bobby's
leg on the railroad siding was a sermon called "The Seven
Deadly Sins."

He continued wandering through the afternoon stopping briefly at an art museum until he turned a corner and
ran face-to-face into an enormous Velázquez that was featured in one of Diane's art books. He immediately left the
museum not wanting for the first time in his memory to think
about Diane. The coolness had remained in his head and

it was grand indeed to realize that Marquette, Michigan, wasn't the center of the world. He liked the new feeling of being nothing, of being empty in the busy world. He had no idea what it meant, if anything, except perhaps that being in a foreign country where everything was a diversion might free the mind of its habits. And what good had his ceaseless thinking about Diane done him? They were divorced forever. What possible meaning could their little affair have? And what did he mean by the word "meaning"? He had no idea. This tongue twister was why he had decided not to go to graduate school.

He sat on a bench in a lovely little mini park noting that the girl in the green skirt, actually a woman, was sitting across the way. She looked at him angrily as she approached.

"Are you following me?" she asked.

"Not in the least. It's my first day in Seville and I'm just wandering around. I was in the museum for a few minutes then got out."

"Why did you stay so briefly?"

"A Velázquez reminded me of my ex-wife and I had a slight feeling of suffocation."

"I understand," she laughed. "I just got divorced this spring, then quite depressed. My father sent me here as a gift because once when he was depressed he came to Seville and the music got him over it."

"Sounds wise. I'm not depressed, maybe a little lost."

"I walked past the bar and saw you in there rather early."

"Let's go there now. I think it's time for a drink."

"It's early for me but I'll have a sherry with you."

He had no idea where they were but she did. They were
cordial and talkative. He had his sexual antennae out but
sensed nothing. She taught physical education in a boarding
school near London. Her recently ex-husband also taught
there so she was looking for a new job, not wanting to be
in the same workplace. She said he was *whinging*. When
they first married he wanted to be a writer but as a matter
of fact, she said, he was too lazy. He liked to drink with his
*mates* and watch sporting events on the *telly*. Before their
marriage when he was still at Cambridge he had won a
short story contest.

"Not enough to coast on," she said.

"The world is bursting with failed writers." Sunderson
should have worked on his essay after his nap but pretended
that he'd forgotten. It was too pleasant eating a room-service
omelet and looking out the window, then heading out for
his walk.

They came upon the hotel from the back and he shook
her strong hand with his own. In the bar he ordered a red
wine rather than the Canadian whiskey he had been ordering for more than forty years. The idea of wine seemed to
go better with this new coolness he felt in his head. The
bartender seemed pleased that they had met. He suggested
they go see La Lupa that evening, the best young dancer in
Spain. She had agreed to meet friends for a late goodbye
dinner at 10:00 p.m. but the restaurant was close to the little
hall where Lupa was dancing. The bartender made the call
and said he had secured the last two tickets. She explained
she was going back to London tomorrow. She said she had
two more paid nights at the hotel courtesy of her father but

she had run out of walking-around money and her English friends were broke. He deftly slid her three one hundred dollar bills from his wallet cache. She was stunned.

"How do you know I'll pay you back?" Her voice was flustered.

"Frankly dear, I don't give a shit," he said coolly.

"You don't look or dress rich," she laughed.

"I'm not. I just had some extra and you might need two more days to have a sherry with me."

That was that. Her name was Laurel. Not cute or pretty but handsome. He noticed her strong musculature, most obvious in her arms and legs. Would making love to her be like writhing with another Boy Scout? That didn't sound attractive. A friend had told him that ballerinas had hard asses. Across the table she looked as if she was deciding something but he didn't know what. He had a second glass of wine, still less than a couple of Canadian whiskies. His new cool head responded well to wine which was without the dreamy confusion of Canadian whiskey. When he got home he would stock up on something called Côtes du Rhône which Laurel had recommended. It was very palatable to him and not expensive, and he would experiment to see if wine was a suitable permanent substitute for Canadian whiskey. He didn't care for American cabernets which were syrupy with an aftertaste that resembled taking a small bite of an oak tree.

They went up to their separate rooms to freshen up for the evening. They had plenty of time before Lupa's dancing and both wanted another stroll along the river. In his room Sunderson perceived a possible disadvantage to his new

cool head. Simply enough, he could see the unchangeable
past too clearly. They never should have stopped camping
which Diane loved. And he had been too far sunk in the
male hoax of fishing and drinking. He couldn't take time
off during his precious vacation from his strenuous detective work to go to France with Diane. She went twice with
friends but said it certainly wasn't like going with someone
you loved. In all of this he had been wrong. A greedy beast
of his own will. What the fuck was fishing, or drinking, if it
destroyed a marriage and the love of a grand woman? He
sat down by the window and reviewed the mournful story
of his divorce, diverted by the sight of Spain out the window
and the errant memory of a college course on the origins of
Latin America. He sat drying off from his shower wrapped
in a big, expensive towel. Spain didn't look big enough, out
the window of course, to have ruled so much of the world.
He rehearsed the defeat of the Spanish Armada, the final
driving of the Moors out of the country, Teddy Roosevelt
kicking Spain's ass.

The doorbell rang. It was Laurel in a beige robe. He
quickly dressed and let her in.

"I thought you might want a snack. I want some olives,
ham, and shrimp. Another sherry?"

He called room service ordering two dozen shrimp and
immediately thinking how expensive they were. He added
the wine, olives and ham.

She was sitting in an easy chair with her robe flopped
open and her nightie under the robe open almost to the
crotch. The man on the phone said in a surprising American
voice that the scampi were a better deal than boiled shrimp.

Sunderson said okay. He looked at Laurel's bare legs with agitation. He had sworn to himself that he would avoid sex in Spain in order to be fresh for Diane when she reached Paris. Laurel told an amusing story about her maiden aunt, her mother's oldest sister. After World War II the whole family was desperately hungry with little food available in the stores and everything rationed. The aunt began dating GI's. She was pretty and soon there was plenty of food. The family was embarrassed having figured what was going on, including dozens of rare eggs and fine steaks the soldiers had stolen from the commissary. When the food situation improved after a year the aunt had told her mother she was going to stay a maiden aunt, and that she had had thirty-some "boyfriends" in one year and didn't want any more sex. One sergeant from Ohio had made love to her five times on his day off and she had fallen asleep at her desk at her office job the next day. The punch line of the story was the aunt had told her mother, "Between morals and food, I'll take food."

"That's a wonderful story," Sunderson laughed.

"So I was thinking in the bar that if you want me, why not? With that money I feel a bit obligated."

"Well don't feel obligated. Of late I've messed up my life with sex. Younger women and all that. Plus I'm meeting my ex-wife in Paris. I don't think repairs are possible but I'll try."

"You still love her. How sweet." Laurel covered herself a bit.

"Yes." For some reason this made him defensive, and he walked over, knelt, and went down on her for a long time.

She was multiorgasmic and he felt proud as a peacock. She pushed his head away finally and said, "English men rarely do that." He stood and she blew him expertly. The doorbell rang just as he came off. He started to fall backward but she caught him in her strong arms. He stumbled into the bathroom. She wiped her mouth on the bedspread and answered the door. It was room service with their snacks on a little rolling table.

Sunderson came out of the bathroom a little shamefaced with his khaki shorts in disarray. It was his room and he should have answered the door but people become nitwits post-orgasm so he had fled. Was he cheating on Diane now? What they had done wasn't sex in Bill Clinton's opinion but what was it, table tennis? The word *Parcheesi* came to him but he didn't know what it meant.

They were quite happy with the food especially Sunderson with the copious amount of garlic on the scampi. They dozed for an hour with Laurel naked. It was warmish but she didn't want the air conditioner on because of the noise it made. At one point Sunderson got up for a glass of water and stood at the end of the bed staring at her. He had a book of memories from his sexual life and he would mentally photograph his lovers for recapture later. The mind fully concentrated is a great photographer, he thought. He also liked to sniff the air because that also could be remembered. It wasn't a long book but it was fun to resort to during boring stretches fishing or driving or watching an inane sporting event on television of which there were many. You had to pay careful attention to the smallest physical oddities. He had never cared for nude photos in magazines or any kind of visual pornography. Everyone looked dead to him whereas the mind could re-create the living woman.

When they were having the first drinks of the evening he stuck to red wine. It occurred to him that there was a bit of a time bomb in the jolts of whiskey that made him not truly notice what was going on in life even if it wasn't much. He was very slow to accept any change in his life but this one seemed to have possibilities. There was the problem that few bars in the U.P. carried drinkable wine but he rarely went to a bar anymore and there was always cold beer. He had read in some dipshit self-help book that Diane had given him that change brought more oxygen into your life which he could certainly use.

The bartender, by name Alphonse, warned him not to look at Lupa directly and especially not to exchange any looks because she was reputed to be a witch. This startled Sunderson who didn't think people believed in such things any longer. He was going to ask but then the bartender and Laurel began to talk about Spanish poetry about which she knew a great deal. She had boycotted Spain all of her life because of the murder of Lorca but then last year she bit the bullet and went to Granada where on a steep hillside near the city she visited the site of the assassination. She said she had wept. The bartender was visibly angry and said goddamn Franco had stolen his boyhood. Laurel felt that the murder of Lorca was like killing the last hero on earth.

For Sunderson the performance was nearly unendurable. Before Mexico he hadn't been all that familiar with flamenco except in college a boy down the hall had a Carlos Montoya record he played very loud and sometimes

Sunderson would stand outside the door for a few minutes
and listen. For the performance the hall was small and the
guitarist very loud. They were in the third row and several
men danced first. Their movements seemed implausibly
violent but graceful. Then a very small man with a huge
voice sang a passionate song that Laurel translated in a
whisper in his ear: "My life has been full of love, suffering,
and death but that is all we humans have on earth if we live
well and honestly, love, suffering, and death." Sunderson's
mind agreed if his body did not. The guitarist increased in
volume and out came La Lupa from the wings at top speed.
Now Sunderson was hearing the music in his spine and felt
her movements in his swollen heart. He had told Laurel he'd
keep an eye on his watch so she wouldn't be late for her dinner but he forgot everything. When it was over he noted that
Lupa had danced for an hour and he wondered if she had
a body of steel. Toward the end, because she was backlit,
you could see tiny droplets of shiny sweat fly off her hair.
He was emotionally exhausted and he had tears in his eyes
when they filed out. He noticed he was damp with sweat
and despite the bartender's warning when Lupa had looked
at the crowd with almost a glare in her eyes he allowed his
own to brush hers with a glance. She had something more
than beauty. He had never seen a woman who inspired such
awe. He frankly didn't care if he was bewitched or haunted
by her. He certainly wouldn't forget her.

　　He walked Laurel to the restaurant to see her friends.
He was invited to eat but he didn't feel up to chatty company.
He quickly drank a big glass of delicious Priorat and was on
his way. He passed the hotel and continued on to the river

because he saw that there was a big moon and wanted to see the reflection in the water. He sat on a bench for at least an hour staring at the moon buried in the river. Maybe he could see Lorca's shadow in the Guadalquivir he thought. Laurel said that he loved this river.

Back at the bar which was busy he had a wine nightcap and the bartender looked at him and said, "I can tell you stared into her eyes, you fool," and laughed.

"I've always been a fool so why stop now." Sunderson shrugged.

He had lunch with Laurel the next day before catching an afternoon train for Barcelona. They didn't make love again. He invited her to Marquette later in the summer saying he would pay the ticket. She said she would think it over, thanking him for the gesture. It occurred to him belatedly that Diane might be jealous. He admitted that he had fallen a little bit in love with La Lupa.

"She would kill you in a week," Laurel laughed.

"I don't care," he said without a smile. That chilled the air.

After lunch he walked two hours to dispel his unrest. Why didn't he make love to this woman? Maybe he caught a moon infection whatever that was. He was pleased he had checked his ticket that morning because he awoke with no idea he was going to Barcelona that day. Normally he over-planned everything. The long walk and a shower helped. Maybe you can walk out of one life and into another. He liked the idea and swore, as he often did with resolutions, to walk a couple of hours every day. *Let's see if I can keep this one*, he thought.

# Chapter 28

He wanted to doze on the wonderful train but didn't want
to miss anything. He bought a small bottle of wine, a demi,
in the club car. He had also bought a nice color guidebook
to Barcelona at a used-book table outside the Seville train
station. There was a lot of information about an architect
named Gaudí. Diane had owned a book about this man but
he had never looked at it for more than a few moments. What
intrigued him is how the Spanish people had commissioned
so many works by this crazy man. It could never have happened in the U.S., a meat and potatoes place compared to
Spain. Of course maybe the man wasn't crazy, just inspired
to do something different. He was delighted to figure out
by the maps that a Gaudí cathedral was being built near his
hotel. He thought that they had stopped building cathedrals
on the backs of the poor in the Middle Ages, a Catholic trick.
Probably current workers were paid well.

He loved the logic of the olive orchards they were passing through, clearly something grand about an olive orchard.
Diane had given up on butter in the home in favor of olive
oil though he had demanded butter for frying fish and for
corn on the cob. His doctor thought butter was worse for
America than drugs.

His seatmate pointed out a bull ranch and Sunderson
stared long and hard at these fighting creatures, Miura bulls.
They looked baleful indeed as if they would be glad to attack the train if there weren't a big fence parting them. For
a college term paper on Hemingway he had read the author
on bullfighting. He found him needlessly technical as if to
say, "You will never know as much as I do," but then he had
never been curious about the sport. At the movies once he
had seen a short film about it but he had liked best the stir-
ring music that accompanied it. At the farm once Grandpa
had shot a steer in the head with a pistol and then he and
Sunderson's father had gutted it. It was a cold, snowy No-
vember day and the guts steamed. They hung up the carcass
with a rope and pulley to the rafters for a couple days to
make it taste better. Sunderson had had quite enough of the
process and didn't watch them cut it up for freezing. He
had liked this particular steer and had petted it as a calf and
nothing seemed fair because it wasn't meant to be.

Despite his best intentions he dozed off and they were
suddenly in Barcelona. He had been dreaming about La
Lupa and felt the music again buzzing in his spine. He took a
cab to the hotel, loved the room and once again found it too
expensive. It was far too late to be angry at his travel agent.
Besides Diane or Mona had probably done it on purpose.

There was a nice sundeck and he drank a small bottle of red wine from the minibar, noting that it was eighteen euros for which you could get totally drunk in Munising.

He continued his train nap waking in a slightly frightened state thinking that far more scary than the Miura bulls was the possibility that Diane would find out he had written nothing, rediscovering that he was a fraud. He ordered room service coffee, got out his tablet, and sat at a desk. He had left Diane's notebook at home because it was too nice. The small passages he had copied out from Djuna Barnes and Nabokov didn't fire him up. They made him want a drink which was *verboten* before the work starts but okay near the end of the session, he had decided. He reminded himself that though Faulkner drank a lot he had also written well for decades. Sunderson tore out his only page, crumpled the paper and made a good shot in the corner wastebasket. He started again.

*Cain rose up and slew Abel, a preposterous murder between the first two brothers on earth, the sons of Adam and Eve. The violence was over jealousy. We shall see as the pages pass (note to self: awkward!) how the Seven Deadly Sins, so central to human life, play off each other and never seem to act alone. We shall also see that they are somewhat connected to sex. Needless to say Cain and Abel weren't sisters. In natural history the two mountain rams noisily butting heads aren't females. Males often seem to be hardwired for violence especially in the natural world but where else are we? Whether you believe it is historically accurate or not, the Old Testament is a bloodbath. I've always thought a mistake was made when man separated himself too radically from the natural world. Even Shakespeare said "We are nature too." The true revolution brought about by Christ was to deliver a theology of love rather than bloodletting. But banded together with the power of politicians, the Caesars of this earth, the bloodletting resumed and flourished down to our time. A professor in college insisted that during World War II there were millions of German Lutherans who persisted in thinking of Germany as a Christian nation. I wonder how many millions of the opposing troops died with a prayer on their lips for the defeat of the enemy. Soon after the Civil War we resumed our extermination of the American Indians, a holocaust in itself in that when we arrived there were thought to be as many as ten million Indians and by 1900 American Indians numbered a scant quarter of a million.*

Sunderson bolted for a drink. Fuck history, he thought. His central lacuna in history had been our Civil War and the so-called Indian Wars. He could not bear either and had wondered how so elegantly intelligent a man as Shelby Foote had managed to do so. When he was still planning on taking a master's degree, before the police force and fishing won, he had hastily read Foote so that he wouldn't be empty-headed on the Civil War during his interview.

He was diverted by the memory of his mother's father Fritz who had a wretched farm near Trenary and a small inheritance from his parents in Chicago. They were adoptive parents as his own had drowned in the *Eastland* disaster, a cruise ferry that tipped over at the docks and drowned 844 off on a company picnic, including all the members of twenty-two different families. Fritz had found out that his

real name was Olaf and most of the drowned were Swedes.
Fritz didn't get out of Chicago until he was fifty and made
his way to the far north to become yet another unsuccessful
farmer. Sunderson's mother had been miserable on the farm
with its outdoor toilet until she met his father at a dance
in Trenary. She was eighteen and they were married in a
month. Youthful photos of his mother were quite attractive
but she went downhill fast in Sunderson's opinion. Fritz was
a cranky old goat who had started his family very late. When
Sunderson was a little boy Fritz would take him fishing on
a nearby lake all the while singing World War I songs in a
horrid, cracked but very loud voice.

> *Over hill, over dale*
> *As we hit the dusty trail*
> *And those caissons go rolling along.*

Or "It's a Long Way to Tipperary," which Sunderson learned
to loathe in the boat. Sometimes another boat approached
them to see if there was a problem what with all the "shout-
ing" and the insulted Fritz would yell "I was singing." Many
years later, Sunderson learned that caissons were wagons
carrying ammunition. He had never figured out Tipperary
because Mona had found an Internet piece on Tipperary
that still didn't say where it was. Evidently "a long way to
Tipperary" meant a long way from a train stop. His dislike
of the computer intensified. He was still to be an antique and
who cared? He would never know the number of Russian
prostitutes in Madrid. Marion showed him pictures and
they were too beefy for his taste.

Sunderson recalled another song Fritz would sing in a mournful voice while fishing, "There's a Vacant Chair in Every Home Tonight." When you said "send a prayer for our boys over there," likely many people did send a prayer over there. His father used to rant about how the demolishing of the Warsaw Ghetto could have been prevented. He recalled that four hundred thousand Jews died there, a number of dead that is not easily comprehended. Each of the four hundred thousand was *one* to somebody. This seemed key to his essay.

On the elevator he questioned once again how we bore up under our own history except by remaining ignorant of it. No wonder he became a detective and alcoholic and a late-blooming sex maniac. He recalled one professor who quoted Dostoyevsky as saying, "I believe that to be too acutely conscious is to be diseased."

On the floor below his own a Spanish woman he thought to be in her fifties came on the elevator. He nodded and she said "Good afternoon" in Spanish and smiled. You couldn't imagine anyone more tastefully dressed and he felt his tired old worm turn.

He nearly ordered a whiskey by mistake then backed away into a glass of house red which was good enough. He quickly drank several glasses and then the attractive, stocky barmaid gave him a glass of water which should ordinarily be drunk first so that you don't drink alcohol out of pure physical thirst. He asked the barmaid about a nontourist restaurant in the area saying that he was only moderately hungry then guessing that tourists by the dozens must request "nontourist" restaurants as if they were up to something shameful. She spoke good English and considered out loud a dozen places before they settled on a seafood tapas place. She drew him a map and he was off.

The place was crowded but he found a spot at the end of the bar next to a short, plump man with a stack of a dozen plates in front of him. Diane had described the protocol to him and he ate four plates of *pulpo*, octopus, in a row adoring the flavor. He broke into this string with a single plate of ceviche, pickled fish, then went back to the octopus thinking he might be the only man from Marquette who loved it. The man next to him introduced himself as a journalist and said he hadn't realized that Americans loved *pulpo*. As they talked he admitted he had spent the last two years of Franco's power in prison. He said that his wife had divorced him and now he was raising a son by himself while the wife kept the daughter. "At least I got him," he said, pointing to a pudgy little boy sitting on the floor intently reading a comic.

By the time Sunderson left Barcelona two days later and three days early for Paris he felt more than a trace of panic. The point was never say you're going to write something until you've already done it. In writing good intentions are apparently crippling. By going to Paris early he had a realization that he was one of tens of thousands of Americans who have traveled to Paris to become writers. Maybe only hundreds. He would stay in a nice hotel rather than eating stale bread in a garret for all that mattered. He had liked Barcelona very much but that first day he had walked himself into painful shin splints. After a sleepless night he had bought himself a pair of puffy walking shoes at a sporting goods store. That helped. There's something in cement

that doesn't love a foot. He could walk for hours pain free
on the soft forest floor but then recalled the same thing had
happened when walking in New York City before his back
had been blasted by a baseball bat. The afternoon of the
second day he talked to the concierge as advised by Diane
and she found a retired architect with an air-conditioned
Mercedes to drive him around in the nerve-dulling heat. The
architect took him first to see a group of geese wandering
around the yard of an old cathedral. Sunderson then told
the architect that he was mostly interested in seeing all the
works of Gaudí. This was partly so he could talk about it
with Diane and also, though he had never had a trace of
interest in architecture before, because Gaudí fascinated
him. The Sagrada Família gave him vertigo and he watched
the men working at the top of the spires and wanted to yell,
"Get down from there!" They gave him a palpable ache in his
stomach. Even monkeys have a fear of falling, he thought.

They went to a park on the north side of the city where
Gaudí had lived and had his studio. He liked this way of
commemorating the dead. The house was small and tasteful, surrounded by greenery that seemed to intrude into
the house. He could not imagine a lovelier place to live and
thought of building such a house back in the woods next to
a river. Not to write in but just to *be* in his coming old age.

He went back that evening and ate himself silly on
octopus and drank far too much wine. He reminded himself
you could get drunk on wine just like whiskey only it took
longer and the transition from sober to drunk was gentler.
He had tipped the concierge twenty bucks for the architecture ride and changing his reservations for the flight and

his hotel in Paris. He felt temporarily like a big shot but then the fear of writing began to nag him in the lobby. She seemed insulted that he was leaving early but he said that he had an important meeting in Paris. He liked saying it as if he were in a movie.

The morning flight was a little turbulent and unpleasant because of a thunderstorm. What an asshole way to travel, he thought. Up in the air but out of contact with birds and beasts.

At de Gaulle he headed for the restaurant to have his salad with *lardons* and a poached egg and, of course, a glass of red. At the hotel he broke into a cold sweat when he was escorted to the same room where he and Mona had made love. In college he had a friend, a literature major, who quoted a French poet, René Char, as saying, "Don't live on regret like a wounded finch." See the bird fly around with a broken wing. He hastily smelled the sheets to see if he could detect Mona from that long ago. Ho, stupid. Likely the worst move of his life, and here he was reliving it. Oh well, it was easy to forgive himself, too easy in fact. He was bad but then so was she. He couldn't imagine her not doing what she wished. He was trying to pretend that he didn't remember the beauty of her ass. She was clearly a punishment, all in all, from the first few times he could see her through the window of his study, cavorting in her nude yoga poses. He never doubted that he loved her but this was love as a disease afflicting his life, the way it used to be described in the pre-Romantic period. He wondered what would happen if she were here right now and decided he could behave on wine but likely not on whiskey. Wine seemed not to leave you so bereft of your senses. In the wine store down the street from the hotel and the Odéon he had picked up bottles of Gigondas and Domaine Tempier. He thought about changing the room but was confident he could overcome the memory.

He opened the Gigondas hastily because of his tension over Mona and drank deeply from the water glass. This was technically illegal as he hadn't written anything yet, just arranged his papers and ballpoint, the long yellow legal tablet he wrote on. He looked at the passage from Djuna Barnes, supposedly there to help him.

> *Her flesh was the texture of plant life, and beneath it one sensed a frame, broad, porous and sleep-worn, as if sleep were a decay fishing her beneath the visible surface. About her head there was an effulgence as of phosphorous glowing about the circumference of a body of water—as if her life lay through her in ungainly luminous deteriorations—the troubling structure of the born somnambule, who lives in two worlds—meet of child and desperado.*

What the hell did that mean he wondered? He only copied it because it contained the word "fishing." How would this help his essay on violence? He was in despair and went out to the balcony and lit a cigarette. She wrote beautifully but what good did it do him?

The long passage he had copied out of *Ada* was even more useless to him. When he read the book he had become infatuated with Lucette, Ada's younger sister. Ada herself was too much a big pail of boiling water for his taste. Lucette wore a green wool bathing suit like girls did in the 1930s, well before bikinis took over.

His room and desk were very neat if you ignored the possible imprint of Mona on the bed. He did not, however, feel propelled toward work. Would he ever be? He decided on a walk and went downstairs, trying to ignore an erotic painting in the hallway. The sin of lust was everywhere and always ready to strike.

He headed for the Luxembourg Gardens a block away, Diane's favorite if she didn't have time to go up to the Bois de Boulogne. He entered by the French Senate building, an imposing place with armed guards. The grass was kind to his sore legs and he sat by the huge fountain wondrously decorated with fresh plantings of flowers. He stared at the water for an hour, dozing off briefly. This dozing was a new factor of age, he thought. It wasn't bad but he recalled being alert all day long. He recalled a brief horrible memory from early in his career near Detroit. Several squad cars had been called to a bar for a slaying and he answered the call. There was a small crowd and a young man propped dead against the building, his throat deeply cut so that his sliced trachea looked like a large squid ring. He was sitting in a pool of his own blood that smelled like burned copper to Sunderson who was not able to eat dinner that evening except for some much needed liquids. He was quite suddenly absorbed in the stupidity of becoming a detective if he had to look at such things. He had always had a problem helping his father butcher a pig at Grandpa's several times. If he had refused he would have been thought a sissy. The same with gutting a deer or field dressing they call it. We easily forget that all creatures are full of blood. It occurred to him that he might include this insight in his essay. The very notion of bloodletting made him queasy. Syria now in the newspapers murdering her own to the tune of a hundred thousand stinking bodies. He reminded himself that Spain had murdered its grand poet Lorca. Why? As if there's ever a reason to kill a poet.

Walking again he came upon an odd but lovely fenced impoundment of fruit trees that he would have to show Diane. They were densely planted unlike an orchard. He sprawled in the thick grass and stared at them. They were obviously fenced to keep people from eating the fruit. He would ask around about it.

Meanwhile, confused by another old bad memory he left the park by the wrong exit and got lost. He was too impatient to retrace his steps. The memory was about a young girl who had been raped, to the point of needing surgery, in an alley behind the movie theater. It was an easy arrest because a cook and a dishwasher were having a cigarette out the back door of a nearby restaurant, heard screams, and saw the guilty man flee. It was a huge lout and ex–football star named Tad, who had never adjusted to civilian life, as many athletes couldn't. Sunderson had been glad he had the patrolman with him in that over the years Tad had accumulated a dozen assault charges and was known for his crazed violence. His first charge had been when he was fourteen and seriously kicked the ass of a big college hockey player. They drove to Tad's small house and knocked. Tad yelled "come in" and was sitting at the kitchen table with his especially big dick hanging out. The patrolman walked out on the back porch from which he returned with a pair of khakis all bloody around the fly. Tad had the grace to look forlorn for a moment at this especially outrageous piece of evidence. Then he smirked widely and Sunderson who was standing at the edge of the table felt his anger rising.

"Hope she's okay," Tad said with another smirk.

Sunderson hauled off and slugged him in the cheek harder than he had ever hit anyone in his life. Tad fell to the floor on his side. The patrolman looked at Sunderson with disappointment over this violation of professional ethics then hauled Tad to his feet and pushed him to the door.

"No funny stuff. I'd love to shoot you," said the patrolman as if he meant it which he did.

Tad got twelve years with very little chance for parole. Sunderson didn't feel this was enough considering what he had done to the girl who never seemed to fully recover.

Now in Paris he saw a top corner of the Senate building off through the trees. The trees and the onslaught of violent memories made him wish he was camping in the U.P. with Diane. He still couldn't believe how stupid he'd been to give up camping with her. It had been a sullen period. He had been promoted but the raise in salary hadn't compensated for the extra work which urged on his drinking, plus he was driving the four hundred miles to Lansing once a month. He loathed state capitals as a matter of principle and fully supported Smolens's desire to avoid that fate.

A pretty girl approached on the path and Sunderson asked, "Pardon, the Odéon?" She smiled and pointed in the direction he was already walking. He was desperately hungry but wanted to write for an hour and digestion ruined the imagination. He suddenly felt the pall of his violent thoughts lift and was thrilled at the beautiful trees, a lifelong enthusiasm along with rivers, both of which brought him closer to religious feelings than churches or the Bible. They filled him with wonderment and whatever the origin of the universe rivers and trees could not be improved on as cosmic inventions. Now he felt a sloppy energy toward his writing and would simply write down everything he knew about violence and Diane would arrive in three days and could help him edit. He wasn't a writer so how the hell could he write beautifully?

When he reached the hotel he asked the shy desk girl about the fenced garden. She seemed to ignore him and rattled with her computer, but then she abruptly handed him a page in English. "This little orchard of 2100 square meters is called Le Jardin Fruitier du Luxembourg. There are about 1000 trees including 370 different types of apples and 247 of pears. It was created in 1650."

The date stunned him. America had barely gotten started back then. At his desk after a long stare at the erotic painting in the hallway he poured himself a full glass of red wine as a reward for nothing in particular. He wrote hard and not well coming up with three pages, a record for him. He recalled the root of his obsession with the Warsaw Ghetto, an ill-advised paper he had written on it and Dresden. It had occurred to him early in his writing that there was nothing to write about except the immensity of hate that had killed hundreds of thousands and also destroyed a beautiful city. The key word was *hate* which despite the wine he could not quite comprehend. So what? He plunged on then rushed out for lunch at a small bistro, Le Bon Saint Pourçain. He jumped into the sin of gluttony and ordered two whole meals, a roasted fish and then the Provençal beef with olives and an entire bottle of Brouilly. He finished the whole meal and sat there like a stunned mullet. The husky proprietor and cook laughed and shook his hand. The proprietor's little dog was allowed in the dining room as this wasn't America. Sunderson loved to pet dogs and before he left Diane had taught him how to ask permission in French, "Puis-je caresser votre chien?" The proprietor nodded, snapped his fingers and pointed, and the dog jumped on Sunderson's lap. He warned himself that the world was getting too perfect and hand-fed the dog a few scraps: fish skin which it loved, an olive which it spit out, a piece of bread swabbed in the sauce of the beef. With this the dog was frantic for more. Sunderson thought that the French love for sauces must be shared by their dogs.

He went back to his room and collapsed in bed from the food. He wished he could get that kind of lunch in America. Maybe you could in New York City, or learn to make it yourself. If he learned to cook better that would help with Diane who loved to cook but had gotten a little tired of doing it every day when she got home from work. His mind made plans for the couple of days before she arrived and they would tour the city. He most looked forward to taking one of those big tourist boats down the Seine. He would go to the park every day, drift around, then come back to the room and write. If he continued at the rate of today he could reach the sought-for ten pages before she arrived.

He slept very deeply for four hours dreaming not surprisingly of trees and his favorite tree place out near Barfield Lakes southeast of Grand Marais where there was a stand of huge oaks. He awoke in the early twilight knowing that a good marriage had to flow, it couldn't be herky-jerky like he had made theirs with melancholy and whiskey. He didn't have to be that way anymore even in the likelihood Diane didn't actually return to him. She had readily accepted the idea of an affair. He had been a little upset when she said she was also going to have her own room in Paris so he could write without interruption. But she would only be next door. She said if he got excitable he could knock on the wall, laughing like the old days when she said it.

He went down to the lobby and had two cups of double espresso, then walked quickly back to the park. He needed to see water to continue his fine mood. He sat down on a bench and stared at the flowers and fountain. There was a row of schoolgirls sitting on the embarcadère behind him. They were laughing at the old man a couple of benches down who was shamelessly turning to look at their bare legs. Sunderson himself didn't turn for a peek. He was quite tired of being as ridiculous as a twelve-year-old boy, an aimless prisoner of sex. Though he could use one now, Diane would be startled that he had stopped drinking whiskey. She would have to go to the wine store.

He walked back to the fruit garden and sat there almost in a dream state. They would walk here together, hand in hand if she liked as they should have twenty years before but they had sunk below the surface. Now they had risen a ways again as people do, rarely but it does happen.